Martha McPhee

Gorgeous
Lies

A Harvest Book

Harcourt, Inc.

Orlando   Austin   New York   San Diego   Toronto   London

The author wishes to thank the National Endowment for the Arts for granting her a fellowship to support the writing of this novel. Also, the writer would like to thank Paul Allman, Jin Auh, Christina Ball, André Bernard, Pryde Brown, Sarah Chalfant, Heather Clinton, Cynthia Hogue, Sara Powers, Andrea Schulz, Cullen Stanley, Mark Svenvold, Andrew Wylie, and all her sisters and brothers (especially Joan) and her many parents for their generosity.

Requests for permission to make copies of any part of the work should be mailed to the following address: Permissions Department, Harcourt, Inc., 6277 Sea Harbor Drive, Orlando, Florida 32887-6777.

www.HarcourtBooks.com

Library of Congress Cataloging-in-Publication Data
McPhee, Martha.
Gorgeous lies/Martha McPhee.—1st ed.
p. cm.
ISBN 0-15-100613-X   ISBN 0-15-602882-4 (pbk.)
1. Parent and adult child—Fiction   2. Terminally ill parents—Fiction.
3. Father and child—Fiction.   4. Communal living—Fiction.
5. Stepfamilies—Fiction.   I. Title.
PS3563.C3888 G67 2002
813'.54—dc21   2002007213

Printed in the United States of America

Text set in Minion
Designed by Linda Lockowitz

First Harvest edition 2003
K J I H G F E D C B A

Praise for *Gorgeous Lies*

"The greatest strength of *Gorgeous Lies* is in its multiplicity of perspectives. . . . It's easy to see why the charismatic figures from *Bright Angel Time* would not loosen their grip on this author." —*The Washington Post Book World*

"An unusually strong novel [that] explores the wild frontier of domestic life." —*O Magazine*

"Some sentences bulge with lyric imagery, while others are blunt with resentment, wielded like weapons. When McPhee strikes the right rhythm, you don't so much read her prose as live inside it." —*Santa Fe New Mexican*

"McPhee brings sensitivity and insight to her account. . . . She is an immensely gifted novelist."
 —*Times Union* (Albany, NY)

"McPhee is a sensuous stylist." —*Elle*

"Fine work: A moving portrait of a foolish, foul-hearted, but impossibly innocent man." —*Kirkus Reviews* (starred)

"Deftly depicts individuals dealing with old memories and new problems." —*The Dallas Morning News*

"*Gorgeous Lies* is a lovely meditation on mortality. . . . Brilliantly and convincingly done." —Larry McMurtry

For Dan
For my mother
and always for Mark and Livia.

MEMO: FROM *THE COURSE OF EMPIRE* BY BERNARD DEVOTO

Autumn softens the bluffs on the river
with a haze, and a fierce, finite light—
Rivers flow into other rivers, and they
flow into rivers that flow into the sea.

Imagine, if you will, Coronado's golden city,
for here he stood—never mind the doughnut factory.
Rivers flow into other rivers, and they
flow into rivers that flow into the sea.

Despite lost tribes of Welshmen,
Israelites, Amazons, unicorns, all maps agree:
Rivers flow into other rivers, and they
flow into rivers that flow into the sea.

Why ask the radar on the mountain
for the latest news? Here's an update—
Rivers flow into other rivers, and they
flow into rivers that flow into the sea.

You want it when? With graphs and charts?
You give me a headache. I'll give you the summary.
Rivers flow into other rivers, and they
flow into rivers that flow into the sea.

First he lost his appetite. Sick days came
and went—by now his bones have learned
Rivers flow into other rivers, and they
flow into rivers that flow into the sea.

How do I love thee, and why? O, congeries
of gorgeous lies, I've lost my way,
and rivers flow into other rivers, and they
flow into rivers that flow into the sea.

—MARK SVENVOLD

CHAPTER ONE

Promise

THEY LOVED ANTON. Every single one of them. Alice most of all. She was his youngest. Eve loved him. She was his wife. Agnes loved him. She was his ex-wife. Lily loved him. She was his lover. They all loved him. The little beady-eyed preacher woman, the woman who sold ducks, Eve's divorce lawyer who always had a different girl on his arm, the Strange couple from down the road. (That was their name, Strange, and they were strange, with dramatic drawn-out English accents, though they were not English—he a poet and a banker, she an aging actress.) The Furey kids loved him, of course. He was their father. The Cooper girls tried to hate him, but what they really wanted was for him to love them. Love them big and wide and infinitely, like a father. The Cooper girls were not his children.

Once, they had all lived at Chardin—all the children, that is. Long ago in the 1970s. It was called Chardin for the Omega Point, and it was Anton's dream that he could create a home that was a perfect meeting place of the human and the divine: a divine milieu, the setting for a profound and mystical vision

of God. Pierre Teilhard de Chardin was his preferred philosopher. He upset the Catholic Church, scaring its thinkers into
thinking about his attempt to combine evolutionary theory
and Christian theology in a seamless whole.

Chardin sprawled on a hill, the highest point in Hunterdon County, New Jersey, blessed with hundred-mile views
and lapped by seas of green fields rolling into cornfields and
forests with creeks slinking through them. And up there,
there was a lot of sky with all its storms and sunshine. In the
spring forsythia, magnolia, lilac, and dogwood bloomed. The
house had been a hunter's cabin, added on to over the years
by Anton and the architect so that wings extended from it,
spokelike, sprouting glass rooms and lofts and decks. At one
end of the house an indoor swimming pool steamed like the
mouth of a dragon, so fiercely you could not see but an inch
in front of you. Steam seeped through the cracks in the sliding doors so that that end of the house seemed alive. Anton,
who was many things—a philosopher writing a treatise on
love, a berry salesman, a dealer in Haitian art, a writer, a
Gestalt therapist, a Texan—had wanted the indoor pool as a
place to hold therapy sessions.

The architect loved him. They had big dreams for what
more they would do to Chardin. Dreams involving silos,
Moorish courtyards, a barn, a tower on the barn, an office
from which Anton could watch the setting sun. On the roof
of this office he would gather all his children and friends to
read poetry in the dimming light.

"I need a small pool. Big enough to fit twenty-five people
or so and it needs to get pretty hot," Anton said to the architect upon first meeting him. Standing in the architect's living
room, he also asked for a whiskey though it wasn't noon.

Outside, Anton's turquoise Cadillac languished in the sun, filled with kids. "Scotch," the architect said, because he only had scotch. Slim and handsome, with a quiet voice and a tendency to stroke his bearded chin, he was a precise man with a tidy mind and a tidy house, and in his world people did not drink before six. On Anton's ring finger the architect noticed an enormous turquoise ring. In his world, as well, men did not wear rings. His name was Laurence—pronounced the French way. Anton drank down the scotch and then ushered Laurence into the back of the Cadillac while all the kids crammed up front. Schoolbooks and boys' underwear were everywhere, and as Anton drove fast Laurence flopped this way, then that, picking the underwear off of him. "A pool," Anton said, looking at Laurence in the rearview mirror, "for my therapy sessions. I believe in finding ways to become un-self-conscious." And Laurence nodded and the kids carried on up front. Anton had one hand on the wheel, the other draped over the back of the seat. He piloted the car like a master, suave Texan that he was. The idea of un-self-consciousness floated like a party balloon in the back. Laurence hoped he'd get to this house alive. And he worried. He was a worrier. You could read it on his tightened face. "I don't know," Laurence kept saying, distressed because an indoor pool was never as easy as it seemed, because his beautiful wife was having an affair, because he had four teenage boys and a floundering practice in a tidy little town. "It'll be fine," Anton said into the rearview mirror—smooth Texas accent. And just the way he said it, just the way Anton held him with his eyes, made Laurence feel possibility. As if Anton's eyes opened up for him and allowed him a visit inside, the mix of enthusiasm and wickedness and faith therein beckoning Laurence, seducing Laurence—as if Anton's dreams, sliding off his lips like truth, were large enough to save him, too.

They became fast friends with their elaborate visions for Chardin. Before too long Anton was inviting Laurence to rebirthing ceremonies on the front lawn in which a person ready for rebirth crawled naked through a canal of arching bodies, teaching Laurence one more aspect of un-self-consciousness.

The steam from the pool caused the ivy to thrive. Ivy crept up the walls, nearly covering the house. It crept through some of the windows into some of the rooms, and though it looked beautiful, over the years it caused the walls to rot, the roof to leak, the pipes to crack. Its roots snaked underground and around the sewage pipes, cracking them, too, and on thick July days the faint smell of waste wafted over the yard.

"It'll be all right," Anton promised. He promised that many times over the years—when the waste backed up into the basement bathroom and overflowed onto the basement floor; when water dripped through the ceiling from the roof onto Julia's pink bedspread; when, indeed, the design for an indoor pool proved more difficult than originally thought and the wall between the pool and Jane's room turned to paste and crumbled. "It'll be all right," he promised when they couldn't afford the taxes and the IRS threatened to foreclose on the house, when cops flew low over the cornfields in helicopters to determine if grass was growing there. Grass as in pot, dope, weed, reefer, marijuana. Anton and the kids grew it back then, in the 1970s, and the cops would fly in low to inspect the fields and Anton would shout to all the kids, "The cops are coming!" His beautiful, wicked grin lit up each one of them. They'd scramble out of the house, slithering into the fields to lay waste to the plants. "The cops are coming," exhilaration in his voice and a thrill running through the kids because they knew that they would not get caught. "It's just ditch weed anyway," one kid would say. The cops would come, would circle, that's true. The loud hum of the helicopters teasing the kids as they lay in the fields against the prickly husks and the corn silk. The wind from the helicopters blew over their backs.

"It'll be all right," Anton promised with all the authority of a Texas Ranger—his sideburns curling, his blue eyes squinting, his Texas accent full. He was six generations Texas on his mama's side. The first oil well in Texas blew at Spindletop on January 10, 1901, not far from the site of his great-great-granddaddy Beaumont's farm. Beaumont had been a French trapper, trapped alligators in the bayous and swamps. In 1824 he sold his land to other trappers and farmers and they made the town of Beaumont to honor him, and the town thrived, growing rich on rice and salt and soy and even blueberries and later crawfish from the Neches River before it became an oil mecca. "If only Beaumont hadn't sold the land," Anton would tell the kids, as if great wealth and fortune were just within their grasp. His great-granddaddy was a journalist for the *Corsicana Star* and one of the few men in Texas who was pro-Union during the Civil War. One hundred and twenty thousand men wore the gray coats and fought for the Confederacy. Just two thousand supported the Union, and most of them were forced to leave the state. But John Darling stayed and made his opinions known. No one was going to throw him out of Texas. "It's the rich man's war and the poor man's fight," he wrote as boys were drafted to fight while slave owners were not required to enlist. Anton's granddaddy was the first in their line to leave Texas. He drove off in a convertible Pierce Arrow with the top down all the way to Hollywood to become the pharmacist to the stars. He bought a movie mogul's mansion and lived his life out there, leaving behind his Catholic-convert wife to die of a female disease and his young daughter, Emma Darling, Anton's mama, to be raised by Ursuline nuns. For the remainder of Darling's life he longed for Texas. Of Texas Texans are proud. It remains in them, the essential ingredient of who they are. That's how it was for Anton, and for the Furey and Cooper kids. Texas became a mythic spot of identity and action, of high-stakes poker where little rich boys lost their daddy's Cadillacs in a game, a country of tall tales where people talked big and lived big and the laws of life elsewhere did not exist.

On March 20, 1930, Anton was born in Corsicana; it was a cool spring morning, very early, very dark, and the air fragrant with first flowers. Winds from the east blew in quietly along with the Great Depression, and Bonnie and Clyde were on the road robbing banks, already capturing many imaginations. But the real significance of this day is that it would later be discovered to be the true birth date of Christ. At Chardin, on this occasion, there would be a celebration: champagne and waltzing and the Serape rug rolled back and toasts to Anton for sharing this with Christ, adding all the more to his power and allure. Anton, big large man that he was, loomed over all the kids—their leader, their guide. They loved him. Whatever the problem, he would say, "We'll figure it out."

"Promise?" the kids would ask. Promise like a ticket to somewhere fabulous, like an answer. Promise, rich beautiful word that it is. Promise. The oath of God to Abraham. That their futures would be safe, clear, understood. Promise like a road map, like insurance. Promise.

"I promise," he would say to them, sipping a glass of whiskey, a flute of champagne. An ascot folded softly at his neck. And they believed him—for a long, long time they believed him.

And the scent of lilac was always stronger than the smell of waste, and the cops were simply on a routine training mission, and the IRS man, all dressed in black, walking up the long driveway with a briefcase in his hand, simply needed help with a flat.

"POP?" ALICE ASKS. It is 1994. Her voice is gentle, but firm with will. She has just graduated from college and is on her way to India on a Fulbright scholarship to study Indian cinema for a year, her life about to open like a flower. "I can't leave unless you say you'll visit." She smiles, giddy with ambition to do good things, contribute herself to the world. "Aim high," her father has always told her. "If a thing is worth doing, it is worth doing badly."

She wants to understand how the dreams of films—Hindu women dancing love dances on broken glass to save their lovers' lives—can lend an entire culture a bit of peace and hope. Traveling movie theaters, screens hitched to the backs of trucks, lighting up a few thousand lives in the countryside. Fairy tales are her belief; her father always taught her to believe in the possibility of the impossible, that fairyland is reasonable, indeed, is common sense.

Anton reclines in his bed, propped against a sea of white pillows. He's an old man, old before his time, aging fast now at sixty-four. Thin and unshaven and weak. His skin is gray. His hair is gray. His tongue is gray. Mysterious cramps dart through his abdomen, crippling darting cramps. Sun streams through the bedroom of windows, and outside is a spectacular

late-May day with a breeze and no clouds and everything
smells of lilac. The room is thick with the purple branches,
the buds like tiny grapes. Alice stands at the edge of the bed,
wanting his permission to go, as if permission will heal him,
hold him here till she returns. She is a practical, disciplined
girl, her father's opposite in many ways. He would tell her
fondly that he has had to be extremely undisciplined (credit-
card debts, chronic lateness, a smoker of fine Moroccan hash
among other things) in order to teach her otherwise. But like
her father she also has a great capacity for dreams.

She wears jeans and a T-shirt and baseball cap (her traveling outfit) beneath which is tucked her long walnut hair.
She's a strong girl with an energy that makes her seem as
though she is always on the verge of erupting—a toughness
countered by an exquisite beauty that softens her, eliciting in
others the need to protect her. A beauty that emanates aloofness and in that an alluring mystery. Determination lights
her face; it's in those fierce gray eyes. Miracles blossom in
front of her. Anton sees a glass wall go up, cutting her off
from him. He wants to reach through the wall and grab her
back. He is beginning to lose his ability to dream. Look at me
wasted here, he wants to say. Her voice wraps around him,
envelops him with exhilaration and the force of her will. "Say
you'll come," she insists.

"Watch out for monkeys, babe," he warns, trying to prop
himself up. "They're devilish little creatures. Beguiling. They
are not your friends, even if they try to convince you otherwise." He squints a smile, forcing it out between his lips and
the pain, a Texas half smile.

"You'll feel better again. You'll even be fat again," she reassures, though somewhere she knows she's bluffing.

That smile of his turns ironic, then hopeless, then boyish.

"I was never too fat, babe," he says, accent thickening. "Just healthy." He's bluffing, too, of course. They're both bluffing. They both know, yet neither will concede. He's taught her— endless games of poker. She's sitting on a full house. Just another ace is all she needs. He wants to cheat and give her that ace.

"We'll see a lot when you come." Her eyes warm, changing colors like wet stones, and it's as if she were singing, a lark, a nightingale with the beauty of the world on her tongue. Rossignol, "nightingale" in French, the name of the petit and very dark-skinned man who married him to Eve at the Oloffson Hotel in Port-au-Prince. Eve in her cream silk standing by his side on the balcony. Pigs and chickens and schoolchildren in their uniforms racing on the streets below and the jolly painted buses lumbering along and the old women with *paniers* of bread balancing on their heads while the Tonton Macoutes keep guard with their AK–47s. He sees the day as if he were there. The ceiling fans move the slow-motion heat and the blessings are read and he kisses the bride. Familiar French songs drift in from far away. That night they'll attend a voodoo ceremony—women dancing wildly to the thump thump of beating drums; men decapitating chickens, painting their bodies with the blood. They'll hike through the mountains to Jacmel, make love in the open; Haitian families will invite them in for a meal, give them a mat to sleep on, a painting for a souvenir, discuss Duvalier and his cure for yaws. The Oloffson was the setting for *The Comedians;* he and Eve had slept in the Graham Greene suite. The romance and excitement appeared visceral in the heat.

Anton has the urge to tell this story to Alice again, but she is singing already, herself. He winces. The cramp slices through the flesh and muscle of his belly to his back, a well-sharpened knife slipping around in there. He closes his eyes and the lark sings a song colored by painkillers and the approaching dusk and he hears everything she has ever said about India... *The full moon suspended over the Apollo Bunder, lighting up the whole of Bombay.* Coming to him in opiated clips. *That big and brilliant platinum moon, somehow closer, somehow different, more moonish, more spectacular. And the rains come and the heat lifts in a steam to reveal a woman dancing in the center of a giant lotus flower, beckoning her lover to descend from the thin air above, and he arrives tethered to a string.* India is one place Anton has never been, one place Alice wants to show him. His love of adventure is a gift he has given to her. He counts the gifts now as if to read her future, glimpse the woman she will become. *The* gopuram *of Madurai sprawling over that insane town. The country roads thick with cars and lorries and bullock carts and festivals celebrating the holy cow, and the fields afire in the evening and the whole world smelling of sugar, and herds of goats, and packs of newborn chicks, and castles, entire towns made of sand, palaces floating in desert lakes, the Ganges at night: pitch black and all the people gone and the river so quiet and big like a beast, a massive sleeping beast—Eliot's strong brown god—and the mist just lifting lightly but hanging on, eerie with the smell of coal fires and of the burning* ghats. *And the lotus flower closes concealing the lovers and then the petals open and the flower floats on a pond and the woman continues her intricate dance.* He imagines Alice, a lark in the latticed windows of the Pink Palace of Jaipur, in the early morning hours at Chardin. How the birds sing, an entire orchestra with their elaborate odes to day. *The red earth of Karnataka and the golden sands of Arabian beaches. The flute player in the smoggy streets of Calcutta, the smell of woodsmoke mixed with sunflower and jasmine and apple and orange.* "Dad, please come?" she says. Let me sleep, please, babe, let me sleep here awhile. *The red-faced and mean and untrustworthy monkeys swinging between the dazzling branches of the banyan trees, rising up the boulder mountain to the place where the monkey god was born.* He opens his eyes and looks at his girl behind the glass and he knows that she will leave, and though he knows it is not rational and though he knows it is not fair or just, he feels betrayed. Don't go, please, he wants to ask of her. Just sit here and let me look at you.

"Do watch out for the monkeys, babe," he says instead, because for only her is he still perfect. He wants to remain that way. "They bite. I don't want to have to come all the way to India to take care of a monkey-bitten daughter," giving her, in this, permission. He rises on the pillows. She leans down and kisses him, holds him tight and kisses him— imagining herself as a monkey-bitten daughter that her father has come to retrieve. He wants to say good-bye simple as that. Have a good time. I'll come. She is just a young girl standing before him, a child who emphatically does not want to grow up. Not yet. Not in this way.

"Don't ever be sentimental, babe. You can be romantic, but never sentimental." He gives her the Texas squint and rubs his belly as if he could massage the pain right out of it like air bubbles in bread dough. "Smoke a good joint for me. Dope's good over there," and from his wallet he gives her a hundred-dollar bill. "For good grass, babe."

She pockets the bill, stuffing it into the front pocket of her jeans as if it were a tissue, feeling light because she knows she's won this hand. "Bring everyone," she says suddenly, greedily even. "What if you all came to visit? That would be fun. Wouldn't that be fun?" She feels like her mother using

that word *fun*. Fun is her mother's word. *We will have fun.*
You're having fun, aren't you? Fun. Fun. Everything fun. Then
she imagines them all in India, the whole clan, all eight brothers and sisters and her mother. And she does believe it would
be fun and it does seem possible, a matter of logistics—that
is all. Her family like a long tail extending from her, trailing
after her across the vast, hot expanse of the subcontinent.
Marching like a tribe. Fun. The image makes her feel powerful, as if she really did have the ability to make this family
whole—perhaps her most certain and central fairy tale.

"They'd never want to come," Anton says, taking the notion seriously.

"Don't be sorry for yourself. And besides, they would,"
she says brightly. "You know they would."

"You really think so?" he asks, perking up with hope.
Hope, like an injection. "What about the Cooper girls?
They'd never come." His blue eyes droop, resigned. Sorry for
himself indeed.

"That's not true. You know that. Why wouldn't they
come?" But then she pauses. Dread seeps inside of her,
spreading out like a stain. She sees her three Cooper sisters
bickering, faces red with it, as they complain about their
childhoods. She paces. Looks around, how neat the room is.
Her mother's doing. Afghan folded over back of rocking
chair. Books in tidy stacks. Photographs of all the kids—
having fun—on all the various family trips. All the ages they
have all been. For twenty-five years this family has tried to be
a family. She feels tired and wants to leave. For half a year she
has been planning this trip. She's spoken with a famous director; he intends to meet her—Sanjay Deep of cinema Deep
fame with five hundred films to his credit. She wants to step
inside a film, learn the dance, the how-to of lip-synching the

songs. She wants to step inside dreams, understand them, explore them, invade them. She looks through the sliding doors to the deck, the yard, the fields, the forests, the deep and distant views of farms and silos and hills and sky. She thinks about the long trip in front of her and of how very far away it will take her from her world and she feels the exuberance of a clean slate and time.

She adjusts her baseball cap, flipping the bill to the back. She has a certain power over Jane and knows that if she convinces Jane to come then Jane will convince Julia who will convince Kate. They are woven together like fabric, inextricable threads.

Anton folds his gray hands at his belly. Very gray against the white sheets, he shuts his eyes. His lips pinch as he eats the pain. No good feeling about this has he, but he will not let her know. Go, he wants to say now. Go quickly.

"They'll come," she says. "For me." She imagines herself as a bridge, the family stepping along her spine. Determined little girl, she's been working this family together since she was pencil-size in her mother's womb, negotiating all their troubles with her extraordinary capacity to be fair. "She'll be a judge someday," her sisters and brothers predict.

Anton holds her. She is warm inside with her plan and everything becomes sweet because there is a plan and there is not yet an explanation for the crippling darting cramps and she will leave. The mystery illness is shrouded in the vast expanse of hope. Hope infused in her simple words, bright and forceful, You will come. (And the family, too!) Hope in her erect stance and her thrilling determination. Foolish hope, corrosive hope. You Will Come.

"I won't go unless you promise."

Gently he squeezes her hand, placing a light kiss on her

large forehead, pulling her close, the soft same newborn smell of her as if she still fit into his palm. He sees her blown to India carried by the force of his breath, rising and sinking on its back away from him. "Promise, babe." A commitment, the authority of the Word. His nose stings. His eyes close. "I couldn't go a year without seeing you. It'll be all right."

CHAPTER TWO

Pro-Life

ALICE WAS LUCKY to be alive. Her older sisters and brothers teased her about this. We had a family meeting. You won. Alice liked to bet; she was good at cards. She liked the feel of the slick new cards in her hands, sliding them apart to reveal her odds. She liked that the odds changed, shifted, improved—and when the odds were truly bad, she folded. Her skill at poker was a talent learned from close observation of her father, her Texas inheritance. She liked holding her face in such a way that the other players could read nothing. She liked taking a risk, refining her sense of the probable. She liked that she was able to read the faces of the other players, sifting out the bluffers by their tics. She liked holding tough until the finish, sweating it out, the last step before the final round. The ante, the growing pot, checking the other cards on the table for the odds to the ace she needed. The sweat. The win. She was lucky to be alive.

IN THE HINDU RELIGION it is believed that when a child is born, Brahma, the First Creator and Lord, is present at the

birth. Brahma comes just at the moment when the child
emerges from its mother's womb and enters the world so that
he can write on the forehead of the newborn his or her fate.
Even Brahma doesn't know what he will write until his pen
writes it. The words are based on the good and the bad of the
newborn's previous lives. Whatever karma they achieved in a
previous life they receive this karma again in the new life—
again and again and again.

There were moments in this life when Alice felt she had
lived what she was living many times before. There were moments when she felt the Grand Mystery was to repeat over
and over again your one life. For ten million years her father
would die when she was twenty-one. The static cycle of birth
and rebirth.

The story of Brahma's presence at the birth of children,
his script upon their foreheads, was one that her father liked
to tell her. He stopped believing too hardily in fate and the
will of God after he left the Jesuits and became involved in
existentialism, but even so he liked myth and story and he
liked the concept of a story foretold to be lived by the unwit-
ting soul.

He liked the irony and futility, the soul's struggle to will
its fate even when the path was preordained. And this he im-
parted to his daughter when he'd tell her of Brahma when
she would struggle too much with a disappointment or a
desire.

If Brahma had been present at Alice's birth—which was
a hot September day in 1973 at Columbia Presbyterian in
New York City, Harlem to be exact, with a view of the George
Washington Bridge (which cost extra, but Anton insisted)
and Anton with a Super 8 filming the whole event, filming
this tiny little long-lashed baby, who for two weeks would re-

main unnamed, now red with blood and white gook, screaming into the camera—Brahma would have written something
like this: This girl will grow up and kill her father.

Does Brahma visit non-Hindus? What would he have
made of Anton and the movie camera capturing the picture
between Eve's bloody legs, capturing the pain etched into her
face?

Anton set the camera down to hold his bloody unnamed
baby, lifting her to the air as she shrieked and shrieked. His
baby girl. He simply had not realized the depths of love, that
there was room for more. That his heart could continue to inflate, to ridiculous proportions, an ever-expanding universe.
Standing there he became all heart, could feel happiness in his
fingertips, could feel joy in his toenail-less big toes, could feel
devastation in his religion, or current lack thereof—that
he had come so close to throwing this all away, like crumbs
vacuumed up on a rug, her brain sucked to mush, this little
treasure, this love, this life. He had saved her from himself
and for that he would always love her more. Her face was
squooshed, her head cone-shaped, her eyes shut tight, her
mouth opened wide. Eve smiled. Anton smiled. Alice in the
air and Brahma in the corner.

There are Indic myths and folktales that tell of people trying to outsmart fate and Brahma's plans. These hapless characters play with the laws of the universe. They stop time,
change the course of the stars—or believe that they do. Some
succeed and others don't. There is a Marathi folktale, similar
to the Oedipus story, about a mother who is fated to marry
her son. When she learns this she disappears into the wilderness. But she drinks from water in a lake that holds the spit of
a king. Accidentally she drinks the spit and the spit impreg-
nates her and she bears a son. Recalling her fate, she throws

the newborn over a cliff but the thick branches of a pipal
tree save him. A barren couple finds the boy and adopts him
as their son and many years later when his mother decides it
is safe to leave the wilderness she finds herself at the home of
the barren couple. She falls in love with their son and mar-
ries him.

If you knew your future, could you bear to go on?

THERE WERE TWO abortions before Alice, and even so she almost got aborted, too. The first was early, a month or so after
Anton and Eve started making love outside his therapy shack
in the long onion grass when Eve for the first time was learning why sex was called a pleasure. Naked in the long dewy
grass with the cars rushing past on the road and her legs open
and that sensation, that reaching-to-the-universe sensation.
The second came after a long trip out west, when the two
families came together, when they lived on the road in a
turquoise camper and the days were long and the desert hot
and everything was possible.

Alice was lucky to be alive. There was a time when Eve
and the Cooper girls spent their nights at Anton's though
they still lived in their big white house in the woods where
they had lived when Eve and Ian were still married. At
Anton's, Eve slept with Anton, of course, and the girls slept in
sleeping bags on the living-room floor. It was a period of
transition. Anton wasn't yet divorced. There was talk, a possibility he would return to his wife. He was discussing the
possibility with his Jesuit friends at the Hastings Institute on
the Hudson, with his Jesuits friends in Brazil and Argentina,
with the Catholic intellectual society. It was a question of
ethics, of morality, and he was still in love with Agnes's gorgeous mind. With her he could discuss anything. She'd been

a Catholic when he met her, a beautiful young woman studying at St Mary's College with the vague idea of becoming a
nun. He'd been at Notre Dame finishing his college degree
after his failure in the Jesuits. Together they had tried to leave
Catholicism behind. She understood the puzzles of his mind.
He was tormented, even so, by the marriage and the laws of
the Catholic Church and the desire for a lawless life in which
imagination reigned. He so hated the Catholic Church for its
power over him and he so hated it for its absurd and imprac-
tical doctrines woven around him like light blue morning
glories—pretty flowers, suffocating vines.

So the Coopers couldn't move in right away. Logistics,
you know, or was it etiquette? Fifty acres on a hill with forests
and fields all around. Anton's goal was to create nothing less
than a paradise for his children, a magical playground that
offered curiosities about the world, for their friends and his
friends, for anyone who found it pleasant to be there. Already
there were two pools, an indoor and an outdoor. The indoor
was heated to 105 degrees Fahrenheit, a steam bath of heat
and mist, with waterproof speakers, candles and ferns, massage tables in the corner, and sliding Japanese doors. Neil
Young's voice singing about old men and burning castles
through water and mist and it all. In the winter the kids
dashed from the pool to the snow and back to feel the prickly
burn of cold and heat playing against their skin.

Laurence was there all the time with his blueprints, smoking a joint with Anton—un-self-conscious now with his
loose jeans and T-shirts and big plans for raising the barns
with the help of seven Polish builders who he, in turn,
wanted to save. His plan involved the Polish builders living in
yurts in the woods behind the house until all the projects
were complete. And Anton was delighted to have the help

and to see Laurence expand. Often the Poles on the early-morning shift would take turns driving the kids to all their various schools. At the house there was a lot of work to be done, always a need for extra hands.

The outdoor pool was tiled with tiny Moroccan mosaics of a deep blue that made the water a sumptuous sapphire and it, too, was heated. Anton did not like the cold, swore to God that before he died he would live somewhere tropical, somewhere permanently warm. Life then stretched into infinity like the arches he'd seen in the Cordoba mosque when he was a young man. Life was easy, filled with possibility, and it was negotiating this possibility that was the challenge. I'll have a bit of this, a bit of that. He started to write his treatise on love.

The house had a Moorish courtyard intricately tiled like the pool and filled with jasmine trees and red geraniums. Anton tried growing groves of olive trees to bring back a bit of Spain, of Greece, of Italy; he tried almond trees, pear, peach, apple, and cherry before he got it right. There were Haitian paintings, wooden carvings and sculptures, Indian tapestries of Rama dancing with Sita before Ravana stole her away, Japanese screens, a geisha fan, Italian pottery. There was a bit of everything—hanging benches from the islands, elaborate Burmese pipes for his strong Moroccan hash, and a house goddess from Thailand. Rugs from Persia and a baby quilt from Rajasthan. Dancing Shivas and Parvatis. A Ganesh carved from stone. Life was for the taking. He had had five kids by the time he was thirty-four—four with Agnes and one with the Italian maid. By the time he was forty-four he would have four more. He was told by someone, somewhere, that a lemon seed could give you an orange tree, a grapefruit seed a lime tree. Citrus was unpredictable, always a surprise.

If you spliced the seeds together you could get a tree that bore lemons, limes, oranges, grapefruit. He wanted a tree like that.

It was Alice who sealed the move of the Coopers to Anton's. Later Sofia would tell the Cooper girls that Eve got pregnant in order to trap Anton. She did it for the money, Sofia would say, and throughout her childhood she'd pray to God that Eve would die before Anton. "If she doesn't," she'd say to her sister, Caroline, and brothers, Nicholas, Timothy, and Finny, "we'll be left with nothing from him. You can bet your life Eve will use all the money for her kids. And it won't be fair because Mom bought the place." Sofia was a wise child, thinking already at the age of fourteen about the nasty complications of inheritance, the strategies. Twenty years later as Anton died she would cart off Furey possessions in a U-Haul, staking her claim to the land. Her shocking blue eyes, Anton's eyes, held no secrets.

In the room at the end of the long hall—still barren of all photographs describing fun, but already flooded with books—Anton and Eve fought. In the room where Anton would die after an overdose of morphine (administered by his youngest) he fought with Eve over Alice's life. Jane heard it first, their voices above the wind blowing bitterly outside. She was more attuned than her sisters to their mother's cries.

They fought because Anton did not want the baby and Eve did. Of course, it was more complicated. The baby had quickened (moving like a little crab in her mother's belly) and it was beyond the time he believed ethical for an abortion. Before the quickening he could justify it, he could refer to St. Augustine. There were those in the Church who would not call it a sin. But the baby had quickened. He was trying to

explain to Eve that he was discussing the issue with his
friends at the Hastings Institute. They were trying to help
him see the way. Another child with a woman other than
Agnes would make divorce definitive. He wasn't ready to
make that decision. He saw Agnes folded over, weeping. He
was weighing the odds, studying doctrines, seeking advice. It
was a catch-22—divorce or murder? A balancing act. Anton
was nuanced. He was not in love with Agnes anymore, but he
was not yet sure if Eve were the Love with whom he could
find utter equality. With Agnes, though, he had a spiritual
connection, an understanding of faith that was as deep as the
deepest depths of religion. He was struggling to explain the
nuances to Eve, the ramifications. The two other abortions
weighed heavily, as well, on the side of allowing this one to
live. He had been able to justify them because the fetuses
weren't yet three months, but three abortions became a pattern. His colleagues at Hastings, his Jesuit friends in Brazil, in
Argentina, were giving up on him. He was terrified by his
mistakes. He pleaded with Eve for understanding, his big
voice rising.

Jane listened outside the door, bolted as it was with a big
brass lock. Jane understood that the fetus had moved, but
Anton's arguments were lost on her, smothered by the loud
pitch of his anger and by her mother's pleas. Eve was tired of
abortions. She wanted this child. "I don't care if you leave,"
she cried. Anton shouted now in a hushed but no less urgent
voice. "I wouldn't abandon a child of mine," he said. He gave
Eve no choice. The Cooper girls thought of Finny, son of
the Italian maid. What had her choices been? Where was she
now? Bianca Maria, her name was like some exotic ghost
drifting through the mystery of their lives.

"Hypocrite," Jane said to her sisters. "Each life is a gift.
Each life is sacred. Each life is a miracle." She quoted him. "If

the baby has quickened it is then definitively and definitely too late." Only a few days before Anton and Jane had had their hundredth fight on the subject. He had raised his hand poised to strike. Dinner. Late. Eve and all the other kids at the table. All the candles lit, their flames reflecting in the dining room's big glass windows. Twenty-two years later, at his death, the dining room would look the same, all the same faces. Their grown-up faces, mere impressions of what they once were. Even Alice was present by the time of this fight, the size of a pencil in her mother's womb. Eve froze. Anton's hypocrisy, almost tangible, wrapped around her, snaked up inside her. For she knew already she was pregnant and she knew already that she would have the child, knew already she would have to defend Anton's hypocrisy to Jane for the rest of her life.

Jane mocks Anton: Says each life is a miracle especially if the mother's been raped, especially if the mother will die as a result of the pregnancy, especially if the mother makes a mistake and gets pregnant with the baby of a man she cannot stand. Quickening. That's just another excuse. It's the woman's body, therefore her choice. "You have no idea what it is to be female," Jane shouts. "And you stand there acting as God." Her face is red and raging. "I started the local chapter of NOW." She persists in mocking him by quoting him. "I'm a feminist who teaches girls to be more like boys." She can't stop herself, though she knows she's going too far. "I organized sit-ins in bars that excluded women." He rises, looming as he did, looming tall and ominous, filling with hate. He's at the opposite end of the table—rising to enormous proportions as he stands, hands braced on the table for lift, thin lacy lines decorating the whites of his eyes, voice sticking, words getting caught in a web of marijuana phlegm. She enjoys the power, like puffing up a balloon.

"*You have Lucifer inside you,*" he shouts.

They say babies can hear in utero. Alice, the length of a pencil, listening to talk of Lucifer. Kate whispers to Finny, asking him what Anton means. Finny shrugs and holds her hand the way he always does when Anton gets mad. His big hand envelops hers, covering it completely like a glove.

What was it like for wide-eyed Alice, born as savior of this family? Her role was already defined at pencil size. Eyes wide inside the womb, asking already, *Who are you, Pop?* Such a terribly complicated question. Eve's secret beneath the palm of her hand resting on her abdomen, listening. Eve's tiny fourth child in there while "Lucifer inside you" hung in the air and eight wise child faces tried to make sense of it. *No one knows,* Eve kept thinking to herself. *No one knows,* thought as if that knowledge contained not *a* secret but *the* secret.

Jane and Eve had run away that night, leaving Kate and Julia at the house while they circled the roads in Eve's beat-up old green station wagon. They had circled and circled with Jane crying and Eve apologizing and Jane wishing that her mother would have the courage to leave, enjoying the intensity of the moment alone with her mother, wishing it could always be that way. She realized that she would be utterly happy if she and her mother could just drive off to anywhere, leaving Kate and Julia with Anton. It was completely black inside the car—the dashboard lights hadn't worked in years— but even so you could see Jane's eyes, big and wide and filled with hope. She would share the shape of those eyes with Alice. Alice had them open, wide and already gray, listening to the mysteries of the world, which were just a few layers of skin and tissue away.

"Mom," Jane said. She was only fifteen. "Why don't you just leave? We'll be all right. You have me." Same question she would ask for twenty-five years, that she would continue to ask even after Anton was dead. "He listens to me," Eve said, eyes tight on the road. "You don't know what it's like to have someone focus everything on you, believe in the depths of you. This isn't him. It's his anger, is all." She needed Jane to see it her way as if that could make everything all right. Jane would always remain one thing for Eve: her firstborn. At twenty-two she had become pregnant with Jane; she'd been a child then, just a few years older than Jane was now. She had kept Jane a secret, too, from her first husband, Ian. But with Jane she had not been sure if she were pregnant. She thought of herself as a young girl, couldn't imagine being a mother. Getting pregnant seemed so complicated, so much like a miracle, Eve did not believe it would happen for her.

Eve kept this first pregnancy a secret because Ian had had a job interview—a very important life-changing job interview—and she knew he would be made anxious by the news so she did not tell him, and since she could not tell him, she could not tell anyone. She waited. She felt the changes in her body—breasts heavy, stomach tight, a light nauseous feeling in her gut clinging there like a barnacle unwilling to abate. And her period did not come and she wanted to call the doctor but she wanted more to simply possess the secret of this inside of her. She wanted something that just she and the fetus knew. And Ian's interview came and went and she did not want to tell him. She wanted the secret to remain forever. Her firstborn, the first time she would feel all these new sensations taking over her body, slowly, emphatically. Together with Jane, she discovered what it meant to be pregnant. She imagined inside her a girl, a tiny version of herself with blond hair and wide-set green eyes, a round bright face. When little dark-eyed, dark-haired Jane was born, the only thing Eve could think was *She is not of me*. And Eve knew that ever since she had been trying to make Jane more like her, more of her. In the car with Jane there was a part of Eve that could have fled, too—leaving everything else behind—as long as it could have been with Jane. She only would have done such a thing with Jane.

"I'M SORRY, BABE," Anton said to Jane when she and Eve returned at dawn. A pale light spread over the day like a veil. He was waiting for them in the living room, sitting on the floor near the swinging couch with a book of poems in his hand reading aloud.

> I caught this morning morning's minion, kingdom of daylight's dauphin, dapple-dawn-drawn Falcon.

The ecstatic beauty and pain of being alive. "Forgive me? Please?" Like a puppy just allowed out of the doghouse, his face red and a little guileless though aware that he'd done bad and in that endearing.

"It hurts," Jane said.

"It's the anger gets ahold of me, babe."

"It feels like you don't love me."

"Oh Jane, darling," he sighed. "You know that's nonsense."

Eve stood there hoping, her thumbnail pressed against her lip, in love with Anton all over again for his appropriate sense of the moment, hoping that everything would always be all right, that she'd be able to have a successful family this time—the one thing that had seemed promised by her childhood and growing up female in the middle of the twentieth century.

Anton's arms reached for Jane, pulling her to him. Big

and sloppy. She could say anything now. He was hers, for a little while he was hers. "It hurts," she said again.

AT THE DOOR to Anton's room, Jane cried. Not for her mother but because she knew that now her mother would never leave. She could tell from the tone of her mother's voice—that power, that urgency so rarely there—that she would have this baby. She could tell, as if she were inside her mother's mind, that her mother had had dreams already about this baby, about what this baby would mean, that this baby would come to save her when she had been left so alone, that this baby would keep her forever with Anton, that this baby would knit the family together for once and permanently, that she could give this baby a good life. This baby would obliterate the life she had had before, making the one she had now complete and right. Jane was inside her mother's mind; they were thinking as one. She knew her, knew what she was thinking behind that bolted door—that this child would solve the trouble of her loneliness, make right what her first marriage had made wrong.

Jane felt the largeness of possibility—big like a universe opening doors on more universe—and at the same time knew how small permanence and decision can be. She would be here in this dance with these people until death. She imagined herself as old as her grandmother—her grandmother who at Jane's age had no idea of the characters that would inhabit, invade, her later life. Suddenly Jane had a love for the new baby. She vowed she would love it like a mother, realized that at fifteen she was old enough to be this child's mother. She would mother this child in order to ensure her own mother's dreams.

IN THE MORNING it was decided and a little later announced. "We're having a baby," Anton said with a jolly tone. The family was gathered for a family meeting in his office, the room where he both worked on his book and saw his patients and where the children were only allowed when invited by Anton. The kids studied the room, trying to imagine what went on in here when Anton had a session. Sometimes in the hall Kate and Finny would put their ears to the door and listen to the crying of the woman who wet her pants, to the identical-twin Indian Parsis who prayed to Anton as if he were a god, to the graduate student and his girl. They claimed Anton saved their lives.

"We want your help, deciding if it's a good idea," Anton continued, though the issue had already been decided. He simply wanted them to feel they were part of the choice. The walls of the room were lined with bookcases. He called this the sexuality library and on the shelves there were books about homosexuality, monogamy, hermaphrodites. The words LOVE and SEX radiated from those shelves. THE END OF SEX, THEORIES OF SEX, SEX AND THE CHURCH, SEX AND THE BRAIN, SEXOLOGY, SEX, LOVE AND THE DEVIL. The kids had stolen hours in there looking at the pictures of vaginas with testicles and men with breasts or with scrotums turned inside out.

Sofia, as usual, spoke first. "All in favor of an abortion raise your hands," and hers shot up. But of course it didn't really matter what she thought. Anton had decided they would have the baby and the baby would be a girl and she would be a strong and fearless woman and her life would be inspired by adventure and the world.

You could tell from the way he spoke about this child that the depths of his love would expand and multiply. It wasn't that he loved his other children less. It was that he hadn't believed that there was room for more love inside of him. She, his baby daughter, would represent the mystery of all that love—above all because he had almost tossed her away. She would represent that choice, and as she grew into a long-limbed, gray-eyed beauty of fierce intelligence she would represent the other abortions as well. A paradox again, he would wonder who those other children would have been. If Alice were so tremendous, how tremendous would they have been? Yet had either one of them been born, Anton never would have had Alice. Alice was all three of them, and her existence alone was a miracle that he would treasure and contemplate and turn over in his mind along with his deep ambivalence and confusion with faith and fate and the will of God.

On the day she was born at Columbia Presbyterian with a view of the Washington Bridge, with the movie camera whirring and Brahma in the corner, all the names that Anton and Eve and the kids had thought up during one of their many family meetings became meaningless. They were names belonging to an imagined child, but not this child. Not this tiny, bloody long-lashed baby whose screams entered every part of him, inflating him with love. For two weeks she would remain unnamed. I'm thinking about it, he'd say when asked, holding his girl bundled in a blanket. This annoyed Eve's daughters—Kate in particular. She resented Anton's claiming this child that their mother had produced. "We should just name her. We should name her Charlotte," Kate said at one family meeting, peering into the face of big sleeping eyes. "Mom did all the work," Kate said. "We should be able to decide, too."

Anton stared at Kate with his face reddening. She could tell he didn't like the notion of having done no work. The baby awoke with the sensation of his body rising. Kate was always scared of Anton. The fear made her never want to say a word. In fact, for the most part she rarely spoke. She saw what happened when Jane spoke out. Kate's face twitched, becoming quite ugly as she wondered if she'd pushed too far. She was jealous of the baby, held there tightly in her father's embrace. She wished he would hold her sometime like that. And everyone said the baby was so beautiful. To Kate it was just a baby and ugly, with an unusually big head.

"I did some work, too, babe," he said, softening. The baby started to scream, hungry. "But the work's only beginning," he said with a smile as he tried to soothe the baby. "Want me to show you how to change a diaper, babe?" The three sisters thought of the night Anton tried to convince their mother to abort. Often they thought identical thoughts; they were connected that way, somehow. Later, the sisters would wonder if their half-sister were connected to them in the same way. Eventually, they'd decide not, that she never could be because she was so much of him.

"Charlotte's a nice choice," Anton said. "How about a vote?" Kate felt embarrassed now with all the attention on her. Part of her wished he'd refused the name without discussion and gotten mad and exploded. Then she could have been mad at him and that would have felt so much nicer. "It reminds me too much of the spider," Julia said, killing the idea entirely.

His baby. His life. His murderess. He wouldn't want to give her up at feeding time. He'd let her suck and suck and suck on his pinkie, wishing it could produce the milk. She was the citrus tree bearing all the various citrus fruits. She had a bit of Kate and Julia and Jane. She had a bit of Nicholas, Sofia, Caroline, Finny, and Timothy all wrapped up within her. Through her he could love them each a little more. She had big gray eyes at birth and their color would never change.

Alice Athene. He chose that name. At a family meeting in the library with the long-lashed bundle in his lap two weeks after Brahma had decided her fate and she had entered this world from between her mother's thighs and onto the film of her father's Super 8, Alice Athene was named. Alice Athene for her wondrous gray eyes. Alice Athene because it was a big strong name.

The world took on a new meaning. It seemed the world, the universe, the sun, the moon, were created for him and his girl. It seemed everything in his life had happened in order to bring him this child—the failure of his first marriage, the Jesuits, the abortions, his very birth. Light was created to shine on them. Jesus, God, and the Holy Spirit. Brahma and existentialism, even. A new faith.

A few weeks later he baptized Alice himself (this was as close as he'd let her get to Christianity). The ceremony took place in the indoor swimming pool, steamy and hot and filled with family and friends. Naked, holding his naked baby, he dipped her once, twice, thrice. He said a few prayers, candles were lit, champagne bottles popped open. The kids swam about in the water, their heads bobbing in the mist. The baby cried. Holding her, he understood that he could die now and he understood as well that for her sake he could not.

CHAPTER THREE

The Proposal

1971

M Y NAME IS ANTON Furey and I write this proposal
on behalf of a small group of people in this town who want to
come together to form an organic community that will develop
a new lifestyle for living more creatively and joyfully. For the
past few months we have been working on a functional community design which includes the following basic ideas.

We hope to find enough semirural land, within twenty to
thirty minutes' drive from the town center, to eventually ac-
commodate about fifty to sixty people. We want separate
dwellings for families and apartment complexes for individuals
with sufficient space to ensure privacy and some land to farm.
We also intend to have separate living facilities for university
students from town who will share in part of the community
experience. The makeup of the community will be as heteroge-
neous as possible.

The architectural aim is toward the aesthetically exciting
and challenging as well as the comfortable and functional.
There will be a communal dining room for the single members
who don't want to cook and for families who occasionally feel

the same way. There will be a building for centralized activities and living quarters for visitors and temporary residents. We will welcome, with community approval, people who are "turning new corners" in their lives and need a place to stay during that time.

We don't want to retreat or dissociate ourselves from the world. On the contrary, we hope that there will be a dynamic interaction between our community and the existing society. Therefore, some of the members will work in the community and some will continue with their outside professions.

Other points of contact with the larger community will be a Gestalt Therapy Center, an experimental school, and a craft workshop. The Gestalt Center will have regularly scheduled encounter and sensitivity-training workshops in which people can work on themselves and on clarity. There are several members of the community who are trained in the Gestalt method and I, Anton Furey, will oversee its direction. Plans for the school, which will be K–12 for sixty to seventy children, are being developed by several teachers in our group including my wife, Agnes Furey. Please contact Mrs. Furey for further information. Essentially, however, we believe in the child and her right to pursue her interests. The Craft Guild will offer an opportunity for people to use their hands creatively—candle making, pottery, sewing, cooking, carpentry. These activities will take place on the community property, but the staff will include those from outside the community.

Each person, including children, will participate in the decisions that affect the total community. Meetings will be held at specified times for the purpose of making decisions and airing gripes. The members themselves will determine how they wish the community organization to function. There will be no leader or guru—it will be a participatory democracy.

*A major radical aim of the community would be a pilot
project to equalize the roles of men and women in terms of
work, leisure, and vocational opportunities. Men and women,
husbands and wives, will be asked to share their common tasks
and to treat each other on a totally equal basis. Each person
will be responsible for jobs devoted to the community good,
such as gardening, cleaning, cooking in the communal dining
room, etc., and each family for the upkeep of its own home.
There will be a collective pool of talents and knowledge to be
tapped.*

*We hope to make the financing of the community a flexible
shareholders' arrangement so that no one need be excluded but
also no one need bear too large a financial burden. Because of
the experiential and humanistic aspects of the community, we
intend to approach individuals and foundations for their
support.*

*A very important ingredient of our life will be an emphasis
on interaction between children and adults. We want to encourage the "extended family" idea in which adults, married
and single, will have a role in rearing the children. Children
will have more opportunity for friends of all ages. We believe
this will mean more freedom for both children and parents to
develop healthy and joyful lives. We want our community to be
a place where each person can be himself and allow others to be
themselves. Therefore the basis of our interpersonal relation-
ships is honesty and openness. When resentments, arguments,
or estrangements occur, we will deal directly with whoever is involved and work the problem through. This may be in a community meeting or privately, but the necessity for facing difficult
and uncomfortable situations will be an accepted pattern. In
encountering ourselves, and others, in this way, we hope to grow
by giving up our manipulative, dishonest game playing. We be-*

lieve that a great deal of energy is thus released and can be used more freely, creatively, and joyously.

In closing, I would like to include a quote from a Look Magazine article written by George Leonard (January 13, 1970) which states succinctly our feelings on community life:

We need bigger, less well-defined "families." We need groups of friends and neighbors who are willing and able to share the strongest feelings, to share responsibilities for the emotional needs of all the children in the group. Thus no one will be childless, no one will lack affection, and no one will be deprived of a rich and varied emotional and sensual life.

CHAPTER FOUR

Chardin

"TIME," ANTON EXPLAINED, "an understanding of its depths is not even two hundred years old. Before Darwin and evolutionary theory, time was thought to have spread back only six to eight thousand years and to have had a future of just about as long. The world's leading thinkers would not have dared imagine a past or a future extending any further." It was a few months before Alice was born. All eight kids sat on the deck. Anton and Agnes had bought the place a year before—fifty acres on a hill, the highest point in Hunterdon County—but before moving in, Agnes had left for an ashram in New York City to try to give their marriage space. Now Eve was quite pregnant and Anton was designing a commune of another sort.

On a clear day, Anton told the kids that you could see all the way to New York City and the Empire State Building and the Twin Towers. It was a clear day, but they couldn't see anything like that. Even so they still, all of them, believed him. Anton had big plans for the deck. The deck was like a stage with levels and tiers and he wanted to put on plays, direct the kids in *Hamlet*, in all of Shakespeare, and invite friends and anyone from town who cared to watch. *"O God!"* he'd think, mouthing the precious words, *"I could be bounded in a nutshell and count myself a king of infinite space, were it not that I have bad dreams."* He wanted to have dinner parties on the lawn, tables elegantly clothed in white, champagne fountains, while Nicholas played the part of Hamlet and Julia of Ophelia. Nicholas had a brooding look that reminded Anton of Hamlet, and Julia—Julia was pure and tragic beauty. But for now he was teaching the kids about time.

"Of course biblically you know the story, that man appeared fully formed. You know Athene, like Athene from the head of Zeus. But with Darwin we learned otherwise." Anton stood up, big tall handsome man that he was with his sideburns and his blue eyes squinting in even the slightest light. He worked on his treatise in a dark wing of the house, the dark study with a big fireplace. The kids liked that the house had wings, as if it were living, as if it could gather speed and fly. Books and newspaper clippings on sex and sexuality cluttered the floor, spilling out of boxes and filing cabinets. He'd spend long hours in there. This was going to be a great work. This was going to change the way men and women think about sex and marriage. A revolution, it would cause nothing less.

The Coopers were still living ten miles down the road in the big white house, but Ian wanted to live in the house again and so it was Anton's and Eve's idea that she would sell her half to Ian's new wife, Camille, and move out here as soon as Anton's divorce was definitive and Laurence had finished the additions.

Anton's five children already lived here. Nicholas, the oldest, had painted his room a deep purple for "Purple Haze"—the color was so deep it looked black. Caroline's room had a collection of rare books that had belonged to Agnes and an ivory rosary hanging from the window. There was nothing particular about the rooms of the others, just kid rooms with football motifs—the Fighting Irish, the Miami Dolphins, the Buffalo Bills, the Cowboys. O. J. Simpson was their hero, everything orange and O. J. They even had a dog named O. J. The additions were lofts which made the Furey children nervous that they'd have to share their rooms—the Cooper girls in the lofts, suspended above them.

During family meetings Anton often talked to the kids about big things. Time was a big thing, of course. And, of course, so was God. Today he was trying to explain to them God's relationship to time and evolutionary theory. Other days he'd explain about Gestalt truth or the myths of the generation gap. Or they'd fight about politics—Vietnam and abortion. Anton was pro and con respectively, in opposition to the kids.

"If you open your eyes and look, Darwin was suggesting, you'd see that species evolve and that the theory of the instant creation of all things was impossible."

The Coopers' green car was parked in the driveway and their dog, Max, a big white sheep dog, sniffed about in the yard. Not on this visit, but on another visit not unlike this one, Max would drown in the indoor swimming pool. Julia would find him floating there, hair matted, drenched, eyes open, dead. But for now he pranced, liking the place. A warm summer breeze drifted over the lawn and the field and if you looked straight ahead, you looked above the trees and it seemed you could look into infinity. The trees in the yard were thick with brilliant green leaves and the lawn was emerald. To the left of the yard, surrounded by crab apple trees, lay the outdoor pool. The kids all wanted to swim. Anton opened a bottle of champagne while he spoke, resting it in a silver ice bucket.

"As I've said, before Darwin we thought of time differently. Time was brief. We could never have believed that it could be so infinite. That isn't what the Bible taught." When Anton had his family meetings, everyone listened. The kids were sitting there, concentrating. He wanted to teach them things he thought they might not learn in school. "But with Darwin, time was forced open like space and the universe were after Galileo. In both cases time and space were extended toward infinity. In the Renaissance, the Italian Giordano Bruno was burned at the stake for his belief that space was infinite. Well, of course, the Church didn't like Darwin, either, declared him a heretic and tried the best it could to ignore, even silence, his work." He spoke seriously, without irony. He wanted the kids to learn. He squinted in the bright light.

The kids knew little things about Darwin. They knew he figured out that man was once some kind of ape and all life had evolved from some sort of slime. They knew as well that Darwin's parents didn't think he was all that bright and that they sent him on the HMS *Beagle* to study wildlife in South America, hoping that it would lead to something, but expecting nothing. It gave Kate hope to think about Darwin's not being too bright because she was terrible in school, though she did not feel at all dumb. What was happening at home was far more interesting than what was happening in school and thus she couldn't concentrate.

"What are you getting at?" Julia finally asked Anton. She never felt dumb. She was a star in school. In fact, she always had to show how smart she was. She was twelve, but thought of herself more as eighteen. "I know you're not having a family meeting to tell us stuff we already know about Darwin."

He smiled at her and winked. The way he did that melted you. In that one wink all his attention focused on you. The Cooper girls were always vying for that wink, as if it pulled them into him, making them feel safe and loved by him. "You're absolutely right, babe," he said. He loved Julia best of the Cooper girls. Her fierce intelligence, her exquisite desire to know. Kate was too quiet and awkward with her crooked teeth, and Jane was too contentious, always testing him. He poured everyone a glass of champagne now, even the little kids. And then Eve, who hadn't been on the deck, appeared from the sliding glass door to the living room, carrying something big beneath an orange towel. She was smiling, too, and she came over next to Anton and stood behind him. Her swollen belly pressed against his back. The wind blew his hair gently, mussing it.

"Now, looky here. What I'm getting at is an understanding of the meaning of evolution." He was all concentration and focus. From the way his eyes squinted alone, the kids understood that he was going to be giving a lesson. A big lesson. "With the advent of astronomy, the geocentric universe, in which earth sits in its fixed place at the center of all things, with the heavens above and hell below, was exploded. With Darwin, with geology and biology, the horizons of time have been pushed backward into the remote past and forward into the far-distant future. As life came to be seen as evolving across the millennia in a gradual succession of living forms, suddenly a notion of progress was born. With this new sense of moving forward in time from the simplest life-form to the most complex, science became more than a method of classifying the facts of life. In fact, science was seen as the specific means by which humanity would move forward into the future." He spoke directly, losing some of the kids. But the kids were used to being lost.

"Like slime becoming human," Finny said, his big blue eyes squinting just like Anton's, his long hair blowing into his mouth, across his cheeks. His hair was so thick that a dozen ticks had once lived in it long enough to turn fat with his blood before he noticed them.

"Well exactly, sort of," Anton answered warmly. Anton loved Finny specially. He was Anton's Alyosha, warm and tender and pure and good—spiritual. "Now you all know I'm trained in theology. And you know that I'm not scientifically inclined, though I respect science." Of course, they all knew that Anton had been a Jesuit: There was a picture they'd all seen of him wearing a cope and cassock, a rosary around his neck, a wizened elder standing a head shorter at Anton's side. It was taken at Saint Charles seminary in Grand Coteau, Louisiana before he'd left the order in '52—deep time as far as the kids were concerned—because he was too interested in sex and his novice master thought he'd do better in secular life. But Anton took a certain pride in how having been a Jesuit defined him.

The wind picked up and stirred the leaves. The smell of manure rose from the field and a farmer on his tractor, slowly, rhythmically, rode across the lower half that was lying fallow this year. They'd all heard rumors that that farmer, named Gable, like the actor, was not at all nice. Gable had Doberman pinschers that he let roam about and it was his firm belief that all of Anton's land should be his. He was known, therefore, to steal slices of it with his tractor, cultivating it as his own. Since he shared the name with the famous actor, the kids believed that he could be a relative and thus they always tried to get a close-up look at him to see if he were dark and handsome. He wasn't.

"Look around," Eve said brightly. She was still holding on to the big thing beneath the orange towel. Some of the kids wondered what it was.

"It's a sign," Sofia whispered.

"Look at the yard, the day, the house, the trees," Eve said. Though it wasn't her house, she loved it as if it were. They all did as Eve asked. They were too young to think much about physical beauty and how it evolved to be so, but this spot was gorgeous up on top of its hill, a sort of paradise—they couldn't help but recognize that. That's what Eve said: Paradise.

Anton studied Eve. He loved her. Her bright smile. Her brilliant enthusiasm. Her gorgeous brain and her exquisite mistrust of it. He never tired of encouraging her to see her worth. He was quite confident now in his decision to leave Agnes. Sometimes he daydreamed about marrying Eve in Haiti—hike through the mountains, attend voodoo ceremonies, swim beneath emerald waterfalls on black sand beaches, meet local artists and politicians and priests. He knew that with Eve they would always have adventures. "He listens to me," she so often told her daughters.

"What's behind the towel?" Timothy asked. His buck-teeth gave him a goofy look.

"A sign, stupid," Kate said.

"Can I feel the baby kick?" Finny asked, and put his hand on Eve's belly.

"This is our house," Sofia whispered for Eve and the Cooper girls to hear. Sofia didn't want them moving out here and was afraid this was all a big preface to that announcement. (She had refused to allow a loft to be built above her room.) Though Anton had bought the house, it was with her mother's money, and she believed that was an indication that her parents were going to get back together. She knew her mother would adopt the baby as she had with Finny, and then good riddance to the Cooper lot. But the Cooper girls knew better. Eve had told them that Agnes had bought the house so that the kids would have a place to live because at the ashram there was no room for kids.

"What's Darwin got to do with the towel?" Finny asked.

"Well, I'm getting to that, babe," Anton said. "But Eve is right. Do you see how beautiful this place is?" The light trickled through the trees, spraying across the lawn. He had enormous plans for this place. He wanted orchards and a barnyard with animals. Vast gardens that bloomed both by day and by night. He wanted them to raise their own beef and pork and lamb and chicken, collect their own eggs, grow their own vegetables and berries. The possibilities were infinite. Eventually he wanted to set up a school for the kids, perhaps have other families move out here so there could be a larger community, an extended family. Already the property had two cabins big enough for families of four.

They all said yes, impatiently. The house was long and flat, tucked against woods with that persistent ivy climbing up the walls, smothering it. It had been a hunter's cabin over a hundred years ago and hunters had come up here to shoot deer with bows and arrows. Before that it had been the site of Chief Himmohaho's tribe of Leni-Lenape and if you searched hard you could find arrowheads. Some legends had the house built on the site of a burial mound. There was a lot of history to this place. George Washington had marched by here on his way to the Delaware and camped in a grove of trees by Indian Creek at the foot of their hill. These were the stories that Anton told the kids. John Ringo, the founder of the town, had buried a pot of gold up here. Later, over the years, Anton would organize enormous parties in the summer and have treasure hunts with all the guests searching the property for that gold. The Stranges were the first to use a metal detector. They combed all fifty acres. "There's no gold here, Anton," Mr. Strange said. "No gold a'tall," Mrs. Strange added. "Sorry to burst your bubble, old man," Mr. Strange would say with a pat on Anton's shoulder. "You've given up too easily, my friend," Anton would say confidently. "It's there." Mr. Strange was a small keen man with keen eyes and a spirit for adventure himself. He'd traveled all of Asia as a young man, writing poetry and letters home that his mother read aloud after dinner to the company that collected in the parlor. One woman collected there was Lilia Morgan, lying on a divan dreaming that someday, though she had never met the writer of the letters and though she was married already herself, she would be Mrs. Strange.

Over the years friends would live in the cabins, erect teepees in the woods, while other friends would come for a long weekend and never leave. *Let our home be a haven for those in need.* The seven Poles came and a whole cast of characters that were friends of Nicholas. Sergio Tate rented Kate's bedroom from Kate for ten dollars an hour so that he could take his girlfriend there. Of course, Kate had no idea what he did in the room, she was only eleven, delighted by the money. Friends of the kids, a friend who had just been released from jail. Friends of friends, old boyfriends of old friends, would come to stay and stay and stay. "Get rid of them," Jane would demand. But now they were still way back at the beginning— sitting on the deck imagining the depths of time, expanding like the universe, as if their future could be as infinite.

"Now I want each one of you to notice something that you find beautiful," Anton continued. Then he called each child by name. He loved it here. You could see it in his eyes, and he wanted the kids to love it just as he did. It was the first time in his forty-three years that he owned so much land. He saw himself a boy in Texas on a small street in a small house with a tiny yard, his mama pleading with him to make something of himself: "Get out of here, out of flat empty Texas." She had wanted him to be a priest, said she'd had the vision when she was first pregnant, before she knew her boy would be a boy. A vision in a field of bluebonnets and in the distance oil rigs pumping up gold and all the dreams of Texas. A priest. He had tried. Now he was at work on a book, an important book, and he saw himself with it, handing the finished book over to his mama—her reward. He saw her taking it and though she would not understand it, holding the object would make her tremendously proud.

They were silent at first. You could hear the leaves, the grass, the terrific velvet wind. "The spiderwebs all around us," Julia said suddenly. "You don't notice them unless you look. It's as if we're inside the web, like we're inside silk." "The air," Jane said, "how clean and cool it feels even though it's summer." Then everyone was speaking at once, excited by Anton's excitement. "You can see the Empire State Building," Kate said. "And the Trade Towers climbing into the sky." "Like castles," Anton said with his smile. "Castles in the air," Eve said. "But you can't see them," Timothy snapped. "On an even clearer day you can." "The trees," Caroline said. "They're like spires rising all around us." "Fifty acres," Sofia said. "All the space and it's ours, Furey land." "The pond in the woods," Finny said, "with the big snapping turtles and the scaly smallmouth bass." "Indians lived here," Timothy said, "and I found an arrowhead, and a pot of gold is buried here for us to find." (He loved to play cowboys and Indians, played all the time. He always pretended that he was a Texas Ranger and he always got Kate to play with him though he'd never let her be a cowboy. If she played she could only be a squaw or a whore—"You choose," he'd tell her.) "The big lawn," Nicholas said. "It's big enough for a football game."

"Pierre Teilhard de Chardin is one of my favorite writers and thinkers," Anton said, becoming serious again. "He was a Jesuit and a paleontologist who worked in China. In fact, he was part of the team that discovered *Sinanthropus*, Peking man, in 1929. He wrote a book called *The Phenomenon of Man*, which was not published until after his death in 1955, because, in this book, he tries to reconcile evolutionary theory and the depths of time with Catholic doctrine. The Church did not like this." The sun, trickling through the leaves, sprinkled over them. They were serious now. When Anton spoke for a long time his Texas accent thickened. It was thick now.

"What's behind the towel?" Timothy persisted.

"The Omega Point," Caroline said to Anton, sitting forward in her chair. "The Omega Point's behind the towel." They held each other with their eyes. He was proud of his girl's knowledge. She always knew how to study a situation to figure it out. Of his two daughters she was the thinker, the intellectual, warm and gentle and not at all silly or frivolous. She always chose her words carefully. Her blond hair was pulled back with a headband. Her eyes clear as the sky. The other kids looked at her curiously.

"Exactly, babe," Anton said, and lifted his glass. Delight lit his face. He was impatient to show them the surprise beneath the towel. They clinked their glasses though none of the other kids knew what they were talking about. Caroline always knew obscure things. She had read a good many of the books in Anton's library. Her favorite writer was G. K. Chesterton. The wind died down and the mean farmer continued making his way across the field. Eve let the orange towel drop to reveal the sign. The word CHARDIN was intricately carved beneath the omega symbol, big and bold in black. Running up the sides and around the top was carved ivy painted green with a spray of pastel flowers.

"That's Greek," Sofia said, "meaning everlasting or never ending."

"What does that have to do with Chardin?" Julia asked, raising her left eyebrow. "And what's the Omega Point?" They all studied the sign.

Anton asked Caroline to explain.

"It's the point at which there is a final union between the human and the divine," Caroline said. Her voice was quiet, but assured. Wise. "The point where evolution reaches its culmination and man and God coalesce. Teilhard writes about it; it's his theory in *The Phenomenon of Man*. The idea is that evolution is not haphazard, but rather it's directed by God toward an ever-increasing concentration in Christ. Evolution is like an arrow, right?" she asked, looking at her father for reassurance. He nodded.

"I don't get it," Kate said. She felt stupid, enormously so whenever she was with the Fureys. They always carried on about these subjects that were so abstract. She looked to Julia and Jane, hoping they'd do something to either change the subject or to make her feel smart. If one of them acted smart, they all felt smart.

"This has to do with the noosphere, right Dad?" Sofia asked, trying to keep up with her sister. "*Noos* in Greek means 'mind.'"

Puffy clouds billowed dramatically like empires in the cornflower sky and the wind picked up and then died down.

"I am the Alpha and the Omega," Nicholas said, "the

beginning and the ending saith the Lord, which is, and which was, and which is to come, the Almighty."

"The rhythm of the wind," Julia said dreamily, continuing with what it was that she loved about the place. It was a dreamy day. The day their home was being named. Their home for eternity, that's what Anton dreamed. Here things would happen. He pulled out blueprints that Laurence had designed to show the kids the idea for the silos and the tower, for the lofts and a new glass kitchen overlooking the fields and big enough for them all. The pages fluttered in the breeze and Julia poked and prodded at the sheets enthusiastically approving the designs. Here Anton would make his family. Here he would write his book. Here his life would unfold, evolve— all of their lives. His book would be published. It would make a difference, receive good reviews, earn royalties, earn him a living so that he'd be free of his dependence on Agnes's wealth. He wanted to be the one to provide. He inflated just a little thinking of that, handing out an allowance to each and every one of these kids. Chardin—the family farm for generations, their own village.

"There's a rhythm to the wind like the sighing and revving of an engine," Julia continued. "I like that we're up here on this hill in our own little world with these currents of wind cooling us. Let's put on some music," she said, sipping her champagne. And then she went inside to put on Mozart's serenades. She loved the oboe. "It's like a human voice," she'd say.

"Who's going to pay for all this?" Sofia asked, fingering the blueprints as Anton rolled them up.

"I am," Eve said. "When I sell my house." She gave Sofia a look. A perpetual duel existed between them. Sofia was too polite to ask, What about Mom? Even so the question was apparent in the expression on her face.

"An excellent choice," Anton said as Julia returned. "And, by George, it does sound like the human voice."

"What's the noosphere?" Sofia asked Julia, testing her though Sofia had long forgotten what the noosphere was. She was jealous of Anton's affection for Julia and was always trying to make her look stupid though she never managed to succeed. And now she was mad that Eve would be putting her money into the house because then, she knew, everything would be intertwined and confused.

"I've no idea," Julia said, unafraid to not know when the subject was something that she might not possibly know. "Dennis Brain. He was the best interpreter of Mozart's music for the French horn."

"He died in a car crash," Caroline said.

"Do you mean," Jane said to Anton, sarcasm curling her lower lip. She'd been quiet up to then, pondering big notions. "That we're living in the Omega Point here at Chardin."

"You've got to aim high, babe. Aim high with me. If a thing's worth doing, it's worth doing badly." And he gave her that wink which Kate noted, knowing that on Jane it was wasted.

"Chesterton said that," Finny said, referring to aiming high, proud of his knowledge. He was almost eight years old.

"It's a name," Eve said, smiling at her daughter. She didn't want Jane to ruin anything. Anton had been so happy to have the sign made; he had designed it himself, drawing it out on paper with crayons in a dozen colors. He had kept it a secret from the kids and had been looking forward to the surprise of showing them the sign. Eve knew that. He wanted to include all the kids in the naming of Chardin, as if they were one. "A sort of ideal," she added. Eve knew well how easily Jane could ruin things. She studied her daughter's big brown eyes to see what she could read in them, which way her mood would go, trying to will it toward generosity. Jane's hair was long and ratty. In the past two years she had changed so much. She was no longer a girl in tight braids. Rather, she had developed breasts. She was a teenager and her bitter opinions were even more bitter. Eve studied her other daughters. They were ratty, too—Kate with her crooked teeth and Julia determined to grow her hair long enough to sit upon. She thought of them not so long ago in their matching outfits, and a part of her wished they could be like that again.

"The meeting place of man and God, where man meets God, evolved to a perfect state? Isn't it just like a Christian to find a way to make Christianity and God the center of everything, even of science? Make science and evolution a Christian notion? At the service of their theology?" Jane said, holding Anton with her eyes. Her hand clutched her champagne flute. But what Jane really wanted was to press him on logistics. She knew, despite all the words and promises, that it could be a long time before he actually divorced his wife. She knew that his wife would accept him no matter what, that she had accepted him back after Finny was born and had even adopted the child. She knew, as well, that Anton did not have enough of his own money to leave his wife. He was caught. No matter how hard he claimed to love Eve.

"You're a good thinker, babe. I like a doubter. It's good to know they're teaching you something in school." He raised his glass to her. "Or perhaps it's just my ornery influence."

"It's an honorable name," Julia said, raising her glass, too. She knew that Jane was on the verge of bringing up the wife. There was silence for a moment, swollen and thick like you could touch it. Jane loved to bring up the wife. It made her feel powerful to make people face things they didn't want to face.

"The baby's kicking," Eve blurted, genuinely in awe of the motion coming from within her, the tiny elbow and knee pushing through. Those near her—even Sofia—put their hands on her stomach to feel.

"It's a lot of pressure," Jane said. She could turn the mood of the afternoon any way she chose. She knew that. And that, too, made her feel powerful. She knew how easily she could make him snap, make him puff up, turn red, get angry enough to want to smash something. But the will of the others was stronger—the will to give Anton this day. Jane was outnumbered so she relented, slowly, gently. What did she care? She knew if they ever did move out here, she would move away. "I think my intelligence has a lot to do with your ornery influence," she added.

"It's a romantic idea, Chardin," Caroline said.

Some small part of Jane wanted to surrender to Anton and be loved and cared for by him, wanted to believe in Anton's dream because she knew it was her mother's dream as well. "Here's to Chardin," Jane said. She lifted her glass and all the glasses clinked.

"It's a beautiful sign." Eve sighed, slumping back in her chair.

"To where man and God meet," and the glasses clinked again.

"To where man is perfect enough finally to grace God."

"To where we're perfect enough to finally grace God."

"Do you think God will be a woman when we meet her?"

Anton poured them all some more champagne and they sat out there on the deck until the afternoon began to fade and the sunset sprawled across the sky. Somewhere Anton had believed it was that simple, way back at the beginning, in the depths of time. He was an ambitious man, or at least an ambitious dreamer—passionate, a sensualist. For him ideals were practical. He wanted to create a place on earth that would be worthy of God, of life, of himself, of Eve, of these children. They all believed in the dream, for all their lives they would. Sure they would fight and sure they would hate each other, but just as soon they'd love again. Chardin was their country. Anton was giving it to them.

"How about a little football game?" Anton asked.

CHAPTER FIVE

Locks

JULIA HAD THIRTEEN LOCKS on her bedroom door. Thirteen locks in one long row. She loved those locks, the clicks they made as one by one she bolted them closed at night. She had one for each year. She was thirteen going on adult. She had screwed the locks in herself—all but the lock on the knob, which wasn't much of a lock, an easy one to pop. Screwed and hammered them in with their bolts and their screws and their keys and their nails. Some of them were pretty, brass and silver. She flirted with the carpenter whom Anton had hired first to build the lofts and now the extension to the dining room until he agreed to drill the holes for her. The carpenter with the long red beard would later steal from them—Tiffany silver and sheepskin rugs, a Haitian painting or two, an erotic wood carving. But for now he was just a nice red-bearded guy, working steadily on the dining room that seemed to hang above the lawn and fields. Other than the drilling, Julia installed the locks on her own with tools she found in the utility closet.

Julia's locks were a fetish, one of her many fetishes like silk pajamas and linen sheets and velvet dresses and her long mane of thick blond curly hair, which she brushed one hundred times each day with a special brush with special bristles. In her room gardenias and jasmine thrived, their white buds in perpetual blossom.

All over the house, as it happened, there were keys. Cigar boxes filled with single keys—beautifully colored keys. It seemed those keys could open countless doors and the kids wondered where all the doors for all those keys were. Everyone had at least one lock on his or her door. Even so, the house had only twenty-seven lockable doors. Julia had counted them. And only eleven of them had actual working locks—though of course Julia's alone had thirteen. Green keys and red and blue and even a yellow key with a metallic shimmer. A rainbow of keys. One thing each kid wanted was a master key that would unlock all the doors. Anton was the only one with master keys. He kept them on a key chain carved with an ivory anaconda, coiling to strike. "There is no master key that could unlock my door," Julia declared proudly to the others, lifting her left eyebrow. "Not even all of Anton's keys could unlock my door. I've made certain of that." Anton would flirt with Julia. He'd chase her through the house until he caught her, then bend her fingers back until she was on her knees pleading with him to stop. Sometimes before bending her fingers, as he was chasing her, he'd snatch off her blouse. She'd try to cross her hands over her chest though she didn't have much to hide. When she said "uncle" the game was over.

Julia's room was like a sanctuary, a museum with rare and precious jewels. It smelled sweet, like a florist's shop. "What's so good about your room?" Kate asked, standing in the doorway. "Why all the locks? I don't see anything so special in here." Everyone hated Julia for having all the locks. "She's

neurotic," Sofia would pronounce. That was a big word in the
1970s; the kids had gotten into using it all the time. People
were neurotic and they went to therapists and EST in order to
find themselves. "Like Kersi and Farhad," Sofia said. They
were Anton's patients—the Indian Parsis he saw to make
extra money. "When Kersi and Farhad die, their bodies will
be laid in the open for vultures to peck clean," Julia told the
kids. She liked knowing details like that. "It's their religion."

"While we'll be eaten by worms," Caroline said.

"You may be. I'll be ashes," Julia said. "Dancing with the
wind."

Of Julia's locks, the kids were jealous, of course. Each kid
secretly wished for multiple locks. They envied the mass of
keys that Julia carried on a silver Tiffany ring. One key, they
were sure, existed to unlock all the locks in the house, and
they searched for it in those cigar boxes as if finding it would
unlock more than her door.

ACTUALLY, KATE ADMIRED the room. She stood in the doorway waiting for an answer. It had petal pink walls and a big
red velvet bookcase that reached from the floor to the ceiling.
In the bookcase were Jane Austen novels and Russian novels
and Hardy novels (Julia had read them all) and a Spanish doll
she had named Mariquita Perez and for whom she had a
wardrobe almost as varied and as vast as her own. One special
shelf was preserved for the music of Mozart. Dennis Brain,
who died in the car crash. The small details. Kids never forget
that kind of stuff. "He died in a car crash," Kate observed.
"And Mozart was buried in an unmarked pauper's grave,"
Julia added. Beneath a set of four windows languished "like
an odalisque," Julia would say, a red velvet couch to match
the bookcase. The couch was upholstered with five humps

and each hump created a seat and each seat lifted to reveal a hiding place for her silks and linens, all of which she ironed herself.

The windows overlooked the deck, the yard, and the field. "I can see everything from my room," she'd say to Kate. "I can spy on people late at night when they think they're utterly alone." Once at dawn she saw two of Anton's patients, the graduate student and his girl, making love on the diving board. The woman danced on her knees with her crotch in his face. Mostly, Julia just saw people after parties who had drunk or smoked far too much. Janis Joplin belting out blues and people skinny-dipping in the indoor or outdoor pool depending on the season. And Nicholas driving home, late, in his yellow MG convertible. Sometimes for fun, when his MG was broken, he would steal someone's car right out of its driveway and drive it most of the way home. (People left the keys in the ignition back then.) On those nights Julia would see him walking up the driveway, hunched over and sloppy. He was never stupid enough to bring the car all the way home. He was a bad-boy type and she loved that about him. He felt dangerous to her, in need of being conquered and then protected. His teenage sexuality spilled out of him with his long blond hair and marble blue eyes, his ability with a guitar and singing love ballads written by hard rock bands— The Who and Led Zepplin, The Doors. On those nights he'd knock on her door, pleading to be let in. "I love you, Julia," he'd whisper through the door. Sometimes she'd let him in and he'd hold her and she'd hold him, patting him on the back. He'd be cold and smell of cigarettes and something sad. She'd lay him down and fuss over him and think of herself as Florence Nightingale, getting him water and aspirin. "You've got to go back to high school," she'd instruct, pinning him down with her hands, her own nascent sexuality pulled by his and the power she could feel she had over him. He dropped out of high school when he turned sixteen. "I like that you're my sister," he told her. Though really, looking at his big blue eyes in his gentle face, what she wanted was for him to fall in love with her.

HER PINK ROOM had been Nicholas's before, the one that had been painted a deep purple to honor Jimi Hendrix. "Janis Joplin loved him," Julia said to Kate tragically, thinking of Nicholas, "But he did not love her back." She sang a bit of a Joplin song about freedom and having nothing to lose. A sand blaster had been needed to remove the purple paint. "She didn't write 'Me and Bobby McGee,'" Kate said. "Kris Kristofferson did." "Bobby McGee was a girl," Julia added.

Julia's room was the only room in the house next to Anton and Eve's. Sometimes late at night Julia could hear them. She didn't want to listen too hard, but sometimes they argued and there was nothing she could do. Mostly, though, she heard the baby—Alice Athene, six months old.

It was just Kate and Julia of the Cooper girls at Chardin. Jane moved in and then promptly moved out. She went to live with her high school music teacher. She left with a knapsack patched with peace signs and ERA and pro-choice buttons. She did not explain to her sisters why she was leaving, but they knew it had to do with Anton.

Julia's bed was a canopy with a mattress made from horsehair. "Horsehair"—the way Julia said it made it sound expensive, rare, unique, though none of the kids understood why she'd want to sleep on horsehair. "Why horsehair? It's like sleeping on hay in a barn. Doesn't it stink?" "Do they have to flay the horse to get the hair off?" The canopy was draped with lace and it dangled past the mattress as if you were inside a tent. "An Arabian tent," Julia would say. On the floor was a Laver Kirman from Persia that came from the dining room of her old house.

With all the lace and red velvet Julia described her room as a boudoir. When Nicholas and the kids made movies with the Super 8 she always wanted to be the whore. Sometimes Kate would fight with her because she'd want to be the whore, too. But Julia always won. She had bigger breasts and was older. "I've had more practice," she would say, staring down at Kate. "I'm more whorish." And she would tie her silk robe tight around her waist to emphasize her breasts. Actually they were quite small. "SS LL UU T. Slut. You can be the whore," Kate would concede.

Julia had these fetishes. She thought of herself as an elegant woman at thirteen, an Austen woman. Or when she was feeling tragic she thought of herself as Tess. At school she taught all the kids to waltz so that they could have a proper waltz. She had learned to waltz from Anton. At Chardin she organized big parties and made everyone come in long dresses and tails and they waltzed and waltzed, deep into the night. Japanese lanterns lit the lawn and Anton made champagne fountains for her with the cranberry crystal, making sure they ran abundantly. He also organized the music for her, making certain that the waltzes were plentiful, promising that at one of these parties, soon, he'd have a quartet. Julia wore Eve's dress from the May Court Ball at Sweet Briar. A pale blue gown of silk organza with a hoop made from bone.

Standing in the doorway, Kate asked again, "What's so special that you've got to have all those locks?"

"I am," Julia said. Her bright eyes held Kate for a long time.

AT NIGHT WHEN Kate couldn't sleep she'd sleep with Julia. The first night she crept upstairs to Julia's door and knocked. One by one Julia unlocked the locks and slid the bolts. The process took a long time. Kate listened in the dark. She could see her breath. The furnace had broken down a few months back and hadn't been replaced yet. The cost was over three thousand dollars—too expensive. Actually, years would pass before they'd replace it. For now, they used kerosene heaters in some of the rooms and the whole house smelled of it. Bookcases lined the hall, the spines of all the books a deeper shade of dark. Kate didn't like to look too hard. The house at night spooked her. The brass knob of Anton's and Eve's door glistened. She wanted to go in there and curl up with her mother as she used to do back at their old home, back before Anton. Finally the door opened and Kate slipped into the cool wrinkled linen sheets of the horsehair bed as Julia bolted all the locks. "Feel how comfortable the horsehair and linen are," Julia said.

After a short while, sleeping together became a ritual. Sometimes Julia would make Kate sleep on the humped couch, but usually the two of them crammed into the single four-poster bed. "It's warmer this way," Julia would explain. If Nicholas stopped by, they'd sister him and then talk about the beauty of having a brother. Nicholas would sometimes come by just to be swooned over. Then Finny would come, then Timothy. Kate and Julia would pet the boys, fuss with their hair, their ears, late into the night, telling stories. The boys' sisters didn't do that with them anymore.

Julia liked that Kate stayed with her. She liked to tell Kate

things, teach her things she had learned in order to encourage
Kate to be curious about the world—that a monarch butter-
fly has a brain the size of a poppy seed, but it can see three
hundred degrees around, far better than a human, and it
migrates over twenty-five hundred miles for warmth. That
Voltaire died eating his own excrement—she thought she'd
read that in *Madame Bovary,* a book she did not like at
all. "Emma Bovary was a brat." As Kate drifted off, Julia
watched. As Kate slept, Julia studied her, watched her chest
filling and emptying. Kate was not a pretty child. Her
crooked teeth, protruding every which way from her gums,
made her entire face look crooked and distorted. Braces will
fix her teeth. I'll fix her mind, Julia thought. But more than
anything she wanted to protect Kate. Julia was suspicious by
nature, suspected most everyone of something. "Always
sleep with me. It's my job to protect you," Julia would whisper, pulling Kate near, deep against her chest.

JULIA KNEW WHERE Kate was when she woke to find her
gone. Quietly she stepped out of bed and wrapped her silk
robe around her and stepped into her mother's and Anton's
room. Everything was still. She figured Kate had had a bad
dream, that Kate had tried to wake her. Kate was always having trouble sleeping, forever waking Julia with bad dreams. It
was Julia's job now to get her back. She wondered what time
it was, how long Kate had been gone. The room was so dark
Julia could see nothing.

   She stopped near the door, waiting for her eyes to adjust,
but the room only became darker. She heard her mother's soft
breath, the baby's gurgling, the light rustling of sheets as bodies turned. Though she could not see her, Julia knew that
Kate was there. She knew that Kate was wedged into the space

where the water bed met the frame, and she knew that Kate had been there for a while. And she knew that Kate was awake and scared and she knew that it was her job to get Kate out of there without waking her mother or the baby. She could hear wind. She wanted to shout Kate's name. She thought she heard her mother cough. She stood there for a long time until she was quite cold. Finally she managed to whisper Kate's name.

"Go with Julia, babe," Anton said. She heard him move. "Take her back to bed, Julia," he said. She heard the water bed slosh; she heard the wind again, the twisting of the baby in her bed, the plastic crinkle of the diaper. But she could see nothing, hard as she tried. She wondered if Anton could see her eyes, chatoyant in the night. "Off to bed now, babe." Kate scrambled out of the sheets and met Julia in the doorway.

In Julia's room they sat on the red humped couch. A very thin, very early dawn light spread across the morning. It was snowing. Julia studied Kate's face, scrutinizing it as if she could read something. "Stop staring at me," Kate said. "It makes me nervous."

"What happened in there?" Julia asked.

"Nothing," Kate said. "I had a bad dream."

"I told you to wake me."

"I tried," Kate said impatiently.

"You can tell me."

"Tell you what?" Kate said.

Julia brushed Kate's long stringy hair. One hundred strokes. Julia opened a hump in the couch, plucked silk and velvet from it in which she dressed Kate. Kate looked almost beautiful wrapped up in the sumptuous fabrics. She smoothed the silk with her fingers. The tall trees were now in silhouette and even though it was snowing birds sang.

"Why all this silly red velvet on the furniture?" Kate asked.

"I had a romantic notion," Julia said.

"From some novel?"

"Probably. You look like a queen."

"Like Livia?" Kate held her chin high, with drama. Julia had told her about Livia, Augustus's queen, mother of Tiberius, and murderess of many.

"Why did Jane leave?" Kate asked suddenly. The question hung in the air for a while, unanswered. The two of them pictured their sister with her knapsack of signs and symbols walking away, walking down the driveway, departing for good. Julia started to brush Kate's hair again and the question, hanging there, dissolved.

"Why did God create light before he created the sources for light?" Kate asked. "The sun and the moon didn't come until the fourth day: And God made two great lights; the greater light to rule the day, and the lesser to rule the night: He made the stars also. Were the stars an afterthought? A romantic notion?"

"So I've taught you some things," Julia said proudly, "but don't get philosophical . . . or biblical on me. It's too early in the morning. Look how beautiful it is out there."

"Do you think Anton loves me?" Kate asked. She pressed her face into the window and created a fog with her breath. She was crying a little bit, but she did not let Julia know. Snow came down furiously now, collecting on all the trees, weighing down the branches. The first real snow of the year. "Oh Kate," Julia said. She pressed her own face into the window next to Kate's, thinking about Anton in the water bed. "He loves me," Julia said, not triumphantly or competitively, but more with a sense of fact and resolution. He thinks I'm pretty and smart, she thought. I like that he thinks I'm pretty and smart. I like it when he chases after me. She thought of Kate, how she could be so quiet and awkward. Julia worried that Anton didn't love Kate. In fact, she was quite sure he didn't love her, but she didn't tell Kate that. "Maybe school will be canceled," she said. The sun would not crack through today. The light was equal, muted, of one note.

"I hope not," Kate said.

"Maybe this is a blizzard," Julia said. It was hard to see too far into the field now. Kate yawned. She leaned against Julia, resting her head and closing her eyes. Julia ran her fingers through Kate's hair. You could hear the whistling of the snow and wind. Both girls thought of how their mother would be happy, how she loved it when it snowed, how the snow seemed to make the whole world clean.

"When did you get the idea for all those locks?" Kate asked softly.

"What happened in there?" Julia asked again, left eyebrow raised.

"You're so suspicious. Stop it." The snow was thick now and silver in this early equal light, spreading out across the lawn and fields to create a sameness of the land like a desert. "I love Anton," Kate said too softly for Julia to hear.

Chapter Six

Fear

LATER, MUCH LATER, twenty years later to be exact. Anton feared most his body after death, the slow expansion of his guts with gases—slow expansion to the bursting point—and the humiliating smells. A form of hell, a metaphor. And he not there to control it, he not there to take care of his own mess. What would happen to his dead body, his shell? He wished it were like a shell, shed off for some other smaller creature to crawl into and inhabit. Like a hermit crab. For Alice.

He asked Eve, in the early days of his illness, if she would promise to be the caretaker of his body so that his body didn't last to humiliate him. He could imagine quite vividly the noxious gases gurgling to the surface, foaming at his mouth, his nose, his eyes, his ears, as he lay dead on the pillows of their bed. She sat by his side at the edge of the bed all determination and will, residual omnipotence triumphing in her green eyes. She did not want to hear this kind of talk. "Think positively," she told her husband. "We're going to beat this."

Like a child looking for direction, like a child desiring to see the future, believing that a parent's words are the Word, the answer to the mysteries of the future, he filled with a gust of hope. He looked at her. He could see his beautiful wife emerge from the depths and ravages of time—the bright smile that had captivated him. He saw her thirty-four again with her three little girls swarming at her legs in their matching outfits that she had sewn. How he had wanted to save her from the desire to sew. How he had believed that she was meant for much more, that any person who could think as big as she did was not meant for sewing children's clothes, keeping daughters clean. "I want to be a writer," she had told him softly, gently, shyly. How he dreamed sometimes that he could go inside her brain and hack away at the fear that stopped her, go in there with a sledgehammer and smash that stubborn obstinate fear, which was as determined as her will. If only he could train her will on writing. How he dreamed she would succeed, be heard with him standing by her side. With all the kids standing at their side.

He feared the fading memories. He feared the family would evaporate while his body slowly, quietly, permanently laid waste to the dreams. He feared the gates of hell, feared deserving entrance there. The black wall at the end, the icy river and God and his reprimanding finger asking where Anton had been—pointing out one by one all of his transgressions. The Truth was now. His body erupting with impurities, not deserving of purity. He had made his choice long ago to leave the Church, to question Christ, to choose the pleasure of flesh, to flood his soul with the beauty and freedom and risk and experimentation of life. He thought of Kate, of Cliff, of his book, of so many things. It was all done with the aim of experimentation, he tried to reason. No, no. He'd been misguided. He'd been bad. He was guilty. Now, simply, he would learn the Truth. For eternity he would know the truth.

CHAPTER SEVEN

New American Family

FOR A WHILE IN THE 1970s they'd been famous. They had all liked being famous. Reporters came from all over to interview them, from Dallas and Trenton and New York City, from Los Angeles and San Francisco. Television channels were eager to do documentaries on them and even the movies got involved.

"It's a lot to organize," Anton would say. He enjoyed it though. It gave him a break from his book, which had been going slowly. He squinted, date book in hand, red pen poised to make a notation, as he scheduled another appointment, phone pressed between ear and shoulder. He stood in the kitchen, sun streaming in through all of Eve's plants. The kitchen was like a jungle. With the movies, it seemed things were finally going to go their way. Inside both of them, Eve and Anton wanted to make the most of this. Eve encouraged Anton with her bright smile.

It had been a terrible year financially. They had had to fire the cook. The furnace was still broken and they couldn't come up with the cash needed to replace it. They still used the kerosene heaters for each room and the house smelled of kerosene.

"This is ridiculous," Julia said. "Kerosene is more expensive than oil." And besides, they were forever running out of kerosene.

The heater for the indoor swimming pool still worked, but to cut back and save they had to keep the temperature low, at 97, except during parties when Anton would raise it to 105. A thick steam would shroud the pool, making it impossible to see. Sometimes, to stay warm, the kids would hang out in the pool.

"Your skin's gonna shrivel and fall off," Sofia would warn, her bright blue eyes shining. "Wise eyes," she would say. In Greek her name meant wisdom, a fact that made her proud.

To add to their money problems, Agnes was threatening to give all of her money to the ashram and the State of New Jersey wasn't recognizing Anton's divorce, in Haiti, as legal, and thus his alimony was in jeopardy. In which case, as well, it meant that the state was not recognizing his marriage, also in Haiti, to Eve. One of the newspapers wrote about that.

"That means," the Cooper girls' stepmother Camille had said, after reading the article, "that Alice is a bastard." Camille stood in the girls' old kitchen—Camille's kitchen now. It was clean and spare. No plants. No jungle. Practical. She had had Eve's french doors removed because there were too many panes to keep clean. "She's just jealous," Julia said to Kate. "She'd liked to have a baby with Dad."

"GERMANS," ANTON SAID to Eve, affecting a German accent that wasn't very good but that made her smile. "Dey vant to make a documentary. Vhen's a goot time." Together they leaned over his date book, studying the days. The kids wandered in and out of the kitchen.

"Is there any money involved?" Julia asked, raising her left eyebrow and ignoring his stupid accent. At fifteen, she had already put herself in charge of the family finances.

"Friday after Thanksgiving," Eve said. "All the kids will be around then."

"But that's Dad's day with us," Kate said. Eve hadn't realized she was in the room. Ian had been granted every other weekend, the day after Thanksgiving, the day before Christmas, and one month in the summer by the State of New Jersey. Always, the time allotted him began at 6:00 P.M. sharp, and often Eve found a way to make him wait.

"Not until 6:00 P.M.," Eve said. "It won't take the Germans all day."

"Friday eet eez," Anton said, winking at Eve.

Alice inserted herself between them, staking her claim to her father. She'd taken to doing this whenever he and Eve embraced, though watching them hug and kiss clearly delighted her. "Dad," she said, drawing out the word. "That's a stupid accent." He picked her up and tossed her into the air and caught her, making her giggle.

"It'll take all day," Sofia said, coming into the kitchen with those eyes. "If I know anything about making movies, it's that it takes a long time." She said this to make Kate nervous. She liked to make Kate nervous. It was easy. Sofia pulled back her long curly hair, twirled it into a knot and gave Kate a look.

Whenever the Furey kids went off with their mother there was never any squabbling. Anton liked for them to go. In fact, he usually arranged it, choosing somewhere exotic like Hawaii or the Caribbean because Agnes was rich. This was a fact that the Furey kids never let the Cooper girls forget. Anton arranged the trips (Eve told her daughters) because Agnes preferred to spend her time at the ashram rather than with her kids. Kate wished that Agnes would give all her money to the ashram and that the Fureys would be suddenly poor.

Kate slammed the refrigerator door and walked out of the room. She knew about time, how it just never seemed to last as long as her mother thought it could.

"Come on, babe, it'll be fun," Anton encouraged.

"I guess she doesn't want to be famous," Sofia said, now picking at leftovers directly from the refrigerator.

IT WAS THE MID 1970s and this interest in blended families was a trend that had begun with the divorce boom, and then the *Brady Bunch,* and now everyone, everywhere, wanted to know how it was *really* working out, was it *really* possible for two old families to merge into one new family? This was the dawn of talk shows, the ordinary person as extraordinary. When reporters came to the house, the family sat on the deck and Anton and Eve and the kids told stories. Some of the girls dressed up, acting famous, posing for the photographers. They wore platform sandals and long polyester skirts with large floral prints and halter tops. Julia draped herself over a chair and smoked a long white cigarette in a long white holder, ignoring Eve's reprimanding glare. The kids said things like, "We're each other's best friends. We love each other like sisters and brothers." "Living en masse"—Julia's words—"you never get bored, there's always someone to talk to, always someone to listen to." "We're our own little world here at Chardin. We don't need anybody else." They sipped champagne and soda and Anton put on some Schubert and the summer days were long and clear and breezy.

They were famous for many reasons. They were famous because they lived on a vast piece of property that was supposed to be a farm but that was not a farm at all, though there were peacocks and goats and ducks and chickens. "Chardin," Kate said to the reporters. "For the Omega Point," Finny added. He had long curly hair and was often mistaken by the reporters for a girl. "That's where the human and the divine meet in perfect harmony," Kate said. "Pierre Teilhard de Chardin," Finny said, stressing Chardin. "A Jesuit paleontologist who spent most of his life in China." "He studied bones," Kate interrupted, feeling quite smart as she explained all this, "and tried to come up with a way to make Darwin's theory of evolution compatible with Catholic theology."

From this vast piece of property the sounds of parties, the music of fun, blew to town making people wonder what was happening there. They were famous because Anton was a Gestalt therapist and in town he had a reputation for holding therapy sessions on his front lawn. The people imagined Bosch-like ceremonies: people naked doing handstands, people naked with their limbs intertwined; nuns in the swimming pool; a drunk lurking in the bushes, peering out at the world with lizard eyes. And children were everywhere, running around in tie-dyed clothes, dancing, singing, swirling, living—alive. They were famous because many children preferred to be at Chardin than at their own homes. "It's because we trust our children to make wise choices," Eve would say.

They were famous because there were so many of them—though Jane hadn't lived there in two years. (Not even becoming famous could lure her back. "You won't tell them the truth," she said to her mother. Jane's hair hung long, her ERA patch shouted from her chest. "Of course, I would," Eve replied. But actually Eve was afraid of what Jane might say.) People were curious to see if they really all got on. They were famous with all the shopkeepers and merchants in town for making late payments on their bills, but even so they still got credit, because they were famous. "Check's in the mail," Anton would say with a sincere grin, a grin that would make anyone believe, and he would not be lying. Only problem these days, sometimes the check was no good. They were famous because Anton had been a Jesuit. They were famous because Anton had divorced his oil-heiress first wife and had won custody of the children, alimony, and child support. This was unprecedented—unique, bizarre—because Anton was a man. They all loved being unique and bizarre. "We're unique, bizarre," Julia would say looking dramatic in her long 1920s flapper gown—thousands of black tassels swishing around her slender body. The dress actually belonged to the grandmother of Sofia and Caroline, but their bones were too big to fit into it so Julia appropriated it. "It's mine," she declared.

They were famous because Anton did not have a traditional job and Eve did, and it was Eve who brought home the money; it was Eve who paid for the vacations, the food, the extras, the mortgage. "Anton is a good feminist and a wonderful mother," Eve would say.

He taught the kids to think. His study was filled with philosophy. Together they read Nietzsche, Husserl, Heidegger, Sartre, Merleau-Ponty, Rousseau and Wittgenstein—to name a few. They read St. Augustine and St. Thomas and Teilhard de Chardin and Chesterton together as a family, Alice on his lap. The kids knew that St. Thomas was extraordinarily fat and they knew that St. Thomas defined humility as honesty and that Chesterton believed that if a thing was worth doing, it was worth doing badly and that fairyland is nothing but the sunny country of common sense. They knew that Beethoven started to lose his hearing in his thirties and wrote his second symphony to express his depression and they knew that it had big moments of humor to balance the misery. "Always remember the importance of humor," Anton instructed. Anton was a Jesuit and learned. He wanted that for his kids. "I want to expose the kids to great thinking," Anton would tell the reporters. "I want them to know how to argue." He was the friend of Fritz Perls and R. D. Laing. R. D. Laing had given Eve a black eye once because she had talked back to him.

There was Anton big as day on the cover of *People Magazine* (actually it was Marlon Brando, but it looked so much like Anton that even the kids, even Eve, at first, thought Brando was Anton). Inside that issue was a five-page spread on the family with pictures, covered by a famous reporter. Anton, for real, on page sixty-five with his bright, electrifying smile, extended even wider by his sideburns, a dustpan and brush in hand sweeping up the kitchen floor. A pull quote from Eve said, "I'm delighted by a man who will clean while I'm at work." All of the kids laughed when they saw that picture; they'd never seen Anton before with a dustpan in his hand. But they liked being famous. They played the role. If America wanted to hear about a new American family, well then they'd give it to them. "He earns a living," Eve told the reporter. "Forty-five hundred dollars a month in alimony and thirty thousand dollars a year playing cards." Actually Anton didn't play high-stakes poker so much anymore. He had, though, that was true, with rich men with names like Heston and Reagan who owned off-shore businesses in the islands. When he won big, he came home and woke up the kids and threw the cash into the air so that it snowflaked to the floor.

"Where should we go?" he'd ask. He'd always spend it traveling somewhere with all of them—Haiti, Mexico, Key West, France.

"Machismo is silly and futile," Anton would respond to the question of how he felt about being supported financially by his wife (and ex-wife). Eve had just started her own catering company and already it was thriving. "It makes equality, and therefore love, impossible."

"I don't know how a conventional marriage can work if the father is away from nine to five and leaves everything to the mother," Eve would add. "If these men want to have families, I think they'd better rearrange their schedules to spend more time at home."

In town people gossiped about them: Anton would not have to work another day in his life. That was not right for a man. And Eve saying, "Women always get alimony. Why shouldn't a man?" or "If the tables were turned and Anton had the money, you could bet the courts would give Agnes what she deserved." Justice. There was justice in the world.

"THE GERMANS are coming. The Germans are coming," Timothy shouted. He loved to hear himself speak. He crawled like an alligator, low to the floor, through the living room, with his left leg broken and in a cast, wearing only a pair of boxer shorts. "The Germans are coming." Nicholas threw a pillow at him, but Timothy was right. The Germans were coming, up the driveway in an enormous orange U-Haul. So what if they were only Germans. One thing always led to the next and soon Hollywood would be on to them and they'd be making money hand over fist. No more worries about the back taxes. The kids wouldn't be embarrassed to get milk from the pharmacy anymore. They could pay for that vacation last summer to Haiti. Hurrah for the Germans! They could even buy a new furnace. The kids calculated potential percentages and royalties, becoming instantly quite rich.

As planned, the Germans came the morning after Thanksgiving, early enough, around noon, so that the house was still a mess. Crystal and china and silver were crusted with food and wine from the night before. The kids picked at the turkey that still sat on the enormous silver platter. "That's our family's platter," Sofia said to Julia. "It belongs to the Fureys." Sofia knew every item in the house and what belonged to whom and how much it was worth. She was already telling her sister and brothers which pieces she would like to inherit.

"This is the best part of Thanksgiving," Nicholas said, dropping a piece of breast into his mouth and then sipping from his beer. His shaggy long blond hair dripped over his bloodshot eyes. He was a sexy boy at eighteen with colorful notions about the ironies of the world, "Fighting for peace is like making love for virginity," he'd say.

"It's too early for beer, babe," Anton reprimanded as he walked into the kitchen in his robe—a short red robe, above his knobby knees. His skinny legs like twigs. He started to clean up for the Germans and asked the kids to help, which they did, and in an instant the kitchen was clean. "One of the many pleasures of such a big group," he said. "Things get done fast." Every other weekend he organized work days, eight hours in which they worked as a family to make Chardin beautiful—although the kids always complained and hid and came up with elaborate ailments. "My knees ache," Kate would say.

"I've got a lot to tell these Germans about my childhood in Montana," the grandmother, Eve's mother, said from the dining room where she sat eating a plate piled high with leftovers, dripping cranberry. "You know you should get a job as an actor," she said to Anton. She was always telling him what kind of jobs he could get. She could not bear it that her beautiful Eve worked her fingers to the bone in a hot kitchen while he lazed about. She believed it was beneath her daughter to be in the service industry, catering (literally) to the whims of others. Others should be catering to her. If her father only knew, the grandmother would think, knowing if he were alive he would never have allowed Eve to marry Anton. And they weren't even legally married! "You look like Richard Burton you know," she said. Anton winked at her, flirting. The grandmother liked it when he flirted with her. Her long white hair hadn't yet been put up and she was still in her nightdress—pink pastel with turquoise flowers. She called it her muumuu. She was visiting for the holidays, though she had spent most of the trip plotting her departure. Once she even carried her suitcases down the driveway, threatening to hitchhike home.

The Germans came in their U-Haul filled with cameras and tripods and lights and light meters and fancy sound equipment—Sennheisers, boom mikes with fuzzy sleeves, topnotch headphones—professional, sophisticated, real ("We'll be rich," Sofia whispered to Kate. "Rich."). A crew of twelve, all speaking German, spilled out of the U-Haul like an invasion, lugging equipment and strobe lights and electrical cords and screens and backdrops and a glittering makeup table with its big mirror surrounded by bulbs. "They're gonna do our makeup?" Sofia asked, astonished and hopeful.

Kate greeted them at the door, her green eyes on all of them, her crooked and braced teeth protruding. The silver sparkled in the daylight. The load of them stood in the doorway. They didn't look like saviors to Kate with their round scruffy faces and tired, drooping eyes. All she'd ever heard about Germans was bad. "You'll be done by six, right? My father's coming to get my sister and me at six sharp so that we can celebrate Thanksgiving with him."

"They don't understand you, Kate," Sofia whispered, squeezing into the doorway next to her.

"DONE—BY—SIX," Kate repeated very loudly, very slowly.

"She's a worrier," Alice said, sliding between their legs. She was proud of being "just three," observant and wise. "I'll be taller than you someday," she'd say to Kate. "I'll loom over you." Loom, a big word learned from Julia. Alice was proud as well of all her words; for a long time she counted them. Turned them around on her tongue, tasting them like rare chocolates. A cute kid with her large forehead and she knew just as much about Aquinas and Chesterton as any of the kids. "If a thing's worth doing, it's worth doing badly," she'd chant. Her hair was in pigtails, gray eyes wide. "Athene's eyes," Anton would say.

Bastard, Kate thought, thinking of Camille. Alice is just a bastard. Kate wanted to tell the Germans that when they started asking questions. In fact, there was quite a lot that she wanted to tell the Germans. For one, Kate had never liked Alice. Alice was spoiled. She had no idea what it meant to have to go visit your father. She only caused problems. Just last year Kate and Julia had had to come home early from their father's in order to celebrate Alice's half birthday. "Half birthday?" Camille had asked incredulously, her sad face framed by her long ginger hair. "Your mother," she had said, shaking her head in despair. When Alice was an infant, Kate had dropped her seven times.

"Don't be bossy, Kate," Eve said, coming out to greet the

Germans. "This one *is* a worrier," she said, and patted Kate on the back. It was cold outside and you could see the Germans' breath even though they weren't speaking.

"Don't you want to be famous?" Finny asked Kate, squeezing into the door as well. Everyone was trying to get a peek at the Germans. Even the grandmother who tapped her cane, hard, in order to be heard.

"As long as I can be famous before my dad gets here." Of course she wanted to be famous. She wanted to be Shirley Temple or at least Cindy from the *Brady Bunch*. "If you really want, you can do that," Eve would encourage. "You're cuter than that girl." And Kate had believed her. Shirley Temple had made over forty million dollars while she was still a child, a fact that entranced Kate. She wanted to be funny for the Germans. She had a thousand stories to tell them and had dressed especially for the occasion in tight pink jeans that she thought made her look grown-up. For days all of the kids had been deciding what to wear.

"I'm Hans," the tallest of the group said. His hand shot out toward Eve. He was the director. Thin stubble shadowed his face and wisps of hair hid his warm blue eyes. His lashes were unusually long for a man's and made him appear delicate and beautiful. He wore shiny black patent leather pants that hugged his legs and that squeaked as he moved. His lips glistened.

The Germans, who were all tall and blond and young and blue-eyed with big and rosy faces, had names like Jens and Rheinhold, Katerina and Klaus. The one American, the girlfriend of Hans, was named Mourning. They all wore sandals with socks and actually they all spoke very good, though loud, English with thick accents—*v*s for *w*s, guttural and deep. Even Mourning seemed to have that accent.

"What kind of name is Mourning?" Sofia asked Kate, rolling her eyes impatiently. Mourning had short fine blond hair that tucked neatly behind her ears, abrupt bangs, and a long slender nose. "Aristocratic," Julia said. "Roman." Mourning, too, wore black leather—a miniskirt—and thick black tights.

"They're gonna do our makeup," Kate whispered to Julia.

Before long the Germans took over the house, telling the family what to do, removing the furniture from the living room, dining room, and kitchen. Setting up the makeup station and the hair station. And before long a makeup artist and a hair stylist were working on Nicholas and Caroline, and the kids were lining up for their turn. In the kitchen a caterer prepared a table of snacks—delicate finger sandwiches and loads of cut-up fruit and brownies and cookies. "Is that for us to eat?" Timothy asked, lying on the floor in his cast. "Of course it is. We're the stars," Sofia said, sitting down to have her makeup done. "My hair's very difficult," she instructed, and gave directions on how to straighten her tight curls.

It didn't take long for the kids to start liking this, for the ones at the end of the line to get impatient for their turn. They could hardly look at the Germans, so enraptured were they with the process—mascara combed onto lashes, lipstick swept across lips, water spritzed, fingertips on face, on scalp, blow-dryers whining. Even the boys and Anton were made up. And there was so much food; the more they ate, the more it was replenished.

"Don't forget me," the grandmother said to the stylist. And the afternoon passed in this way.

"I could get used to this," Julia said. "Who couldn't?" Caroline responded, taking a bite of brownie. Her hair was in curlers. A German fussed with her lipstick. "You look scary,"

Nicholas said to both girls. Their eyes were so dark and their faces so pancaked they looked more like caricatures than people. "It's for the cameras. It will translate to beautiful on film," Sofia reassured.

I'm going to look beautiful for Dad, Kate thought, looking at herself in the mirror.

Julia waltzed into the living room in a long green gown, singing *Life Upon the Wicked Stage.*

"Kiss me, babe," Nicholas said to her, and then so did Timothy.

"Little Antons," she said, and planted full wet kisses on both of their lips, showing off for Hans.

Hans and Mourning and the technicians arranged the set. The room was bare except for two blue velvet chairs on which shone spotlights. Microphones dangled from the ceiling. A bench was placed between the chairs. The lights made the room hot. The soundman fiddled with the mike. Big headphones crowned his head. "Airplanes, damn airplanes," he kept saying. All the kids thought this cool since they could not hear the airplanes at all. This was how the movies worked. Hollywood. Money. Salvation. "Practice for the big leagues," Julia said.

Hans threaded film into the camera. Mourning held a clipboard close to her chest, directing the Germans. They were all scurrying about. Cords snaked across the floor. Anton and Eve sat in the velvet chairs. Eve's girls stood to her right, Anton's kids to his left. "I'm in the middle. Of both sides," Alice said emphatically, with seriousness, sitting on the bench between her mother and father.

You're just a bastard, Kate thought.

The grandmother inserted herself on the bench by Alice though no one had invited her. "I'm Grammy. Call me Grammy," she said directly to the camera.

It was awkward at first. None of them actually knew how to act famous, what to say. Even Anton was shy, sitting there almost baffled. Julia had held a meeting earlier with all the kids. "What they want to know most of all are the intimate, juicy details. Provocative things." Of the kids, she was the one who most aspired to being an actress. She told them she would be famous by the time she was twenty—and she'd be right. "They want us to reveal what's in our guts, our souls. They want to see us emote," she said, clutching her chest, head back with drama. "To what?" Timothy asked. "To cry," she responded, looking hard at him. "Tears. They want tears."

In front of the camera they froze. All but the grandmother. "It was the Germans' fault, the flu epidemic of 1918," the grandmother said to the lens. "Germ warfare. They sent it to America in envelopes. Germ as in *German.*" Her teeth were out, causing her mouth to pucker like dried-up fruit.

"Put your teeth in, Mother," Eve said.

The Germans spoke in German, they fussed, adjusted lights. The soundman complained about the planes. The lights made everyone sweat. "Well, I know a thing or two," the grandmother persisted. "And those Germans sent the flu over here in 1918."

"Who will begin?" Hans asked.

"I've begun," the grandmother snapped.

"We're all in love with each other," Julia blurted suddenly. "We've been so for years."

Then everyone was talking at once. Julia was saying who was in love with whom: she with Nicholas, Kate with Finny. Sofia was telling the story of how Anton and Eve met, how he had been her therapist and how he'd been married. The juicy details. Nicholas was saying that Julia was a romantic. "A gorgeous romantic."

"A romantic?" Hans asked, looking up from the lens. "I love Tchaikovsky," Julia said brightly. "And the oboe. Mozart's oboe." Julia captured Hans, and then the camera, with her marvelous eyes. *Oboe* hung in the air, sophisticated instrument, wonderful word. Oboe. The sound of the movie camera made soft and reassuring clicks. The lights were on her face, her chin cocked toward the mike. Oboe. "It's like the human voice." Later she would say that Hans was devastatingly handsome with an air of vulnerability that made him sexy. But for now he was just a means, a savior. "Tchaikovsky's big and romantic. My favorite is Mozart, though, but I am romantic. You can't grow up at Chardin and not be a romantic." Her lips curled. She wanted Hans to fall in love with her. "And my philosopher is Kierkegaard. He's fabulous on love." Hog, Kate thought, hogging the spotlight.

THEY HAD tried to make money in other ways, of course. Not so long before, Anton had received a stock tip from the sister of a friend of his in Dallas. It was for gold, Newmont Mining. He had swept through the house excitedly, big smile, gold filling shining from the depths of his mouth, and had taken up a collection. Julia had given him five hundred dollars that she had earned cleaning the house of a pack-rat friend of Anton's and Eve's. Freezers filled with frostbitten meats and fish. Kate had given him fifty dollars she'd earned selling sympathy cards door-to-door to little old ladies. His ex-wife and some other friends had contributed substantially to the pool. Stocks were down and so gold was up, inclining. Fast. Gold was meant to multiply. Rich. Fifty bucks could become as much as five thousand dollars. Kate dreamed of what she would do with all that cash. If fifty dollars could make five thousand dollars, the possibilities were infinite. Five thousand dollars to $500,000 and she'd never have to worry about money again. But alas, of course, fifty dollars quickly turned to nothing, and that was that. "I'll help you get it back," Eve promised Kate. "You were brave to try, but I'll make certain you get that fifty dollars back. That's a lot of money for one little girl."

They tried to make money by importing Haitian art from Haiti and selling it at a gallery in a nearby town. After Anton and Eve married in Haiti it was his idea that the kids would love it there and so they'd rented a house in a breadfruit grove at the edge of the Caribbean in Jacmel for a summer. Anton flew them all down there along with some friends. In Port-au-Prince they'd stayed at the Oloffson and then with George Nader, a Lebanese art dealer who intended to help Anton get his business off the ground. Nader's house was in the hills above the capital with a view down through coconuts and almonds and pineapples and mangoes and coal fires and the smell of grilled goat to Duvalier's white mansion in the center of town. They were swept away by the exotic beauty of the country—all the graveyards with handsome cement headstones, the incessant thwacking of grass with machetes and the sound of sweeping, the dust, the heat, the marvelously cheery painted buses, the trips to black-sand beaches and the long trek across the mountains, eight thousand feet above sea level to Jacmel on a terribly in-progress road that French engineers were donating to the country. "Are we going to a voodoo ceremony?" the kids kept asking. Little Kate tried to sell Chiclets in the market alongside the people from the mountains who came to town with their loads of onions and meats thick with flies. The flies were everywhere.

With the help of Nader, Anton learned about the best Haitian artists—Duffaut and Ducasse and Joseph-Jean

Gilles, Gerard Paul. He met some of them, bought the work of many. He paid cash. The pictures were primitive versions of scenes such as Adam and Eve with the snake, a black Virgin on a half shell, a funeral procession in a jolly little village, Christ on his cross in a brilliant green jungle, a repetition of pink flamingos, of turkeys, of people. He bought chairs and funny old carved walking canes and wood panels of couples copulating and light summer dresses and cotton tablecloths and napkins. He bought and bought and bought at top market price, eager to help the Haitians, to be fair, promising to come back often and buy more.

The gallery thrived for a little while and then began to fail. Anton's customers didn't quite share his enthusiasm for the paintings and the crafts and before long the walls of Chardin were covered with Haitian paintings.

Another reason the gallery struggled was that Anton was too generous, couldn't help himself from trying to help others. A friend had invented a massage aid called a Body Buddy—two wooden balls that rolled at the end of a smooth and thick wooden handle. *To be used with oils,* the instructions read. He bought hundreds of them, picking them up at the docks in Newark with some of the kids. Boxes and boxes of Body Buddies. "They look like dicks," Nicholas said. "What fun," Julia agreed. The friend had needed help because he had no luck peddling them and thus he wasn't making ends meet and he was desperately depressed and talking about suicide. Anton said he'd try to sell them for him; they were clever. For another friend he sold square egg molds, a mold that turned a hardboiled egg into a cube. It was a gimmick for Easter. Neither the Body Buddy nor the square egg mold sold well. But Anton had paid for them. They belonged to him. For years they'd remain in boxes in the basement, hauled out at Christmas, Easter, and on birthdays as joke presents.

Anton moved on to growing berries in the fields and selling them to fancy restaurants in New York City. All the kids in the fields picked raspberries and strawberries and blackberries, depositing them delicately into the quarter-pint boxes. They were organic, expensive, unique. With the damaged berries the kids made preserves and pies—low sugar, low pectin, high fruit content—The Berry Best Jams and Pies (Alice came up with that name). Anton bought an air-conditioned van, installed custom berry-carrying racks, and drove the boxed berries carefully to New York City where he peddled them, taking orders for more. The Four Seasons, Lutèce, Lespinasse. He was well liked by the chefs and for a while he was making $25,000 a year after expenses and taxes. Once again, though, Anton was let down by someone he'd tried to help. The farmer whom Anton had hired (and then partnered) found a way to steal the business. Without a farmer there would be no berries and thus he went back to his book.

Now they sat in their living room, emoting for the Germans, the kids believing that this time things would be different. That this time things would go their way.

"Anton could be a famous movie actor if he ever put his mind to it," the grandmother continued, speaking directly to the camera. "He looks just like Richard Burton and you can bet he makes love like Richard Burton, too, given all these kids. But he doesn't like to work."

ANTON AND EVE were telling the Germans about their bad financial year and the court's decision to grant Anton alimony. It was Mourning's idea that each person would take a turn telling a story to the camera. Mourning scribbled notes on the clipboard (in German). She seemed impossibly skinny and pretty with her long legs and blond bob. Her smile was severe. "You've got to be severe to handle all these Germans," she told Anton. She referred to herself as the Very Boss. "I've got to keep them scared, on their toes." The crew worked fast, all but Hans who had a slow, precise manner. Confident. His leather pants squeaked. "We need more story," Mourning had said to them all. "Where's the story?" as if it were hiding. This worried the kids. They saw the orange U-Haul retreating down the driveway. "Emote," Julia urged. "About what?" Timothy said desperately—desperate grin on his desperate face. He dragged himself around the rooms with his broken leg. "Use your imagination," Julia bossed. "It's just a movie," Sofia said, as if a movie didn't matter, as if a movie couldn't change their lives.

Anton had tied an orange silk ascot around his neck, but even so, he was nervous, stuttering as he spoke—a remnant of his youth in the Jesuits. He sat up in his chair. "Worrying about money was refreshing, enlightening actually. It made the world seem more real." Everyone was trying to be quiet for the soundman. The sun set over the cornfields, turning everything outside golden then gray. Anton's voice was Texas thick. He was telling about how he and his first wife had decided to live off her wealth so that they could devote their life to intellectual, philosophical, and religious pursuits, so that he could write his book. "I had to advance an original idea when I was completing my work at the Sorbonne," Anton said. "And that was that the Catholic Church has never fully recognized the sacramentality of marriage. Sexuality always took second place to celibacy. My book springs from this concept."

"What kind of Ph.D. do you have, anyway?" the grandmother asked him. She had asked him that question many times in an attempt to infuriate him. He ignored her.

"I fell in love with Eve because of her energy and gut strength," Anton added, leaning over to kiss his wife.

"I'd lived life vicariously before I met Anton," Eve said, looking straight into the camera, serious. Her coiffed hair gave her that little-girl look and at forty she still had an uncanny way of looking sixteen—fresh and innocent. "Like Doris Day," the Furey kids would say. "My husband was the one with the exciting life. I watched it from the sidelines while I taught my daughters to iron. I'd never written a check before he left. It was like recovering from a stroke and learning to do the basics all over again. I needed a man willing to stay at home and help out with the kids because once recovered I was determined never to go back. And there came Anton worrying about dentist appointments and his little guy wetting the bed. Now since we're both living, not sitting on the sidelines, we can give our excitement to the kids. The kids live an exciting, rich life out here. When I was a girl, I was prepped for marriage."

The room was a mess. Everyone wanted to speak. They all knew how to act now. During pauses in the filming (which were frequent) everyone started talking at once. The baby kept insisting she had stories to tell. She hated that everyone still called her the baby. She felt older than most of them. "It's like I've got ten parents with all these sisters and brothers," she declared. The grandmother demanded her turn. The light man fidgeted with the lights. Bulbs burst, reflections were too strong, too weak. Everything went wrong. The makeup artist and the hairstylist would fuss with everyone's face and hair between takes. Between takes, Anton flirted with the Germans, knitting them into the Furey/Cooper lives. He offered them a swim in the indoor pool and a joint. But they were workers and worked hard. Mourning tapping away on her clipboard. The soundman kept hearing those airplanes, as if a whole fleet were flying incessantly overhead. And to make matters worse, the film kept catching and breaking, and Hans had to fix the camera.

Lights appeared in the driveway, shining through the dining-room windows. Nicholas was speaking to the camera now. His hair was neat, feathered back with hair spray. Black eyeliner ringed his blue eyes. He was telling about being arrested by the police for filming a Western in town with his Super 8. He'd thrown a dummy off a building and it had been mistaken for a real person by a dental hygienist. She had stopped cleaning teeth and called the police who came and, upon spotting Kate's BB gun in the glove compartment and believing it to be more than a BB gun, radioed for backup. The whole street swarmed with cops. "Are we going to prison?" Kate kept asking Nicholas.

The lights in the driveway grew bigger, filling the dining room. Kate saw them and froze. It was Ian, of course. It was six sharp. He was never late. For him an hour was an hour. Six was six. At the head of the driveway, he honked once for his girls. All Kate could think about was her turn. Finny was already posed in the spotlight in the other chair, waiting for the cameras to start rolling on him. Finny never said much. In fact, for two years once he didn't speak at all. He'd be quick, Kate thought. Then she could go, then Julia. Their father would only have to wait a little bit. He could do that for them. But then when Finny started speaking it seemed he liked the mike and wanted to speak forever. It seemed he would never shut up, carrying on about trips out west and

stupid details about his mother's ashram in New York City—
how they grew all their own food on the roof of the building.
They were even trying to start a vineyard up there, he explained. When it seemed there was nothing more to say about
his own life, he engaged the grandmother in a conversation
and the two of them were a duet talking about her childhood
in Montana and little Irish harlots in Butte, and Kate was just
about ready to scream. Her brain was racing. She couldn't see
anything but lights. She hated Finny. She wanted her turn.
She hated her father for always being so precise. She hated the
Germans for taking so long, for being so fussy with their
equipment. She thought they'd be here all night.

"I want my turn," Kate blurted. "Dad's here. Can't you
hurry up?" she said to Hans and Mourning, but they were
too busy to notice her. The soundman swore, it seemed, in
German, as her words scratched across the recording.

"Dad can wait a few minutes," Julia said, raising her left
eyebrow. She, too, dressed specially in her long pale green
sleeveless satin gown. It looked ridiculous, like something an
old lady would wear to try to look younger. Nicholas teased
Julia about the dress. "Gown," Julia corrected.

"Let Finny finish," Eve said. He kept talking. It seemed
hours were passing, but it was only a few minutes. Ian
honked again. Alice sat snuggly in her father's arms, watching. Kate was definitely going to let the Germans know that
Alice was a bastard.

"You never say a word. We have to pry words out of
you," Kate said. Finny's blue eyes grinned at her as if he
knew, as if he enjoyed torturing her. The spotlight lit him up.
"What are you talking on for now?" He was a bastard, too,
and she was going to let the Germans know that as well.

Ian sat in the driveway in his little white VW. Kate could

see the car from inside the house with its dome light on. He always brought along something to read because he knew that he would be made to wait. Inside the house all the kids were making noise and teasing each other as the Germans tried to make their movie. The house was warm with people. Anton had turned the pool up for the Germans and steam from it drifted down the hall. The night was clear and very cold and the moon was a big smiling shining face hanging there above it all.

Ian had waited before—when they had had to buy the Jeep on Christmas Eve, when their auto-train to Florida had had to leave a day early for their spring trip, when their van had broken down in Mexico. Once he had waited three hours before realizing the house was locked up tight and they had been gone for a good long time. "It's only a few minutes," the Furey kids said. But it didn't feel like that to Kate. Time did funny things inside of her; it seemed just ten minutes were ten hours. They wanted Kate to tell the story of renting out her bedroom to Sergio Tate and his girl. But Kate decided to leave. She didn't care about being famous anymore. She went to her room and got her bag.

"I need to go," she said, returning to the living room with her bag slung over her shoulder. "Get your things, Julia."

"But it's your turn now, darling," Eve said tenderly.

"I don't want my turn anymore. Get your bag, Julia. It's not fair to make Dad wait any longer. Dad doesn't like to wait."

"It's only a few minutes," Eve said.

"No, it's not," Kate shouted. Suddenly she hated her mother, felt her mother was trying to trap her here. And as easily as igniting fuel she ignited her mother. Kate knew how to do it. It was easy to make Eve mad if you pressed. "It's not fair to make Dad wait," Kate repeated. There was silence for a moment, thick and oppressive.

"Not fair?" Eve asked softly. Hans looked up from the camera. His lashes were so long it seemed they, too, had been polished with mascara. "Not fair," she repeated for emphasis. "He doesn't like to wait," Eve said, mocking the idea—thinking of how he'd made her wait, wondering if he'd ever come back to her and his girls. She no longer looked sixteen. She sat down in an armchair. The grandmother continued talking even though Hans wasn't filming her. Not fair that Ian left her with three children. *He never said a word to me; he never explained a thing.* "Always your father," Eve said, still quietly. Kate wished the Germans would get busy and capture her mother on film. Mourning absorbed the situation. "Always protecting your father. What about me? What about protecting me?"

"Why don't you film my mother," Kate snapped at Mourning. "She has a story to tell."

Mourning nudged Hans. "Film the little one, let's see what she has to say," Mourning said.

"I don't want to be filmed anymore," Kate said as the camera and lights turned her way, pressing her with their heat, smooshing up against her face. She couldn't get away from the camera. It seemed there were hundreds of cameras, capturing her—a thirteen-year-old American girl in pink jeans and braces and a T-shirt and sneakers, trying to look grown-up. Made up fine with her blow-dried feathered hair and her thick mascara and her blue eyeliner and blue eye shadow. "To enhance your green eyes," the makeup artist had said. *I'll look pretty for Dad.* Kate stopped refusing, realized that if she just did it she'd be able to get out of the house more quickly. The makeup person swept a powder puff once around her face. Kate imagined her father, could see him with his head sunk into the steering wheel. She could feel his breath, cold in the car, knew he was wanting to come inside and get his girls but afraid. He did not like Anton; he did not like going into the house. He stayed in the car in part because he knew this was Eve's punishment. For as long as she could, in her eighties, her nineties (if they were still alive), she would make him wait for his girls. Somewhere he accepted the punishment as if the waiting were giving something back to Eve. I'll wait, he'd say to the night, to the day, to the circumstance. See how long I can wait.

Kate cried into the camera—with her bright red nose and glimmering braces, black-and-blue makeup dripping down her face. Oh, she emoted brilliantly. Little American girl emoting for all of Germany, ambassador of the New American Family. Love me please. "I want to go to my father," she said. The kids watched, feeling not so jolly anymore. Her face was red and blistery, her voice cracked. Surely Ian could hear that voice all the way in his car. Maybe he'll come in and get me, she thought. Eve continued to hang her head in her hand. She could not look at her daughter. Her third-born knotted to a chair. Leave, Eve wished, get up and leave. Punish me and leave.

Kate was the star. Something happened. She liked it, the release. The desire for her father articulated, spilling out of her, skidding across the film, the ocean, continents. Will people really hear this? she wondered. Are people listening? Would this make the family famous? She said bravely that she loved her father, wanted her father, missed living with her father, that her mother wouldn't let her love her father. She felt beautiful emoting. Red face sloppy with red tears telling why her father waited, how he always had to wait, that she wanted to go out to him and stop the waiting once and forever. Cindy from the *Brady Bunch.* Shirley Temple. Forty million dollars. She imagined them rich quick because of her. Anton giving her a warm and gentle kiss on the cheek saying, "Thank you, babe." Her mother smiling proudly, Kate the superstar. It was always Alice who was the superstar. "AA Superstar," Eve would say to her baby, hugging her big and tight in her long warm willowy arms together with Anton. Ever since Alice was a tiny baby she had loved to watch her parents kiss and hug. She'd giggle and squirm exquisitely whenever they did, inserting her own lips into the embrace. Then Kate saw her father again with his head on the steering wheel, waiting patiently, too proud to come in the house.

"The father," Mourning said. "Can we get the father in here?" Hans agreed that was a good idea. "*Zehr gut, zehr gut.*" They looked at Eve as if it were up to her. Julia laughed with the absurdity of the notion.

"Leave my father out of this," Kate said. Suddenly she felt dirty and the desire to leave came again. But Mourning asked another question. "I'm finished," Kate declared, standing up. The camera continued to roll. "Answer the question, Kate," Eve said. She couldn't help herself. What Ian took from Eve, he took from Kate as well. "Tell them about when your father left. Tell them about Camille, about betrayal, neglect, desertion." Eve was crying. Kate was crying. She hated the Germans. She saw Alice reclining in her father's arms. Alice looked at Kate, held her with her wide Athene eyes, studying her with a cool remove, it seemed, a distance, as if Kate were drowning. Those wicked gray eyes, but there was warmth in them. Stop staring at me, Kate wanted to shout.

"I want to go now," Kate said quietly, directly to Hans. "Please." Little word, tiny word. *Please.* The reassuring click of the film moving through the camera. Click click click.

Light caught Kate's tears, turning them into a rainbow of colors. "Someone tell my mother to let me go."

The baby sank back against her father's chest. She felt the warm embrace of his strong arms pulling her a little closer, deeper into him. Comfortable there as if she owned that spot, lounging there as if she were always meant to exist. As if the world had been made for her existence. Alice turned in her father's arms, twisted to face him. "Make this stop," she said to her father, as if understanding something big yet simple yet complicated all at the same time. She wiggled out of Anton's arms and made her way to the spotlight, standing in front of Kate in front of the camera. She wore her pajamas now, the kind with the padded feet, an all-in-one, zipper up the front. Her toes poked through holes in the fabric. "Her daddy's waiting," Alice said boldly to the lens. "Mom, let Kate go." She looked at her father with a commanding, confident look. Kate had the urge to shove Alice, to scream at her. Instead she choked on her tears. Alice spoke slowly, enunciating each word. A little grown-up in her pink pajamas, justice in her tone, fairness, big gray eyes filling the frame—adorable girl for all of Germany to admire. AA Superstar. Then, just as gracefully as she stepped into the picture, she stepped out.

Eve was still crying beside Anton as he stood and stated firmly, "This is over now. The show is over."

Hans looked at Kate. He looked up from behind the viewfinder. Little Kate in tight pink jeans, trying to be grown-up, reflected back to her in his big long-lashed eyes. Madeup face, mascara drooling down her cheeks, sticking in the flesh beneath her eyes. She was ugly sitting there on the stool, afraid, gasping, sucking up air. Hot room, hot lights, boom mike drifting toward her little braced and sparkling mouth. The clicks stopped. "Cut," Hans said. "Cut."

CHAPTER EIGHT

The Big Concerns of Their Lives

"Do you know what Ian used to tell me, Alice? You know what he used to say?" Eve would say sometimes to her daughter. It was hard for Alice to imagine that her mother had a life before Anton. That she'd been married to Ian, had three daughters—a life that had had nothing to do with her, a life in which, had it continued, Alice would not exist. Hard to imagine that her mother had once been a woman who ironed, cooked, sewed, when now she was a businesswoman with a thriving company. Alice laughed at the idea of her mother teaching her daughters to iron—so impossible the image seemed. She laughed at the image of her three Cooper sisters in matching outfits that Eve had sewn out of Liberty fabric, standing primly in their big white colonial home, hair curled into sausages. That life like a long-passed historic era—the Greeks, the Romans. Remote. She loved hearing her father describe the Cooper girls when he first met them. Neat and clean in party dresses with black Mary Janes—but they were fighting and swearing. "These three proper little girls screeching at the top of their voices, shouting very naughty words," he'd say. "My own boys didn't say such naughty words."

"You know what Ian used to say to me?" Eve would say. Perhaps she had had a fight with Anton. Perhaps she just wanted Alice to know the complexity of the picture. "He'd say that if I ever had a child with another man he would love it as if it were his own. Ian loves you as if you were his own, Alice." He had said this to Eve shortly after he left. She always wondered if the declaration indicated that he loved her still (she hoped) or if it were simply an expiation of guilt.

On the lacrosse field during her senior year of college when her father was mysteriously ill and could not attend her final games, Alice would think about what her mother had said. During one important game she saw a slender, tall dark-haired man across the field, alone high up in the bleachers above the small crowd, wearing a beige trench coat against the misty weather. She knew without being able to define his face that the man was Ian, here to watch her game because Anton could not. A tall bearded man alone in the cold watching her. He had driven over a hundred miles to watch her play. That was something, made her feel just a little bigger, like she had just a bit more.

Ian was a scientist with a string of successes that spanned his adult life—a driven, solid, practical man and her father's opposite in every way. She understood that Ian with all his acclaim and as her mother's first husband was an object of her father's jealousy. Somewhere the fact that Ian cared for her made Alice feel powerful, that she was indeed able to transcend the rules and laws of love, that this New American Family could work, did work. That was her job after all.

Alice remembered the long-ago night of the Germans. She remembered wiggling out of her father's arm to stand in front of the movie camera, to protect Kate. "Mom, let Kate go." The Big Concerns of their lives. "Kate's daddy is different from mine," feeling the complexity of that idea for the first time, how that truth would be the great fissure that crept through their lives. And she knew, as she recalled the night, the way one remembers having done a good deed, that she'd put herself in front of the camera's wide stare—the camera clicking away like the ratcheting of machine-gun fire—to save Ian too.

CHAPTER NINE

White Mary

I WAS THE BASTARD. That's what they called me when I was a little boy. Finn the bastard. I was different from them, my brothers and sisters. I was the youngest and had black hair. They were blond. I thought being a bastard meant something to do with having black hair. It was Timothy who teased me most, as if being a dark-haired bastard boy were something funny. For a while I thought it was something funny, too. We lived in London and then France and then Dallas and then we traveled on the road in a turquoise camper in the deserts of California and the West. All this before I was five years old. The mother I thought was my mother left for an ashram and my father met Eve. And Eve and her kids lived in the camper with us and it was crowded and smelly and we had nowhere to really go except that Dad wanted us to see how beautiful the world is. Then Eve's kids started calling me the bastard, too. Little Kate spit the word out from between her crooked teeth and she did not laugh, which was the first time I thought it was a bad thing. And I asked my father when we were out there in that lonely land where it seemed nothing could grow, where all you could see for miles and miles and days was nothing, not another soul except our camper and all of us trying to see the beauty of the world. I asked Dad what *bastard* meant. I was four, almost five. A tiny boy with long hair that looked like a girl's.

On my birthday Dad took me for a walk far away from the other kids and he explained, squatting down on his knees, squinting and looking me in the eye. I probably squinted, too. We had the same squint, as if the sun were always in our eyes. I have always loved that squint; it's how we look alike. He hugged me for a long time before he spoke. "You're my little boy," he said. "You're my little boy." He ran his hands through my hair. I always loved it when he did that, the feeling of his fingers on my scalp. I remember the other kids far away at the picnic table. Later I knew they knew what I was being told. At the time I could hear them laughing and shouting and their voices swallowed up by the emptiness because there was not even a cottonwood tree or a mesquite bush for their words to bounce off of or get snarled around. They were sitting at the picnic table with all my presents (several of which were IOUs because we hadn't seen a store in days). At first I was glad to be alone with Dad on my birthday, have him all to myself, all his attention focused on me with his fingers running through my hair. Then I wanted to be back with the other kids; I wanted blond hair cut like a boy's.

My father told me I should forget the word *bastard*, that it had nothing to do with me. He told me that I was half adopted and he explained adopted and then he explained what half adopted could mean. He explained that he and Mom (the woman I had thought my mother to be) had been angry with each other and that she had left him for America and that during this time he'd fallen in love with another woman and that together they'd created me. She was an Italian woman from the island Sicily in the south and she had loved me more than her eyes, loved feeling me in her belly. I was all hers there. She would lie for hours watching me move and I never caused her any problems, no nausea or anything. But she had had to go back to Sicily and since she wasn't married it was impossible for her to keep me because then she would have had nowhere to go because her family would not have welcomed her and she was too young to be on her own with a son, floating in the world. They were strict Roman Catholics, Dad told me. Her name was Bianca Maria, White Mary. And with time, my father told me, his wife came back and they fell in love again and she adopted me so that I would be hers. That's what he told me on my fifth birthday. It was August—hot and dusty and I was thirsty and everything I had thought to be one way was now suddenly another way and I wondered if the woman I thought was my mother loved me and I wondered where the other woman was, if she were still in Sicily and what was Sicily? Did she have dark hair and did I look like her and would I ever see her and did she ever think of me and did she really love me and if she had really loved me why would she have left me? And I wondered if I'd always be her boy and I wondered if my father had loved her and if he had loved her why did he stop? I couldn't ask these questions then because all the things I needed to ask were too big and didn't make sense. The world looked different and I wished I hadn't asked what a bastard was. And all my questions swelled my head and half of me vanished. Out there in the desert there was nothing and I had no idea where I was or where I should be or what an island in Italy looked like, what a woman named White Mary looked like. I imagined her as extraordinarily white, floating like the Virgin through the clouds. And I didn't know what to think about it all so I stopped speaking. I didn't speak for two years. Nothing made sense and I knew my words would least of all.

WHITE MARY. She came from Sicily to London in the summer of 1964. A friend had found her the job. It was billed as an adventure, a chance to see London and learn English while caring for four small children of intellectuals who wrote books at home. Bianca came from Taormina on the slopes of Mount Tauro, the Mountain of the Bull, which seemed to crash into the Ionian Sea. It was a resort town for the very rich filled with Rothschilds, Krupps, Vanderbilts. Greek ruins and gardens thick with bougainvillea and olive and citrus trees surrounded the town, and in the distance to the south Mount Etna glowed a brilliant red at night. Most of the year the land was brown and barren like a desert, with Mount Etna rising snowcapped like a god. In spring, though, the land became as green as Ireland, hiding all the scars—an Eden of figs and oleander and jasmine, and just as fragrant.

Bianca was the youngest child of six daughters and her dream of London made no sense to her parents or her sisters (all of whom were married), but they remembered the war and they loved Americans so it didn't take much to convince them to let her go. She would be earning her way at least. The Furey family would fly her to London and offer her a small stipend, and when they traveled to America and Africa and anywhere they needed to go to do their research and write their books, Bianca would travel with them. The small stipend was a lot of lire and the chance to learn English worth even more.

Bianca had big dreams. She saw the Rothschilds in their fancy gowns. She knew the world was larger than her small town. In the encyclopedia, she had read about the brain and thought it the most beautiful thing in the world. It all begins and ends with the brain. She wanted to study it, become a doctor. She could get carried away with her dreams.

At first she was shy because she knew only a few words of English and this family knew no Italian. They had a house in South Kensington and clearly they were rich even though the house was a mess and it seemed it was run by the children who ran around it fighting, ignoring Bianca. The only word they knew in Italian was *Mafia*. They said it all the time. She wanted to learn English simply so she could scare them with stories about the Mafia. The baby, the newborn Timothy with a head nearly as big as Anton's, had a will to cry, but stopped crying in her arms—a small victory that gave her hope.

Anton worked in a sunny room on the top floor that was flooded with papers and he spent hours in there at a time and it seemed the room was filled with thousands of books. When she came up there to clean, cleaning was the one thing she felt comfortable doing at first, he didn't mind the interruption. He tried speaking with her, making her feel warm and welcome as he sipped coffee from a large mug. With his shining eyes he had a big friendly smile that she wanted to step inside. He was tall and big and handsome and just being near him warmed her, made her feel safe. He would pick up small objects—a toy soldier, a paper clip, a pen, a book—and teach her the word in English, and then she in turn would teach him the word in Italian.

The wife, Agnes, was kind, too, and would take Bianca shopping for blue jeans and T-shirts and anything else that would make her feel more at home. For the most part Agnes did not care about managing the house. She did not discipline the children. She was a tall thin woman with dark rings beneath clear blue eyes. Her hair was gray though she was just thirty-two. Mostly she liked to read and write and talk to Anton at the kitchen table for long hours with her chin in her hand, pondering large questions about religion and philosophy while the children played and the baby fussed. A pack, a tribe, a force. Agnes oblivious to their rampages. This was how Bianca imagined it, though she had no idea what this American couple spoke of, but just from the way they looked, the intensity, she could tell the subject was important. She wanted to learn English as well, so that she could understand what they were saying.

When they traveled, it seemed anywhere they went, Anton and Agnes made friends and they were always having big dinners and Bianca was always included as part of the party and the children did a fine job taking care of themselves. Sometimes she wondered why they needed her at all. The arrangement was strange for Bianca, that they wanted her to be like a member of the family.

At the dinners Anton and Agnes would tell her not to worry after the children, but rather to enjoy herself, and she drank too much wine for the first time with them and she smoked a cigarette that was not really a cigarette, making her dizzy and eager inside. Bianca Maria was young, nineteen, with long black hair, black observant eyes, and thick dark brows that defined her beauty.

"Bread," Anton said, lifting bread at the dinner table in the crowded restaurant in the South of France. "*Pane*," Bianca said. Platters of fish on the table, candles dripping their wax, glasses of wine, jugs of wine. They were there with a group of people they had met on the beach. "Wine," Anton said. He tilted the glass to his lips and drank. "*Vino*," Bianca said. "*Vino rosso dell'Etna*," she said. "The red wine of Etna."

Gorgeous drawn-out garbled words slipped off her glistening lips. "Drink wine," he said. And then he put the glass to her lips and tilted it so that she could drink and then he took his napkin and wiped her lips because a bead of the red wine lingered there. A spark shot through her so electric she was afraid that Agnes had felt it. She imagined her sisters watching her with their big accusing eyes. *Servants don't behave like this. Servants are not a part of the family.* But I'm not a servant, she would boldly respond. A part of Bianca rebelled against conformity, defied her position in the world, believed that nothing was set in stone and she did not have to remain a girl from Sicily whose life would be lived out there. "Lips," Anton said, and he touched her lips with his large index finger and her lips curled into a smile. Then so did his, a dangerous smile that seemed to suck her into him. "Lips," she repeated. "Teeth," he said, running his tongue over his teeth. "Tongue," he said. The restaurant was loud with chatter and the clatter of glassware and silverware and the noisy children. The tables were beneath a canopy at the edge of the beach and you could hear the Mediterranean lapping at the shore and the full moon lit up the water and the night. The smell of garlic and grilled fish permeated the air. She stared at Anton, feeling her own teeth with her own tongue. "Kiss," she said bravely, and puckered her lips and kissed and knew for the first time that Agnes was oblivious to more than just the children. "Kiss," she said again, and then reddened as his smile continued to devour her.

In the fall Agnes's father got sick. She flew home to America to care for him, and Bianca, now in her jeans and T-shirts and with her garbled English, was left in South Kensington to care for the kids. It seemed Agnes would be gone just a short time, but weeks passed, then months. Long enough for

Bianca's garbled English to become quite fluent. For the wild kids to come to like her. For the wild kids to start teaching her English, too. "Fuck," Nicholas said. "Fuck," Bianca repeated, knowing that they were teaching her obscenities, that they were teasing with her because they liked her. She knew they were wild simply because there were so many of them. She read to them, put them to bed on time, took them for walks in the park, to Speakers' Corner on Sundays with Anton. "Karl Marx got his start here," Anton said. A boy no older than Nicholas stood on a box, expounding the virtues of communism.

Caroline and Sofia laughed. "Fuck off," Nicholas said. "Fuck off," Bianca repeated. And then they were all laughing. Sofia played with Bianca's hair, combing and combing it, twirling it into buns and french rolls. Sofia's small fingers scurried across her scalp. Bianca liked that Agnes was gone. She hoped Agnes's father would be sick for a long time. Sometimes she would go through Agnes's clothes, trying to find some small piece that she liked so that she could try it on. But Agnes was bigger than she, a small triumph that made Bianca proud.

IT HAPPENED SLOWLY because she was a virgin. His White Mary in her American blue jeans with her sad dark eyes. At first there was a light touch of the arm, then his fingers gently in her hair. Piece by piece he took off her clothes. A sweater one week, a camisole the next, then finally her bra. He loved everything female and would buy her silk stockings and velvet scarves. He held her breasts in his two hands. This was her adventure, her mystery. She had come from an island in Italy where lava burned a brilliant red against a black night, where her sisters were all married, in order that they repeat the life their mother had lived and her mother and her mother before her, reaching back to Greek temples that withered and crumbled in their yard. Their accusing eyes were simply jealous eyes. Her breasts in his mouth, the children carrying on below, the baby crying, his wife in America, Bianca had never before felt delicious. "Kiss," she loved to say because it made her feel brave. God watching down on them. "Kiss."

Anton encouraged her and for that she fell in love with him, encouraged her with his Texas drawl and his Texas-sized enthusiasm, his twinkling, mischievous eyes. She told him her dream to be a doctor. He had no doubts about what she could achieve. He made life seem easy, the impossible seem possible. Just within our grasp if we tried. He confirmed her notions of will. "You can be a doctor, babe. Work on the brain. Magnificent." The word *magnificent*, in the way it floated off his tongue with a smile and belief, made her realize there was nothing impossible about the idea. It was as if he wanted to save her, help her step outside the obvious. He had friends, lots of friends—friends met on the beach in the South of France, in a pub, a café, at the theater, from Texas even. They came to the house in South Kensington for a drink, for dinner, for a week, a month, and she could see they were feeding on him—on his ability to inspire the confidence to turn expectation inside out. Bianca plunged into the dark abyss of hope, a tingle in your finger, a thread you need to follow to its source.

Then she was pregnant, scared, and humiliated, and Agnes's father died and Bianca wished Agnes would die along with him. The baby grew and it began to kick and Anton fucked her hard and she fucked him hard, the baby between them, kicking still. Her baby, her blood. She imagined carrying it back to Sicily, a bundled newborn in a blanket—a pure and unbaptizable sin. Then began the long period of bewilderment and tears, of shame and then its slow erasure. "It'll be all right, babe. I'll help you. We'll help you. We'll see you through." Under his tutelage she began to shed herself, to see this new magnetic wisdom that people were drawn to, as if "seeing her through" could be the answer. The scornful sisters faded into a past that didn't exist. He made it seem that before too long the world would be perfect again.

"Feel it," she'd say, intoxicated by her new life, placing her hand on her tummy. They would lie on the floor of his study, sun spraying light over them, warm yet cool like a crocheted blanket. "It's a boy, I'm sure from how it moves. *Un figlio.*"

"A powerful little *figlio*," he said as some little part of this little guy pushed through her skin to touch Anton's big hand resting there. "*Nostro figlio*," he said, and kissed her. He kissed her tummy, sang to her tummy, read Shakespeare and Byron and Tennyson and Dickinson to her tummy. Kissed the kicks. He swallowed tears. "I'm sorry," he said after a while. His voice strong, yet consoling. "I'm sorry, babe, for this pain."

"It's hard for you, too," she said. Just a young girl with life in front of her—fancy dreams about the beauty of the lobes of the human cortex. "Like coral," she'd say.

"We'll help you," he reassured. "It'll be all right. I promise."

As Catholics they were at an impasse: she could not abort; he could not leave his wife. The kids down below dizzying, running around like some intense weather system, oblivious—Mafia, Mafia, Mafia—wanting to know anything and everything there was to know. Truth was, she knew nothing and wanted them to shut up. Together with Agnes, Anton would see Bianca through. She wilted so utterly and completely inside. "See you through," the meaning of those words she learned very well—coming from his gentle lips and eyes.

Agnes returned, all tenderness and warmth. A loving hand on Bianca's shoulder, her arm, her belly. "It will be just fine," Agnes said. Her gray hair had become even grayer. She looked positively old. Bianca had no idea what Anton had said to Agnes, no understanding of how Agnes accepted so easily. Was this their way? Were all those other children mothered by other mothers? Bianca wanted her own mother, wanted to curl into her big warm lap, wanted her sisters to tease her sweetly as they had as children. Tease her about her curiosity, about eating flowers, about listening in on the confessions of others in the church. But not this. She wanted Agnes to hate her. She was unnerved by Agnes's equanimity. It didn't seem human. Bianca felt her shame welling up. She hated Agnes. What right did she have to walk around like a saint? The more Bianca hated Agnes, the more generous Agnes became. When Bianca least expected it, the baby would move like an octopus in her womb, tickling her. Her belly grew so big she thought the baby would come forth through the skin. She walked around the house, sweating, legs swelling, feet puffing. The kids screaming, "Bianca's got a baby!" Did they know?

"Why don't you hate me?" Bianca wanted to ask.

"Because I'm Christian," she imagined Agnes would answer.

"Because I know this is not your fault."

"Because you're just nineteen."

"Because you're carrying my child."

Bianca didn't know that Agnes was familiar with Anton's betrayals. That long ago she had accepted and forgiven this as weakness.

The birth was easy. Agnes held one leg and the doctor held the other and they instructed her to push. Anton was in the waiting room pacing, cigars in his breast pocket. It was late in the night and through the windows of the hospital room, white and sterile, were the lights and sounds of London. Police sirens and bells and speeding cars. And then quiet. In a vase on the radiator were two-dozen champagne-colored roses from Anton and Agnes. Agnes's hands were soft and damp as they pushed against Bianca's leg, pushed her leg back against her chest, offering Agnes a wide view of Bianca's vagina and the dark head of hair that was trying to emerge. Bianca was drugged enough not to feel the pain, but she was aware of Agnes watching for the baby, aware of Agnes's damp hand on her forehead between contractions, soothing her, aware that Agnes would take this baby and become the mother of this baby. "Push, Bianca, harder Bianca," the doctor said. "You can do it," Agnes encouraged. All friendly and the elegant rose blossoms and Anton outside in the waiting area, her family in Sicily with no idea.

Afterward she would shrink back to the woman she had been and she would return to Italy and no one would know that she had given birth to another woman's child. Her body would be what it had been, keeping her secret. Bianca, a girl of nineteen, a mother who was not a mother. "Push," the doctor said sternly, and she pushed. She pushed with her guts and her brain, pushed out her blood, her life. Agnes by her side, Agnes massaging her back through the contractions, Agnes teaching her and telling her how to breathe, paying for the doctor, cutting the cord, holding the baby first. That gorgeous baby with the headful of black hair and his newborn eyes so big and bright and already a stunning blue—Anton's blue. That baby sliding out from between her legs. That baby on her chest with his eyes latching on to hers. Those eyes pleading, pleading with the mother, claiming her. That baby searching for her nipple. "I don't think you should get started on that," the doctor said softly, gently. Didn't cats get six weeks with their kittens? "But I'm not yours," Bianca whispered to her son.

Her American dream in London. Anton took Bianca once, before they knew about the baby, to the house of a friend. The man, Mr. Laing, was a philosopher and he was clearly not so rich as Anton. He lived in a basement apartment with just two rooms. Anton and Bianca went together to this man's house and it was as if they were a couple. They went to talk about their dreams. Bianca had liked the idea because she liked feeling that she belonged to Anton and Anton had explained that this visit concerned his work. She liked being a part of his work. It made her feel more like Agnes. The visit involved a form of psychoanalysis, necessary to experience for the writing of his book. He held her close. He cared not what this man thought about their relationship. They were to lie on the floor and simply describe the dreams they had had. But first they would take a drug she had not heard of. It was called LSD. It came as just a tiny white square of paper, as delicate as tissue. The man had a big forehead and whitish hair above his ears, though he was still young, and he wore a crooked tie and a big grin. He placed the small piece of tissue on her tongue, which he asked her to stick out like a supplicant receiving the Eucharist. The body and blood of Christ. She told him this. Interesting, he said. Very interesting. And I the priest, my dear. And then he told her to lie on the floor and to wait patiently and then to tell him and Anton what she was seeing. We want to catch your dreams, my dear. He and Anton did the same and the three of them lay staring at the ceiling and after a time she started seeing her town in Sicily. She started seeing the Greek temples become whole again and magnificently white and then magnificently painted. She saw her church where she was baptized and saw her priest holding her in his arms in her long white dress and all the images swirled together and she saw her sisters one by one in their white wedding gowns and the gentle smile of her father and his gentle hug good-bye as he escorted her to the steps of her plane with a hot Sicilian breeze brushing over them. *Brava ragazza.* As she climbed the steps, as the plane climbed into the air. The room was spinning, Mount Etna was erupting, then she wasn't making any sense, spewing lava and fire, then it was calm, a perfect cone and snowcapped. Bob Dylan was singing about changing times. She tried to explain. It became imperative that these two men understand her. Anton wanted to kiss her as she talked. His lips felt enormous and hot and dry on her lips and his hand grotesque at her breasts and she saw her church and her baby self in the arms of her family's priest and her father's gentle hug and the beautiful normalcy of her Sicilian world. Anton's tongue in her enormous mouth. His mouth ate her words. She thought she'd swallow his tongue, like the snake that eats its own tail. She wished she could swallow the tongue, and then she'd swallow him and he'd be inside of her. And Anton's friend, he thought this was interesting. He hovered above her wanting to know more, see what she saw. She sweated. Mount Etna raged. Mount Etna poured blood all over town, devoured her town, her sisters, her mother, her father, her baby self in her priest's arms. His tongue, she slurped it and it grew and it pulled him from the inside out and into her. She kept sucking, slurping, making him smaller and smaller until he was entirely devoured. "Interesting," the friend said. Until Anton was nothing inside of her. And for a long time she would think of this, Anton becoming nothing inside of her, an accident in her early life, swept along with the currents—her child, the wreckage. Forever she would think of this. And forever her boy's eyes would plead with her. Her boy's eyes would plead with her at the most unlikely times. Those big bright magnificent newborn eyes.

SOMETIMES WHEN we were little, Kate would sit me in front of a mirror and take apart my features. "Like an equation," she would say. "Like math." She would tell me that my blue eyes belonged to my father. "Their squint and color and all." But that my dark curly hair, my long face and strong jaw, my full red lips, my olive skin—all that, she told me, belonged to my mother. Sitting on the counter in the bathroom with the bright bathroom lights illuminating us, she made me imagine from my features my mother's beauty. And I could almost see her on her island. White Mary. I could almost touch her, like in a dream, she was that close—hidden in my face.

For my birthday once, Kate gave me a compass. It was a joke intended to say, You're lost, now find yourself. She came to this because I don't like to have a plan. I don't want to be pinned down. I like to wander, to drift from one notion to the next, from here to there and not know where there is. I've not finished college. I take jobs as they come, if they sound interesting. I work with my hands. "Finny's genius is in his hands," my father used to say. Kate says I'm floating. She thinks I'd be better off in one place like herself, in a stable with pretty things all around. Kate says I should be angry with my father, that that would help me find myself. She says I should own up to how he's hurt me. But I tell her she has no idea what she's talking about. "Presumptuous," I say. What should I be angry for? For my father falling in love? He loved love. For cherishing me? I can still see him squatting out there in the desert, holding me tightly as he tried to explain, knowing what I needed to hear most. "I loved your mother," he said. "I'll love her always because of you." It was as if that love were visible, a road I could wander along.

I wasn't clever with the compass. I throw maps away. Instead, I like to float. I like the light way it feels. Above an island, a country, a continent, a world untethered on the road.

CHAPTER TEN

Truth

EARLY JUNE. Anton is lying in bed. He knows what day this is. The bamboo scrapes against the windows and sun floods through the sliding glass doors. Birds sing and the cardinal, a cardinal who's been around for years, stuns himself by flying into his own reflection in the window. Stupid bird, Anton thinks, wants to mate with himself. Anton is alone. Eve is at work. She knows what day it is, too. She'll stay away until late, a busy day at the office. She will not remind herself once about what day it is, but of course she knows. She knows. He knows. They all know. Alice flew halfway around the world to avoid the day.

"She shouldn't have gone to India," Kate had said to Jane and Julia. The three sisters were talking on the phone, a three-way conversation—they had had their phones programmed specially. They always had three-way conversations, unless they were in a fight. Usually when they were in a fight it was two against one and the two had a two-way conversation discussing how horrible the third was. But it was never too long before they were all in love again. Sometimes they would stay on the phone for what seemed like hours, saying nothing, phone pressed to ear as they went about their business listening to one another breathe. The three shared the same doctor and they all had husbands or boyfriends named James, Jim, and Jimmy, who were all some form of beleaguered artist. Jane was the only one who was married, married since she was twenty-two to an English hitchhiker that the family had picked up long ago as they traveled through the deserts of the West. They became friends, he went back to England, became a painter, and eleven years later they fell in love. Julia and Kate were both divorced and newly involved with their Jim and Jimmy.

Woven together like fabric, Alice always thought of her Cooper sisters, wishing, on occasion, that she were part of the weave.

"She's in denial," Julia said. "And so is Anton for letting her go. He knew he'd hear about the scan only three days after she left."

"Alice told me that he promised he'd go visit her."

"Right," Kate said sarcastically. "It's intriguing to see denial so transparently at work."

"How's the new part?" Jane asked Julia, changing the subject. She was starring in a new show off Broadway in which she was to play the part of an older woman—a show she didn't want to do but did because the money was good. Of the three sisters, she had a bit of fame and loads of money from doing commercials, and as a result the other two were jealous, though they pretended not to be. Jane, too, had loads of money. She lived in a mansion in Georgetown, impeccably designed. She even had her own dressing room, but she envied (a little) Julia's fame. The kind of work that Jane and Kate did would never bring fame: like her father, Kate was a geochronologist and taught high school students in New

York City while she tried to finish her dissertation, which she had put on hold during her marriage because that life had taken her to Italy. Jane, following after her mother, had a successful catering company in Washington, D.C.

"I'm only thirty-four and now they'll label me an old lady. The shelf life of an actress is somewhere between cottage cheese and milk. I'll get hammered. Whatever I do, they'll destroy me," Julia said, speaking of the critics.

"You always say that," Jane said dismissively. "They always love you. This is a good opportunity. Another chance to be adored."

"Don't be so vain."

"Actually, I'm quitting. It was a stupid choice and the choices make your career. Nicholas says he's going to try to write a feature with me in mind for the lead—a young lead."

"But he makes experimental art films," Kate said. He'd been doing this for several years and had a few of his films featured in shows at the Museum of Modern Art in New York City.

"What are you going to do, just sit there while the camera catches every flicker of your brow for minutes on end?"

"Or you could give someone a blow job like the Warhol film."

"Nicholas wants to try something different. He wants to try a feature," Julia said.

"Do you really think you'll ever do movies?" Kate asked, somewhere hoping that Julia never would because that kind of fame would be too much to bear. "Aren't you too old for the movies?"

"That's mean," Jane said.

"I saw a great pair of shoes at Varda," Julia said, changing the subject. She knew that she could only go on for so long about her career before her sisters became jealous. Sometimes she enjoyed going right to the brink, taunting them and then pulling back. Talking about shopping was something they all enjoyed. "Platform sandals for summer with very thin straps around the ankles."

"How much?"

"Two fifty."

"A bargain."

"Spend now when you're young and beautiful! I'm still beautiful, aren't I?" Julia said with her bright smile.

"Poor Alice," Jane said. "She's going to have to come right back home from India." Kate sighed impatiently. "Just imagine, Kate, if you knew your daddy might soon die." Your daddy, said as if they didn't share the same father. It was meant as a stab. Jane and Julia claimed that Kate was their father's favorite.

ANTON WONDERS if Eve will call to check in. He hopes she will. He wants to hear the enthusiasm of her voice. It's a moment of peace from the cramps. He thinks that he would like to work, get up and go to his study. *Eros and Irony,* the latest title of his book. The bedroom is very clean. The white spread freshly ironed. A vase of lilacs. What if the cramps just disappeared completely? he thinks. If they disappear completely, he promises, he will finish his book. He says a prayer. He has not thought about God in a long time. "Get out of bed today," Eve had told him before leaving. She had bent over him and kissed his forehead. As if it were just that easy. Get out of bed and miraculously your life will be as it once was. But he knew well what day it was. He had given her a hopeless smile that she had ignored. He knew how much she hated illness. He knew how glad she was to get out of the house. He was jealous of her.

If I die, he thinks, before finishing this book, my life will have amounted to nothing. In general, he did not think like that. A life was lived and enjoyed and then it was over. Even so, he had wanted to give his book to the world. He had promised God that he would; he believed that God had promised him—long ago when he left the Jesuits. Almost like a pact. If I die without completing this book, my life will have been for naught. But he can't think about that. His death is still an abstraction. It's a sunny day. He steps out of bed, he is weak, his skin sags off of him. He opens the sliding glass door and looks out over the lawn and the vast field, and he feels hope. Hope—beautiful, infinite hope. Hope with its layers, layer after layer after layer, peeled back to reveal even more layers. The depths of hope.

Anton knows that shortly his doctor will telephone to tell him the news. This doctor is a gastroenterologist because the family still believes (hopes) that the cramps are caused by some mysterious tropical disease picked up from eating red snapper in Jamaica. The gastroenterologist will call and he will say that there seems to be pathology in the pancreas. Adenocarcinoma seems to be presenting itself. Do you know what kind of hope there is with adenocarcinoma? None. Or at least very little, such a tiny shred you would have to be at the very core of that hope to scavenge any. Eve, blessed Eve, she could crawl into that tiny spot and by sheer will drag the entire family in with her and they would try to thrive in that shred.

Your pancreas is a small organ, only six inches long, narrow like a thin pear and animate with a head, a body, and a tail. The job of the pancreas is to make enzymes and insulin that help digest food and sugar. It lies in the upper abdomen and is connected to the small intestine and is surrounded by the stomach, the intestines, the liver, and the spleen. Its deep location, smack up against the spine, hidden by the other vital organs, makes cancer lurking there hard to find. And there where it hides, it presses into nerves, triggering phenomenal pain. Cramps. Anton knows all this. His father died of pancreatic cancer. His father's tumor had been "operable," but he'd died shortly after the operable operation.

Anton breathes in the spring air with the full force of his lungs. He looks out over the hills, the same view he's been looking at for years—stunning variations on green, this time of year. Cowbells clank together. Birds dart about searching for worms. They can feel the worms beneath their feet, in the ground, squirming about. Chardin. The Omega Point, the point at which there is a final union between the human and the divine. He laughs at himself, the hubris of his youth. He wonders what will become of his home and his family after he is gone?

The phone rings. He can hear it ringing throughout the entire house. Loud, impatient rings. He hopes it's his baby, Alice calling from India to say she has arrived. Hope, beautiful hope, with depth, like a quarry, like the universe, like time. But he can tell by the ring that it isn't Alice, but the gastroenterologist from the big New York hospital. Funny how rings can define the caller. He's calling to tell Anton that indeed there is a tumor in his pancreas. That damn, deceptive little thing. Just a wee tumor, just one centimeter long. Hiding there. No matter how wee, this news means one thing alone.

But still he is hoping that it is his baby so that he can hear her wonder at the world. Elephants on the streets, a camel, cows everywhere. The big moon over the Apollo Bunder, more moonish in India, somehow closer. As if you could lean a ladder up against it and climb onto the moon for a walk, a nice long stroll, that big and fat and splendid Indian moon. For a moment he sees the whole family in India visiting Alice, a clan, a traveling caravan marching over the subcontinent— united, whole.

But it is the doctor. When Anton puts the phone down he holds his head in his hands and he tries to think very clearly. He thinks, Before too long I will die. A few days earlier he and Eve had taken a short walk to the peach orchard. They had sat on a boulder looking over the fields and they had smoked a joint together and the joint eased the pain, and for a while he was able to forget the cramps until a pain originating deep within him shot through his body like a lightning bolt, blinding him for a full five minutes. "This isn't good, Eve," he had said. "I don't have a good feeling about this." The air so warm, like velvet, embracing them.

"Don't be ridiculous," she had said. That's all she had said.

I'll be dead and Eve will be alone. She knows what day it is, but she will not call. He does not dwell on this. In fact, before he can be terrified for himself he is terrified for her. He is worried that the news alone will give her tachycardia, that is atrial fibrillation, a rapid fluttering of the heart of up to 500, even 600 beats per minute—risk of heart failure, heart attack, a stroke. He knows she is out of heparin. He knows she is at work and that it has been a busy day. That she'll be tired when she comes home. He thinks of her surrounded by stoves and mixers and young chefs in their checkered uniforms, trying to please her with tastes of their sauces, their tortes, their mille feuilles. The farmers stopping by with their loads of fresh produce, fingerling potatoes, baby beets, and mâche. "I want to be a poet," she had confessed to him when they were first together. She read to him from her work, confessing as well that she had never shared it with Ian. How

Anton had wished he could help her, save her from a life of ironing and sewing her children's clothes. Anton had been proud that Ian never saw this beauty in her, the beauty of her words, her ability to see the finest details of the world, that it was all his to celebrate and explore. He wants to tell her to write.

Anton calls Julia first. When he hears her bright voice he cries and she knows the news, though he does not speak and though he tries not to let her hear that he is crying. He remembers Julia as a little girl with her hair all done up perfectly in pink ribbons and how that contrasted so magnificently with her intelligence and her competitiveness. He sees her by the side of a road on their long-ago trip out west, lining the boys up to have a pissing competition. Desert and sagebrush and tumbleweeds tumbling in those hot dry winds. He smiles. "I can piss farther than any of you," she had declared. He thinks of her romantic notions, begging him to teach her to waltz. Waltzing with her through the dining room out onto the deck back into the living room. Round and round, swirling her in a long ball gown. She is a younger version of Eve. He thinks of her rosy face, her electric smile, he thinks of a flower blooming—of how she loves the oboe, of how she delights in Mozart. He thinks of her twirling across the stage as flirtatious Bianca in *Kiss Me Kate*, singing about an oilman and checks and a Paris hat—glittering like a gem. He thinks of Ophelia, how he had wanted her to play the part on the deck, how he had never done that, so many things he had not done. His book shoots to mind and then vanishes.

Even though Julia has known for a while she, too, is silenced. The sunshine makes a blur of the bedroom. The bamboo scrapes against the windows. The cardinal knocks. "I love you, Anton." Her sweet words melt into him. He doesn't know what else she says. He asks her to pick up some of Eve's medicine at the pharmacy. He is all concern for Eve, terrified for her having to live without him, terrified that the news alone will kill her.

Julia calls her sisters. Anton calls his children. Those that are near descend on the house. The sisters arrive first. Anton is kneeling at his bed, praying. Julia embraces him without hesitation. She cries, unafraid to hide the truth. Kate doesn't know what to do. She's afraid, staring at a dead man, afraid she'll say something wrong and stupid—that he'll think of her as stupid. Jane sits on the edge of the bed and takes his hands in hers. Her hands are long and slender. His are still big and fat. The two sisters comfort him as if he were a little boy. They want to make it somehow all right. For months Julia will say that she wishes she could die in his place, "Like a mother would. I feel more like his mother." "Well you aren't," Jane would snap. Kate just stands there awkwardly, feeling death pervade the room, sliming up around her and her fears of stupidity. In the car coming down from New York they weren't so generous.

"Does this mean he's going to die now?" Jane had asked. She was up from D.C. visiting her sisters for the weekend and had now extended her trip because of the news.

"He's a dead man," Kate had responded, though she had no idea what she was saying. "Dead man," she said again for emphasis.

"I hope that Mom has finally legally married him," Jane said. "You know Sofia will have her out of Chardin in a flash if it's not legally hers."

Mostly they spoke about wills. They contemplated how rich the Furey kids would be when Agnes died and then they contemplated what the Furey kids would do with all the money. They enjoyed speculating. "They won't be as rich as we've always been led to believe," Jane said.

"Agnes has been giving them ten thousand dollars a year—for a long time now."

"Finny's even got a will. He's leaving everything to Alice. He tells her she's just as entitled to it as he is."

"Nicholas can only talk about his movie and investing. He's invested in La-Z-Boy."

"How rich is rich?" Kate asked.

"I think they'll have about three million apiece," Julia said.

"That's nothing these days," Jane said.

"Poor Mom."

"She'll be better off than ever once this is over."

"Let's just hope she doesn't get involved with another man. I can't deal with another man of hers."

"I THOUGHT GOD was going to let me finish my book," Anton says to Jane, Julia, and Kate. "I thought he was keeping me alive for that." Then Julia starts speaking about options, finding the best doctors, Sloan-Kettering, experimental treatments—cryosurgery, macrobiotic spas, herbal remedies. She gets out a pad and paper. She's all business and efficiency. Other kids arrive. They're all hugging each other and telling one another how much they love each other. They collect in the bedroom. Candles are lit. Bibles are opened. Rosary beads fingered. The day blows on. No Eve. No sign of Eve. No call from Eve. She still does not know. Anton makes sure that her medicine is there on the bedside table. He has a glass and a bottle of cool water with ice chips. He went to the kitchen to get it himself. It's there waiting for Eve. His shrine to her.

How he wants her to have an attack. He had needed her optimism the other day in the orchard, that unrelenting strength; he'll need it again later. But today he wants her to crack if only so that he can save her. How he wants to be prepared to save her. Hold her in his arms and tell all the kids to leave the room so that they can have this moment to themselves. Kiss her cheeks, her nose. How many things he wants to say to her. He wants to apologize, tell her that he always loved her and that sometimes he was bad and couldn't express it and sometimes he was selfish. He wants them to go through this together—for it to be theirs, beautiful even. He remembers her as a young woman, just like Julia now, a blooming flower. He remembers making love to her for the first time in the long onion grass by the edge of the road. He remembers all the daffodils and he remembers the exquisite promise of that day, how the whole world smelled sweet and he truly believed he had found love, the love he had tried to write about, lifelong love, equal love—the love promised by the Jesuits.

Even the kids can feel his anticipation. "The glass, the glass of water is right here," Caroline and Julia keep reassuring him. "It's right here if she needs it." Their faces close together—his daughter and Eve's, sisters—comfort him. Caroline's bright eyes, the gentle worried creases of her brow. Love each other like sisters and brothers, he had encouraged them for all these years.

Several times he had to drive Eve to the hospital to stop her heart from racing. Once had been his fault. They had had a fight. He saw the doctor in the emergency room take the long needle and plunge it into the muscle of her arm. "She'll be all right," Jane promises, then so does Kate. But that is not what Anton wants to hear. Now they are all waiting for Eve to return. The daughters wonder if this will trigger her heart. He knows it will because she doesn't like to be alone. He waits for her, for this. He's entirely focused on Eve. The family swirling about is a blur now. He wants to see Eve's face. The sun disappears; the sky fades to evening to night. The birds come out in their chorus, then they, too, disappear. The cardinal continues to fly into the glass. Then, finally, Eve is home.

What is it like to tell your wife that you will die? He wants to study her reaction, as if he will learn something new, feel something unfelt before, perhaps a love like when Rossignol married them in the slow-motion heat of the Oloffson with the familiar French songs, the great bed of the Graham Greene suite waiting for the pleasure of their bodies. They made love to get cool, the chill once ecstasy subsides. Perhaps in her reaction he will learn about their love, what has become of it, that love that seemed promised long ago among the daffodils. In her face, in all the lines of her face, in the fierce determination of her eyes, he wants to find their love. Find something in that face that for such a long time has been misunderstood.

Eve looks tired. She is oblivious to the news. Bags are hanging off her as she comes into the room. She dumps them on the floor and asks brightly, "How did you do today?" She brings with her the strong smells of a kitchen—rosemary, chocolate, steak, sweat. She notices the kids, her daughters. She smiles. Happy that they're all here. "What a surprise," she says, noticing nothing unusual on their faces. Wavering not one bit from her belief that she can stop time, change the course of the stars. Residual omnipotence. It was this ferocity that Anton had fallen in love with.

Anton is lying on his bed. The room is dark, lit only by a few dim lamps. The faces of all the kids, like shades. A Bible lays open on the bed. Rosary beads are entwined in his fingers. But she doesn't notice any of this. A smile on his face. She sits down beside him and quickly, like a shot, he tells her. Eve is no longer oblivious to the news. Anton looks at her chest, her big supple chest, as if he could look through it to her heart. On the table is her medicine and the cool glass of water. Need it, he thinks. The dogs bark. But he should be looking at her face, at her left nostril flexed, straining in that pricking way for air, at her eyes where the tiniest tears are forming. She pushes her hair back, quietly she breathes, she swallows. He should be looking at her face. All the kids in the room like armor, like interference. What if they weren't here? What if he had called her first? Why didn't he call her first? Why doesn't he look at her face? Why is he so determined to look at her chest, her heart? Her answer is in her eyes, in the flexing of her nostrils—they ache while her heart goes still.

At first, she doesn't know what to say. She wants to say something that will please him, that will support him, make him love her. Reality antagonizes her. She antagonizes it right back. He keeps studying her chest; it is steady, silent. Something tremendous wilts inside of him. Her heart has been triggered for much less, Anton thinks. The first time was when she was seventeen and Ian took her home to meet his parents. The second was when she was in divorce court. The third was when she and Anton fought and he slammed a door in her face and a nail protruding from it caught the skin by her eye and ripped it. Five stitches, she still had the scar. The fourth was when she had stolen daffodils from an abandoned house and the police had arrested her. The fifth was when Alice had been hit by a car in Mexico City. His insides close up like a fist. He shuts his eyes. He does not want to see her eyes. He cannot look her in the eye.

Eve's face is illuminated by the dim lamp now. She looks young and beautiful in that light. Her cheeks brighten. Her eyes flood with determination. She thinks this is what he wants, what he might need most. This is what she knows. She is pushing reality away from her. She is crawling into the shred of remaining hope. She is entirely inside it, stretching its borders, making room enough for all.

"We'll beat this," she says with calm. His eyes are fixed on her heart. "We'll beat this," she says again, and he will never hear her believe anything else.

CHAPTER ELEVEN

Never Say Die

THE FIGHTING BEGAN and it seemed it would never stop. Everyone was fighting. It was a terrible time. Anton was dying and the family was dividing. The Coopers against the Fureys. The Fureys against the Coopers. They were all plotting against one another. Alice ran between both sides trying to knit them back together. "Don't fight, please." Jane held Alice, trying to protect her. She cried for hours in Jane's arms, her hands patting the girl. But the will to fight was strong. No one trusted anymore. They fought over jewelry and furniture that belonged to the Furey family and that the Fureys thought the Coopers would try to annex. They fought over property and wills. A will? Did Anton have a will? Would Eve be protected when he died? Were they even legally married in the State of New Jersey? Jane fought with her mother about whether they were married. Married three or four times, in Haiti or by friends with no vested authority. "That's no good when it comes to the law," Jane said. A will? There was a will. Anton left the house and most of the land to his kids, the Furey kids, and two acres apiece of the fifty-acre farm to the three Cooper girls. "Two acres and a mule," Julia said, raising her left eyebrow. Kate smiled. "Two acres and not even a mule," Jane said, with a cutting look. Eve made excuses for Anton, saying the will was old. He'd been mad at the girls when he wrote it.

All the kids came home, living together as a family once again, as if fifteen, twenty, years had somehow passed yet never passed at all. Alice came home from her three-day adventure around the world. Everything was suspended except for Anton's life, which ticked, fast, to its ultimate conclusion.

Lily, Anton's mistress, came with her Perrier bottle filled with vodka. Of course, no one was supposed to know that she was his lover, but of course, they all knew. His ex-wife, Agnes, came—a New Age woman with death crystals and uncomplicated thoughts about how it was not so bad on the "other side." The little beady-eyed preacher woman from down the road came, trying to calm them with her prayers as a procession of friends came and went. Laurence came; the lawyer came. The Strange couple came, declaring this a tragedy. Everyone came. (Everyone but the maid, who had given notice because death terrified her.) Anton wanted it that way. He wanted to apologize and beg forgiveness of them all. Secrets lurked beneath the surface of everything, like worms beneath the yard.

They fought over dinner jobs and beds and who'd get to sleep where and who'd do all the food shopping and who'd pay all the food bills. Bills? Julia had excavated a mass of debt and was fighting with Eve over it and the back taxes Anton hadn't paid. Julia always took care of their financial messes. She always said she felt more like the mother of Anton and Eve than the daughter. "You're going to be stuck with all that," she shouted at her mother. "And you won't even have his alimony to help pay it off." Forty-five hundred dollars a month was what the alimony amounted to. After twenty-five years of divorce Anton still received the alimony check from his oil heiress ex-wife—a settlement agreed upon so that he could continue to live in the style he had become accustomed to and one of the reasons for which he begged forgiveness. Julia came up with figures, figured he was at least one hundred thousand in the hole. "You have to keep him alive as long as possible," Julia snapped at Eve. Eve rubbed her thumbnail against her lip and stared blankly at her daughter.

Anton was in bed dying. Everyone gathered around. They said the rosary, read psalms and mourning prayers, pleading with God for one more chance. Heads bent in prayer and meditation. Incense burned. A candle flickered. They held hands. A bolt of pain shot through Anton and he cried out. At one point or another all the kids, the wife, the ex-wife, and the mistress had wished Anton dead. Some of them wondered, had they wished too hard?

Cool, crisp summer days. Mysterious rains in the middle of the night that left the trees and the lawn a magnificent emerald green and thriving with life. The big field in front of the house that was usually a cornfield was wheat this year. The farmer's change of heart. Red wheat with a current of wind running through it like a stream. The white peaches in Anton's orchard were enormous and succulent. "The best peaches we've ever had," Eve said. "Eat a peach, Anton," she pleaded, as if the stunning life of that juicy peach would save his own.

The field was the only other difference; they all took it as a sign. Corn to wheat. A premonition of sorts? Five months, that's how long the death took. Summer turning into autumn and those lovely fall days.

Anton was in bed with a whistle in his mouth, whistling for help because each day brought something new that he could no longer do: walk, lift his right arm, shit, pee. Lily helped him shit. The Cooper girls helped him pee. "Massage my belly, babe. Please," he'd plead. Kate and Julia would take turns kneading his belly. Soft and flaccid flesh beneath their hands. "You're so beautiful, babe. So kind," he'd say to each of them. His penis dangled into the portable urinal. Eve couldn't stand proximity to disease. His own kids didn't want to see their father's penis. And Alice, his Alice, couldn't bear to see her once-strong father, so weakened, so debilitated, so absolutely gone. Anton, the apex of the family. Anton, the cornerstone, the one who had made it all happen, he was dying. His foot began to bulge with a clot, the catarrh accumulated in the back of his throat. His toes and fingertips grew cold. They say the extremities die first. All that was left, it seemed, were two huge blue eyes bulging from his big head, terrified. "Big eyes," Eve would call him, smiling down on him in his bed, a smile full of hope. A smile that believed she would be able to reverse his disease. "Die? He won't die. That doesn't happen to us. We don't die!" They always had found a way out of disaster, loving the high of the near miss.

"I DIDN'T EXPECT to come into this life. Coming into this life was a surprise. Death is just as much a surprise as birth," Anton said, trying to believe his words. A beautiful late spring day, clear and blue, with an electrical storm smashing overhead and not a cloud in sight, not a drop of rain. Family meeting. "My disease brings up the issue of death so we need to discuss it as a family." Anton cleared his throat and spit. You wouldn't have thought him sick if you hadn't known him. A thin, handsome man with a big head and graying hair that receded gently, he had managed to dress for the meeting. A new pair of khakis that Lily had bought and an ironed shirt, an ascot around his neck. The family sat outside on the deck overlooking the front lawn, where he used to lead the kids in football games, drawing pass patterns on his palm as they bent in a huddle; and beyond the lawn the field of wheat that should have been corn, where, in the 1970s, Anton and the kids had grown the pot. The grass in the yard was too long. Had Anton been healthy, the lawn would have been mowed. Anton had always kept the lawn mowed. Ticks dropped from the trees. Someone said all the ticks were a result of the long grass. Lots of ticks this year. They picked them off with tweezers, scared about Lyme disease. All of the kids crumbled inside but appeared strong, following Anton's cue. His blue eyes held all nine of them. Nothing was going to beat him. He was a strong man. The one in control of every situation. He'd chased Sofia's boyfriend out of the house with a loaded Colt .45 once when he'd caught them making love. He was still the same man. "I don't think I'm going to die, my coloring is good. But we need to discuss the possibility of death as a family." My coloring is good. That one thread of hope. He looked strong and handsome, but even so, for those who knew, the cancer had already ravaged his body. He'd lost forty pounds to the cancer that for four months had been misdiagnosed with possibilities ranging from some tropical disease picked up from eating red snapper in Jamaica, to a psychologically induced disorder, to irritable bowel syndrome that the doctors suggested Metamucil would cure. "I'm not going to die; my coloring is good."

Anton laid out the terms of his new will, sitting forward in the chair, trying his very best to appear the strong big man he'd once been. "Eve and I have decided"—he cleared his throat—"that everything we have should go to Alice—the house, the cars, the property, the Haitian art." The Cooper girls, he reasoned, would inherit from their father and the Furey kids from their mother. "Of all of you, Alice is in the best position to keep Chardin together once Eve and I are gone."

"What about the two acres?" Julia whispered to her sisters, left eyebrow raised.

"And the mules," Kate whispered.

"We were never promised mules," Julia whispered back.

Alice sat by Anton's side, her long walnut hair twirled into a bun, her shoulders shrugged forward. She wore sneakers, jeans, and a T-shirt. Her gray eyes were wide and tired. India appeared before her, screaming chaos with the scent of clove and she saw herself standing in the middle of a hot street in Bombay (dressed in these same clothes) with cars and rickshaws and bullock carts and cows and people and even elephants swerving around her. A sea of life gathered, crushing together, for some festival or other. She took in the yard, the field, the glistening pool, her home, her father, fixing the image permanently in her mind—thick branches and thick leaves on thick trees rioting in the yard against this news.

Daylilies in abundance. Warm. Fireflies just beginning to emerge in the early evening light, flickering over the front lawn. The family said the rosary, chanting with Anton as their leader. "Chant as the Muslims do. The idea is to contemplate God in the repetition of the words." All of them thinking, because all of them had been at one point or another to Morocco to Fez, of the call to prayer reverberating above the red roofs of the city, drifting from the minarets: *It is better to pray than to sleep.* The family contemplated the glorious mysteries of Christ—the Annunciation. They read poetry. They put their hands on Anton's body, from head to toe, all of their hands, and asked and pleaded with God to remove Anton's cancer. "Each life is a miracle. It's absurd not to believe in miracles," Anton said, lying there on a white chaise on the deck overlooking the yard and field and only then did he begin to cry.

ALMOST EVERYONE believed it was unfair for Alice to inherit everything. "That should mean she gets all the debt, too," Kate said.

"Well obviously," Julia said.

"Don't be ridiculous," Jane snapped, defending Alice. "It's only fair she get everything. What else will protect her?" Jane would steal Alice away to D.C. for days to spoil her with elaborate meals and shopping sprees to distract her.

"Easy for you to say, you're rich."

"And you aren't?"

"It's not normal, the way you love Alice," Kate said. She was jealous. Jane was her older sister, should love her exclusively in that way.

Timothy had decided to marry in the midst of all this (black-tie affair in Dallas), and as a result everyone fought with him. He shouldn't marry now—the nerve. Nothing good should happen to anyone.

Caroline, on the other hand, decided to become a nun. Gentle Caroline with her soft grace. A nun? What did that mean? Worse than marriage. It was another death and as a result everyone fought with her. "We've lost her," Finny said. "Lost her."

Sofia and Eve were fighting over a diamond that had belonged to Anton's mother and which Anton had given, accidentally, to both his wife and daughter. Sofia wanted the ring as if it could restore a sum of what was vanishing. "Let her have it," Julia instructed her mother. "It's small and cloudy. Worthless." But Eve was losing her husband; she wasn't letting go of anything else. Jane was fighting with Kate because Kate wanted to leave and because she did not care about staying around to protect Alice. "That's your job," Kate shouted at her sister. Julia was fighting with both of them for their narcissism. "This is real," she'd say. "Real. Don't hide." But they continued to fight, fighting about their wretched childhoods as if it were vital to their very essence to believe in the darker shade—fighting as only sisters can fight because all three of them no longer had their lives.

Anton's illness gave free rein to their suffering, gave voice to pain, and so all the pain they'd ever suffered came pouring out. Years of it. There was articulation now for the sadness. You could scream and shout and cry and hate and everyone would understand. So they did.

Everyone fought with Nicholas because he was filming the whole event with his 16 mm. He had his camera propped up at the edge of Anton's bed, rolling—hours and hours of film gliding by. He intended to use the footage in a film he was making for the Whitney Biennial. He'd do anything for his art. "It's okay, babe," Anton would say, staring at the lens. Years from now this footage would surface, surprising everyone—loosed, like a long drowned body bobbing to the surface of a lake. "It's his way of understanding," Julia said. She had always defended Nicholas—claimed she'd been in love with him since she was thirteen.

Alice fought with herself, disappearing for hours. Screaming one moment. Silent the next. "It's all right, baby," Jane would say. But her father was dying. She would live most of her life without him. She saw her life stretching on to infinity and her father locked back there in her twenty-first year, his image and memory fading. He lay in his king-sized bed. "Don't leave me, babe." His big eyes bulging. "I'm so afraid, babe." He'd become someone different entirely. She did not know this man. His fear repulsed her.

Timothy was fighting with Finny. Finny was fighting with Kate, remembering their childhood and how she had made him her slave for a day, promising to be his slave on the next. How she'd never done it. Betrayed him. Loss of trust. No one trusted. The family was disintegrating with Anton's disease.

EVE TRIED TO save Anton. She really thought she could. Thought all you had to do was want something badly enough and you'd get it. She tried to save him with shark cartilage hidden in fruit smoothies. The shark cartilage was Sofia's idea. She explained that sharks never get cancer. You could hear that being chanted around the house. "Sharks never get cancer." Sofia was proud of her attempt at a cure and Eve would try anything. She tried to save him with a dose of twenty-five pills of bovine cartilage and forty pills of pancreatic enzymes a day. She tried to save him with Chinese teas and Tibetan mushrooms brought by Federal Express from the Far East. When he could no longer eat, she still managed to get these pills down his throat. "Eat these or you'll die," she screamed. "Let me die, babe," he screamed back. She tried to save him with coffee enemas. She tried to save him with fat-free foods and an alternative dietary approach known as the Kelly treatment. When he lost too much weight from the fat-free foods, she tried to save him with milkshakes and ice-cream sundaes. Anything. They'd done a round of chemo-therapy—cisplatin, leukovorin, 5-FU, and something else and something else that both sounded as deadly as the first three, like they could kill anything. They considered cryosurgery and placenta treatments. A specialist in Russia. A specialist in the Bahamas. A macrobiotic spa in Massachusetts. A slew of alternative specialists visited him, including a Chinese doctor from New York. "The doctor says Anton looks good," Eve said, smiling hopefully. "The doctor says he has a good chance. The tumor isn't growing." Somewhere there had to be a cure. "Insurance doesn't pay for all this," Julia said, waving the bills at Eve.

"Let Alice worry about the bills," Kate snapped.

Eve read New Age literature on fighting cancer with the mind and meditation. She tried to get Anton to fight with the mind and meditation. "Image," she would urge him. His cancer took on the image of Joan of Arc and he waged war with her. "Image," Eve would urge, hiding the morphine and feeding him the bovine cartilage. Eve didn't want to be deserted.

"IS HE DEAD YET?" the grandmother kept asking from her perch in the living room—Eve's mother, who lived with the family now. "Some hot tea, please," she'd say to whoever walked by. A huge pile of corn was at her feet waiting to be shucked. Eve couldn't tolerate her mother sitting there doing nothing. So the grandmother always had some peeling project or other, some enormous pile of vegetables that needed tending to. "I'm combing my hair with a can opener," she would add to whoever it was walking by. Her white hair swirled into a beehive bun. Her sharp green eyes studied the situation. She did not like Anton, never had, though she enjoyed flirting with him. He used to come to her old Victorian home in Maine with a camperload of kids who would sprawl all over the house, getting her precious things dirty. She'd make them all wash their feet before bed. At night he'd smoke marijuana, trying to get her to take a puff as she complained about the smell and the hazards of fire. "He's ruined you," she'd say to her once-beautiful daughter. The grandmother was ninety years old. Anton was sixty-four. It was cruel of God to take Anton first. "Is he dead, yet?"

"Have you finished the potatoes?" Eve would ask.

ON OCCASION you could hear Eve say, "Anton's in remission. Look at how well he's doing. His coloring is good." The kids would want to believe that. The new spots on the lungs were from the weight loss or from the Lyme disease he'd once had. It was one giant mistake. The doctors had gotten it all wrong. But Anton continued to wither. Two hundred and ten pounds to one hundred and thirty. All the fat disintegrating and layer after layer of him being peeled away to reveal him naked. Big eyes bulging from his head. Big scared eyes, searching all of the kids for the answer to what would follow.

No one had a life anymore. Career? What did that word mean in the face of this? As the months passed and the kids tried to get back to their lives, a schedule was set up and a rotation worked out so that at any given time two or three people were at home with Anton. If you claimed you had to work, if you claimed responsibilities to your own family, your own life, in order to get out of the rotation, you were selfish, self-centered, egomaniacal.

"He's dying for Christ's sake! He's dying!" That's the way this family worked. Solidarity. Unification of the whole. This was not, under the reign of Anton, even though the kids tried to convince themselves otherwise, a society of individuals.

"We've all got a fatal disease," Jane said. "Called life."

"Don't be sentimental," Kate said.

"You sound like Anton," Jane replied.

"This psychodrama is ridiculous," Julia said.

"Is he dead yet?" the grandmother interrupted from her perch. "I want my gun back." She was snapping a huge pile of peas from Eve's garden, her strong fingers working fast and effortlessly. Her toothless mouth pinched in a small and unattractive way. "It was my father's gun from the Spanish-American War. I want it back. Anton won't be needing it anymore." She'd given Anton the gun when he'd been strong and healthy.

"Put your teeth in, Grammy," Julia said.

"I thought pancreatic cancer killed you in a few weeks," Jane said.

"We've all been swallowed up," Kate said.

"Don't be sentimental," Jane snapped.

SOFIA CARTED OFF Furey furniture in a U-Haul—a bed, a dresser, Anton's bedside tables—and as a result Eve fought with her. "He's not even dead yet," Eve screamed. Eve fought with everyone. She fought with Lily for being Anton's mistress and for coming around too much. Lily had taken charge of the kitchen, cooking enormous and abundant meals to feed everyone. The kids were all sorry to see her go. The kids fought with Laurence because he tried to protect Eve—tried to stand up for her, comfort her. "No one's comforting her," he said to the kids. Eve fought with Agnes who continued speaking holistically about the benefits of the "other side." Eve didn't have to tolerate these people anymore. She could kick them out. It was her house, finally, now. Free rein. Her reign.

Sofia and Julia were fighting over the disposal of some secret computer files Anton wanted destroyed. Everyone was fighting over what they believed the files to hold, what secrets of Anton's they would reveal—another will? hidden money? more debt? a secret family? That's what Sofia believed: another family with a wife and kids. Anton begged them not to fight. The one thing he wanted before dying was for the family to be united, one family, whole.

Everyone was fighting with Eve because she refused to let Anton die and Anton wanted to take the long sleep. He started talking of euthanasia. "He wants to die," Nicholas would say to Eve. "He doesn't tell me that," she'd respond, shoving bites of food and pills of bovine cartilage down Anton's throat. Residual omnipotence, Anton used to call it, her determination, her belief that she could stop time, change the course of the stars. It was what he loved about her.

Everyone had an opinion about how Anton should be nursed and everyone was fighting with everyone else to make that opinion heard. But mainly Anton was fighting with Eve, and Eve was fighting with Anton. "She's killing me, babe," he'd say to the kids, "Stay near." "Eat these pills or you'll die," she'd say.

Everyone was confused. Nobody understood what she or he wanted. The family was falling to pieces like a country of many religions newly emancipated from the hold of an empire—for so many years the citizens had fought against the empire, but now that it was gone they waged war among themselves to stake their claim to the land.

It was a terrible time.

CHAPTER TWELVE

Soldiers

On Alice's fifth birthday a clown fell out of the sky and floated to the ground in a parachute, landing in the middle of a swarm of partying five-year-olds on her front lawn. Ponies and goats and ducks and peacocks and dogs and chickens strutted across the yard, nibbling on the grass. For her big present this year Anton was giving her her own small farm. In the lower field the carpenter had built a third barn (clapboard this time, designed by Laurence). The noise of the plane made Alice and her friends look up. It was high above the yard. "That's the lawyer's plane," Alice said, and she was right. He would do anything for Anton and Eve, even deliver a clown. He was always flying them here and there, flying upside down over the yard simply to say hello. He flew them to Haiti to be married, twice.

Alice saw something tumble out of the plane, something big and sloppy with enormous feet, and then a parachute burst open. "What's falling from the sky?" Anton asked, seemingly astonished. A bright clear sky. The clown began to wiggle and dance like a marionette as the enormous orange feet descended to the ground. "By George, what could that be?" Anton looked at Eve with mischief on his face and then Eve looked at Alice. Alice studied hard and then she smiled, knowing, because she knew her father, that on this birthday he was also giving her the sky. Gently the clown drifted toward her. Oh, that smile of hers was so bright, so wide, so deep, so big and gaping as if she wanted to fit the whole universe inside her mouth for sheer joy. "The surprise is in the sky," Alice screeched, clapping her hands. Each year the surprise came from a different spot—the field, the pool, the roof. She ran to greet the clown as he settled on the lawn with a thump and the parachute collapsed around him, enveloping him. Alice tugged on the folds of the parachute until she managed to free him.

All the older kids were there, too. Each one dressed up in a costume to add to the sense of occasion. Kate was Snow White, Nicholas was Dracula, Sofia was a Greek goddess wrapped in a white sheet, and so on. Alice's birthday was a big day for the family. Always. It was just as important as Thanksgiving, Christmas, and Easter. Some of the kids even flew home from college.

Presents hung from the clown for all the kids to pluck. The clown bunched up the parachute and gave it to Alice. Later, in the woods behind the house, Anton would use the parachute to build Alice a fort within the trees, a safe place to go even when it rained. Together they made a big couch with leaves and hay and they collected wood and kindling for fires and in the late summer they'd go berry picking so they could have some food. Anton would lift a branch. Hiding beneath the thickets glistened hundreds of plump sweet raspberries. On the fire they grilled corn stolen from the mean farmer's fields. "How long could we live out here without anyone else?" Alice asked. "A long time, babe." "What other things could we eat?" "Why, fish, babe. We could catch them in the creek with our hands." He squinted and smiled, enraptured by his baby's enthusiasm. Sometimes they'd go to the creek that was deeper in the woods and see if they actually could catch fish with their hands. "We could get a wild turkey," Alice suggested. "How?" Anton asked. "With stones or a slingshot," Alice answered.

Beneath the parachute they would play even in the rain and come up with possibilities. She'd play with his hair. She loved his hair. It was dark and unruly and seemed to have a personality of its own, always a little greasy and determined to fly off in its own patterns no matter how he protested. She'd play with it, trying to tame it. "It's just like you, this hair—animated and irregular. It doesn't play by the rules of hair." "What are the rules of hair?" he'd ask, amused. "Everything that your hair is not." And then he'd call her fresh and brazen and then she'd warm up inside, proud to be fresh and brazen for him.

Sometimes they'd bring things from real life into their fort—blankets, in particular, and pillows—so that they could keep warm and comfortable in the rain. They liked to be comfortable. Later she would be glad that her father did not believe in moderation. The idea made her think about their Christmas trees, how they were always so tall because they had tall ceilings. How she was proud of having high ceilings and big Christmas trees, of how she felt sorry for, and liked feeling sorry for, those friends of hers who had parents that were practical. Or worse, who had fake trees. The thought that someone would buy a fake tree to save money or avoid a mess was hideous to her. She would be able to remember their trees as if they were friends, each chosen at a local farm run by the farmer's son. He gave them a discount because of her. She knew that life would be something else entirely if her father had ever become moderate.

They'd lie in the parachute fort listening to the rain patter against the nylon, dribbling down its sides. Sometimes he'd teach her to memorize poems. *And indeed there will be time To wonder, "Do I dare?" and, "Do I dare?"* And she was proud of being able. *Time to turn back and descend the Stair With a bald Spot in the middle of my hair.*

"Tell me a story, Pop," she'd ask. He was all hers in the fort. In the fort, time slowed, the days long and safe. "About Ike Scarborough?" he'd ask. "About when I was a boy and Ike was a boy?" About Texas? About his hat? His head, so big it was nearly impossible to find a hat to fit it? About being a Jesuit? About the brotherhood of friends? About poker? About winning big? About poker face and betting? About his aunt who had a habit of killing her husbands? About when Alice was first born and unnamed and baptized by him in the indoor swimming pool?

"About Texas."

"About Ike's two Cadillacs?"

"Tell me."

"Well," his voice thickened, became more like Texas. She imagined Texas big and wild and very far away and very flat. Texas was a foreign country as large as her father's large forehead. It contained the story of her father as a boy. He had told her once about his collection of toy soldiers made from bronze—heavy and substantial—with their bayonets and rifles, chipping paint, in their blue and red uniforms. They lined a bookcase in his office now. His mama had thrown them away because of the chipping paint. She'd thought them dirty, unsanitary, most of all ugly. So she dumped them in a box and placed them on the street—a humble Dallas street, lined with walnut trees that stained the sidewalk with black patches—for the garbageman to collect. Anton had sneaked out there in the night and stolen them back, hid them under his bed, hid them in his closet, hid them in the backs of drawers throughout his childhood so that he could have them to give to Alice. "How did you know about me then?" she asked, holding him with her big gray eyes. Looking at him, she would always see herself. His eyes were blue and he was a man, but otherwise they were identical. Same big round eyes, same vast forehead, same high cheekbones, same skinny legs of which both father and daughter were proud, same invincible smile.

"Ike Scarborough was as rich as Croesus. By the time Ike was fifteen he had two Cadillacs all his own. He didn't have a driver's license but he had the cars so he drove anyway. In those days back in Dallas everyone had money; oil wells were pumping up gold all over Texas—oil rigs as far as the eye could see. Ike had parties. Boy oh boy, did he have parties. All the kids of Highland Park were invited. Thousands of Chinese lanterns lit up the night, sparkling like so many stars. It was hard to tell the difference between the universe and the lights. I was there with my girl Annie. She wore a long gown and I wore a tuxedo. We went skinny-dipping, us boys, and even some of the braver girls. Annie was a brave girl. And then one of us tasted the water. 'It's beer, by golly,' someone shouted, then we were all tasting it and those who weren't in the pool dove in to swim in the beer. Later Ike's mama hung herself. People all over Texas were hanging themselves when oil went south. And then Ike lost everything he had in a poker game."

Alice saw Anton there as a teenaged boy with Annie, holding hands. She liked to imagine her father as a boy. She liked the stories, how they leaned back into a time long before her, it was as if she were back there with him. She liked as well that there was always a little drama at the end. "It's the Irish in me, babe," he'd say. "I saved the toy soldiers for you," he told her, and she asked again, "But how'd you know about me?"

"Ah darling, how couldn't I have known about you?"

CHAPTER THIRTEEN

"Cry, Baby, Cry!"

ALICE LEARNED THE NEWS of her father's cancer in Bombay, India, on the third day of her Fulbright scholarship to study Indian dreams. The news arrived in the form of a telegram brought to her in her hotel room by a very dark-skinned Indian in a white punjabi suit and turban. "Message, madam," he had said after knocking, and when she saw the white slip in his white-gloved hand jutting through the door-way, she had known what it contained and she had not wanted to be alone. She had wanted to ask the very dark man in white to stay, but already he was gone. Instead she opened the telegram on a street just outside the hotel, thick with people and cows, cars and fumes and grit and dirt, with a beggar stooping at her knees. The air smelled of jasmine and oranges and smoke. The telegram read only COME HOME BABE, and she had known then in the swirl of chaos, a dope tout trying to sell her hashish and a decorated elephant thumping by on its way to a carnival, that he would not die fast and easily, with dignity and grace. She stood there for a long time, a curiosity for a while, this tall American beauty looming over the road. At first people gathered around her, enveloping her like a blanket, offering the vast comfort of humanity. They wanted to help, truly they did. They asked if she was all right, offered themselves to her, suggested a cup of tea in their stores. Silk floated by in bolts and men passed carrying enormous movie posters or guiding carts stacked high with pyramids of fruit—mangoes and papaya and mangosteen and coconut and bananas. She stood there so long that finally she became just another obstacle in the road that had to be swerved around. The moon was the color of milk against the dark blue sky. Sea air and the scent of salt blew in from the Apollo Bunder. She knew that her father would hang on by a thread of steel. He would not be her father, just some faint impression that would seem to live forever, and she knew that the longer he lived in this way, the more she would wish him dead, until finally she would kill him.

ALICE SLEPT most of the trip home from India, waking only to see the man sitting next to her snatch a bite off her untouched food tray. He was a fat man and hungry. She smiled and offered him the whole tray and fell back to sleep. Her sleep was infused with visions of India, of chaos and beauty and a woman dying on a street as people passed by—dreams of the dreams of Indian cinema becoming merely a residual joke. Cradled in a fuselage, propelled forward beyond her will, she slept in the sky, with a fat man devouring her food.

At home the family was gathered, running around in a dizzying way. Alice walked through the house in a daze, constantly dizzy herself. Doctors called and New Age specialists arrived. The house was a mess. Anton lay in his bed the same as she had left him, propped against a sea of white pillows. His big blue eyes watched her as if trying to define in that instant the nature of their new relationship—the one in which he would become more like a child, a greedy child unwilling to share. They held each other for a long time with their eyes. A truth or dare. A test of wills. Who would speak first? She could see he had lost his sense of humor, that this man would not speak about monkey-bitten daughters or warn against sentimentality. Rather, this man was an impostor, a thief who had entered her father's body while she was away. With her hug and averted eyes, he won. He smelled sick. She hugged him and left the room.

"Let me tell you why I love your father," Laurence said to Alice, offering her insight she was not sure she wanted. A little sloppy and sad he was, with a whiskey in his hand and a tone of mourning in his voice as if Anton were already dead. They were in the living room. She sat on a swinging couch, bought years ago in the islands, that had fallen on her when she was a baby and her parents were off in Haiti getting married for a second time. It had knocked her unconscious for a few minutes, but it had not hurt at all, and she remembered that the fact that it had not hurt terrified Jane (who was in charge of watching her). "You're suppose to cry," Jane kept saying. "Cry, baby, cry!" Alice had felt proud of not hurting—of being fine and not hurting, sustaining the great weight of that swinging couch.

Laurence was there along with other friends. Anton's brotherhood friends from high school flew in from Dallas— a bunch of cowboys invading the house. Friends streamed through, some would simply sit in the living room too afraid to witness Anton transformed. Like jumping into cold water, they didn't want to make the journey back to his bed. *Let me tell you why I love your father.* Laurence claimed Anton was his best friend. That Anton had saved his life. From what? "From myself," Laurence told her. He was a slender man with a long bearded face and the slightest French accent because he was born there. Alice knew that he was proud of that accent, but otherwise she did not know him well. She had heard from her sisters a secret of his, that after he fell in love with his second wife, the pair dropped white dried fava beans in a glass fishbowl each time they made love. They wanted to be able to count the times, so in love were they. The bowl had soon overflowed and they'd bought another bowl and they kept the bean ritual up for a while and would have kept it up still if the bean bowls hadn't started to take over their house. She liked that story about him. It made him seem softer because he had always struck her as one of those adults who have very little patience, especially for romantic notions and children.

Laurence tried to articulate his love for Anton, to give it to her as a gift as if he could restore her lost father. He, too, had been crying, swollen faced and red eyed, though he was the kind of man who could not cry publicly. Is this what her father had tried to save him from?

"If you think I'm rigid now, Alice, you should have seen me before I met Anton. I was made of glass, living as I'd been taught, the man providing—tidy in my box. Then your father showed up in his turquoise Cadillac with his turquoise ring and his Texas accent and the car filled with kids and boys' underwear and dreams spilling off his lips. Dreams that he thought I could help him make. He brought me in and kept me. He saw an unhappiness and he didn't ask about it, just embraced me." Laurence was trying to be compassionate with Alice, to love this child. But she could not hear him. Instead she saw her father, a young man again, holding her, a newborn, in the palm of his hand.

"Anton made it seem so easy," Laurence was saying. The indoor pool had been covered over with plywood for a good dozen years. It had become too expensive. Alice barely remembered swimming in it. The heating system for the outdoor pool had long since broken down; the tower had not been built; the kitchen never really completed. The man who had done the carpentry on the glassed-in dining room had stolen from them. And she had never understood the silo fantasy.

Laurence put down his whiskey and took her hands, getting ready to say something important. She could see from the slight curve up of his lower lip. "You have that in you, Alice. That gift is yours," Laurence continued. She wanted him to shut up. She realized now that there were others in the living room, the friends coming and going, looking at her for her signs of grief. *Cry, baby cry.* How we love to know that others can grieve, how we adore witnessing it, savor it on the tongue with the knowledge and reassurance that no one escapes. How we try to read their misery to see if it is equal to our own. The other kids orbited in their own orbits. The Haitian art on the walls told stories of death and rebirth and repetition—the endless cycle. Laurence wanted to help her because she was Anton's. But it wasn't Laurence whom she wanted. As Anton transformed, perhaps so did she. It doesn't hurt, she wanted to be able to say.

HER THREE DAYS in India floated across her mind—the path of her other life. Then came the endless games of Battleship, of beating Anton, wounding him, life crashing toward its end. The Alpha and the Omega, the grand sequence flourishing at her feet.

The games of Battleship were played on the deck extending from Anton's bedroom. She managed to keep killing him, sinking his ships no matter how hard she tried to let him win. He rested against pillows on a chaise, the leaves rustling overhead like silk skirts and a cool and gentle breeze. They didn't speak of his condition, or hers. He slept. She watched him. He woke. They played. She sank his ships. With each ship she felt she stole a little bit more. Alice was in her cool analytical mode, that detached mode that allowed her to watch her life as if it belonged to someone else. She wanted to stop playing the game, but Anton did not. "One more, babe?" he pleaded. And once more she beat him. One more, like a gambler who's betting now with the bank's money. One more so that he could lie there drifting in and out and watch her win to each loss of his. Was it that he wanted to see her win? Or did he take pleasure in watching her watch him lose?

The summer went fast, summer turning into autumn and those lovely fall days. In August, Anton had a stroke as she lay on the bed reading to him. Slowly it crept over his body, taking possession of a foot, a leg, an arm, his face, his brain, and along with it came more fear, extreme fear, filling him up like water rising in an empty tank. She was at the bottom of that tank, holding on to her belief that he was king, looking up through all that water to the sky.

In September his body healed from the stroke and he could walk again, and as it healed, the cancer spread to his lungs, his liver, his stomach. But he was walking, a soft step in the soft emerald yard, unaware of the cancer's progression. How simple and beautiful a step is. His toes gripped the grass and the mud from the rains that lay beneath it. A few people held his arms and then let go; he was like a child on a bike without training wheels for the first time. There was applause. Anton walked all the way across the yard, down into the field. It amazed Alice how the body can heal while destroying itself elsewhere so completely. But in that healing it was impossible not to find a shred of hope.

Jane held Alice close; she'd been holding her close since she returned, and together they cheered for Anton. In October, Alice and her father went to visit yet another specialist who confirmed the spreading cancer; it was now everywhere, rippling out from his pancreas like a stone skipping across a pond. "But I need to finish my book," Anton had said, eyes pleading as if it were up to the doctor, as if by flirting with him just a little, he could alter the prognosis. "I would get to work," the doctor said.

Alice went to all the appointments. She sat at the edge of his bed. He spoke to her of nothing substantial. He told her no deathbed truisms. It seemed now he believed in nothing. He refused to offer her even the smallest reassurance, to say sweetly and simply the small thing, that she'd be fine.

Chapter Fourteen

Sane

With her father Alice had picnics all over the world, all over America and Europe anyway. They had picnics in the rugged mountains of Ballydavid in County Kerry where Anton's father's family had come from. The kingdom of rugged mountains and green and rolling hills. "They came to Texas with the potato famine of 1890," Anton told her. Came on a boat carrying their good and simple faith, the knowledge that they would be all right. He taught her Irish ballads lying on a blanket, "The Ballad of the White Horse."

> For the great Gaels of Ireland
> Are the men that God made mad
> For all their wars are merry
> And all their songs are sad.

He replaced his Texas accent with an Irish one and sang in his raspy voice. He resurrected her ancestors, her great-grandmother and great-grandfather on their boat to America singing forlorn songs. Standing on the plains of Texas so very far from the green hills of Ballydavid.

They had picnics in fields of blooming desert in the West, in the Kansas grasses, a night picnic beneath a Texas moon. Picnics in the South of France with views through cypress out to the open sea. Anton had a special basket. It contained forks and napkins and plates, wineglasses and salt and pepper shakers, and a checked tablecloth for the ground. He brought the basket on all trips. To Haiti and Mexico and Morocco and Spain. If he forgot it, halfway to the airport, he'd turn around just to get it. "The plane will wait. If the plane won't wait we'll get another." But, by George, he'd have the basket.

It was the special arrangements to eat outside that Alice loved, a form of plan her father could tolerate. The food always tasted better outside and she loved to feel a breeze as she ate or to look at an ancient monastery or up into the intricate web of leaves and branches that formed the canopy of a tree, up through to the sky. Outside they could be entirely alone and far away. It was also that he would do it for her, that he cherished this whim and desire and pleasure of hers.

Once on a snowy day in January he asked her what she'd like to do for the day and she suggested a picnic on the Delaware—a picnic spot in Point Pleasant near a footbridge that crossed the canal and that had been designed and engineered by John A. Roebling, the man who built the Brooklyn Bridge, a fact that Anton would make sure that Alice knew, for he wanted her to know what there was to know about the world. "It's snowing out," Eve said, considering the idea. "Look outside, sweetie. Not a day for a picnic."

"That's a brilliant idea," Anton said. His face beamed, he moved through the kitchen eagerly, delighting in his little girl's will. "We've never had a picnic in the snow." And before long he had the basket packed and he had her bundled up in a snowsuit and scarves and hats and mittens. "Warm enough, babe?" he asked. "Warm enough, babe," she answered. The snow flurry had turned to a blizzard as they ate beside the Delaware. Alice and Anton had watched it swirl in, sipping soup and gnawing on huge chunks of baguette. They did not worry about getting home, being safe. Anton would not teach his little girl to live like that. They watched the blizzard, they watched the canal, they watched the river. Both the canal and the river were frozen. Even so, they could still hear the sound of flowing water as they walked on the ice across the canal to the river, as they walked on the ice of the river toward the center. "Like walking on water," he said, as if they were mightier than the river. "Imagine that, babe, that you and I can walk on water." With her father at her side, behind her, there were no limits. There was nothing she could not do.

"Pop?" ALICE ASKED softly. Late November, cold. He lay on his bed of pillows, his body making not even a dent. The late day was brilliant. Sun flooded through the sliding glass doors of his room. The Christmas cactus raged with its fuchsia bloom. It would continue to bloom straight through to April. The debris of his illness cluttered the shelves and tabletops: pills spilled over the dresser, shark cartilage and pancreatic enzymes, books on how we die, on cancer, on miracles. And the smell—stuffy, sick.

Alice stood in the doorway watching her father. His mouth and lips were white. His eyes were all there were to his face. They were open, but it seemed he was sleeping. His cheeks were sunken beneath his unshaved and yellow-hued skin. She felt like a spectator. She had felt like a spectator since he was diagnosed and she realized that she wanted to do nothing for him. She had not wanted to touch his belly; help him pee, shit, eat; make him shark shakes. She watched her

Cooper sisters race around him. She was sorry for their desperation as they tried to extract her father's love like bees on the wrong flower. She had always watched them dance around him, knowing that he was hers whenever she chose, that she could claim his love in front of them and make them wince a little. Now it was simply pathetic. His whistle rested on his cheek.

On the floor, leaning against the closet doors were the remnants of his book—collages of paintings of beasts adoring beautiful women; milk crates filled with index cards with his red-ink scrawl.

The "cosmic snigger" at romantic love is but the faint echo of the Galatic jibes aimed at the joke of human sexuality, and this is, in turn, only the barest imitation of the colossal irony hurled relentlessly by men over the ages at women.

He had been reading to her from his book since she was a child, ambitious for and with him. Now she saw that it all added up to this—a few collages and crates of notes, more debris at the foot of his deathbed.

Just his hair was the same, black and thin and greasy, swishing this way and that as if on whim. She went to the bed and put her fingers through his hair. She wished she could be different this time—want nothing, give everything. Little hope, she wished.

"Fresh and brazen," he said very faintly. But she heard it.

"You're awake," she said.

"I've been thinking about sanity," he said.

"What about sanity?" she asked.

"Ice water with chips," he said. He stared into the ceiling. He did not look at her. Speaking was the only gesture of his pose that had changed.

"Look at me," she said. If he didn't look at her, it was as if she were talking with a dead man. He continued looking into the ceiling.

"Sane as in how many minutes you would stand there and watch me."

"Look at me," she said again, a little rush of urgency in her tone. She was scared, alone at Chardin. She didn't want to be there alone. It was a sharp bitter day with a clarity that made even the smallest detail precise.

"If I look at you, you will turn away." He paused to sip in a breath. "The straw in my ice water is sane. The sane versus the insane. The world is divided in two." Staring into the ceiling. His big blue eyes sunk deep in the sockets. The field that should have been corn was golden in the afternoon light. It made no difference now that it had been wheat instead of corn. Insane, Alice thought. A quiet against which so much could be heard. The house had a breath of its own, a living breathing organism. "Finny's sane. His genius is in his hands. Has he ever given you a massage? Have you ever seen him catch a football? Why'd you cut your hair, babe?" he asked without turning. "Cut hair is insane." It wasn't cut, just pulled back in a rubber band. "Insane is the Cooper girls when I first met them. A flock of girls in pretty ironed dresses. Like tulips. Swearing. My own children didn't swear as much. Fuck and shit and piss and cunt and dick shooting from their mouths as they fought with each other. And those pretty faces and dresses. Like tulips. Insane, babe." His blue eyes turned to hold Alice steady as he struggled with his breathing. And he had been right, she turned away. "Insane," he said, and closed his eyes and tears pearled at the corners. "The dream I had last night. I'd been alive, breathing with the full power of my lungs, one long luxurious deep breath, a cool drink in the desert, my lungs billowing and full. Alice. No, Alive. Your name, babe, one small *c* away from what I was. Insane. I was eating peaches and cream and pound cake. The kind Mama used to make, a special Texas recipe—one-two-three-four cake. Little Kate, bless her heart, with her screwed-up teeth and her pigeon toes, she had learned to make it just for me. In a few days," he said to his child, "I won't know what peaches, pound cake, and cream are. Mama's insane." She thought of Aunt Mama as she was called because she had not liked the word *grandmother*. Thought of her with her hair swept into a french roll standing tall, arriving from Dallas with presents from Neiman's beautifully wrapped with candy canes in the bows. Born in 1900 she used to say, "I go with the years," riding a bike at eighty, eye exercises to keep her vision perfect at ninety. She had faded slowly, ending up in a local nursing home. When he was healthy, Anton visited her three times a week and brought her to Chardin for all the holidays. Alice remembered he'd once sent Aunt Mama home to Dallas with a few joints because she'd enjoyed smoking them. She carried them in her underpants, but halfway home she became afraid of the law and flushed them down the toilet.

"Are you keeping tally? Tallies, insane. Alice, insane. Rotation insane. It's your turn in the rotation. Otherwise you would not be here. Can't you say good-bye?"

"It's all right, Pop," Alice said, and she stroked his hair, pulled her fingers along his scalp, sitting behind him so that she didn't have to look at him. She lifted his head up gently and placed it in her lap.

"It's not all right," he said simply. Then, "Look at me. You couldn't look at me before you went to India. Look at me now. Please. Why don't you say something?" he pleaded.

"You're impish sitting here. You were once impetuous, belligerent, righteous but not impish. My daughter is not an imp," he snapped. Dying people got mean, she knew that. "You die as you live," her Cooper sisters liked to say, as if it were some sort of vindication. He had not lived like this. She tried to find some wisdom. Why wouldn't he be mean now? His life was being stolen pound by pound, organ by organ. Half of who he had been lay on this bed. The other half had fled. Her jaw hung, her eyes drooped, her face stung. She swallowed.

"You're gonna cry now and make me feel bad? I'm the one who's dying. I'm the only one allowed to cry." His voice was big. With effort he rose higher on the pillows away from her lap. "What do you want from me? What do you want me to say? That you'll be here for a short time and then that you, too, will die?" The veins at his temples pulsed. She wanted to be rational, wise. The tears fell slowly down her cheeks, scratching the delicate skin. She looked hard at the door, willing someone to walk through it. She wondered if she could leave, drive off, go back to India, vanish. Her chest cracked. She saw her father seated on a checked cloth in the kingdom of Ballydavid eating a potato, a whole peeled potato with butter on the tip.

"I'm here, Pop. It's Alice here."

"Stars flutter like red moths. Can you see them?" he asked, deep sunken eyes turning on her. "Look where we are. All the stars. It's beautiful. Look at them with me. Join me here, babe, please."

"I want to," she said. "Help me," she asked.

"Did you know I wanted you to go to India? So badly I wanted you to have that."

"I know," she said.

"Isn't that something?" he asked. India floated by, leading her through all the muck—outstretched arms of a child chasing after a firefly eager to trap the beauty. "I'm sorry I ruined it for you, babe."

Dusk came on in a sweep of red—swathes of color against the indigo sky. He breathed heavily against his white pillows. "I don't want to be sick anymore," he said, shutting his eyes. "I'm so tired of being sick. It hurts so much. Rub my back, please." He cringed with the pain. She did not want to touch him.

"You need morphine," she said. She helped him turn over so that she could rub his back. His skin was warm and sweaty, covered with bedsores. She massaged him, thinking of Finny's big hands, the genius that they held, of how easily they could work his skin.

"Mom's hidden the morphine," he said. Sweat beaded on his face as he struggled to move the parts of his body he still had the muscle to move. Alice searched the room for the morphine, pulling open drawers, looking in the trunk at the foot of the bed, in the closet. It relieved her to do something. She wanted her mother. When would her mother be home? Kate and Julia were taking her to the opera so that she could have a break. When her mother returned, everything would be all right. "I think it might be hidden in her shoes," he said. Her mother would prop him up against the pillows, make him comfortable, and ignite her infectious belief in the impossible. Indeed, the morphine was hidden in the toes of Eve's shoes in the bottom of the closet. Patches and liquid in bottles stuffed in shoes and boots. Her mother's belief that less morphine would save him. The morphine made Alice nervous, giddy even. If he had been her father, she would have told him of the impulse taking possession of her just now and they would have laughed about it. "Not you, babe, not my daughter. Promise. You're not capable of that." She saw Ian at her lacrosse game in a trench coat in the mist. She wanted to call Ian on the phone, hear his voice, and simply say, "I'm scared." Perhaps he would come and sit with her. Perhaps he would keep his promise, love her as if she were his own. She wanted a father. She would be responsible with that love; she would not take too much. She saw his little white VW of long ago driving up the driveway to get her sisters for school, coming like a thief to steal her family. How she had wanted to get in that car with them, even as a tiny child, and fight for her family.

"I'm sorry," Anton said. He watched his little girl, with her hair pulled back tight in a rubber band, her fierce gray eyes, and started to cry. "I thought I'd been left alone. It made me anxious. I'm so afraid to be alone that when I saw you I was relieved. Let me love you," he said. She folded into him, hugging him, taking what she could, desperate and greedy like her Cooper sisters for his love. His one good arm was cold, but it still felt good. He stroked her. He smoothed her hair and she closed her eyes and lay there for a while before It came again. It always comes again. Because time rolls forward, predictably, cruelly, because you can only hide for so long and because there is only so much grace.

"I want Mama. In a few days I won't know Mama." Anton struggled to sit up. "I haven't seen Mama since I've been sick. Mama won't know I'm dead. Help me see the way, babe. I haven't been good. I've been bad to the Cooper girls, bad to Mom, bad to so many people, babe, and I'm terrified. What's going to happen to me? I need to tell you some things. I need you to know some things. It's so dark and the wind's so loud and... Can you hear the peacocks? Can you? They're ruining the roof with their shit. Kill them. Wring their necks. They'll destroy the house. Kill them." His eyes were on fire, hissing snake eyes. "Fatima. I can see the children glimpsing hell, all the souls falling into hell like snowflakes, babe. Countless. Looky here, can't you see it?" He pointed to the ceiling. "Like snowflakes. Can't you see? Look this way. Look at me. Please. You refused to look at me before you went to India, otherwise you wouldn't have gone."

"I'm sorry," she said simply, and smoothed his hair. Give everything, she reminded herself. But what she wanted was to be violent. To smash the brains out of something. To kill.

"I've failed. I've wasted my life. My book is in that box," he said.

"You didn't fail," she said so softly it would seem he had not heard.

"I saw you looking at the box, the collages."

"You're my only hero," she said, again so softly it would seem he could not hear.

"Hear me, please. Will you hear me?"

"Hear what?" Ever so slightly her hands shook.

Anton held her hard. "I need you to know about Mom, Kate, the Cooper girls."

"It's all right," Alice said, soothing him with her hand running over his limpid flesh because it did not know what else to do. She didn't want to hear about Mom, Kate, the Cooper girls. She wanted him to shut up. She wanted him to die. She hated this man. Her father would have protected her, even from himself.

"You're gonna listen, babe. I need you to. Your mother, Cliff, Agnes. Hear me out. Please," he pleaded like a boy. He collapsed back into the pillows. She had no idea who Cliff was, but she did not want to know now. She had the morphine in her hand. She didn't want to know. She was afraid that he would start speaking and she'd have to hear. "Explain what's happening. I don't understand."

She wanted to be mature, do something smart, take care of her father. Be rational, poised, disciplined. She put a morphine patch on his arm. He blew the whistle though there was no one else to whistle to. She peeled the backing paper away from the adhesive strips and stuck the patches onto his skin. "Listen to me, babe," he tried again. She put on more patches. He blew again with force, meaning to be heard. She measured a spoonful of the liquid morphine and filled his mouth with it—spoonful after spoonful of the pink morphine, pink and tasty like the cold medicine she used to take as a child. Pink morphine spilling on the white sheets, but some of it, most of it going down because he swallowed.

Terror pooled in those blue eyes. He said, "Don't," but he swallowed. Alice shoved the cold metal spoon down his throat until he coughed. He swallowed because he wanted to die, because he wanted her to kill him, wanted her to be linked inextricably to him, bound to his death. His baby, his Alice in her football uniform joining Pop Warner's as a six-year-old, shoved morphine down her father's throat. "I will. I will join your team. It's sexist to keep me off," she had said to the manager. "I'm as tough as any of these boys. And bigger." Anton wanted her to be brave. He wanted her to act.

Everyone who ever died appears before Alice. She sees God, Brahma with his pen, Shiva, Buddha, Vishnu, Jesus, Mohammed. She sees Krishna blazing like a thousand suns, death, the devourer of man. She sees the Virgin Mary and Mary Magdalene. She sees herself. She sees her father sitting in the big ash in the yard. "I don't want to leave Chardin," he says to the sky. One of those glorious sunsets, all red and violet, and the yard a brilliant green and the air cool and pleasant drifting through the wheat field that should have been corn. His father comes down from that sky and takes his son by the hand. "Son, it's time for you to come," he says lovingly, the first words he's spoken in some thirty years, talking gently like a father who wants to put his child to bed.

Alice held the spoon, looked at it shining silver through the pink. There were tears in his eyes. He was not crying. They were simply pools of sadness—a mask between him and the world. "I miss you. I'll wait for you." He took Alice back in his good arm and she lay there heaving, because he understood her so completely as no one else ever would. He stroked her hair the way he did when she was sick. His big cold hand on her large hot forehead. He always knew her temperature exactly with just the back of his hand. She lay there with all the quiet and cold of the night. Her father's pain subsiding. He stroked her so gently she could feel each strand of hair against her scalp. She lay waiting for the drug to take full effect so that she could leave—until his hand became lazy, drooping, until it was a weight, a tremendous pressure on her forehead, until his breathing slowed. Each breath a tiny struggle. Gliding away, gently. *"We're swimming in the emerald river that runs among the ruins."* Her voice very far away and soft and soothing, her fingertips exquisite on his neck and scalp. *"And the afternoon is shrouded in a milky mist."* Lumps in her throat and her own face stinging. He has come to India. It's a hot day and they're swimming in the... smooth, smooth, dreamy voice, receding so he can hardly hear. *"We drift, the water like velvet enveloping us, past paddy and groves thick with mango and banana trees. Gopurams in the sky and an elephant being cleaned at the dhobi wallah ghat. The family floats in the river like we did down the Delaware with picnics and champagne. Your kids, all nine, their faces shining in the blue light of the rising moon."*

This was everything she could give.

CHAPTER FIFTEEN

Notes for a Sermon

(St. Charles College—Grand Coteau, 1950)

ALL OF US ARE looking for happiness. Every minute of our lives we are working for it and planning for it. When we are children, we look to our mother to give it to us, and she tries to make us happy—and at the same time she wants us to understand that some things we ask for are bad for us and won't make us happy. And many of us grow up thinking that our mother can give us almost anything—that she is a queen.

Anton, dressed in black robes, wearing cheap brown sandals that crush his big toes' toenails. (In a year he'll lose those toenails. Ingrown, they'll be cut back to the roots at some Louisiana clinic that the Jesuits use.) Anton, kneeling in his cell with a block of St. Charles stationery and a gray felt-tip pen, kneeling, knees pressing into cold stone, scribbling notes for the sermon he will give—his first in the novitiate. A cell like the ones in which Fra Angelico painted his frescoes, Anton likes to imagine, though the room is actually not referred to as a cell at all. Outside he hears the soft murmur of

other juniorates and novitiates at rec and relaxation as they
float in pairs in their black cassocks through the pecan trees,
trying to be solemn and serious. The bright jolly faces of a
hundred boys held here in the palm of God.

*But when we grow older, we understand that our mother really
can't give us everything—and that even she is looking for something that she doesn't have. And then we begin to look for it
ourselves. We think it must lie in being popular, so we try to be
popular. We think it lies in having a good time, in not worrying
about being popular, in taking care of ourselves, in being independent. Then we decide it is better to be married, settle down,
have a good job, have kids.*

Anton sucks on the end of his pen, bites it, stares at the
page, mostly blank. Did Augustine ever worry about "being
popular"? He grabs the sheet and crumples it in one swift gesture and throws it into the corner with a heap of other sheets.
In a week he'll give this sermon. In a week his mother and father will drive down from Dallas in the company Packard,
across the dusty plains and into the lush country of mean-
dering bayous where live oaks drip with moss, to hear him
address the religious at St. Charles Borromeo Church—this,
one step in the process of taking his vows.

A thin ribbon of black ink leaks across his lip. He taps the
pen against the bed he is using for a desk. The block of stationery looks up at him. He makes a design with his pen.
Dramatic clouds billow in the sky, swollen, shaded in a hundred variations of gray. He would like to write a sermon
about Catholics and sexual repression, but instead he goes
straight to the sex, drawing a naked lady with dark erect
nipples, sumptuous thick nipples and a sumptuous thickly
haired pudendum. Sex blossoms on the page, hardens him in

his robe. He reaches for himself, lets go of the drawing, thinks of breasts and lips and tongue. Now he's warm to his task, truly working it. Outside, the novitiates, naked under their gowns, stroll beneath Spanish moss while Anton is suspended in a singularity that cuts through the good and the beautiful the way the ax seeks the tree—in perfect violation—then deposits him back into himself, back into his clammy cell.

His cheeks flush. Then he shivers and looks around as if spied upon. He hears the footsteps of the novitiates returning. He crumples the sheet, rising to light the candle on his desk. With the flame he burns the sheet; the superiors examine all waste for sin. He says, "I'm a sinner. Forgive me God for my will." Anton watches the body burn. The flames eat her, her nipples become even more full until they burst. *In revelation Christ said, "If you want to be perfect you must let nothing stand between you and me; there must be nothing held back: no deliberate affection for anything opposed to my will.* He rubs the ash into his cassock and then rubs his hands through his thinning hair until all the ash has vanished to become a part of him.

Is Christ watching—even this? "He knows who you are and loves you, anyway," his mama often reminds him. Anton shakes his head—*Impossible*—and shivers again. He sees his mother with her impossible halo of chestnut hair sitting tall in the Packard, driving down through Nacogdoches or Shreveport, down among the sugar plantations with their towering cane, through the whole sweet world of Louisiana to get there and be proud of him. *Impossible.* Daddy is small in the driver's seat, the car outsized for his frame. Mama's imposing figure shades the sunlight from his eyes. Daddy looks hard at the road, something sad in his eyes. The day streams past like so much water. "Keep your faith simple," he has told his son. "Don't delve too deep to rouse any doubts."

He begins again. *To pray if it is easy, to pray if it is hard*— Well goddamn! Another sheet gets tossed across the room. Each day it's been the same. As he studies The Constitution of the Society of Jesus, as he works his cincture beads, as he engages with other novitiates in discussions during legal talking time, in the back of his mind he is pronging away at the female form. It's there during his morning prayers. It's there during evening mass. In his dreams he is one big pronging penis cloaked in the cassock of his hypocrisy. He is, shall we say, having trouble with the idea of celibacy. He is doubting. No marriage for priests. No female priests. The lack of shading between good and evil. Distribution of grace. Inculpable sin. Original sin. The Virgin birth. His list is long, but there is one item at the top of his list that pitches him into a bewildering spiral to the bottom of the world. His hands smell of ash. His dick smells of ash.

"Dear boy," Father Master comforts him with his bald and wizened face. (Later, Anton's bald wizened toenail-less toes, pinched from the stitching, will stare up at him, reminding him of this face—innocence, faith, belief—and of the Jesuits.) They talk in Father Master's office separated by the wide expanse of desk; they talk in the chapel, solemnly at prayer; they talk in the rose gardens, beneath the oaks. They talk about everything under the sun except the thing that troubles Anton most. Sex to Father Master is like Antarctica. He knows it exists but he knows he will never go there. He's a slight man, fragile yet strong. His head is flecked with freckles and liver spots and the sprouts of a few remaining hairs. Anton is his jewel, the precious sum of God's will. The old man radiates warmth and a deep belief that the Lord has sought Anton. Anton's mother shares this belief, the dream of the bluebonnets. Why can't Anton? Father Master is eyes, all eyes, tremendous eyes, red-rimmed, glowing eyes. For he sees in Anton more than Anton could ever see in himself. Anton holds the Father's hands, both of them, and close. The Father is Grand Coteau, he is the Church, Christ's messenger, God's servant, the Word. His hands are big, enormous for such a small old man.

"It is a sign of wisdom, of your intelligence, to doubt," Father Master says.

"N-n-no," Anton stutters, an impediment recently developed. "I...I...I—I'm wrong, unworthy. You don't understand."

"We cannot know the essence of God with natural intuition," Father Master warns.

The other boys float among the pecan trees in the sulfur-colored light, trying to be serious. At rec time Anton teaches them to play football (tackle not touch), has even started a team, and they love him for it. He has found little ways to breach the rules. Those boys feed off him, think he knows the Truth. And he loves to watch their seriousness crack. It's then that they descend down to him, in laughter, his amusing misdemeanors joining him with them. Christ was human, after all—fallible. Doesn't wisdom mean being wrong—doing wrong—sometimes? Their laughter sails through the yard like a protective cloak over winking Anton, ironic Anton; for isn't Anton basically good? And isn't that what matters?

And sometimes the Virgin defeats the whore. *Life. Death. Divine judgment. Our Blessed Mother was able to remain calm at Calvary, to never seek the riches or fame or wisdom of this world—simply because she lived by her faith. She said to God and knew it to be true, "You are the way and the truth and the life. You are the vine and I am the branch. Without you I can do nothing, therefore be it done unto me according to your will."*

Sometimes he wants to be lost again in his mother's eyes, she the pillar of his tiny soul—the whole world simple. He tries prayer, but instead he is twelve again and spiking a rock and jumping for joy, riding home on the air because Annie has kissed him. She had been asked, "Who do you like best?" in a game of Truth or Consequences played with five boys. Delicate Annie with her long lashes and bright brown eyes, her large forehead and slender birdlike wrists. She stood beneath the large canopy of the walnut tree in fading sunlight on a small Dallas street. Her consequence: Kiss who you like best. She passed by two boys and then kissed Anton. She ran up to him and kissed him softly, warmly, on the cheek, and then ran away. Chosen by God. Anton in his sweet awe of victory, the four other boys watching him ferociously, felt a little baffled knowing he had been delivered and that she was unaware of it.

JUST A FEW MONTHS before, Anton had been a boy. He had been part of the brotherhood—a gang of friends that rode wild through Dallas in a pickup truck, pulling pranks, riding fast beneath the Mobil building and the flying red horse. They turned off all the lights in Highland Park; they opened all the fire hydrants. Their bright faces shaded beneath wide brims of cowboy hats. They drove into the plains late at night and drank beer beneath the stars at old O'Connell's ranch. They fished and they camped and they hunted. They played poker, high-stakes poker. They gambled for dares. James and Rick and Johnny, Buck and Stewart—sons of oilaires and bankers and manufacturers of farm equipment. And there was Ike Scarborough, rich as the sun—not Catholic, not part of the brotherhood, but a friend just the same. He threw big parties, filled his swimming pool with all that beer. "It's beer, Anton,"

Annie declared, with her big brown eyes brilliant as jet—his
girlfriend now for five years, since she delivered him. Her
long taffeta gown floated up at her waist as they waded in the
beer, drinking it from their cupped hands. Then they were all
skinny-dipping, the lanterns in the yard—so many—lit up
and twinkling, easy to confuse with the stars.

The boys, they were boys. They dated, they danced, they
dreamed of futures filled with long legs and the gentle curves
of soft bellies. The gentle touch of a woman, silk hair, the per-
fumes of the female embrace, the thrill of touching chiffons
and taffetas and velvets, delicate stockings and dainty shoes.
And here Anton is now, a virgin in the Jesuits, at St. Charles
College in Louisiana, one of the oldest and most respected
seminaries in the country, and he is afraid he is not good
enough, worthy enough, to serve the Lord. Even the statue in
the courtyard is sexual to him. Her lips have been painted a
pale and sumptuous red, her mouth pouts, her expression
beckons, her robe falls seductively off her shoulders. He
imagines peeling back those robes—dark nipples, dark patch
of hair. Who shall serve the Lord? they ask in evening prayers.
But I'm not in love with God, he thinks. Indeed, he disdains
the simplicity of foolish nuns and emotional priests who de-
clare, "I love Jesus." "I've not fallen in love in a final way," he
confesses to Father Master because that love is the promise,
that love is the reason, that love will become his life's quest.
"Patience, dear boy," Father Master reassures.

Anton studies Latin and Greek, ethics and theodicy—the
differences between the Suarezians and the Thomists. He
learns about music and art. (He can draw fine wanton women
with astounding precision.) His mind expands. He searches
for models in a parade of saints: St. Thomas, St. Augustine,
St. Ignatius Loyola, St. Charles. Why am I here? Because

Mama had a vision in a field of bluebonnets? He wonders sometimes.

"God created man simple," Father Master says. "And we inevitably destroy our simplicity both individually and collectively. Sometimes," Father Master tells him, "I put on some Mozart music turned very low so that I can pretend it's coming from a distance. Then when I close my eyes, everything seems (or is, maybe) simple again."

Anton imagines himself with a sweet virgin girl. He imagines himself very big and defined and knowledgeable, untethered from the burden of Christ. I was not born to save you, Mother. Little Annie and her soft kiss become a woman in a pool of beer.

Racing through the streets with the brotherhood in the beat-up old pickup, out beneath the stars to old O'Connell's ranch, such a short time ago.

"Our Anton's gonna be a priest," Buck said, his hair blown back in a swirl from the wind. Buck had enormous ears and thick dark eyebrows. He was an ugly boy. He held his hat in his hands. The lights of Dallas dimmed with each mile until the night opened up into one vast and blackened world. "A virgin. A goddamn virgin," Buck said with awe. "How you gonna do it, man?" They were all virgins still, though they never spoke of it. Instead they spoke of going down to whores in Mexico. It was the idea of the infinite that so confused Buck—the permanence and commitment of forever, so strict and unyielding. "Forever, man, forever."

"You'll have to confess all your carnal sins to me," Anton shouted over the wind. His eyes squinted. "I'll live vicariously through you, Buck. Although I fear I might be a little bored." Buck didn't want to bore Anton. He wanted to live big if only for Anton. The road bounced them, and even so Anton stood up to preside over the boys. He imagined himself standing tall in a bejeweled pulpit, the arms of God holding him tightly. "I'll want all the dirty details." He liked to feel himself worthier than these boys, or at least wiser. But these boys knew Anton well and they knew how to tease him, knew that he saw himself in the bejeweled pulpit or even higher up, in the clouds with Christ.

"He looks more like a goddamned emperor," said Rick.

"Emperor of what?" Buck asked.

"My ass," said Rick.

"It's big enough," Buck said.

"Already been colonized."

"Boys," Anton said, with a flourish of his beer bottle that took in the whole crew, "sodomy, you'll recall, is a mortal sin."

"You'll learn that one real good in the priesthood," Rick said.

"Well," Anton corrected.

"Sodomites, all of 'em," Buck said.

"Now, looky here," Anton said, pointing upward to the heavens. "This is why we come out of town."

"Oh, no. Here we go," Rick said.

Anton just smiled, staring upward toward the numberless stars, the wind in his hair. "Boys," he said, "behold the mind of God."

The great star sieve lay above them, the Milky Way like a scrim across the sky, the engine thrumming beneath the hood of the Chevy, carrying them out into the darkness. They took sips from their beers.

"Infinite," Anton said.

"Forever," Rick said.

"Forever's a long time," Buck mused.

"Without pussy," Anton said.

"Look at that, our savior is a dirty old priest," Rick said.

"They're all dirty," Anton said. "Why else become a priest?"

When he was with his friends his Texas bravado thickened. He was a cowboy at heart, he knew that. He wanted to get on a horse and ride and ride and ride through the whole expanse of Texas. In the Jesuits even he would ride. They would have horses at Grand Coteau, a stable. And he'd ride to the great old outdoor kitchen of the Madams of the Sacred Heart and promise to say mass for them. They'd adore the blue-eyed boy showing up on his horse in their kitchen, and they'd feed him pies and biscuits and cookies thick with pecans and sugar, smiling flirtatiously from beneath their black veils. "How many is the mass you'll say for us," from the pink lips of a young novitiate, coy soft smile floating on a pretty round face. He wondered what color her hair was. He'd ride through the tall wet grasses and ferns, full of snakes, a mist rising, lingering over the land, to make promises to the Madams. Giggling girls, they'd be clustered in the kitchen, waiting for him to arrive. But that was later.

A gold cap sparkled from deep in his mouth, caught by the faint running lights. A semitrailer with livestock sped by, rocking them. They held on tight. In the cab, Stewart's and Johnny's heads were lost in the dark, but you could see the bobbing amber tips of their cigarettes and imagine where their heads should be.

"It'll be our job to tempt you," shouted Rick.

At O'Connell's ranch they hopped into the field. Silos and grain elevators rose like skyscrapers, and a tremendous quiet spread over the night as the truck's engine settled. The barn looked lopsided and haunted in the dark. The boys tried to scare each other, but they'd been here too many times to be scared by a barnful of sleeping animals.

"I'd have liked to have found a lamb," Rick said, dragging a calf from the barn. The enormous doors swayed on their broken hinges, a shade darker than the night. The calf bleated, struggling against the pull of the rope.

"We're gonna tempt our priest here with a calf," Rick explained to Stewart and Johnny. His bald head shone like his cowboy boots. He grinned wide, which made him look really ugly—so ugly he was almost cute.

"You look like the devil," Anton said. The calf pissed, a warm and steamy piss.

"Holy Father please pardon me"—Buck's big teeth glowed and he fell to his knees at Anton's feet, folding his hands in prayer—"once I make it with the calf."

"The calf's for Anton," Rick said. "We can't send him off without a little experience." The calf was weak-kneed, wobbling. Beers popped open and cigarettes were lit—the boys' faces became full moons in the cigarette glow. The smoke mingled with the dusty animal smell, making it sweeter. In the dark the boys talked more easily. They weren't so afraid of the truth.

Anton studied the animal, his friends, the mesquite in silhouette. With a thin half smile, he tipped his hat up so that you could see his eyes. He began a little song, his voice big against the night. Somewhere he wished they were all going to Grand Coteau. He was afraid of being alone.

He saw Annie standing beneath the canopy of the walnut tree on his small street, carrying a clutch and a stack of textbooks, crying. And the idea of becoming a priest seemed very real and wrong. He and Annie had spoken once of their own ranch with children. "It doesn't have to be big even," she'd said—small and simple, not daring to squeeze too much out of the dream. Annie was off at college, engaged to a different man.

"Wasn't Christ a homosexual?" Stewart asked. Stewart had long sideburns, a leather jacket, and was a relation to the Clebergs of King Ranch in south Texas—so big the whole state of Connecticut could fit inside. And though this relationship dangled by a thread, the size of the ranch was a fact that made Stewart proud, that made him feel big—just a bit bigger than all the others.

"Is that what you'd like him to be?" Anton asked. "You're gonna make me work extra hard for your soul, aren't you, babe?" Fear, too, could make his bravado swell. "Christ wants to love with a million hearts instead of just his own." The calf stomped her feet. The boys paced, just killing time before high school finished and their lives changed. "But I'll make a bet with you," Anton said to Buck. "A good old-fashioned bet. I'll bet you don't make it with the calf or with a lamb or a goat or a pig or any other kind of animal. I'll bet you're pure chicken rather than the stud you're claiming to be.

"But if you do, son," Anton said, adding "son" for authority. He placed his palms on Buck's head. "If you engage in relations with 'that there calf,' as long as you do it in front of us, well son, I'll absolve you of all your sins."

"What kind of priest are you?" Stewart asked, in mock outrage. He came up close to Anton and looked him hard in the eyes, so close their noses practically touched. They both swayed back and forth and stared at each other.

"Stewart?" Anton said at last.

"What?"

"Would you like to kiss me?"

A spontaneous spray of beer sprayed from the mouths of

the boys like hissing pipes. And just as suddenly Stewart and Anton began waltzing around the corral, tripping over each other. The cool wind blew through the mesquite and the boys paced around like shades, howling at the stars. No one would have the courage to fuck the calf, of course, and the calf seemed to know it, standing a few paces away, wide-eyed, darting off when one of the boys lunged for him. Just boys standing there, kicking the dirt, rosy-cheeked boys.

ANTON's FRIENDS at law school receive letters from people requesting free legal advice. They've been wronged. They want to sue. Anton's daily mail contains letters of petition for prayer, letters from his mama's friends. *Pray for me*, they request. *We know you're praying all the time, include us in your prayers.* He's not even a priest and here they're hoping to get in on the ground floor of salvation. The letters accumulate. He arranges them in neat bundles on his desk, meaning to respond to each one, but the rigors of his study prevent this. One night, he smuggles them out of the seminary. In the darkness, under stars, with the crickets and the cicadas sawing away, Anton races across the yard to the garbage complex. Raccoons and possums scurry. He pauses, blesses the letters in a batch, then tosses them all into the dump.

I'm not a good Catholic. I'm not worthy of the Lord's grace. I'm unfit to serve him. Summon the sermon. This sex thing. The urge. If there were only someone I could speak with honestly about the sex thing. He wonders if other juniorates, novitiates, regents, ordained priests, suffer as he does. He wonders if Father Master has the urge. Impossible. Antarctica. Has he questioned the innocence of a newborn child? Has he asked, Who am I? This question eats away at his core like acid until he is in pain—a crumpled heap on the bed. *This life here doesn't ask much, only what is due, and when*

*he is understood even the sacrifices become minute in relation to
what must be the depth and purity of his love and goodness.*

Anton wants to change the structure of the Church. He
sees this as his duty, perhaps his calling. The Church seems
wrong. Priests lack worldliness; they're superficial. Communism is devouring the faithful all around the world and the
unyielding Church is partly to blame. In the summer North
Korea invaded South Korea—one more vote for atheism and
the violation of natural law principles. Catholics around the
country are saying novenas to pray for the conversion of the
Russians. Anton thinks of Fatima and the apparition of the
Virgin to those three children, of how the Virgin inaugurated
her own prescient war against communism. "If my requests
are heard," she told the children in Portugal in 1917, "and the
world is consecrated to my Immaculate Heart, Russia will be
converted and the world will have peace; but if my requests
are not heard, the evil doctrines of atheistic Russia will spread
over the whole world." *If some do not understand the justice of
hell it is because they do not understand the evil of sin in relation
to the infinite love, forgiveness, and mercy of God. Love, grati-
tude—from this will flow humility and here is the eternal source
of glory.*

Anton wants a revolution in the Church. He wants to
change the way Catholic thinkers think. He wants to save the
world. He wants more.

"Son," Father Master says, "the Devil works on us
through our virtues, getting us to take on more than we can
handle." He rests a soothing hand on Anton's shoulder, all
bones and age and wisdom. In a year Anton will help this
man die. Help him struggle to catch his last breath as cancer
eats him organ by organ, teaching Anton just a bit more
about the nature of humility. "Many is the mass and communion I offer for you," Father Master says.

"I'm afraid Christ will let me go," Anton says. He's crying. It's all so tremendously big. "Christ won't let you go," Father Master responds. "He does not let his friends go so fast. He will not permit weakness or any other defects that aren't deliberately clung to cut his friends from him."

The letters from his mother's friends continue to arrive, pleading with him for prayers, as if prayers floated off his lips like breath. *Please be so good; include me in your prayers. Pray for me vigorously.* His mother has told all her friends, My son chosen by God. He receives rosebushes for the monastery garden from a florist friend in Corsicana. Christian greeting cards from another in Nacogdoches. Endless quantities of gift-wrapping paper from Mr. Dorman, the owner of the paper-packaging company his father works for, Dorman & Sons, in Fort Worth. Anton tries to remember each person by face, to keep each request close to his heart during prayer. Mr. Dorman with his bad heart; Lolly Pratt with her broken hip; Susie Dale and her husband who ran off with the secretary. He wants to save them all. He wonders, speculates, asks God and Father Master if it really is within his power to help these people. Can he give them the blessing of faith with a prayer? Simple beautiful faith, the ability to trust and believe. He adores the attention. Chosen by God.

"Is this a desire of power? Is this shameful? The exhilaration I feel keeping these souls in my prayers?" Anton asks. "Is powerful how the clergy feel?"

What a beautiful prospect to receive our Lord every day for the rest of my life. Love will be something less if it is not something more.

Anton surprised all his friends after just three months at Grand Coteau. Upon coming back to Dallas in his robes, he was treated like a king, invited to all the Christmas parties as the guest of honor. He'd been allowed the visit because his father had had a heart attack, a mild one. He was recovering well.

The friends expected Anton to be quiet, subdued, contemplative, reserved, and older by a thousand years. He presided over the festivities, joining everyone in prayer at his mother's request—heads bowed, eyes closed, hands clasped. "By making us his friend God binds himself to answering our prayers," Anton said, speaking easily and spontaneously because he shined with an audience. He spoke of the beauty of Christ teaching us forgiveness, humility, the generosity of spirit. He spoke of the Blessed Virgin's Assumption. His arms gesticulated, this way and that. He was on fire with the faith of our Lord. The brotherhood of boys watched his grace with admiration. They noted Anton's effervescence, the enthusiasm of a kid on a school picnic. He was glowing, toasting everyone, promising that he had kept them in his prayers.

"Bet he'll no longer fuck a lamb," Buck whispered to Stewart.

"Or a calf or a goat or a pony," Stewart responded.

"Or a woman, poor soul."

HER COLD FINGERS sneaked around his big head covering his eyes to surprise him. "I miss you," he whispered. Not at all surprised. He turned to kiss Annie, bowing to her forehead. Those leopard eyes of hers, in them he admired a man in a long black cassock.

"I could kiss you in that cassock," Annie said.

"Then kiss me," Anton said.

"You're losing your hair."

"Too much grace. No need for hair."

"What about our ranch?"

"It will still be there."

"Will it?"

"What about your marriage?"

"What about yours?"

A cream lace sash tied her red velvet gown at her slender waist. She wore a strand of pearls and pearl studs and her short hair curled just above her shoulders. She was a brave girl; she'd taken her dress off first to skinny-dip in Ike's pool of beer. "You won't end up a priest, Anton," she said with seriousness. "And I'll be gone."

Anton's mother stood in a corner of the big ballroom of that redbrick Highland Park mansion, holding court with a collection of women who praised her on the accomplishments of her son. This was where she belonged. She wanted to live in a house like this rather than in her quiet little bungalow. Admiring her son, somehow the dream seemed possible. The guests formed a sea of wide round eager rosy faces around Anton and Annie was swept away, receding into the current. They wanted to touch him. They were cupped in his palm, safe and warm and secure, giving all of their faith to him. He alone was the guardian of their faith. He could still feel Annie's cold fingers on his warm eyes. He was glad she was gone. He was afraid of her. He held his rosary beads tightly. Tonight, he would pray. His mother caught his eye and gave him a loving look—an I-believe-in-you look. Christmas hymns drifted through the room, cups of eggnog were served. Someone played quietly on the piano. Servants rushed past with silver platters of fancy foods. Anton avoided the eyes of his brotherhood friends because he did not want to think about the long night rides in the cool Texas air. Or his head gently sweating beneath the brim of his hat. Or the silken underthings of his pretty little girl. The party was a jubilee and all these various people were so variously dressed in

cheerful colors—reds and greens and golds—that Anton
stood out even more starkly in his black robe. His toenails
ached, they bled. A Christmas tree blinked, crowned by the
guiding star. Anton beamed, waltzing among them, the king
they wanted him to be. His mother watched proudly. "I hope
he doesn't change," Mama said to her friends. "I hope none
of us changes. I'm happy with us the way we are."

ANTON IS NO LONGER KING. Instead, he is a young novitiate
writing a sermon, imagining a closing, a deathbed scene. It is
death that comes to him, that makes its impression. That is
what people fear most, of course—all those people begging
for prayers. They fear the arrival of the Lord at the moment
of death when they are truly on the brink of judgment. They
can deny the Lord, but they are never really sure, and they
know they'll find out as they die and they know that if they've
been wrong about the Lord there will be no chance then for a
change of heart.

   Bring them to their death scene—a sunny room (perhaps)
all their children and friends around—perhaps weeping, per-
haps laughing and trying to cheer you up—perhaps even a
dirty joke, or perhaps someone is talking/arguing for birth con-
trol, and maybe the priest is on the way, and you feel yourself
unliving your past—will you be listening to these prattling
people? NO. You'll be thinking of one thing as judgment gets
closer by the second; you'll be thinking only of—The Past. How
often did I commit this sin—or deceive the Church in this
point, refuse to obey when the Church told me to listen. Snap!!
You're gone. The priest never got there. What greets you? I beg
you to listen now. Make your choice NOW.

   For he knew. At twenty death terrified him as well. No
matter how much time he spent with his knees pressed to the

cold stone floor, he knew. No matter how hard he tried to be king, he knew. He feared judgment. With the advent of doubt, he felt he was losing his peace forever. And it was his own deathbed scene that he saw, years from now, far away from the Church, surrounded by a posse of children that belonged to him, smart, strong-willed children arguing about abortion, the Jesuits a distant memory symbolized only by his toenail-less big toes and a memory of gathering pecans on a cold November morning. A dying man in his bed, a skeleton resting against a sea of white pillows. His mother's blue eyes hazy now, depthless, lost to senility and cataracts.

Imagine, my dear brethren in Christ, that you are here at the foot of this pulpit in the center of the aisle in your coffin. Your friends and relatives are here praying for your soul, praying that you lived a better life than you did. Imagine that I am here giving a sermon on a subject that your friends don't understand and that you did not understand in life—that God is merciful, that he wanted your love every second you were alive, wanted you to do things for him so that for eternity he could do things for you.

A friend from these years would write to him in London after he had left the Jesuits. Anton would have five of his children by then. He and Agnes would be involved in dream therapy with R. D. Laing that required the acid trips for elucidation. Yea verily, far away from the Church and learning about Gestalt therapy and studying existentialism, living off of Agnes's extraordinary wealth. I'm not a non-Catholic, he would say. Just an anti-Catholic. The Jesuit friend would write,

You have a greater capacity for enjoyment than I have, and therefore are in the greater danger of wasting your life—not in

any horrible way, of course, although, more or less, by the way,
you have that possibility, too. It's just that, by your own fault,
you might end up not having accomplished anything and hav-
ing taken away from yourself the chance of doing anything to
retrieve the situation except writing your memoirs so that others
can have the same enjoyment without having to throw their
lives away to get it.
  Yours in His Heart.

There in the cell at Grand Coteau in 1950 his past was
pure, marred only by thoughts of sex and doubts about the
doctrines of his faith. In the vase on the simple table blossomed one long white lily. He contemplated the lily. *Consider*
the lilies of the field . . . O you of little faith. He was just a boy in
black robes, youth rosy in his cheeks and smile, with a gray
felt-tip pen in his hand, trying to write a sermon. The lily
burst with a spray of perfume, deeply sweet. Yellow pollen
drifted with dust to powder the table. The lily was fully open,
in a state of perfection, not yet yellowing, the tendrils of its
core bursting like the perfume, like hope. That one bit of
beauty in the sullen room, lying in Mary's empty tomb,
springing from the sweat of Christ in his final hours of sorrow, from the tears of Eve as she was expelled from Eden.
Somehow that lily seemed to promise a lot, perhaps even all
the beauty of the world. *O you of little faith.*

Imagine that as you lie here in your coffin God sends your
soul back to your body, and suddenly, before the whole congre-
gation, you rise into the air in a brilliant light and you tell us,
plead with us, beg us to change our values, to think more
about what Jesus Christ on that crucifix should teach us. Why
wouldn't God let this happen, let you taste this? Because even if
he did, you would not listen.

Anton would write this sermon, though he did not like the pressure. On his knees, he held on tightly to his rosary and prayed. *May I have the grace to be penetrated with a salutary fear of hell. My prayers and sacrifices can daily save people from hell. We will all know people who go to hell. One mortal sin equals hell. I should thank God for bringing me a vocation that gives me so many chances of avoiding hell.* He was afraid— simple, ordinary fear. He would write this sermon out of fear, though in the end his mother would become just a mother. He would write this sermon out of fear, though his head remained wild with ideas about virgins and masturbation and a delicate girl named Annie. The future was his to mar or regale or adorn with faith and glory. For what he knew was that without God that vast slate would be his alone, and it was this that scared and excited him most.

CHAPTER SIXTEEN

The Small
Democracy of Family

It was the boys Eve liked best. You could see it in her eyes. She'd have done anything for them, even sold her daughters right on down the river. She wouldn't have been able to sell Alice. Dad never *ever* would have allowed her to do anything to Alice. She was Dad's favorite. He spoiled her rotten. Whenever we were eating out he'd give the rest of us kids a two-dollar limit. But Alice could get anything she wanted and she always got steak. For breakfast even!

In fights Eve always defended the boys against her daughters. The boys were right, no matter what. Golden boys, blond hair shining in the sun. (Finny didn't have blond hair, but it was as if he did—so brilliant was he for her.) It was sad to watch because my brothers didn't love her much—but they liked getting her love. Who doesn't like getting love? Sad to see her daughters screeching at her, shouting about how it's not fair. "Stick up for me!" they'd each say. Eve knew her girls would always be there for her or at least that they'd always need her even though they'd shout and scream and storm off and disappear dramatically for hours, days, and later months, even years. I'm a mother now. I know the nature of a child's love. They think everything's their fault and run around trying to fix it all up. Once Kate was screaming at Eve so hard, she gave herself a bloody nose. Nicholas had to pick her up and carry her to the bathroom and away from Eve because blood was spurting all over the place. But Eve knew the power of need, the inextricable bond between mother and child—knew that she could do anything and her daughters would always want her.

It was because she didn't have her own boys that she loved my brothers best. Imagine giving birth to one girl after the next. Each pregnancy I can see her hoping, because boys love in a different way from girls and everyone wants boys whether they admit it or not. All I've had are boys. A friend told me that you get boys when the mother has an orgasm. The orgasm helps the male sperm swim the distance, helps pull them up to the egg much faster than the female sperm, which swim slow and steady. This makes sense given the fact that Eve's almost proud about how much she doesn't like sex—the reason, I am certain, that Dad had affairs. Satisfy your man, is what I say!

As far as my sister Caroline and I were concerned, we were the unfortunate stepdaughters, ranking way below our brothers and her daughters on the totem pole. But because of Dad she had to pretend, at least, to be fair. She couldn't boss us around. She couldn't tell us what to do. Ever. Dad would have hollered at her until she was the size of a pea. But he could tell her kids what to do. That didn't seem fair, either, but I was glad to be his child and not hers because he got to boss her kids around and she never complained or never told him it wasn't fair. "Don't bully me, babe," he'd have said. She knew better than to say a thing like that, and besides, I think she liked that he bossed her kids. It was as if he really were the head of the family, a normal family, which is what they wanted after all. It's what most everybody wants, of course— that safe place of family, the bosom of my family, our tiny countries, magnificent empires that exist by a string. But the whole situation, it's like seeing a whole world of impoverished kids, as we did in Haiti, starving on the streets with their big distended bellies, and feeling sorry for them because you're rich. But no way are you going to give up your wealth to become one of them. I felt sorry for Eve's girls, but not enough to trade places—or to negotiate with Dad.

Eve and Dad got together in 1969. We were in Dallas with Mom and didn't know about it at first. Dad was spreading the Gestalt word and women's liberation and had come east to start a chapter of NOW in New Jersey and to find land to start a utopia where all of us were to live with about a dozen other families. Mom was making her plans to bring us east. Part of her plan was to design a free school for kids to give them an alternative possibility for their education. Her school was called Erehwon, *nowhere* spelled backward. All of us were going to attend. But Eve had been dumped by her husband and she had nowhere to go and some friend of hers suggested that she do therapy with Dad and she seduced him and that was that. Mom and Dad's dream for a utopia disintegrated. Eve couldn't see her own way to raising three girls so she had to grab a married man—a happily married man. It took her a long time, though. It took her until she had Alice to get Dad to finally give up Mom. Mom was the love of Dad's life. Sure, they had problems, but he wouldn't have left her for all the diamonds in the Congo if it hadn't been for Eve. It's not that Eve was better than a Congo diamond, it's that she had a determination, a will, that was terrifying if you ask me. No was never a possibility with her. She'd have found a way to the moon on her own two feet if she had wanted to get there badly enough. As a matter of fact, she had two abortions before Alice, that's how determined she was to have Dad's child and to make him stay. But I wouldn't have wanted to be her. Dad always spoke about how great Mom was, about what a marvelous mind she had, what a great thinker she was—so smart and all that. I'm certain it made Eve feel stupid.

When we met Eve we had no idea what Dad was doing with her. She looked just like Doris Day with her pearl clip-ons (she would never have pierced her ears) and her matching sweater sets and her three girls dressed alike with bows in their hair. We did not get what Dad saw in her at all. He said stuff about her imagination, but Dad was an intellectual and we wondered whether this woman even had a brain. Dad explained to us that Eve had a great brain. It had just never been encouraged. He always tried to explain everything to us because he wanted a fair and just society. He wanted us to have opinions and express our ideas and vote for what we believed. The small democracy of family. In the end, of course, our votes were worthless if he wanted it his way and we didn't agree. For example, none of us agreed about wanting Eve and her girls in our life. We had a private family meeting, excluding them, and the vote was unanimous. But they became part of it anyway and Dad tried to teach those wimpy girls to be tough. He gave them punching bags and boxing gloves and BB guns and footballs. The only one who tried to play with each and every one of those things was Julia because she was a flirt and had to be the best at everything. She shot into my life like an arrow and ruined it, hit me right in the heart. Dad loved her. She was the only one of the three of them that he loved. She had bright eyes and she could never stop smiling and she was smart, knowing everything about Mozart and philosophy, and she would learn things about subjects that interested Dad just so she could discourse with him—on Kierkegaard and love, on cant, on Kant. She loved that cant. I don't even know what it means, but she'd talk all the time about cant and I know it was just because it's one of those words that you think you know the meaning of, but actually you don't. It made her seem smart. Sometimes it seemed Julia wanted Dad's love for her to be like his love for Eve. Sometimes I think she would have even slept with him had he wanted. And you know what? Eve would have allowed it. Eve would have encouraged it because it would have bound us up all the more tightly. Aren't there tribes where intermarriage and incest are the way of life? When Julia was fifteen she marched around declaring it a tragedy that she was so in love with my brother Nicholas. She declared that she would marry him when she turned eighteen.

But we just couldn't see what Dad saw. Eve had a will certainly, but a brain? She cared about things that Mom wouldn't be caught dead caring about, like china and silver and antique furniture and freshly pressed clothes. She couldn't stand to see us running around in our T-shirts and jeans, our hair all messy. But that's like the bourgeoisie, that's what Nicholas told me way back then. The bourgeoisie care about material things because they can't have them. And that Julia. I'll never forgive that I had to tolerate her. She was the true definition of *snob.* "I don't sit on sofas. I sit on couches. I don't hang drapes. I hang curtains, and I never give gifts. I give presents," she'd brag, proud of knowing the social differences of those words. Who cares? She was jealous because we could have anything we wanted. Mom's family owned half the oil in Texas and these were boom years. (Well, not exactly half, but quite a fair number.)

When Mom left Texas for the ashram she simply abandoned her house. She didn't care about an heirloom in it. Eve reminds us that we have her to thank for saving those treasures. She reminds us, but lets us know that since she saved them, they should be hers. Hers if she chooses to keep them. Mom locked the door on that house in Highland Park and handed the keys to a realtor. Dad drove all the way out there with Eve in a U-Haul and packed up the most important stuff. There were valuable antiques and loads of Tiffany silver from their marriage and even some Tiffany glass. And then rare objects like fifteenth-century swords and nineteenth-century guns. Dad told us he was taking it for us, so that we could have it later, when we were older, when we'd be able to appreciate it. In the meantime, Eve used it. Eve fingered it. Eve pretended it was hers. Once I caught her polishing a silver bowl and it seemed she was trying to scrub out the inscription. It read: ANTON & AGNES, ETERNALLY IN CHRIST. 7–14–1955. Bastille Day, their wedding day.

Other stuff they got from the Highland Park house were my grandmother's clothes and jewels. One ring was a Cartier emerald and Eve snatched that right up. My own mother wouldn't be caught dead wearing something like that. But Eve wore it. I suppose Dad let her. The idea was that it was too small for our big-boned fingers. Eve would take it off when she gardened so that it wouldn't get clogged with dirt. Well, Caroline and I decided that we would steal it and make it look like she lost it, just to teach her a lesson about who it belonged to and what she was playing with when she left it casually on the bathroom sink. There were so many people traipsing through that house and so many things were always getting stolen that it was very likely some carpenter or drug-addict friend of Nicholas's could have taken it. Caroline and I pocketed it, hid it in Caroline's leather pouch where she kept her rosary. And all afternoon we waited for Eve to discover that it was missing. It was a test: Would she tell the truth or would she lie? Well what do you suppose she did? You're right—she lied. She took her shower, showered off all the dirt, cleaned her fingernails, and went to slip our ring back on her finger and it was not there. We took turns standing on a ladder, peering in through an outside window—Caroline pinching at me for her turn when I stayed up too long. Eve searched the bathroom counter, looking under creams and in jars. Nowhere to be found. She was just in a towel, ripping apart that counter, tearing into the hamper beneath the counter. She spent a good hour searching for it. At one point she sat on the floor and cried. She put her head in her hands and sobbed as if this were all too much for her. She was terrified of Dad. And we saw this as small justice, a vindication of our mother's loss.

On the bathroom floor, her wet curly hair dripping down her cheeks, "What will I do?" she kept asking herself. And that's exactly what Caroline and I wanted to know.

Well, she did nothing. She got dressed, brushed her hair, came out to the kitchen, started bossing her girls around to help with dinner, made dinner; we all ate dinner, and some of the kids drove off to the drive-in. It wasn't that we didn't have fun. At times, we had a lot of fun. Nicholas and I would sit in the front seat of the Cadillac, pretending to be lovers on a date, and we'd cruise into the drive-in at dusk with a bunch of the little kids hiding in the trunk so that we didn't have to pay so much. We made movies all the time, taking turns on who'd be the star, though Nicholas was always the director.

We had fine parties and listened to good music and ate well and read poetry to each other on the roof of the barn while the sun set into the fields. We traveled all over the world, or the Western Hemisphere, anyway. But I'd trade it all—who wouldn't?—for my mother and father to have remained married.

Caroline and I let a few days pass to see if Eve would tell Dad. Sometimes we would go into Caroline's room and open the leather rosary pouch and look at the emerald, how it sparkled in the light, turning it over and over like some kind of truth.

"I don't even like it," Caroline said with guilt. I could hear the guilt coming out of her like sweat. Her round face a little long with it. I'm certain it's because she kept the ring in that rosary case, too close to God.

"Well I do and it's ours," I snapped. I liked acting tough; it made me feel powerful.

On the third day we said something. "Where's your emerald ring, Eve?" I asked. I enjoyed using the word "your" as if it were hers to lose. I enjoyed being wicked when a person deserved it. Caroline blushed, which made us look guilty. I could have killed her. Dad gave Eve a look, looking at her finger first and then her face. She was too wrapped up in her own guilt to notice Caroline's. "I've been gardening and don't like to get dirt in it. It's back in the bedroom," she lied with her fake Doris Day smile, her smile that seems to think it can fix anything.

Caroline and I liked watching her squirm out of this one—well, at least I know I did. It was a no-exit situation because we knew that Dad would persist now until the truth was revealed. He asked her to go get it. Eve got up from the table and went to the bedroom and stayed there for a long time. So long that most everyone forgot what she was doing. Then she came back. "I can't find it," she said. Her face was pale and solemn, afraid. I felt sorry for her then, too. So did Caroline. Caroline knew we had pushed too far because she saw Dad inflate a little the way he did when he was on the verge of getting mad. His face either seemed really friendly or really angry. There wasn't an in between. "Where is it?" he asked—the angry face of course, round red swollen. "That's the girls' ring," he said. "You've got to be careful with it, babe." Just hearing that acknowledgment was glorious indeed—the girls' ring. He thought of it as ours. Well then what in the world was he letting that manipulative woman wear it for! "I left it on the bathroom counter," she said, getting impossibly small. Her voice hard to hear. "When I went to garden." Dad was sitting on his big thronelike chair at the table, eating a muffin and drinking his big cup of coffee, sitting there in his ruby-colored robe. "But you haven't gardened in days," Anton said. That was true, too, because it had been raining, rained so hard the whole yard and her garden were mud. He had the newspaper. He drove to the pharmacy every morning to get the newspaper. Sometimes he drove in his robe if he felt like it. Dad could accept a lot of things, but not lying, and when he discovered that she had been lying his lid would flip. Well, his lid flipped then right in front of her daughters and us. I felt sorry for them, too, having to watch Dad scream at her. She was that tiny pea, with him swollen, looming over her. He no longer cared about the paper or his coffee or his robe coming loose at his waist. "Don't you misuse my kids' things. Don't you lie when my kids are involved. Don't you ever lie." He was a tyrant. I'd never have married him, ever. I kept thinking of that little ring in its little leather hiding place, of how tiny it was to be causing all this trouble.

"Go ahead, do your tyrannical thing," Eve said suddenly, standing tall to meet him—as if she didn't care, as if bravery struck her, knocked her silly. She walked right over to him and stood in front of him. Her hair was curled from all the rain and she looked beautiful. Her cheeks flushed. She seemed to be someone I didn't know. I couldn't keep my eyes off of her. I was actually rooting for her. I wanted to help her unveil that strength. I almost could have confessed, but I'm no martyr. How important our lives seemed, how easily we threw them around.

What is it we all want anyway? What is it that she wanted from Dad, that her kids wanted from Dad, that we wanted from her? Love, of course. We all want love. Caroline and I wanted her love—deep down, that's what we wanted. The Cooper girls had their own father, but they wanted Dad's love, too. They fought for it, danced for it, showed off for it—learned about Kierkegaard and Kant for it. That's all Caroline and I wanted from Eve. If she'd have given it to us, we'd have given it right back. But how many annexed countries do you know where both sides get along?

It took a few days for it to come out that Caroline and I had the ring. In the end, Caroline's relationship with truth and faith and Christ made her reveal that we had it. Dad was just relieved. He apologized to Eve, of course, and then begged forgiveness in that way that made everyone melt. "How could I have doubted you, babe?" He wasn't afraid to become weak, to show that he'd been wrong, and that made him seem vulnerable and like he needed to be protected. Eve rushed in with her "Don't worry's" and "It's all right now's" as if she couldn't bear him to be weak. He was standing up for her. Gently he kissed her head. I rolled my eyes. I wondered, Did he love her? And a truth tore itself in half deep inside of me. He reprimanded us in front of her, making us apologize. "It was just a lesson," I kept saying. "Don't tell me about your lessons!" he snapped. Eve looked at me warmly with her green eyes, holding me, hugging me with her green eyes—no love, just a wee bit of triumph, malice, even. I could feel it coming from her eyes as if they were casting heat. Afterward, though, the ring was ours. It didn't fit our fingers, but it was ours.

CHAPTER SEVENTEEN

Hope

FOR EVE IT WAS THIS WAY: They were in Jamaica for Christmas with a few of the Furey kids, Alice, and several of their friends. Eve was happy because she was having a good time, feeling loved by the Furey children when her Cooper daughters had abandoned her. Her own daughters wouldn't spend any time at Chardin anymore. If she had a problem in her life, it was her Cooper daughters. Otherwise she was happy.

The winter days were long and warm and Anton and she were quite fat. They drank too much, but had just come up with a compromise: they would no longer drink during the week. Just to say that felt good. The rented house came with a cook and a maid, and local children played on the patio overlooking Billy's Bay and the Caribbean. Alice fondly called the house "a Chardin by the sea" because of all the people. Even the lawyer and his girl and Laurence and his wife were there. Even the grandmother was there. She flirted with all the island children who hung around the house. "Little natives," she called them, telling them she was going to bring them all back to America and teach them to make ice cream in a washing machine so that they could get rich. "Grammy," Alice reprimanded. At night the family built bonfires on the beach and drank good Jamaican rum.

After Christmas, close to New Year's, Anton organized a boat ride to a lagoon where they would see alligators. On the trip, Anton got seasick. Like that. *Boom!* He came back clutching his stomach, complaining of cramps. He took his nausea medicine, he drank special concoctions, but the cramping would not go away. Eve had little patience. She could not bear a sick man. "It hurts so bad, babe," he'd complain, eyes wincing with a bit of despair.

December turned into late January and they were back at home and it was cold and snowy—the worst winter in years with drifts making it impossible to drive up the driveway. "You see, it's just alarmism, this talk of global warming," Eve would tell her daughters. Then, "This is the way winters should be." "Oh, Mom. Oh, Mom," they'd say, tired of her optimism.

Outside, the world was covered with snow and she liked it like that. Fresh. All the scars hidden. Each day or two a new blanket would fall. She didn't mind hiking up the driveway in knee-high boots or being trapped at home with her mother and husband. In fact, before the big storms they would drive to the market for supplies, enough to last a week. They counted on being trapped. They loved to be trapped. These snow days reminded her of when the children were young and they had just recently moved to Chardin. The snow would blow in and the cars would get stuck in the driveway and soon be covered by the drifts. All of them in the house for a few days, off from school and excited, feeling as if they didn't need anybody else. How safe that made her feel. The kids would take turns cooking fancy treats—Kate with her brownies that always turned rock hard no matter what she did. "Rockies," the others called them. In the afternoons they would pull out the toboggans and race down the hill with long scarves trailing behind them. This was how she remembered the past, so nineteenth century to Eve. By the frozen pond deep in the woods, wrapped up tight in their wool, they would skate. All of them skated beautifully, executing twirls and figure eights. Anton would build a fire at the edge of the frozen water, sometimes it would flurry, and they would heat hot chocolate and toast marshmallows, and all of them would wish for the snow days to last.

Her daughters now refused to remember these moments. If it were up to them, the past would be pure misery. Eve wondered, Is it fashionable to be miserable? It hadn't been miserable. It had been fun. She thought of how their lives would have been had Ian stayed with her—so conventional. They never would have traveled to Haiti or Mexico or camped in cornfields in Kansas or argued about Nietzsche and Marx and communism and Beethoven. She was mad at her girls for their determination to see only the ugly. She was also jealous of her girls, that they had each other, that they talked several times a day; she wished she had a sister. She knew her daughters stayed on the phone with each other even if they no longer had anything to say.

THE SNOWSTORMS tumbled in with the regularity of waves. But even so, despite the fun, Anton's cramps persisted.

"Something's wrong, babe. I don't have a good feeling about the outcome of all this," he said. He had lost ten pounds.

"Nonsense," she said, and kissed his forehead. "You're looking good. I wish I could lose ten pounds."

In early February he saw the doctor. His blood work was fine, but an X ray showed three spots on the liver. "Spots on the liver!" skidded across Eve's mind. They were standing in the doctor's office. White walls, beige chairs. Muzak in the outside waiting area leaked through to her ears. "Spots on the liver." With those few words her life drained from her. Anton's cold hand clutched her arm. She could feel it, her life pouring out of her. She watched it like a puddle on the floor. She would have to help this man die. In that instant all the times she had hated Anton left her. She had always loved him. There had never been any fighting. He was always good. She looked at him, her strong handsome husband, and thought of everything they had had. Hiking over the mountains in Haiti, just the two of them. They were invited into the hut of a couple and the couple offered them tea and then a meal of stewed chicken and vegetables. They had had hardly enough food for the trek from Port-au-Prince to Jacmel. The stew was warm and thick with sauce. The hut had smelled of rosemary. The couple with their dark skin and bright eyes gave them mats to sleep on and in the morning, porridge sweetened with sugarcane. "The kids would love it here, babe," Anton had said. "Let's bring them back." His face lit up with the promises of life.

She thought of how he had believed in her mind when they had first met. Believed that her mind was smart, that she could do anything she dreamed. She saw her younger self standing in his small blue-lit office, crying in her taffeta dress. Her mind, described by his words, blossomed into a coun-try—uncharted territory to be explored and exalted. He was the only person to have believed in her in this way.

In the beige doctor's office Anton looked to Eve, but she could not look him in the eye. She could not bear to see the terror she knew would be there. Cancer. The word continued to skid across her mind. She refused to look at Anton. He touched her arm, gave it a gentle squeeze. She could feel his eyes on her. She wanted them off of her. She could not help him die. She would not help him die.

The doctor ordered a CAT scan. They went home. They waited. The unknown swirling through their lives, wrapping around them like the roots of weeds. Their futures opened and closed like a fan.

People would say things to them like, "Doctors these days are very cautious, afraid of lawsuits" or "There are other things that this could be" or "You don't know until you have the facts" or "Let me tell you a story about a friend of mine who..."

Had this news been delivered to one of her daughters, they would have been on the phone with each other, a three-way conversation. Talking and talking and working the problem and crying and soothing one another until the news was so fully integrated into all of them that it lost some of its power because they knew that they were each there.

IT TOOK FOUR DAYS to get the results of Anton's scan. In those four days Eve saw him in the casket, saw the casket lowering into the ground. She would stare at him when he was not looking and imagine what he would look like dead. Wanting to divine the unknown, she read lives that came before: Anton's father had also been sixty-four when he had died. Eve's mother had been fifty-eight, same as Eve now, when she had lost her husband. Eve saw these facts like a road map to their lives. Tea leaves.

In those four days time stopped. They had no future, just the present. "Live in the present," Anton and Eve used to tell the kids, though they had always enjoyed living in the swirl of dreams. And in these four days they tried hard not to think about trips back to Jamaica, the piece of land they wanted to buy in Billy's Bay, the workshop at Esalen they had planned to take Sofia to in hopes that they would come to some sort of understanding.

As the four days passed, Eve's love for Anton grew to enormous proportions. In those four days anything Anton wanted was his. Eve bought him new clothes, gave him a thousand dollars for his bank account, which was low. She loved doing this—it was as if she could buy him back to health. She liked having him so clearly dependent and vulnerable. She felt reassured and safe. He needed her so absolutely. "I'm afraid, babe." And in giving, she became able to manage. It was as if he could never leave.

When the news came that the spots on the liver were only hemangiomas—there since childhood—their futures burst open. A deluge of possibility. All they had ever wanted they decided would be theirs. Anton applied for the loan so that they could buy that land overlooking the water in Billy's Bay, so that they could add on to the house, restore the indoor swimming pool, replace the outdoor pool's heater. Their lives became dreams again.

The doctors, like God's messengers in their white robes, had come to Anton and Eve in the white office with the beige chairs and Muzak (that suddenly sounded beautiful—trumpets and horns) and gave them back their lives. The doctors (there were two of them now) said, "The spots on the liver were simply hemangiomas, there since birth most likely. Nothing to be alarmed by." Nothing to be alarmed by? Relief settled into every part of them—the exhausted beauty of birth. Eve liked the feeling. The intensity of the last few days, the worrying, the anxiety, the frantic running around. She thought, All that worry had worked. I've done it again. The power of my will. Residual omnipotence. And then she knocked wood. She knew better than to brag about good fate. They went home and drank scotch and toasted each other and their long list of plans. They called all the kids to tell them with relief that Anton had once again emerged from danger unscathed—like being on that desolate Mexican highway late at night, rolling into town on empty.

"Babe," Anton said to Eve. His head rested in her lap. She stroked his thin hair. They sipped the scotch. The room was dark. The fire blazed. Snow covered the ground. "I was scared, babe." The fire hissed and crackled, its light dancing across the room. "I was afraid that I wouldn't have been able to be brave."

"Oh, you would have," she said with glee because illness was not something they were going to have to face now.

"No, listen to me. Hear me out. It's my book, babe. If I'd been sick, I wouldn't have been able to finish my book." She kept running her fingers through his hair. She said some encouraging words about his book, and then stood up to get started on something—dinner perhaps, straightening the living room. Her life had been given back to her and she did not like to sit still. Or had it been given back to her? she wondered for an instant before banishing the idea. "Please, babe," he said, trying to keep her with him, there in that moment. He needed her. "Without it done..." He stopped. She knew how to finish the sentence. "It's over now," she said. "It's over," she said again. Soothing him. "You still have the chance."

CHAPTER EIGHTEEN

To Deny Our Hearts

SOMETIMES ANTON would drive. Mozart or Beethoven or Chopin or Bach or anyone classical on the radio. His car gliding over the roads—smooth roads, wheels rolling over tar, rolling, going, driving. Somewhere. Anywhere. It gave him time to think. The possibilities were infinite on the open road. Cornfields and soy fields and pumpkin patches and wheat fields and grain fields and all of it parted by road—slick black road, the great American road. He had always loved to travel. Feeling the force of movement, momentum, propelling him. The soft wind caressing his face, running through his hair like fingers—like the tiny fingers of his tiny Alice, playing with his unruly hair. On the road he had time to dream.

I just need a little time, he would say to himself—a bargain. Just a little more time and I'll get it finished. That "it," that little "it" was his book.

On the road he thought about the book, made mental notes, made notes on index cards. *"To Deny Our Hearts,"* he mused, turned the phrase around in his head, where it blossomed into the physical object of a book—a hardcover book that he could hold in his hand. A good title? He would ask Alice later. Do you think it works? He would pose the question. She had listened to the notes for his book since she was first born. He had kept her with him in his study in her cradle and he had read to her for a good long stretch. She was the only one he could share his work with at this stage. Eve wasn't interested enough to be critical. But his Alice was, or certainly would be. Later, as he lay dying, she would tell him she felt like an experiment, his experiment. He would never have put it that way, but he had wanted her to know everything that he knew; he wanted to teach it all to her himself. He wanted her to be free from the burden of unconscious sex stereotyping that plagues girls; he wanted to teach her to hear and discern. He could see his tiny daughter sitting in the big and overstuffed chair in his office, listening. Her feet dangling toward the floor, her big eyes wide with concentration.

Rolling down the window, he practiced his title on the air. "*To Deny Our Hearts: Contemporary Attacks on Sexual Passion.*" Road beneath him. Road in front of him. "*This book is a revolutionary attempt to depict sexuality as the integral desire for the other rather than as something apart from the self's deepest essence.*" He had been writing this sentence for days.

He was a philosopher. He had his *doctorat d'état* from the Sorbonne. He had worked beside R. D. Laing—taken acid with the man—and studied with Paul Ricoeur and Norman Brown. He had published plenty of articles. All he needed now was a book. "*A major goal of this work,*" he shouted to a jolly farmer driving his red tractor across the field, "*is to suggest that there has never been a 'genuine' sexual revolution, and that none is in sight.*" The farmer waved as everyone did in Pennsylvania. "*Which would answer Rilke's plaintive cry against repression and self-division and give us a 'home' within our sexuality.*" The deeper he drove into Pennsylvania, the more religious the world became. Signs poked up from the edge of the road promising another chance: YE SHALL BE BORN AGAIN.

"What is Rilke's plaintive cry?" his little girl had asked him—all eyes, big gray eyes. She spoke, kicking her toes into the shag rug.

"Well you see, babe." He hesitated. He couldn't explain to her about the Catholic Church and repression and the fear of allowing eros with all its perversities and enigmas to be integral with the id and fully human. He couldn't acknowledge to her that human sexual experience with one beloved has been disappointing because it has never been accepted as integral to human experience. "Well you see, babe." He couldn't explain sex and sexuality to a tiny child. But Rilke, perhaps Rilke could explain—sexuality becoming animate like a soul adrift, searching for a home, afloat in the universe, and Rilke, standing at the edge of it, shouting with the full force of his lungs, begging to feel complete.

She had sat in his office and listened to him many times. She knew that what he said was important. She sat and listened patiently, her eyes surveying his study with all its books and newspaper clippings and note cards scrawled with his thick red ink. Against one wall were his gynocracy collages, the latest branch of his work—poster boards covered with pictures of women cut from art history textbooks, newspapers, brochures. Women being adored by men; virgins shunning beasts; temptresses tempting innocent, unsuspecting men.

"What is Rilke's cry?" Alice asked again.

"Imagine your foot," he said to her. He was trying to make sense for himself, of course, and she was his ear. All ears. His echo. He imagined someday they would really be able to have a dialogue and, like a family business, she would train with him. Maybe she would even help him write a book. "Imagine that for centuries you had been taught that this foot was separate from you and when you used it to walk you had to be conscious of it, acknowledge with guilt that it was carrying you somewhere." He lifted her foot and held it in his big hand, her sole fitting neatly into his palm. "But the foot is integral to who you are. It isn't anything special. Well, that's how sex should be—not semidetached like a colony or a motherland that the ultimate and inner self has to use or abuse."

"But it is special," she declared emphatically, her eyes holding him, because she was smart, his wise child. "If I didn't have my foot, I wouldn't walk."

"Precisely."

"Sex is like a foot," she said, and she looked at her foot, as if trying to grasp the meaning. "Integral to who we are."

"This is the essence of my book." It seemed so easy.

Driving gave Anton time. That time, just a little more time. He would get in his car and drive, drive all day, first thinking—doing work—then exploring. Exploring the small back roads of New Jersey and Pennsylvania, exploring signs that looked interesting. He tried to find things, places to bring Alice and Eve, places that would surprise and delight them. A vineyard, a junk shop, a private zoo of cats of the world—African lions and Bengali tigers, cougars abandoned by zoos. A lady who had a farm with one thousand ducks, ducks as far as you could see, quacking, shitting ducks, and it seemed the woman had a name for each of them. He'd run errands, have a coffee at the coffee shop, argue with the pharmacist about the hostage crisis, be teased at the lumberyard about the second bounced check, visit Laurence at his studio. He flirted with them all. He planned the elaborate trips and parties of the years for the family—up the canal on a mule barge lit with fairy lights to celebrate Jane's and Caroline's graduation from high school. Always he would think about his book. He had so much to say. There was so much that had been misunderstood about sex, about love. It was his job, his calling, his contract with God, with life, to say it. "It" little "it," his book.

To the duck woman and all of her ducks he explained. Standing there with the ducks pecking at his feet, the woman's house spilling a chaos of junky furniture and old clothes and clothes on a drying line. Her big brown eyes looked at Anton. He spoke with her all afternoon, surrounded by ducks, until he bought a dozen ducks for Alice—black and white and brown speckled ducks. The duck woman punctured holes in a box with an ice pick she carried in her pocket like a comb, and then she crammed in the ducks.

"I'm a writer," he told her boldly as she shoved the last duck in.

"I've never met a writer," she said. "Mostly I'm with the ducks." There was one duck in particular, a black duck spotted with white polka dots, a fierce duck that bit, that waddled at her side. "This is my assistant," she said, noticing Anton's stare.

"Your assistant? What does he help you do?"

"He helps me keep all these other ducks in line. Ducks can be quite mean, but not with my assistant helping me out." Twelve ducks were crammed into the one box. Anton didn't know what he'd do with them once he got them home, but he knew they'd delight Alice as they waddled, one after the next, out of the small box. Twelve ducks on the front lawn. Duck eggs, he thought.

"Are duck eggs any good?" Then he had an idea, a

menagerie at Chardin with goats and pigs and ducks and chickens and peacocks and mules and calves and even a llama to keep away the foxes. He would build a barn and have a real farmyard, give it to Alice for her birthday.

"The best," she said. "They're gamy." She wrapped a bandanna around her head, pulling her hair back. With her hair back she was beautiful. It seemed her face was there just to hold those two huge brown eyes, like a box designed specially for jewels. With her hair back like that she reminded him of a young nun from Sacred Heart in Grand Coteau. He felt a charge, all warmth. "What kind of a writer are you anyway?"

He told her that he was a philosopher and about his book and that we come from a long tradition of people who had been antisexual and self-alienated and that we are still today and he was trying to write about this in order to liberate people from the trap of the loneliness of their own sexuality. Just speaking, hearing his own voice and his own ideas, filled him with a confidence and the desire to love this woman. He thought again of the young nun. To lie her among the ducks and take her bandanna off and make love to her there with the vicious assistant watching.

"Do you have a husband?" Anton asked, lowering his eyes shyly.

"Only ducks." She smiled, an alluring little smile with her head cocked ever so slightly to the right. Ducks as far as he could see. At their feet were ducks and beneath their feet was duck shit, wet and muddy. He stepped closer, telling her more about his book, about love and sexual equality and Rilke's plaintive cry and the need for a home. She was thin and bony in his arms, but alive and warm and welcoming. He felt like a cowboy in Texas one hundred years ago. He was determined to be passionate and free and unconstrained by the world, by the ducks. The duck lady led him to a clean patch of hay near a little shack and they lay on it and somehow it was as soft as down. The ducks parted. The assistant looked on. A car went by on the road. A plane flew low overhead. A thin breeze blew over them, ruffling the feathers of all the ducks.

We are the heirs, not of a series of profoundly affirmative sexual revolutions, but of a wearily ironic and detached vision of all things erotic that pervades and stretches through every spiritual tradition, Eastern and Western, every therapeutic or esoteric wisdom, every philosophy, meta-psychology, literature, and art in the world.

It was good sex and it seemed to last a long time, the ducks like an audience, the assistant silenced, its beak gaping open, the woman beneath him, on top of him. Mud. Sex, like a foot, integral to who we are.

"I gotta get back to work," she said, wiping herself off.

"Do you do that with everyone who buys a duck?" Anton asked, becoming possessive. He wanted her for himself. He wanted to come back frequently and have her there, waiting for him.

"Are you gonna start thinking I'm yours now?" she said softly. They were silent and awkward for a while. But he could see a little hopeful upturn to her lips.

"Can I visit you again?" he finally asked.

"You know where to find me."

"This was a surprise," he said. "Magnificent." He picked up the box of ducks. "Do you think they're still alive?"

"They're alive," she said. He walked toward his car. It was late. Once again he was going to be late to pick up Alice. He imagined her sitting on the curb outside her school, reading, waiting. They would drive home to the house filled with kids and it would be time to organize dinner jobs and to negotiate fights, to become someone else—the day slipping off of him like clothes.

"That's some pretty racy stuff you're working on," she said to his back. "Not exactly a romance novel, though. Who's gonna read it?"

Anton turned around. He saw her standing there with her big eyes. He still felt like a cowboy—exhilarated, triumphant, knight of the West. After he picked up Alice he'd go home and work for a while. Close the door to his study and tell the kids not to bother him. If only he could make love to Eve as he had just now, with ducks, with nothing interfering, with her belief in him strong. "Everyone," Anton said. He wanted a revolution, nothing less. "Everyone. I hope."

FOR SIXTEEN YEARS he drove. Sure, he did other things as well. For a while he had the art gallery, then the berry business, his practice, his book. But always, Anton drove. Long endless roads. A breeze in his hair, a warm and hopeful wind on his face. By the side of the road he would pull over sometimes to light a joint, turn up the Mozart—Dennis Brain horn concertos, first and third and Julia's favorite. Sweet, beautiful Julia. He would lean back into his seat and inhale deep and long. His lungs filling, big, billowing. Alive. This was long before he got sick, when his baby Alice was just beginning school. Many years before the pains in his back. His future still seemed infinite and though he had gone away from the Church he vaguely believed that Christ was guiding him. His head swirled with the smoke in his lungs. Particularly when he was stoned, it felt more as if he could trust that

Christ stood by his side and thus he did not feel alone. He felt
the elasticity of time—the full illusion of its infinite reach.

*And yet, human sexuality continues to baffle the cynics—
in music, in the resonant zest of young lovers, in the interior
confessions of the aged—"The world will always welcome
lovers" because they seem like remnants of some lost Atlantis,
emissaries of an innocent, unforgettable truth. Perhaps there is
something in this continuing "triumph of hope over experience"
mocked by Oliver Holmes, that suggests something untried between man and woman. Perhaps what Chesterton said about
Christianity, that "it is not so much that it has been tried and
found to fail, as that it has never been tried at all," applies as
well to human sex. Perhaps there is something about the
"human," which has not been noted or explored. Perhaps the
Romeo-Juliet quality of fairy-tale love has a hidden intention-
ality or promise, which might lead humanity to the only inte-
gration, or nonalienation, which is possible—a triple unity of
self with the beloved, with God. Is our bemused response to
such a naive question not itself a piece of armor?*

Thick red ink on small index cards. He loved the feel of
pen on paper, the urgency. The whole car infused with Brain's
Mozart and the smoke of marijuana. Turn some Mozart
music on real low so that it seems it is coming from a distance, Father Master had said. And then the world seems
simple again. Anton leaned back in his seat by the side of the
road. He saw the wizened old Father Master in cassock and
cincture beads, could feel his big warm hands and his penetrating eyes. Anton saw the neat rows of marble tombstones
in the cemetery at Grand Coteau where Father Master lay—
and the lazy cows of the farm just beyond. He wondered for
a moment if Father Master could see him. Sixteen, ten, eight

years in front of him and an infinity of ideas. *Eros and Ego,* he thought of as a chapter title. *The Self against Sex.* The ideas kept coming. So simple. He was writing the book in his head. Potential blossomed, the will and desire to be heard. He thought of something simple: showing his hardback and published book to his mama. Handing it to her. Just that, handing it to her. His mama standing tall in front of him, her white hair crowning her large head. Her baby boy had made something of himself as she always knew he would. He had gotten out of flat empty Texas and into the world. She would be standing on the porch of their Dallas home with that same broad smile, that same proud grin on her face—the one she had when he told her he was going to Grand Coteau. "The Lord has chosen you," she said. "You Anton, my son. The Lord has chosen my son for such a miraculous vocation. My son, imagine that." And then she told all her friends, hoping to instill in them not a little envy.

HE BEGAN DRIVING first, and so extensively, when Alice went to kindergarten and he no longer had her to take care of. It was 1978. The end of summer. Outside hot and thick with humidity of the New Jersey kind. You could swim in the air. Anton dropped Alice off at school, just a half day for that first year. He watched his little life walk into the lime green cinder block school—all determination and fearlessness— leaving him at an absolute loss. He stood in the parking lot for a good fifteen minutes, feeling part of him drain, wishing he could go in there with her, sit and watch her learn, protect her from stupid teachers. What could she learn in there that he couldn't teach her? They had already read and discussed Hegel, Marx, Kierkegaard, and Chesterton and Teilhard de Chardin and Castaneda and Rilke. He had read to her the outline of his book on love and sexuality. Together they listened for hours at a time to Beethoven, Handel, Verdi, Chopin, Mozart, Mozart, Mozart. (He could not imagine the world before Mozart.) His girl had gone inside the school and his life as he had known it for the past five years was about to change forever.

"Pop," her little voice said. Alice had reemerged from the lime green cinder blocks. She stood half in, half out. "I'll be all right, Dad. I'm curious about school." He just looked at her, her large forehead, his forehead, her head, his head, her long skinny legs, his legs, her mind, his mind.

"I know you will, babe," he said. He wanted to grab her, snatch her back. He couldn't remember what he had done before she existed.

"I'll tell you about the teachers," she promised. She studied him. She wanted him to let her go, but he wouldn't.

"You'll know about them just by looking in their eyes. Don't be afraid of their eyes."

She studied the ground. Inside, homeroom was in progress, all the children saluting the flag. The young voices drifted across the parking lot, pledging allegiance to the United States of America. Alice stepped all the way outside now, lit by the sun. The sun caught in her hair as if she could shake it loose. A vast and hazy sky. A jet overhead. She walked toward her father. He didn't speak. "Go home and work. After school you can read me what you've done. Go home and work, Pop. You have time now." His little wise girl. Time. More time now. Big and infinite time. He had sixteen years to be exact. She smiled at him, a big squinty-eyed smile, his smile. "Why don't you try not being late for me?" she laughed, teasing him.

And then she was gone again.

When the bell rang and the parking lot was quiet except for the sounds of settling engines, he got in his car. Slowly he started the car. He looked at the clock, 8:45, and wondered what he would do for the next four hours. He thought about going home and working, sitting at his desk and thinking, just taking a few notes, reading a few passages, clipping a few articles. His office was a jungle of clippings from the *TLS, The New Statesman, The New York Review of Books, Modern Psychology*—reviews for which he had written once upon a time. He thought of his office: Index cards and poster boards dripping from the rafters. Filing cabinets spilling articles on love, sexuality, feminism. The pictures of women cut from art books. He needed more space, another office. He would go home and organize his office. He loved organizing his thoughts on index cards, taping them to the walls, the rafters. His office itself was an outline of his work. He'd prepare something to share with Alice later.

The accumulation of substitute love-objects is fascinating, ranging from God to self to seamless humanity to science to "sex" itself. But the rub is always the same: sex is separated from the essential self, and then destroyed either by "use" or "non-use." My own hypothesis centers on the new union of equals that the sexual liberation movement makes possible, and which, in fact, was the only union ever sought by human eros.

Yes that was it, a great part of his quest: the union of equals. "Love will be something less if it is not something more." It is what he sought with Agnes, with Eve—his ambition, one of his dreams.

It had been a long while since he had had uninterrupted time to work. Simply, slowly, not too much pressure. One sentence, one paragraph, at a time. But instead he started to drive. He thought, Just for a little while, just a short drive, just to see the country, the Delaware, the subtle hills of Bucks County.

Out there in Texas—large empty flat—his father used to drive. Anton and Mama would accompany Daddy on trips to sell paper and paper packaging for Dorman Paper and Box Company. They drove to east Texas and west Texas with all its knobby hills, to the Gulf of Mexico and the Mexican border. They drove in a company Cadillac with Anton in the back next to the neatly stacked samples and brochures. Outside was hot and dry and dusty, northers swirling debris in mini typhoons. They held handkerchiefs over their mouths so they wouldn't breathe it in even though the windows were shut to protect Mama's hair. Texas as far as you could see.

His father peddled packaging for breads and towels and frozen foods and teas and even dental floss. It was his job to win the contract for Imperial Sugar, say, or Borden or Gulfwax or Kroger's or Gandy's or Chiffon. So they drove wide and far. On his father's and mother's mind was work— how to bring in Sunbeam, Holsum, Lipton, Decker, Glen Eden. "If only you get Lipton," his mama would say, her eyes bright. If Lipton were a client, Anton's father's account would double with just one customer and then attract other big names. "We could get a bigger house and I could get some new clothes," his mama would say. "I'm tired of that stuffy house." Each morning when they took Anton to school they passed the mansions of Highland Park. "I want to live in Highland Park." Mama would pause, her dreams swirling in her head like the sharp wind outside. Anton saw his mama in the grocery store holding up a package of frozen peas with pride and a grin that said, Daddy. "How about a ranch with a pool." Smiling and sitting by his side on those long Texas roads. Road, just road, cutting through nothing. On the radio the Loudermilk Brothers sang about being broad-minded and Mama hummed along, caught up in a brighter future of velvet dresses and silk hats. She sat up straight and proud, Daddy's manager, his encourager, his boss. Daddy was her vehicle transporting her to a better future. For the moment she believed in him, believed he could protect her, provide for her, make her life safe. When she was a girl, her daddy drove off to Hollywood in a Pierce Arrow with the rooftop down to become the pharmacist to the stars, leaving her with a sick and dying Mama and some Ursuline nuns in a convent. Her husband was her savior, saving her from all that.

Anton, too, in the back, would think about the possibilities that a Lipton account would bring. Anton, a skinny long-legged little boy in shorts with suspenders pulling over an ironed short-sleeved shirt. "Loudermilk's a crazy name," he'd say, finding hope in the strangeness of the name. He unrolled the window to let the air smack against his face. Even Daddy sat tall, believing in himself. Then the car would go silent with all of them far away. Even the radio music would seem to pause. It would seem to Anton that they were praying to the Lord of Lipton and that would feel both bad but necessary. Necessary because just a little more would make their lives a little easier. Bad because his mama spoke against materialism. She taught that faith alone should be enough. "My hair, Anton, Mama's hair. Put up that window."

The Lipton building was low and flat and sprawling like a kingdom. Daddy walked toward it, slow and confident—a man with time. It seemed it took forever for him to disappear into the buildings, but Anton and Mama watched each step. Even after he was gone, sitting in the Cadillac, Mama chanting prayers in the front seat, it seemed Anton could still see his daddy walking—impossibly small against those buildings.

Mama kept checking her watch, as if she could discern in

the crystal their fate. And when Daddy walked back toward the car she looked at the watch again and knew that one hour was too short. But she kept hoping until he reached the car.

"Well, we gotta stay in there and pitch," Daddy said, trying to light his face with confidence. "There'll be other accounts," he reassured.

Mama sank down low in her seat and they were just there, in Texas, the big bouncy car bouncing over the road. "You weren't forceful enough," she said, all ideas of being saved, of being able to rely on him, disintegrating. "I bet you let 'em see how vulnerable you are. You can't ever be vulnerable. People know it. They sense it. If you're vulnerable, they flee." Her face fell into her hands and she tried to cry, but it was a fake cry because she knew better. Luck doesn't change so easily or so fast. But she knew her crying would hurt Daddy and she wanted him to suffer. If he suffered, somehow she would be able to feel a little special, that he cared. "If I'd been in there. If I'd been in there . . . Oh shoot. Anton and I should have stayed at home. We like it when it's just us. Don't we, Anton? Don't we?"

Daddy's hands rested on the wheel, eyes hard on the road. His face stained with that almost grin. Inside he thought life was suppose to be something more. "The northers are driving me insane. I've got a headache all the time now," Mama said. If she knew how she tortured him, how he loved her, she would not have persisted. She may even have been happy. Mesquite trees hugged the ground, desperate for water, crouching low as if trying to hide from the sun. They drove in silence. Then Mama leaned into the backseat. "You're too smart for here." Her eyes latched on to Anton, holding him—he her potential savior now. Anton looked at his daddy, the forced cheeriness hanging beneath his eyes, the weakness of his posture, which held the frame of failure, and he never wanted to be like that. Outside, the world—the dust of Texas—a shroud around them.

THE LIGHT FAILED in the late afternoon, whiskey-colored and warm. It was time to go home. Anton would work tomorrow. Tomorrow was always better, always smoother. His mind would always be clearer, tomorrow. Tomorrow the light would do stunning tricks on the fields while his imagination cleared. He would listen to a little Mozart. He would not smoke. He would take a day off from smoking. The possibilities for tomorrow widened. A clean slate. He'd finish his book, sell it. He wouldn't need alimony from Agnes anymore. He'd be a provider. (What man doesn't, somewhere, dream of that.) Eve could quit catering. Perhaps she'd even respect him more. The thrill of tomorrow. A clear and lucid mind. He could stop for today.

Then he found Lily at the farmers' market selling raspberry pies. She had a stand of raspberry pies, dozens of them, beautiful in their rows—the crusts bleeding a sweet and juicy red. They were arranged beneath the shade of a willow tree on a picnic table and he bought them all. He had the berry business by now and he decided, on seeing the pies, that he would hire her to make pies. She was blond and smiley and interested. All of her attention was on him, zeroed in and focused.

What do you do?

Where do you live?

You're a philosopher?

A therapist?

You're writing on love and sexuality?

She told him a story. Her teeth were white and perfectly aligned and her smile big enough to feature them. She had married a man who discovered he was gay when she was six months pregnant. He left her for New York City, waiting several months before he bothered to contact her to explain. He left with his clothes and the car and the television set. After the once she never heard from him again. Now she made pies and sold them at farmers' markets, and sometimes by the side of the road, and wondered how this had happened to her.

Anton wanted to save her. For a few weeks he came to her stand and bought pies. She sipped her vodka from her Perrier bottle discreetly, he lit a joint and smoked, she took a puff. After a while they went to her house and listened to *Nabucco*—long afternoons of *Nabucco*. He talked to her about sex and love and equality. Then came Rilke's plaintive cry. He spoke to her about his book and she lay there naked by the fire, naked on her bed, and she listened and they fucked and she listened and then she gave him a long and caressing massage, listening some more, encouraging him, contemplating with him his ideas. Before long she would have an office arranged for him in her house so that he could work there. Before long she wanted to save him, too. It was the first time he felt understood. Fucking her, he would feel guilty, he would feel that the eyes of God were watching and judging and later he would ask God why Eve couldn't listen the way Lily listened. If only Eve, he'd say. He'd say it for the rest of his life and Lily would be his last affair.

"*To Deny Our Hearts* will be your *Nabucco*," she whispered to his ear. *Nabucco* had made Verdi's career. He had only had minor success before *Nabucco*, and his wife and children had all died in illness and he was alone and isolated and frustrated. *Nabucco* was a big opera, lots of brass with a big chorus and it was metaphorically about the unification of Italy—the joining of many to make a large and coherent whole. That was all Anton wanted. He wanted his book to do that with sex. He wanted his life to do that with his family. And Lily understood this and wanted to help him achieve these dreams.

Then he'd say to God, to Eve, to himself, You're not gonna stop me from loving Lily. I'm not gonna feel guilt.

"The beast in the belly," he said to Lily, kissing her belly, in explanation for his uncontrollable desire for her. "Lovers are a curiosity. Like remnants of some lost Atlantis. But why?"

"Why not stop thinking for a while?" she said, and dragged her fingertips over the length of his body. Just the very tips of her fingers until she made goose bumps rise on his skin.

WHEN ANTON DIED there would be no tombstone. Eve would make promises to the kids, to herself. She would draw designs, Irish crosses, search for the perfect poem or phrase. But her ideas were always too ambitious, too expensive, and there were always other more pressing bills. It is in death as it is in life, some old truism explains. After the funeral Lily would have to hunt for his grave before finding it. A tiny metal plaque nearly buried in the grass would read ANTON NICHOLAS FUREY, JUNIOR, 1930–1994. So small she would nearly miss it. Once she found it, she planted flowers, kept the grave up. She planted lilies, in the spring, maliciously so that Eve would know she had been there. After a while she realized that the lilies had gone unnoticed by Eve and if any of the children came, they probably thought Eve had planted them since Anton had loved lilies. After a while Lily realized her visits to the grave didn't need to be secretive. Eve never went. If Lily had had money she would have bought a marble tombstone.

Sometimes she dreamed that she would erect one, that she would have enough money before Eve. What would Eve do? Take it down? On the tombstone Lily would make it clear that it was her gesture. On hers she would have written Anton's dates alongside her own name and birth date—leaving her death date blank. Eve would concoct some way of rationalizing it and then she would forget about it. But until then Lily planted flowers and made up stories about how she and Anton would have lived the rest of their lives. She would lie on top of his grave and shut her eyes and imagine that they had been emissaries of an innocent and unforgettable truth, remnants of some lost Atlantis.

"YOU DIDN'T WORK, POP," Alice said as Anton showed her his discoveries. He could see it in her wise expression, what she was thinking. "You were just driving and what's that going to do for your book. If you write your book, Pop, you'll be happy. If you write your book, it'll make things easier for you." He looked at his child and saw his mother, saw himself handing her a book and making her proud. "You helped me, babe," he would say.

"But I had some good ideas," he said. "I was able to think. Don't be too hard on your poor old man. It'll get done." He smiled his melting smile, a grin with squinting eyes—vulnerable yet strong.

Then Alice would be gone again and he would be driving again. Inflated, deflated. By the side of the road he lit a joint and cried, softly, then with gentle rage.

"Why are you so angry?" he could hear his little girl ask.

"Because of fear," he would answer. Fear of what? Well, for example, at his death he would have produced fifty-four outlines and no book. Thousands of index cards with scrawled notes and no book. Thousands of index cards with quotations from famous men who had produced books. Ten collages and no book. His mind would be an archive of knowledge, but no book. Eve would find all this tucked away in a safe in his office—locked up tight in there for safekeeping, for posterity. An unburnable, unmeltable, unsinkable safe containing unreadable jottings from an unrealized book. She would have to break into the safe with professional help and as she did so, she would be hoping, praying, to find a manuscript. His *Nabucco*—she, too, had hoped. She would read each outline carefully, willing it to blossom into a book, a coherent book. She would never have the heart to throw the notes away. The remnants of his work would stay in the basement for as long as Chardin was theirs.

He cried because he had no purpose. He cried because he was a philosopher pregnant with ideas that he could not birth. He cried because there were nine children needing him and how he wanted to be needed but felt he had so little to give. And this caused him to rage, to swell with impotence. Why was it so difficult to put a simple idea on the page, string one after the other together, create a book? Why was it so hard to be a priest, live in the world, make Mama proud? Sometimes he felt as if he, too—his person—were one of his many outlines. He saw himself as the little boy in the back of the Cadillac watching his father in the front seat with his sad round ridiculous grinning face. "Stay in there and pitch, son," his father would say. How he longed for his father. He saw his father on his deathbed with that same grin—secure and unafraid in his faith. On that Texas road, the world utterly flat and empty and hot and dry. "You're too good for this place," his mama had said. And he had believed her. He saw himself, a young priest in training with his knees pressed into the cold stone floor of his cell, trying to keep all those people in his prayers, trying to come up with sermons while sex and desire tugged at him, slithered up his leg, wrapping around his torso like a Louisiana cottonmouth. He took another puff of his joint. Smoke laced his mind. If he had no purpose, then he had betrayed his pact with Christ, with Eve, with the family. "The life of a religious is a soft life," a Jesuit friend had said. A pact for purpose, definition. "Please. I'll try harder. I'll write every day. Forgive me, please." He was bargaining for his life.

He was not negative. He was simply sad, trapped within the delicate walls of a bubble, the universe and all its beauty just outside for him to see, just through the thinnest film, to admire.

He got out of the car and walked into the field. A field of dead soy. The ground crunched beneath him. He walked for a long time, as if he were his father walking toward the Lipton building. They never had moved to Highland Park. His mother had become a better Catholic and had given up dreams of velvet dresses. Fields spread out, fields rolling into more fields, rolling into hills, then mountains, then sky. A white silo, a red barn, a black stallion running wildly in someone's yard, a herd of cows grazing on grass. He'd get the book done! Slopes and textures and colors. Rolls of wheat like polka dots against the dry fields. The smell of fresh pure drinkable air. Dry leaves swirling with purpose, the skip of squirrels, the music of birds. A wide pale violet sky hiding stars and the moon. Glorious inconstant moon. He promised. He swore.

CHAPTER NINETEEN

Quo Vadis

FOR A LONG WHILE after her father died Alice would ask herself, What would have happened if? Who would I be if? Where would I be if? The great What If. What if he hadn't gotten sick? What if death had remained something distant and vague and mysterious and far off for a few years more? Something that happened to others, but not to them?

On the night she killed her father, Thanksgiving was less than a week away. On Thanksgiving for the past twenty years she had been given an advent calendar—something small for sure, but something all the same that marked a ritual, that kicked off a tradition. On the tenth of December, Alice and Anton cut the Christmas tree. On Christmas Eve, they went to midnight mass. Afterward Anton read from *A Christmas Carol;* Santa visited even after she stopped believing in him. This was Anton's way of protecting Alice from time, of insuring for her—assuring her—that life would remain the same. A tacit promise of a father to a daughter that he would never go away.

What if she hadn't received the telegram in Bombay? What if she hadn't had to walk into the street with all those different things swerving around her—the rickshaws and the bullock carts, the cars and the lorries and the elephants and the cows—and what if she hadn't experienced the feeling of a complete and utter ending of a life that had seemed to be just beginning?

She was on the hot street in Bombay. She could smell the clove and the woodsmoke. She could see the stumps of the man with one arm and no legs on the skateboard who looked into her eyes with studied despair, not at his own condition, it seemed, but at the horror that he saw in her eyes.

She had flown halfway around the world to India. She had just graduated from college. She had won a fellowship and her life had spread out before her like a dream. Her father was sick but it was still early enough to deny it. Immediately she hated India, hated her Cooper sisters for romanticizing the country. She arrived at 2:00 A.M. at the Delhi airport, flying on to Bombay later in the morning. She walked from the terminal into a glass atrium and was greeted by thousands of faces pressing up close to the glass, a sea of faces beckoning.

One of the faces approached her as she walked out into the hot and muggy night and said he was a taxi driver and offered her a "cheap, very cheap" fare to Delhi, which she accepted. On the way, his car stalled. "Dead, madam," he said, glancing back at her. Just then another taxi approached and her driver leaned out the window and spoke fast in Hindi. It was very dark, with no moon, but on the road hundreds of small fires made the air creamy and mysterious. In the cab— a black Ambassador—mosquitoes swarmed at her feet. "Madam, you will have to go with my colleague here. This buggy is broke." The lilt of his words landed emphasis on *broke*. She looked out her window at the driver in the other car. He smiled a big red smile. It seemed his mouth was bleeding from whatever it was he chewed—betel it was called, making her think of beetles. He gestured for her to come. She unrolled her window and asked how much. The price was triple. "Sorry," she said. "But madam," her driver insisted. Other cars and trucks lumbered by. "But nothing," Alice said, leaning into the front. "You're trying to take advantage of me and I don't appreciate that." He wobbled his head and pretended not to understand. The other driver smiled the big red smile. He had a black and perfectly combed mustache. Some skinny men walked past with their dhotis wrapped up like bloomers. All the faces in the atrium had been male. She wondered if it had been so wise to take a taxi on her own. "What to do, madam?" her driver asked. "To start the car," she replied with a ferocity that surprised even herself. She was not easily intimidated. "The buggy does not work," he said, stressing *work*. "Yes, it does," she insisted. The other guy waited, smiling. There was nowhere to go. The triple price for the new ride was only a few dollars, but it was the principle that mattered. "Let me try," she said. "I'll start the car." And she reached up to the ignition with her long arms, fast before he had a chance to stop her, and she grabbed the key and turned it and the engine started easily. She slumped back in her seat, clutching her bag close to her chest and said, "Drive." This exchange, simple as it was, conferred on her the freedom of the traveler—outside of time, responsible to nothing, coming from anywhere. The car picked up speed heading toward the lights of the city and it felt finally as if she were leaving so much behind.

What if she had been able to stay in India? What if her father had never gotten sick? "Don't play the what-if game," her mother used to say. What if he had gotten sick a few years later? Would some cure have come along to save him—gene therapy, stem-cell miracles, human cloning? If... if. The possibilities were infinite for that tiny word. Alice liked tiny words that held big promises.

If things had unfolded in a different way, for one she would be whole. That much she knew for certain. The rest was conjecture, a matter of circumstance. Perhaps she would have fallen in love with an Indian. Perhaps she would have become a Hindi film star. Perhaps she would have been bought. An Indian man had asked her if she were for sale. He asked her while she was walking down Dalal Street near the Bombay stock exchange. The market had closed for the day but stocks were still being exchanged on the streets, crowds of men pulsing and surging as wads of rupees were handed back and forth. It seemed appropriate that if one were to be asked if she were for sale, it would occur in such a setting. Stacks of rupees a foot high. She wondered how many stacks she could get for herself. And she laughed at the preposterousness of the idea, but she speculated. *If,* wondering where he would have taken her *if,* what he would have done with her *if,* how many rupees he would have paid for her *if?* Would he have come to love her? He had a handlebar mustache (which, had he bought her, she would have insisted that he shave off) and he was half her size with glimmering light brown eyes and very dark skin—so slender she thought she could break him. Where would he have taken her? Would he have loved her? Would she have come to love him back? She stared at him, taking his proposal seriously for an instant. For an instant he looked hopeful.

Perhaps the *if* would have had a more banal imagination. Perhaps she would have come home after her year in India and India, as it had for her sisters, would have stood in her memory as simply a country, a year abroad in her young life. Receding like a dream with all its smells and beauty and contradictions. "The cliché," Kate said. "I went to India to discover myself. Well, if that's the case, I discovered I hated myself—squabbling with people over pennies because I would not be cheated."

Alice had been asked to act in a Hindi film. It was those fierce gray eyes, goddesslike, and her goddesslike stature—though she walked with her shoulders slumped forward—that drew people to her. She had liked being asked, thought she'd use the other half of her name, Alice Athene—how she loved the play of it, but how rarely she used her full name. Rather, Athene was like a secret, her father's private ambition for her to aim high.

There was something vulnerable about her, the way she cocked her head when she asked a question, or perhaps it was simply her beauty, that made strangers want to protect her. She liked being protected by people who did not know her. She remembered a man bending down to tie her shoelace on a crowded subway in New York City. "I didn't want you to trip," he had said.

She was in the hotel Taj Mahal on her three-day trip to India, for a breakfast meeting with a director. The hotel was an island of wealth in the midst of India. She went anyway, even though she had already heard The News. The director was to talk to her about Bollywood. Gucci and Vuitton luggage and women clad with gold made expensive sounds, a chorus, around her. She went because even though The News was fresh she wanted a glimpse of where she would have gone had she been able to stay in India. It had taken her months to arrange this interview. And she was killing time—an expression she hated because she loved time, wanted to be greedy with time, horde time in order to always have plenty, like money. Her plane didn't leave until 2:00 A.M.

She sat at a table that could have been anywhere with the

director, Luca. (Luca was his nickname, used in honor of his love for Italy. His real name was Sanjay Deep—of cinema Deep fame with his credit of five hundred films, which he claimed was not that many.) "Sorry, sorry, madam." He wobbled his head and spoke again. "You look so tragic. An angel of tragedy." Well dressed in a Nehru jacket. Warm eyes, small tidy man. He carried a cell phone that rang constantly. Each time it rang he checked the number of the caller and then did not answer. "Not important," he said, making her feel very important indeed. He shrugged his shoulders. He told her he would be happy to talk to her about Bollywood and Indian film. He had an enthusiasm for his craft that emanated from him seductively, like you could hold on to it and go for a tremendous ride. His wife was a movie star. He had a dimple that deepened each time he smiled. "Like Meena Kumari, very famous." Of course, Alice knew who she was, quite famous in America—she held the one available spot for the exotic. But this wife, he told Alice, would no longer work in Bollywood, only Hollywood or art films. His words drifted around her almost visibly as he spoke about actresses with names like Dimple, as he spoke about Lata the sweet nightingale of Indian singing, as he spoke about fantasy and lip-synching and stage design and working with unwritten scripts and difficult actors and the sheer number of films that had to be produced to stay afloat and be competitive. She couldn't keep up. She had not prepared herself. She had no questions. She was mute. Luca fell silent and it was as if an engine were just shut off. She could feel him study her, her dull response. She felt bad for wasting his time. She saw her father on his sea of white pillows. She was leaning over him, telling him that she would not leave unless he promised to visit. Her walnut hair spilled down her shoulders. How possible a visit had seemed, just as easy as stepping inside a dance sequence—shimmying ladies in the desert calling for rain that soon comes; star-crossed lovers reunited in the center of a lotus; a woman dancing on shards of glass to save her lover's life. To escape for a moment, a day, a year, a life. "I believe because it is absurd," her father had said often and with a smirk of wisdom.

If? Perhaps her family would have raised her father from his sickbed and followed her to India, dipping him in the Ganges so that the holy river could restore him to health. She pictured them all at the edge of the Ganges. Perhaps he would have felt better and flown them all to Khajuraho so that he could have studied the erotic carvings for his gynocracy collages and his book on love. Perhaps they would have watched her star in her own film at the edge of an emerald river and an ancient empire, dancing a love dance for her father. "Oh come on, babe, you're getting soft." Texas squint, inviting look, head tilted forward. She knew the gesture well, how it implied a romantic readiness, that whatever exchange was about to take place, be it with a child of his or a stranger, it was going to be both a pleasure for the other and for himself.

An Arab in all his Arab grandeur walked in with a harem of women and Luca asked just then if she wanted to try working with him in a film; she would really understand Bollywood by doing that. "I love your height and your big eyes and your high cheeks and forehead. With a little kohl you could look quite Indian." He smiled with delight at his idea, though the truth of her father kept gnawing away inside. He said more things she didn't hear, but spontaneously she laughed. He told her there was a long tradition of Westerners in Hindi films. She saw herself as a star in India, smiling brightly, five hundred feet tall, on one of those big painted movie posters that triumph over every city, town, and road. She saw herself tap-dancing across the keys of an enormous typewriter, belly dancing in the center of a giant lotus. Tough girl that she is, a sex symbol—she liked the notion. No one truly knew what she held in her core. Secretly, she had always wanted to be an actress. She wanted to be more talented than Julia, shine on the silver screen way above the lights of Broadway—both vulnerable and strong. A waitress served her coffee that she did not want. Muzak lurked beneath the murmur of rich people. She would call herself Athene most certainly! Her laughter rose above it all until the Arab and his harem turned to look at her, until all the noise in the restaurant stopped. "Where am I?" she asked Luca suddenly. He was silent looking at her, absorbing her gently with his warm eyes. "I like going out with Alice," her mother always said. "Strangers take such good care of her."

"You suffer," Luca said simply. She wanted to collapse against his chest and have him protect her, this stranger, this busy businessman with his incessantly ringing phone. If he gave her all of his attention it seemed that somehow she would be fixed, strong and able again. He put his hand gently on hers. "You must eat," he said. He held her eyes with his. They were big and warm and old, a little filmy. He asked her nothing, but made sure that she ate. Then he paid the bill and took her to his car. The day was extraordinarily hot, a thick heat you had to wade through, a thick heat catching dust and debris, holding on to it firmly so that you had to push it aside like gunk on top of a pond—unlike any heat she had ever known. For the rest of the afternoon Luca drove her around, not showing her anything really, just driving her through the streets, up into the Malabar Hills with views out to the Arabian Sea and a cool breeze. The car rocked her in the back-

seat, rocked her soothingly like a baby, and quietly he drove
and quietly she cried. At 2:00 A.M. he put her on the plane
and she flew home to her father.

ALICE LEFT HER FATHER in his bed. She put the morphine
back in the toes of the shoes, changed the pillowcases, rinsing
out the morphine stains. Hiding the evidence, she thought.
She wiped the morphine off his chin. Then, wrapped up
in hat and coat, she stepped into the bitter rainy night and
was soon on the highway, driving fast in her father's blue
Toyota van. Past farmland, dark expanses of shorn wheat and
cornfields. Past silos and barns and the silhouettes of cows
standing alone and in herds. No moon to speak of. An open
window and a cold wet wind on her face. November 20,
1994. She was etching the night into her mind. The farmland
dissolved into a pink and dazzling sky lit up with the neon of
Newark. On the bumper of the van ISRAEL PEACE NOW and
PRO-LIFE stickers shouted their message to whoever rode on
her tail, and Alice chuckled dully. She prayed to God for the
first time in a long time and thought of PRO-LIFE. She asked
God for forgiveness, asked him to try to have heart and understand. A PRO-LIFE sticker on the van, and she laughed
some more at the irony. She had just killed her father and
when she was no larger than a pencil he might have killed her.
She heard her sisters and brothers teasing, "We had a family
meeting and we all voted. It was a close call but you won."
She had never minded being teased like that by them as long
as they were all teasing together and in the same way. Fureys
and Coopers, no distinctions. Her father had asked his friends
at the Hastings Institute, weighing the moral consequences of
abortion and divorce. She imagined a bunch of Jesuits, ears
pressed to phone, granting her her life. She was twenty-one

years old and pro-choice, though pro-life had saved her. She had seen a bumper sticker once that read MOM WAS PRO-LIFE. THANK HER TODAY. Was her father at the gates of hell? she wondered. Or was St. Peter getting out his keys? Should she have listened to his confession, the impostor's final betrayal?

She had no idea where she was headed. The road stretched long and wide in front of her. In her pocket she had her father's bankcard and alimony check to cash. Forty-five hundred dollars. "I need cash, babe," he had said. "For what?" she had wanted to ask. She had her passport and a valid visa for India. The pink night welcomed her. She drove fast, toward India perhaps. Toward Luca perhaps. She wanted to be cradled in the back of his car, his gentle eyes warming her. Smokestacks spit fires which swirled into steam in the dazzling sky. Airplanes lifted into the clouds. Trains and cranes and cars—a conglomeration of highways, byways, cloverleaves. Big trucks. Church spires and church bells and the emphatic Budweiser sign and already the blinking decorations of Christmas on lawns that cut through industry with hope—Santa's reindeer and a blinking crèche. Newark rose up around her. She had known a boy in college, a pale fragile-looking boy with delicate eyes, who had vanished while on a trip to the Midwest. Gone. Just like that. It wasn't known if he had been murdered or if he had gone off to a future all his own. He had had three hundred dollars, enough for a new beginning.

Bars and car dealerships and convenience stores and department stores and stores that sold dishwashers and stoves and refrigerators—aisle after aisle of all anyone, anywhere, could possibly ever need. BUY NOW, BUY NOW, BUY NOW. All the promise of NOW. The planes thundered in and out. On the radio an Indian reporter spoke of the transmission of

AIDS in India, how truckers get it from prostitutes and carry it back to their wives. "We have sex two or three times a day. You see, madam, it is the heat from the truck's engine that warms us up and makes us eager." Live from India. You could hear the revving of diesel engines in the background. "As a result we must relieve ourselves," in that distinct emphatic lilt—emphasis landing on *relieve*. She thought of her taxi driver from the Delhi airport, how proud she had felt of herself then to be alone. They relieve themselves with roadside hookers and AIDS spreads across the subcontinent like the slow and devastating ooze of lava. India appeared before her, a woman dressed up brilliantly in a gold lamé sari beckoning her with a thin seductive smile. India, both magical and horrifying, trapping her future like a fly in amber. Her father lay in his sea of white pillows with the morphine drooling past his tonsils.

She thought of herself as a young girl setting a place at the table for Athene, lighting a candle for Athene—an offering to her very own god. *Wise Athene, great counselor, Teach me waking and sleeping. Send me omens true and dreams wise. Instruct me in your great wisdom. I open my heart and mind to you, Wise One. I ask for your all-knowing counsel and guidance. That my good may come quickly.* Alice saw the conviction on her younger face, infallible faith. Some nights she would wait for the food to disappear and the candle to burn out. "But she won't come, babe, until you're asleep. You know Athene doesn't like to be seen." In the morning, of course, the food would be gone.

Suddenly, she wanted her mother. She wanted to drive to her mother and confess to her as she had done as a child whenever she did anything bad. Her mother spread out like a country. "I pray and confess to her like a priest," she told

Kate. "That's dangerous," Kate warned. But Kate didn't understand. Her mother would listen; her mother would hold her, wrap her up in those long and comforting arms, and extract the pain like a thorn from skin. "I killed Pop," Alice would confess. Eve would kiss her gently on the forehead and say that everything would be all right. It wasn't her fault. Eve would make big promises, inflating truth into impossible proportions. Perhaps she would even be relieved. "Good job, Alice. *Brava, ma petite chère.*"

The bar appeared like a premonition. She had seen it a thousand times as she drove to New York. A Roman theme dive, small and square and lit up in the center of a vast parking lot. It was called Quo Vadis. She had always wanted to stop there simply for its name. Quo Vadis at the edge of the highway, floating in a sea of concrete beneath an apocalyptic sky. Steam and fires and airplanes lifting into the clouds. The letters of the name flashed one bright letter at a time. Plaster-to-look-like-marble statues of Peter and Jesus on the Appian Way held court at the entrance to the bar. Sirens howled on the road, the planes thundered overhead, tires screeched to a halt. Everything smelled of exhaust and of refineries. Alice thought of Peter fleeing Rome to escape the martyrdom and meeting Jesus, asking him, "*Quo vadis?*" and Jesus answering, "To Rome to be crucified again." Peter, the fool, returned to Rome, to his duty; Alice hoped she would not be returning for a while.

This area was so different at night, almost beautiful. The sky held so much. It seemed invincible. She parked in the lot next to an old pickup and a Chevrolet. Quo Vadis would smell of stale beer and stale cigarette smoke. A jukebox would play some old song and there would probably be a pool table. Alice was good at pool, a show-off. A few men would be sitting on stools at the bar, tattooed, smelling of that bitter alcohol smell. Wives ringing on the phone in search of their men. A couple fought at the far edge of the parking lot. "Always dragging me to these shit holes," the girl screamed, and stormed off. She had big hair and tight jeans and she crossed the highway effortlessly, dodging all the cars like jumping rope. Alice was glad for their unhappiness. The guy walked to the bar and flung the door open, unleashing a blast of music.

Alice grabbed her bag, slipped the keys under the driver's seat rug—the way they always did when they left the car at the station for some brother or sister coming down from New York—and closed the door.

At the entrance, she studied the statues of Peter and Christ, standing guard. Her face was red, her big eyes weren't so big right now. A strange concept to have the pair of them at the threshold of the bar, she thought. The plaster was getting wet in the drizzle. It seemed it had gotten wet and dried many times before. Christ's face looked like it had a skin disease, pocked and splotched and blistering. The lovely white had become an ugly yellowish brown. His eyes were light gray and vacant. Someone had forgotten to draw the pupils. Peter, by Christ's side—same skin disease, arms hanging long.

A car pulled up and a guy got out, slamming his door. "Hey, pretty. Challenge me to a game of pool?" He brushed past her, disappearing inside. A shock of light and that nagging music. "I'd beat you too easily," she said. But he was already gone.

"I'm going to India," Alice said out loud to no one, to the statues. "There's a man there that's going to turn me into a movie star. I've always wanted to be a movie star." She saw herself as Athene, five hundred feet high in a gold lamé sari with a golden bindi on her brow. As she heard herself speak, it did seem like a good idea. Just a drink before I go, she thought. A beer and a shot or two like a good Texan.

She looked at Christ. "Go then," he seemed to say as a dare.

"Have you let my father in yet?" Alice asked Peter. She was punchy. She wanted to box, to knock the figure down. The door opened. The man who had challenged her to a game of pool poked his head out. "Are you coming?" he asked. He was a young man with thick dark hair and a ruddy handsome face with old acne scars on his neck. He wore construction boots and jeans and a white T-shirt. The left sleeve wrapped a pack of cigarettes. She hated smokers, had no sympathy for their stupidity. Tammy Wynette's voice wafted through the thick cloud of cigarette smoke that hovered inside. She looked at the man as if he held an answer. She could go inside, play a game of pool with him, knock back a few with him, see a movie with him, sleep with him. She could tell him anything—that she was a Texan here en route to India. Make up a much more fabulous scenario for herself, be carried away for a while to a different land.

"It'll be all right," he said, staring into her swollen face. Soft and gentle voice. Yet another stranger coming to her rescue. She thought of the long-ago man in the subway tying her shoelace. She thought of being a child in New York City for her mother's birthday, of how her father had rented a limousine for the night to take them around. The big kids went to see *The Exorcist* and her parents went to a fancy restaurant to celebrate and left Alice with the limousine driver to baby-sit. He'd driven her up and down the avenues to show her all the fabulous buildings of New York. A nice safe fat man with a clean-shaven face and black uniform with golden buckles here and there on the fabric. Twinkling eyes. Through the canyons of lower Manhattan, "Look up," he'd said. "The beauty and all the surprises are above." Gargoyles and majestic colonnaded balconies, gardens in the sky.

"Do you come here often?" she asked.

"Not really, only when I want to play pool. It's the specialty here, and cheap beer."

"It's sort of nowhere New Jersey. A strange theme."

"It's run by Italians." Said as if that explained everything.

"Eye-Talions, my father used to say. He was Irish."

"From Ireland?"

"From Texas."

"And you?"

"New Jersey born and bred. All that good corn and tomatoes. I ate sixteen ears once, a fact that made me very proud as a child." She wanted to talk. She had so much to say. She was grateful for this gentle man. She remembered the picnic table on the deck piled high with corn, her grandmother shucking it, her hands working at a furious pace. Silver Queen, Bread and Butter, platters of sliced beefsteak tomatoes, red and juicy with basil from the garden—everyone there, all getting along more or less like any family. How simple, as if she could drive back to it. The man went inside and came back with two double whiskeys. "Drink this," he said. "It'll help."

"Thank you," she said. Drinking it made everything sting and then everything warm. "Aren't the planes beautiful?" she noted. The big engines screaming into the night.

"You're getting wet," he said.

"I killed my father," she said.

"How?" he asked just like that, ordinary. Sane. He shifted his feet, finished off his whiskey. She liked saying bold dramatic things.

"Morphine. Tonight. I did." The rain nested in her hair, many fine beads. She studied him hard with that aloof, impenetrable gaze of hers.

"Injection?" he asked. This question made her aloofness waver, throwing her off guard. Now she was curious about him. Clear blue boyish eyes with charm.

"No," she said.

He was silent for a moment, sipping his whiskey. He lit another cigarette and smoked it, sucking in the smoke as it flirted with his mouth. She'd heard blind people don't smoke because they can't take delight in seeing the smoke. "I like the planes," he answered. "Sometimes I lie on the hood of my car in the long-term parking at the airport and watch them glide in and out."

"Whenever we drove through Newark, Dad would say, 'A mecca of transportation, the biggest intersection of transportation in the world.'" Her father felt very far away, but here. It seemed she could still get to him if only she drove on. "Newark always seemed like the root of possibility. Dreams begin here, a sign should read."

"You didn't kill him," the man said.

"I heard blind people don't smoke," she said.

"I know a blind person who smokes," he said.

"What's your name?" she asked.

"Sam," he said.

"Sam I am," she said.

"And yours?"

"Athene."

"Beautiful. You didn't kill him, Athene," he said again. She liked hearing him say the name. It felt invincible. She would become Athene. She wanted suddenly to tell him everything, have it spill forth like a flood. Her sisters and brothers who couldn't stop fighting, her father who was stolen by a thief—reduced to believing in nothing, not even in her. It seemed if she could just tell it all she would be fine.

"You don't believe me?"

"Perhaps you tried."

"Are you a doctor?"

"A cop."

"No, you're not." She bristled a little. Cops had always scared her. It had always seemed they were the one force that could bring her father down. Though he always seemed to get away from them, outrun them in the turquoise Cadillac, or get pulled over by just the cop he happened to play poker with, or if in a real jam he'd use his J-87 badge, "Texas State Department of Transportation." All rich Texans had them. She wanted to tell Sam about her father and the law.

Sam showed her his badge. His face was lost in shadow now and so was hers. The statues remained well lit. "Go," Jesus seemed to dare.

"I put patches all over him, would have covered his entire body had I had enough. The rest was liquid, poured down his throat. He wanted to tell me things I didn't want to know. This impostor trying to destroy my father for me." She put her hands out toward him as if to be handcuffed. He took them, wet from the rain. His hands were soft. She wanted him to pull her farther toward him, envelop her with those hands.

"What does he have?"

"Had," she corrected. "He had pancreatic cancer."

"I'm sorry," he said. It seemed he knew that form of cancer was a death sentence. It had taken her a few days and many explanations for her to believe there was no hope. "Can I help you somehow?" he asked. "Give you a ride somewhere?"

What made her trust strangers so implicitly? Another girl could get in a car and be carried to her death.

"Thank you," she said, indicating no. She stood up to leave.

"Next time," he said, "we'll play a game of pool."

"If you don't mind being beaten."

"Not by you," he said.

She swallowed back a hard nugget of pain, the way her father had done when he was still her father. Sirens and the Newark sounds of night. "I've got a plane to catch," she said as if trying to convince him, or herself. "I'm headed to India. I was on my way there before Dad got sick. I was going to make movies and do good things and have ambition." Don't be sorry for yourself, she'd said to her father.

"It's still there," the cop said as she walked away. "Be careful," he added a little louder to be sure she heard. She slipped past the blinking lights of Quo Vadis. She walked out onto the highway, crossing it easily like the girl in tight jeans. She wondered where the girl in tight jeans had gone. She wanted to follow her home to her cozy house and sit on her sofa and talk about how awful her boyfriend was. The whiskey warmed her all over again. I did kill him. I did. I promise. I did. It was a ferocious desire, for sure, as if killing him proved that she still believed in something.

With each step the weight of her father, his death, her family, fell from her. She was shedding sisters and brothers and mothers and fathers and the ex-husbands and the ex-wives of those mothers and fathers. She was shedding the father's lovers and the father's mother and the father's father. All going going gone. She followed the pale boy from college, wondering where in the world he could be.

Alice saw a lot of things—that big imagination of hers. The promises of life, the promises of God, of Athene, the promises of statistics: that if you're lucky enough to be born, you'll be lucky enough to grow up with a father not far from your side. Numbers. Odds. They, too, made promises. How many fatherless daughters do you know? The things she saw... airplanes thundering overhead, steam snarling up the sky, the blinking red lights of Quo Vadis with a gentle soul at its door, trying to release her.

CHAPTER TWENTY

Score Corner

KATE MOVED BACK to New York from Italy a few
years before she got divorced. I was about to be thrown out of
an illegal sublet and was just finishing film school and needed
a place to live. We found an apartment together on the Upper
West Side, thanks to her. Through a realtor and an illegal deal
(loads of cash in a paper bag) we paid a key fee and moved
into a palace with stunning views of upper Manhattan—St.
John the Divine and the George Washington Bridge. The
apartment was so big it took us a few years to furnish it.
Kate's like her mother in that way, determined to live in the
best manner possible and find a way to do it even if she does-
n't have the money. They share the great gift of hope. I helped
her out with the key fee with my mother's money. The rest
she borrowed from a wealthy friend of Dad's and Eve's who
owed them a favor. A bear of a guy who wore diamond pinky
rings and floor-length white fur coats. She got a job in a high
school teaching rich kids geology and in the early morning
and late at night she worked on her dissertation so that she
could eventually get a job at a college. I, meanwhile, became

a drug addict. It turned out we lived on the best corner in New York City for crack and cocaine, sold by Mexican gangs. At first I was simply curious about how it was done, how you met the dealers, how they sifted you out from the rest of the people walking down the street. Not hard: White Boy on This Corner meant one thing alone. It's the whisper I soon learned. If you listen carefully, and drug addicts do, you hear the whisper. This was the early 1990s and New York was still a mess, people smashing into cars for radios, broken glass all over the streets, car alarms buzzing off in the middle of the night (no quality-of-life laws, no urban paradise yet). I'd slip out to hear the whisper, make eye contact with the guy (which they did not like to do, not wanting to be known), glide my hand through his, slipping him a fifty for a quarter gram. Our hands barely touched. By the end I was so good at making the deal it seemed I'd hardly stepped out of the building onto the street before I had the glassine envelope in my hand. Then I'd get high (any method would do—smoking, shooting, snorting, freebasing—they each had their own benefits: turtle, coyote, kangaroo, jaguar, respectively) and go out wandering the streets in the middle of the night, thinking grandiose thoughts about the films that I'd become famous for. I'd been making films since I was a kid at Chardin. I made a film when we were little about all the tools from the utility closet coming to life and taking over Chardin. I had the others help. We tied them to transparent strings and worked them like puppets. They marched from the cornfield to the deck, advancing on the house like an army. I did that one simply to see what I could do with inanimate objects, if they could become characters and alive. But mostly I was interested in people, in my sisters and brothers and Julia especially. Already back then she had enormous talent, always

dancing through the house singing some song from some
show—*The Boy Friend, Showboat, Kiss Me Kate*. She played a
fine whore for a Western I shot in town. The whore was the
star, a Western from the female point of view. She kills a man
who doesn't treat her right and since she's a woman the law
wants to punish her more severely because it's all right for a
man to take the law into his own hands but never is it all
right for a woman, etc. You could see just from the way she
held the gun and looked at the camera—left eyebrow raised,
a sort of sparkle in those eyes of hers—that she'd be a star
someday. She knew how to seduce the camera, make it follow
her, want her. New York in the first light of day is a strange
place because you have bums blending with those more for-
tunate in equal numbers. You have people spaced-out like
me, wandering the streets hoping to find some answer to
some problem long forgotten and you have those who carry
paper bags and smell like the piss they're wearing, offending
early morning joggers who seem to have it all. I'd wait for the
full light of day to disguise the mess I had made of myself.
But even so, I liked my addiction. It was mine, my disease. I
owned it entirely, held it in my core like a tangible soul.
"What's wrong with you, Nicholas?" Kate asked. She's blunt
that way, doesn't beat around. That was the beginning. I'd
been drinking seriously since I was a teenager, so it wasn't
much of a surprise. She started watching me and I started be-
having more overtly so that she'd understand, I suppose.
"You're going to end up like Anton, just getting stoned all the
time." "Leave my father out of this." "How? That's not possible." A fight ensued. But I knew just as soon as Kate took
"my illness" seriously she'd be telling Jane and Julia. I knew
they'd put their heads together and come up with a solution,
knew they'd have more theories about this all being Dad's
fault, that he and Eve had never bothered with reality, etc. Be-

fore long (I was right) Kate and her sisters put me into a drug rehabilitation center for rich people, at Yale. I was there for thirty days, watched all the time in case I'd sneak something somehow. Watched when taking a piss, even a shit—the indignities of failing. Some part of me liked the idea of a crash landing, falling onto a soft pad and never having to get up. I feared I'd fail at the films. I had become less interested in narrative, more interested in using film like a moving series of photographs, training the camera on a subject to watch it perform: a mouth as it reads a poem; Grammy's gnarly old-lady hands picking at the corn, each strand of silk, just working that corn, the white teeth of that ear oozing water when pricked by her unfiled nails; Dad as he meticulously rolls himself a joint, as he brings the joint to his mouth, as he swallows the swirl of smoke, Eve behind him sweeping. "Tell us what you find beautiful about Chardin," Eve had asked on the day Dad named it. We were kids, didn't understand appreciation for beauty, but we each could have gone on for hours. The fat white dogwood in the yard. If you blink you might miss it, the bloom is so brief. At Yale, women were the only other patients for some reason. I know that most drug addicts are male. But not there. Those women were all in their early twenties with trust funds that supported their habits. They spoke about molestation and rape and self-image. They spoke of cutting and vomiting and stuff that I'd not experienced but could imagine, because I was empathetic, because I tried to put myself in their shoes. (I was like Dad in that; I could make it seem, when dealing with someone else's troubles, that I had none of my own.) They adored me, fawned over me as if I were their big brother. I liked the attention. It's nice, of course, to be appealing. A few years after I got clean, the mayor of New York City parked police trucks the size of semitrailers on score corner, as it came to be called, and swept

out all the riffraff. From our window we could see SWAT
teams (men in their dark blue sporty uniforms) on the roofs
of lower buildings, staking out the streets and apartments inhabited by Mexican drug lords. In a matter of months there
was no more whispering. "They would have caught your
skinny ass for sure," Kate said as we watched the cleansing. I
started working on a feature that would take a few years to
write; eventually I moved to Los Angeles and lived happily
ever after, unafraid to fail. There is always something to hope
for. I had Julia in mind for the lead. She always declared that
she'd only work on the stage (which, frankly, I didn't believe.
And by the way, I was right). The other thing Kate did back in
my drug days, just before Yale, was organize an intervention
with a therapist. She collected everyone, even my mother, and
we went to the therapist's office on the Lower East Side to talk
all about me. I admit I liked the idea of all that focus. I knew
I could count on Kate to take charge and organize something
to save me. I was tired of being strung out and hungover and
feeling the world spin and my mind fuzzy, tired of being unable to read write think—words blending into other words
and needing that next fix and bleeding through Mom's
money and having to come up with excuses for why I needed
more. All the lying involved, I'm not good at it. We talked and
cried and talked and cried without really saying much. It
seemed no one had much to say about me in particular, but
that I'd always been prone to drinking too much (recalled: a
wedding of friends of Dad's and Eve's, an old patient of
Dad's, got so plastered I pissed in the punch), that I needed
help, etc. After fifteen minutes the focus of the discussion
moved on from me and I observed silently as an avalanche
formed. Everyone sat on the edges of their seats all bursting
to mouth some truth, but too afraid that Dad would erupt
until he did. You could see the Cooper girls, eager to say and

have heard what Dad had done to them, looking at Alice though—weighing the need to protect her with this one opportunity for all the ghosts to be paraded. Living with Kate, I knew the stories. Igniting Dad was easy. He punched me in the lip once when I spoke back to him. He erupted in the therapist's office because he didn't want to hear what the Cooper girls would say, didn't want Alice to hear, and an explosion necessarily would silence everyone. The therapist jumped out of her seat, lit by fear, and the next time we came she had another therapist at her side for protection though she claimed the young man was simply a student on rotation. After each session we ate hamburgers at a local pub. We attended six sessions before realizing that we were far away from my drug issues and that this can of worms was far too vast. I am a hopeful person by nature. What else is there to be? The year I got sober was also the year I had my films shown at MOMA for the first time. Those therapy sessions were awful, but every single one of us was collected there for all six of those sessions—first for me, then for the family. We all know it's our ship and since it's ours, necessarily, we don't want to see it sink. We'll tangle ourselves up in a net of gorgeous lies, but we will not let it sink. Not a single one of us, no matter how we complain. I remember being sixteen, walking through the fields at Chardin, feeling the way kids do, when time is irrelevant, a shotgun in my hands to shoot targets (a pyramid of beer cans), swaggering my hips a little, trying out toughness, desiring to be a little dangerous with my gun and long blond hair. Lazy afternoons with clouds like islands drifting by. An excitement filling me up like a thirsty plant being watered because the Cooper girls were coming to Chardin for the day, because of the inevitability that the Cooper girls, arriving like freshly picked flowers, would stay for a while.

CHAPTER TWENTY-ONE

The Green Box

ANTON LEFT THE JESUITS in 1952. He was twenty-two years old. He had an affair with another young novitiate and he told his superior because he could no longer hold the sex thing (as he called it) inside. *The most important thing about my confession is that I be wholly open with my confessor, concealing nothing; no matter what, no matter how great the consequences,* he wrote in his journal. The rules. The law. *For my spiritual profit, by means of humiliation and submission—I must be willing and glad to have my superiors know my faults.* He could no longer fight with his conscience. His conscience was a raw and open wound.

Father Master was dead. The new superior told Anton he was secular and that he should not pursue religious life. *Sins can serve as stepping-stones to God,* Anton had been promised. Now he was thrown out, defrocked, adrift in the pecan trees floating up and out and away from the bayous and the plantations of sugarcane and the live oaks with their moss.

His mama wanted him to go to Europe. They scrambled for the money. "I don't want to know the details," she said to

Anton. "Don't tell me the details. Let's just get you off to Europe for several months—time enough for this to pass." She closed her ears and eyes and pleaded with Daddy to take a loan and send the boy to Europe. She was afraid of driving out in the car. She did not want to be seen by friends. She bought herself a new black dress and hat at Neiman's and wore it all the time. "But Mama, I want to come home," Anton pleaded into the phone like a lost boy.

When Anton returned home Mama could not look him in the eye. In fact, she could not look at him at all. He was ugly and awkward, so very big. She looked at him and saw sex. He was all sex and sex with a man. If that ever got around the gossip mill, she would kill herself. She'd been too proud and God had punished her for her pride. His eyes were big and he'd all but lost his gorgeous thick dark hair. He revolted her. She pleaded with Daddy for Europe. And Daddy tried. He asked Mr. Dorman for an advance, hoping for that big account, borrowing against retirement. But Daddy's heart was bad, his health fragile, and there was nothing extra so, alas, Europe was not affordable.

Anton came home and he sat in his old bedroom and he waited for the days to pass, for some plan to miraculously appear. It seemed there was no one in the world who cared and that the direction that had been so clear was absolutely gone and the world that had seemed so big suddenly seemed small. After a while he began to go out late at night. He was on the prowl. He looked for girls and he screwed them, paying for some, buying a drink for others. The brotherhood of boys were scattered off at college. The streets of Dallas filled with a younger set—boys still in high school running wild, excited by the thrill of all that time in front of them. The sex thing gnawed in the most delicious way, and Anton felt God's eyes

watching and even that gave him pleasure for a time—a sense
of triumph and release. He no longer had to report to anyone.
No more daily examens. *I don't care about you. You let me
down. And soon you'll see the magnificence of what you lost.* He
became defiant. He was going to show them what they lost; he
was going to prove them wrong. Them as in the Jesuits, as in
Christ and our good Lord. The girls were faceless. He didn't
remember the details of them. They smelled like girls. One girl
had a scar on her arm a foot long, an inch deep, like a trench.
He licked it, slowly gently. Driving around, he wished he were
a boy again, with Annie as his girl. The Church had gotten it
all wrong, celebrating celibacy above the sacramentality of
marriage. This quest to set the record straight, this quest to en-
lighten people—for surely this paradigm seeped through to
all persons—would become his life's work.

Maybe he and Annie would be married by now, with that
ranch. Maybe he'd have a solid simple job like his daddy selling paper and paper packagings all across Texas with Annie at
his side egging him on, giving him mock interviews. Her soft
lips and birdlike wrists. He'd be earning money for retirement. He'd be safe, like other people. At night he'd slip between the cool sheets of their bed and gently slip inside of
Annie. Warm and entirely his. She had known the truth
about him.

IN THE BASEMENT at Chardin there is a box—a green box,
sage green and of metal. It has been there for years, at least
since Anton moved to Chardin in 1972. Like Duchamp's
Green Box I imagine it—a box to receive notes, scribblings
that might unlock the mysteries of a life, an art. Rust creeps
up its sides, corrodes its edges like a disease, eating the box.
Duct tape straps the top down, crushing together a mass of

letters and papers spanning the fifth decade of the twentieth century and the third decade of Anton's life. There is a metal handle on the lid and there is one half of a lock (also on the lid, on the lip of the lid). The other half of the lock has fallen away. A smallish box, it is hidden in the depths of the storeroom with other boxes and notes, journals from Anton's Jesuit years. Down there in the basement, thick with warping LPs and old crystal and a bounty of Haitian art. (I remember when we were small the cranberry crystal belonging to the Furey kids, very expensive stuff, was stored down there. The boys had a BB gun fight and all that crystal shattered. "That's your crystal," Julia had said to Sofia. "Furey crystal.")

Anton's journals outlined the customs and constitutions of the novitiate, describing an earnest forthright boy who wants to do good, wants authority to love him and see him as a clever man guided by the will of God. I did not know this man.

Know you not that you are the temple of God and that the spirit of God dwelleth in you? But if a man violates the temple of God, him shall God destroy. For the temple of God is holy, which you are. The devil's plan is riches, honor, pride.

Temptations:
1. Relaxation of fervor
2. Negligence in the performance of exercises of piety
3. Sadness and depression
4. Thoughts of dislike for one's vocation
5. Dangerous readings
6. Dangerous conversations
7. Particular friendships

I read greedily. I take the broken lock as an invitation. I steal the box, take it home to my apartment in New York City and pore through the letters and journals and spiral-bound notebooks. I find love letters to Agnes, from Agnes, letters from friends of Agnes's on trips to Europe, a pen pal from the Jesuits, Anton's mama, his daddy, Agnes's parents. All these lives come forth like butterflies released from a net. Anton is dead now and these letters mean nothing to him anymore and to me they may be clues. Clues to what? To who he was? To whether he had been capable of loving me, Kate.

The green box, so small, holds story. In 1950 he entered the Jesuits. He made his mother proud. He struggled with his physical desires and with understanding the laws, so tight and restraining. They kept him rigid, locked in a pattern of order and ritual of exhortations and penances and mortifications and permissions and daily examens and cassocks (which should be worn at all times) that were supposed to set him free. He was a twenty-two-year-old boy with a vast forehead and thinning hair. He had long skinny legs and loved to laugh and make people laugh. He could ignite them with his bold and wicked grin. He saw this as a power. People were drawn to that power, pulled in as if to comfort—as if they could surrender the quest, the hard work, of being alive. He met another novitiate named Cliff and they kissed.

Open your soul to your superior. Obedience, poverty, chastity. If there are any questions in your mind about anything concerning the matter of sex, you should make them known so as to receive the proper instruction and advice.

Then the two boys sneaked into Anton's cubicle and made love, quiet, delicious love. He had not imagined the relief. Cliff's warm hand on Anton's mouth holding in the joy. All those cassocks asleep and it seemed just the two of them were alive. I am not a homosexual, he thought. How could this be deviance?

At first he said nothing. He thought he would work through it by himself. It was just a curiosity. He thought prayer and meditation would help. He prepared for a retreat where he would work on this issue alone. The sex thing gnawed like rust corroding him, but he would be strong. *When in temptation get your rosary quick and hold it tight and hard.*

But then after the retreat he abided. He told his new superior.

Taking off his cassock was like taking off lead. He shed it. It fell to the floor. But the impression fixed on his form like skin and though he tried he could not rid himself of it. He called his mama. She wanted him to go to Europe. He embarrassed her. *My son chosen by God.*

The green box is similar in size to one used for holding an urn of ashes. It crushes letters and the letters sing. The first paper that I hold is literally a song:

> Mine eyes have seen the glory of the coming
> Of the Lord
> He is trampling out the vintage where the
> Grapes of wrath are stored;
> He hath loosed the fateful lightning of
> His terrible swift sword;
> His truth is marching on.

I hear the whole past singing it, all these voices alive again and screaming to get out of the box. I hear all those young boys at Grand Coteau singing it. I hear his mama and daddy and all those souls he tried to save, all those people who wrote him so regularly—he an earnest young man trying to save them. I hear us singing it as kids driving across the country in the turquoise camper, my stepfather at the wheel teaching us the words, the warm wind in our hair as we drive across America in search of hope. I remember once on that trip

Anton drove thirty miles out of our way to get me apple juice because all we could find was Coke and I didn't drink carbonated sodas. We found the apple juice at a filling station deep inside a cooler of ice. I was so thirsty I didn't put my shoes on. I leaped out of the back of the camper and plunged my hands deep into that ice. The pavement softened in the heat, sticky beneath my feet. Anton picked me up just then. "You've gotta wear shoes in a filling station, babe. It's dirty here." Together we fished out the apple juice. I could count those moments on my fingers. I remember and save each one like a rare photograph. The whole place smelled of gas and ice and then apple juice and then when he picked me up it was as if that camper weren't there, the other kids, the filling station—all of it was gone except for me and Anton.

He was my stepfather and I loved him—big and wide and infinite like a father. I met him in 1969 outside a shack he referred to as a farm where he taught young housewives and clergymen to trust by falling backward into the arms of strangers with their arms at their sides and their eyes shut. My sisters and I were outside waiting for our mother who was inside falling in love. We waited patiently for her and then to meet him, the three of us all curiosity. He was to be our savior, the answer to our mother's deep and penetrating sadness that leaked through her to us. What I remember best about meeting him were his hands, enormous hands with an enormous turquoise ring, and then I remember they led me to the rest of him—so big, big enough to save us. His large smiling face suspended on his shoulders like a globe. Three tiny girls all dressed alike and clean in Liberty print dresses our mother had sewn, selling lemonade outside his therapy shack waiting for our mother while she fell in love. I was seven years old. Julia was nine years old. Jane was eleven years old. For the first time we felt sexual, a squirming slippery delicious sensation within us, oozing through our veins.

> Glory! Glory, Hallelujah!
> Glory! Glory, Hallelujah!
> His truth is marching on.

Then he met Alice. She was home from college for the summer. It was 1953. A smart beautiful girl who wanted to be a poet. She was a poor Protestant, but she and Anton didn't speak about religion much. She attended Radcliffe on a scholarship. She loved sex and she loved Anton and he loved her. Her eyes were big and brown and her hair dirty blond and her legs long. He borrowed his daddy's Packard and then drove off into the plains while she sat at his side with the wind whipping her hair against her lips and she laughed. *I'm going to marry her, by George,* he wrote to a Jesuit friend named Tim. One of those smart, bubbly girls who seem not to know unhappiness. *I like the sound of this one,* Tim wrote back. *God be with you (pretentious but sound).*

The notes slip out of the box along with a tiny cross in a tiny black leather billfold. A picture of Freud and a letter from Jacques Maritain, responding to a letter asking him for advice on the treatise on love that Anton had intended to write.

Dr. Mr. Furey:
   Pardon me for telegraphic style.—Unwell now.—Have not changed my views on your work as expressed earlier.
   Best wishes and sincerely yours . . . JM.

I can feel the blush in Anton's cheek—can see him like his father walking toward the car, his wife, and child, as the Lipton factory towers behind him, that look of forced confidence spreading over his face like a tide. Then a note from his daddy, Anton married now to Agnes, living in St. Louis, studying for his masters in philosophy:

I sure hope you and Agnes keep on having a deep faith and realize that nothing else matters. I was talking to someone about your thesis and they thought that LeSenn or LeCan or whoever he is, was an existentialist and that is supposed to be someone who has gotten away from the straight and narrow, or is it? Ma and Pa had the most simple and satisfying faith I ever saw and I never gave it a thought when I was your age. They never doubted this or that but went right on believing the truth as they knew it. And they never delved too deep to rouse any doubts.

Living in St. Louis with one child born and faith slipping away, receding like the days.

A tooth presses through an envelope—a child's tiny tooth belonging to Finny. *Knocked out in a match with Nicholas—11–17–72. Worth 50 cents,* Anton wrote. Stuffed into the box as an afterthought, a place to save something worth saving, something sentimental—his Alyosha's tooth.

Alice comes before Agnes. He wants to marry Alice. Alice is my sister. Anton's favorite. Present tense because though he is dead she remains his favorite. Alice named for Alice. Clues. In the fall of 1953 she went back to Radcliffe. Scraps of paper that describe a life. She sings.

Caro, she writes in a fast and passionate and swirling script. I can picture her—bouncy and smiley, sitting at her desk in Cambridge. A pile of books tower around her. Perhaps it is snowing and she's thinking of the summer warmth of Dallas and driving fast with Anton in his daddy's Packard and their love seems plausible, highly likely. She's drunk with it, wrapped up in wools, a scarf flipped around her neck, her long hair a pleasant mess, cascading over her shoulders.

Caro,

*There is a line in Virgil which is what you do to me but I
can't remember it—simply I can't. Can't! Well damn I'll find
it—if I can find that word—Ha! I found it—". . . tum selvis
scaena coruscis desuper horrentique atrum nemus imminet
umbra." Now I'd better interpret this for you or you'll go off to
bed in a black prodigious temper. The passage is from Book I
right after Aeneas and the boys have been through pitched hell
in a storm. Suddenly the waters are still and they see the island
harbor on both sides of which "vastae rupes geminique minan-
tur," and the dark protective grove. That is how you threaten
me—with still waters and wonderful bristling depths and the
embracing cliffs forever challenging the sky, forever challenging
the small small creature at their feet to climb and climb to challenge with them by accepting their challenge.*

*Well all that effusion gave me a nosebleed—no—it was my
own fault—I blew my nose so hard and then when it began to
bleed it was so pretty I had to let it bleed so I could watch myself in the mirror. The color is, no kidding, really beautiful if it's
on paper and you could hold it up against the light. I would
send you a bit but I know it'll only be brown and dulled in a
few minutes—the oddest things are beautiful. Do I love you?
Do I breathe?*

> Christ was born across the sea,
> With a glory in his bosom that transfigures
> You and me,
> As he died to make man holy
> Let us die to make men free
> While God is marching on.

"Do you love him?" our mother used to ask us. "Do you
love him? Isn't he something? You don't love him. I can see it.
You've always hated him." Her face would turn from hope to

betrayal like the sun disappearing behind a cloud. Through us she always expressed herself. She didn't mind that I looked through the green box. In fact, she gave it to me. "Maybe it will make you understand him better. Maybe you'll find sympathy for him." Anton was dead and he was just one part of her life as was my father as was her childhood. He was not her entire life as he was for my sisters and me, looming large on its threshold with so many promises. Promise. If he loved me, simply then things would be the way I thought they were supposed to be.

"Save the box though," my mother said. "Alice might like to have it when you're through."

"I didn't know he had loved a man," I said to my mother on the phone with the letters in my hand.

"He didn't love the man," my mother said. "He just succumbed. He was so lonely at Grand Coteau." And she paused and thought for a moment and then added quickly, "He didn't sleep with Cliff. They only kissed. It was nothing serious. Don't make up lies."

Then: "You didn't love him."

"Did he love me?"

ANTON DID NOT TELL the new superior at first about Cliff. He would have told Father Master, but Father Master was dead. Father Master would have rested a soothing palm on Anton's head and have said something wise about Christ's capacity for love and his even greater capacity for forgiveness. Sometimes Anton would find hope in his faith, know he'd be forgiven, know that it was a struggle on a human level here at Grand Coteau and that it wasn't always easy to be pure. He could see all the boys and knew they were lonely, too, that friendships were few and hard and that legal time was sparse and the transition to this solitude so sudden. Saw himself standing tall in the back of the pickup, racing out with the brotherhood to old O'Connell's ranch.

Both boys were asked to leave the Jesuits. Cliff first because he confessed first without indicting Anton. Cliff went to Hollywood. Anton went first to the retreat, then confessed, then went home to his childhood room. The first thing he told my mother when they began to fall in love, my mother tells me, was of his affair with Cliff. "He needed me to know, as if confessing," she said. "Guilt tormented him. It crippled him. He told every woman that he ever loved. He told Alice and Agnes, he told me. It tortured him."

For a while I thought this affair would answer something about him. I told my sisters. "Did you know?" They hadn't known and we gossiped about it and fed on it until it lost interest, becoming just another part of a life plagued by sex and questions of love. The who of who he was clouded by his black prodigious temper—swollen, ugly beast.

On his retreat, Anton carefully composed a letter to Cliff. It is the longest document in the green box, seven single-spaced typed pages trying to convince Cliff that he should abide by the sex restriction:

And if you ever really thought of it, you believe more in God than you realize. But you choose to vacillate—to have your sex and your liberties (which really give you no more freedom than if you hadn't taken them), and straddle the fence, full aware that a merciful Church and God will always forgive you. It is much easier to assure others that they are bound to die, perhaps suddenly, than to realize it ourselves. Yet if you should now, you would most assuredly go to hell for an eternity. And if you sin and procrastinate with the idea of future forgiveness in mind, recall these words—

"If thou be lukewarm, I shall vomit thee from my mouth."

Anton is fully aware as he writes this (the pages aswirl with red ink correcting and rewriting each sentence multiple times) that it will be read by his superiors.

Cliff went to Hollywood, rented a cheap motel room with a fading carpet and ripped floral-printed curtains where he used a sheet to a make a rope, and hanged himself from the lighting fixture in the center of the room. "Anton blamed himself," my mother said.

When we die there is very little we think of except the past. I would like for you to picture your deathbed scene when you are on the brink of judgment and eternity. Our past then is what we're living right now, and we may never have a chance at even the shortest act of contrition. The children at Fatima said they were given a glimpse of hell, and that souls were falling into it like snowflakes. But if we know how to pray, and could learn to pray primarily with our minds and wills instead of trying to feel good in our hearts (which is only spurious and superficial generally), then we will have learned a great deal.

Anton drove to our house in a turquoise Cadillac with electric windows that hummed like flies as he put them up and down. He gave us punching bags and BB guns and footballs and taught us to be tough. He took us to the far corners of the Western Hemisphere to make us aware of the world being larger than ourselves. He put us together with his kids and promised a family. Twenty-five years passed and then he lay dying on his bed with a whistle in his mouth, whistling anyone to attention. Anyone who would come and comfort him and tell him he would be all right, that he would not go to hell. Promise? *Imagine your deathbed scene.* "You don't believe I will?" he asked me. "I hurt you," he said to me. As if I alone could save him from hell. "Let's not talk about hurt," I said. Because what was there to say that could be answered or understood in the hours before he died?

Once he had driven into New York City to talk to me about having hurt me. He arrived eight hours late and I was quite drunk by then from vodka, lying on my bed. He took me to a local bar and spoke about the Francesco Clemente show he'd just seen (and the reason for his tardiness), paintings of vaginas in men's heads and some sort of stuff like that. Then he spoke of a television show in which electrodes had been placed on the heads of ten cabbages to record their sense of fear. The cabbages were lined up on a long cutting board. A woman with a well-sharpened carving knife came along and one by one chopped the cabbages up. The lines on the monitor recording the data from the electrodes were static for the first cabbage but became increasingly jagged as the woman made her way down the line. For the last cabbage the lines ricocheted all over the screen. Who was frightened here? Anton or his children? Or, Anton of his children? Was I his child? We drank eight beers between us. Then he told me that when he was a young boy a neighbor had fondled him. He'd walked by the house many times, a small Dallas bungalow, in which lived a thin old man with enormous eyes. The man invited him in, did his deed, and then instructed Anton never to walk by his house again. "Of course I didn't want to. But I think all the time about you, if you were afraid of me, you couldn't choose to take a different route."

He was molested? A clue? You can dig into a past and find the reasons behind the shape of a life. The further back you go, there's no one to blame and there's no one who needs to take responsibility.

For a long time I would think about a Christmas party at Chardin when I was sixteen. I drank far too much, became

sloppy and pleaded with Anton to waltz me and waltz many
waltzes and then I led him to the sexuality library, to a mattress lying in front of the fireplace, and I lay him down on the
mattress and asked him to hold me, to scoop me against his
belly the way parents like to do with their babies, the way he
did with Alice. The fire hissed and crackled and soon I fell
asleep—passed out, rather. I woke up in the middle of the
night; it was dark and the party long over. I forgot about the
incident until it was so sufficiently buried that I didn't know
what had happened and could speculate. What had Anton
done to me? For I was sure he had done something. I wondered this long before he died and long after. I thought about
lying on the mattress there. Anton holding me against his
chest, rubbing my hair, trying to help me fall asleep. I wanted
to be his baby Alice, loved the way he loved her because that
seemed to be the most beautiful love I'd witnessed. If I could
not be his baby then I wanted to be his lover. To crawl inside
that man and excavate all the promises. To crawl inside that
man and have him make good... on what?

But what happened was simply this: The party carries on.
When Anton knows that I am asleep he quietly rises from the
mattress. He puts some blankets over me and a few more logs
on the fire. He tucks me in and in his gut there is a pain at my
humiliation, at what has led me to this. Ugly little Kate trying
to seduce her mother's husband—at the ache he has caused
in this young girl.

Another memory: at the funeral service for Jane's mother-
in-law I sat in a chair alongside my father. Anton walked in a
little late to a room crowded with strangers—English artists
and intellectuals and Georgetown elite. I saw him looking
around. He looked lost, a little nervous, shy even—big strong

man that he was, omnipotent swollen man. His eyes caught mine, holding me for an instant, asking me in a flickering half smile to help him. He was the emperor of my kingdom, but here I was in another country and he was powerless—a balloon deflating as it rises high into the blue air. His power only existed at Chardin, inhabited by children and others who found his authority seductive and appealing. Those weak eyes of his, they were sort of pleading with me, giving me a little power—the power of being needed. I relished it and winced as he became someone new, as the cocoon of my kingdom was cracked open and held up for me to see objectively. A part of me wanted to go to him and save him and put everything back the way it should be. To be needed can erase a lot.

ANTON LAY ON THE BED looking already very dead—I had no idea yet what death looked like. I wanted to talk to him about his life, acknowledge it bravely as it was coming to an end, as if death were not that much, as if we weren't all afraid. Instead, I sat at the edge of his bed and held his cold hand. I would not see him alive again. The day was crisp and blue and bright and cold—one of those days when all the fruits of the fall are so recently gone and the world feels empty. His room was warm. The cactus bloomed. His cowboy hat, with its hole he claimed was a bullet hole, perched on a bookcase holding all his stories of Texas. I did not know that I would never see him alive again. Instead, I thought he would remain sick forever. He needed me when he was sick. I plunged my hands into the flesh of his belly and massaged until I massaged out the pee. I was not afraid to see his penis, so limp and useless—the "sex thing" defeated. I made him ice shakes when ice was all he could eat. His need of me was some kind of answer.

This is what I believe . . .

That there is a God, and that he made man and the uni-verse, and that he put in man a certain quantity of good and desire of virtue and happiness, and that being the giver of these qualities, he must possess them himself, to a much larger, an infinite degree. And I believe that evil is simply the absence of good, and is permitted by God, who did not want slaves, as a means of testing our will and gaining merit, which is a real thing. God preordained that some would reflect his glory more fully than others, and he thereby predetermined to make some souls brighter, as it were, than others, and give them more grace, though, he still does not want slaves, he would test every one of them at least once, but should one of these souls ignore his opportunities, or flatly reject the grace, then all the further and more horribly will he be punished in hell, for his was the greater gift that was abused, and thus Satan suffers more than anyone.

Anton was thrown out of the Jesuits. Cliff killed himself. And the letter Anton wrote, of course, was written to and for himself. Anton didn't marry Alice. (My sisters and I, in our characteristically ungenerous manner when it comes to things Anton, were certain he did not marry Alice because she had no money.) He met Agnes and married her in the summer of 1955 at a small nondenominational church in Popham Beach, Maine, presided over by a Catholic priest. Agnes's family had a summer home on the beach—a brown Victorian cottage in the dunes overlooking the Atlantic and three small islands, two of which were connected to the mainland by sand spits revealed at low tide. Like arms, the sand spits reached from the beach to the islands as if to pull them ashore. It seemed when people walked to the islands that they were walking on water.

Agnes was a Texan, an oil heiress, and a Catholic. Together she and Anton were going to pursue an intellectual life. Alice instead married a famous English poet and like someone else we all know she put her head in an oven and fell asleep and died. She was twenty-five years old. Lives slipping through your fingers like so many grains of sand. And now so was Anton's life and I stood there (and sit here) attempting to catch it.

> Glory! Glory, Hallelujah!
> Glory! Glory, Hallelujah!
> While God is marching on.

But the final decision to come back, Cliff, is up to you. Remember, we really don't realize how big the stakes are, nor how much God loves us, and how much Christ suffered so that fools like you and I might be taught charity and humility and love, and what it really is, and where it really should be directed. Without him, we would never have existed, and would at this moment be completely annihilated, and all he asks is that we love him and acknowledge him as the creator and sustainer of our very being, who created us through love, and who died on the cross for us through love, and who constantly encourages us through his Church and by as many miracles and visions as we care to count. Yet we have, by his power, an inner citadel that not even he will touch, and that is our will, the tremendous implications of which we do not even understand.

In 1954 it cost six cents to mail a letter from Maine to Dallas. Agnes lay on her bed upstairs in the turret of the

Victorian cottage and wrote letters twice a day and mailed them at the store in town to Anton in Dallas who sat at his desk and wrote letters, twice daily, to Agnes in Maine. Passionate letters filled with desire and the will to be united through a mutual respect and deep understanding of faith. If a letter didn't arrive with the morning mail and the evening mail, both were equally furious, scared, tortured, worried, jealous.

Agnes's parents had met Anton and they did not like him. They sip cocktails on the wraparound porch, looking out over the dunes and the long dune grasses thick with plovers to the Atlantic and the little islands floating just offshore. An American flag flutters in the stiff sea breeze, flapping and flapping patriotism. The sun sinks behind them and the world turns a tremendous red. Their daughter is upstairs writing endless letters to Dallas. What can we do? they ask. Shortly, mother will stop speaking to daughter. It is instinct; they've only met the boy twice.

I'm sure that ours is the best and deepest human love, my sweet, on this earth, and that I have the finest gift of God since— well—Bethlehem. Really, Agnes writes. Letters back and forth daily with their six-cent stamps.

Agnes lives down the street in a Highland Park mansion with a three-car garage and three shining Cadillacs. She's a Catholic because her mama is. Her daddy is a Protestant. She has a trust fund with enough in it to last several lifetimes. She has a bob of blond hair and bright blue eyes the color of Anton's. She was studying theology at St. Mary's College in Indiana while Anton studied at Notre Dame. The year after leaving Grant Coteau he had come to Notre Dame to finish his college degree. Anton and Agnes met on a snowy day. He threw a snowball at her because he thought she was cute.

Sanctity. I want it, love it—more than anything—and the fact that you do, too—in a personal love of Christ, and a clear-eyed pursuit of good whole vigorous growth toward God—this to me is everything.

In the early summer, before Maine and just home from college, they made love in a hammock suspended by the branches of a walnut tree in the backyard of her parents' home while her parents cleaned up dinner inside and convinced themselves that this romance was just a passing fancy. Agnes screamed out so loud that Anton had to muffle her, because of the pain then because of the pleasure then because of the guilt—they were not married and her parents did not like the boy and she was at St. Mary's College with the vague plan of becoming a nun.

Anton, my dear I miss you. Blow in on the breeze hard hurting me in your arms, push my hair back gentle in your big hands, pull my eyes forever into yours and we'll lie and laugh and cry and pray in joy and I will pull your heart inside open and touch all that's there.

Agnes's mother was tall and painfully thin with many sharp angles on her body and her face. She wore ankle-length skirts with pressed blouses buttoned up to the throat even while on vacation in Maine. She wore them boating around the islands and up the Kennebec; she wore them walking on the beach with big hats to shade her from the sun. She liked precision and timeliness and the intricate exercise of peeling her grapes. She had four daughters and for each one she had a different, but equal, love and ambition. Agnes was her third born. Her one boy she had lost in the war. Her eyes were very large and very brown; they seemed to be the concern of her entire face. She told her husband, a small gentle man with a warm round face and a great capacity for patience, that her job as mother was to stop boys from seducing her girls.

I had a long talk with Father Stanley tonight—and have calmed down enough to be slightly more "with you" than I was this afternoon. I had to see him about a paper regarding my dispensation from vows, but the conversation turned to Husband and Wife relations; he was foggy in parts, very good in others—I wish you could have heard part of it—but one point of it was that he didn't think you'd ever be as reasonable as I am, because of your female temperament, emotional, illogical, defensive, weak and needing protection, etc. I wanted to laugh but remained polite.

They had been planning their marriage since the night beneath the walnut tree. "My parents don't approve." "They'll come to love me," he reassured, convinced of it himself.

Her mother didn't understand what it was her daughter saw in Anton. He'd been a failure in the Jesuits. She'd heard the rumors. And he came from very little. He seemed hardheaded and unable to accept it when he didn't know something. "You must understand the responsibility of your wealth," she told Agnes. Wealth was supposed to be nurtured so that it could grow, nested into a safe spot, entrusted to someone who had his own wealth so that all could multiply into a pleasant cove of more. It was not to be scattered to the winds of fancy. "I love him," she told her mother. Her mother read her letters. It reminded Agnes of the stories that Anton told about the Jesuits—about every letter, every scrap of garbage being pored over by the superiors in search of sin. Agnes took to writing and mailing them in secret. Soon she had an entire life planned without her mother's knowledge. "He has nothing, comes from nothing," her mother said. "That's ridiculous," Agnes snapped. Agnes was a pretty girl, with her blond bob and gorgeous, serious eyes. She loved to laugh, but humor was secondary to intellect and all came after love. That love, she held it in the core of her chest and it pulsed and it ached and it caused her not to eat and to lie on her bed for long hours scribbling out words to the source. At low tide, she watched out the window. When the sand spits were revealed by the parting waves, the gulls would swoop down to devour the crabs that hadn't had time enough to hide. Theirs was a spiritual love, a love understood in their understanding of God. "He wants your money because he has none," her mother persisted. "I know the type. I want to protect you. If anything happened to you, any unhappiness befell you, I would—" "Die?" Agnes interrupted, staring at her mother, seeing in her the sorrow of nothing soft. "That's cowardly, Mother. It's not his fault his family didn't discover oil. It's only a little oil that separates you from him," she was shouting now. It was evening and her mother sipped her cocktail as it started to get cold outside. A big full red moon rose above one of the islands to disappear into a mess of black clouds.

Sex has been fine, thank God, fine for a few days. If your letters don't get me hot and bothered mentally—or even if they do—I'm going to try to keep a clean slate forever now. Looking forward to the release of the marriage bed . . . in our bed soon together, our minds merging.

In July that time of evening thickened with mosquitoes. The tide came in carrying the sound of the waves. Agnes had just learned that she was not pregnant from their escapade in the hammock and this relief made her desire for Anton ferocious.

"I'm going to marry him," she said to her mother. "I love him. You and Father are going to believe in us. I love him, Mother. I love making love to him." Her mother dropped her cocktail and the glass shattered on the floor as her hand slapped Agnes. The sting spread out from her cheek in concentric circles, stunning her. For a long time they did not talk.

I'm so happy I can hardly write—I think for the first time I feel the smart powerful ecstasy in us—along with the love and peace deep down I've always had—I'm excited so deliriously that nothing can seem bad—I had gotten so I figured you would never really will it and decide on your own—and even felt all along that I wouldn't get you—but now I feel so tremendously unbelievably glorious—glorious in the Word—I'm confident in your acting and willing and deciding and doing it the right way, even before I got your letter and then the idea of you being mine, Agnes—giving yourself to me with all you know and have and can be—yep, it's a right good piece of weather we're having—the insecurity of what you would do has been a lot of the sex trouble, I think—tonight I cared not a whit for other bosoms, faces, legs, hips, etc ... My darling, God was good to us about the baby—or good to our parents—let's pray hard that he will give us a lot of children, later, when it's time. We will soon be in each other's arms for years and years—days and nights of legitimate mischief, arms, legs, breasts, the works—by George—my sweetheart—let us talk and talk and talk of what we feel and want and love—good night, my beloved.

The sex thing would dissolve in their marriage bed, she believed. She could smell the ocean, feel the cold salt air on her back. Smell the pine. She closed her eyes and the day wasn't very far when she'd be saying the Kyrie with her husband, Anton Furey, and she, Mrs. Anton Furey, and their firstborn, Anton Furey, III, and everything gloriously Anton.

His mama could look at him again. She loved Agnes. Agnes was her answered prayer. Mama ran around Dallas trumpeting the good news with her chestnut hair swirled into a french roll. At Neiman's, on credit, she bought a lavender dress, something to make her look elegant and smart. Agnes's family had one of the biggest names in Dallas. *My son chosen by God.* God had seen him through.

In the months before the wedding Anton could think of one thing alone: a present for Agnes. He wrote to New York and London, to the biggest recording houses in the world for the best recording of Edward Elgar's *Dream of Gerontius*—the journey of an old man's soul after death. The poem was by Cardinal Newman and had been given to Elgar as a wedding present. Anton's hunt for this music was infectious. His mama and daddy helped him, a friend in London helped him. No matter the cost. He knew that it would delight Agnes. The mischievous grin lit his jolly face as he teased her about his hunt for her perfect gift. The soul traveling with its guardian angel first to heaven then to hell then resting in purgatory. He was twenty-five years old and the day came finally, July 14, 1955.

A thick fog spread over Popham Beach—you couldn't see but an inch in front of you—and after the ceremony they returned to the house for a reception. All of her bridesmaids fluttering like exotic birds. One hundred guests, butlers and waiters, and champagne and the tiered white wedding cake sprinkled with blueberries. Agnes's mother, rising to the occasion, planted a kiss on Anton's forehead, was enthusiastic and welcoming to Anton's parents. On her arms she wore white gloves extending past the elbow. "My son died in the war," her mother said to Anton as if he didn't know, as if it explained and forgave her behavior. Anton, her first son-in-law. He prayed he'd be worthy of these people. He was a good

boy. He did not aspire to letting people down. She welcomed
him as a son and Daddy gave Agnes away.

Anton led Agnes from the guests to the beach in her long
silk wedding gown with its train trailing behind them. Short
sleeves revealed her long pale arms. "Like ivory," he said as he
kissed them. The newlyweds disappeared into the fog and he
ran away from her and then sneaked up on her, scaring her
and then she did the same and then their bodies surprised
each other like visions coming through that creamy mist.
Agnes in her dress, a swish of organdy and organza, he played
peek-a-boo with his bride. What could they care now about
her mother? He sneaked up and kissed her warm cheek—*The
Dream of Gerontius,* the music of the soul. The world was
filled with grace and wonderful to them. They had been
searching long for this. He knew her soul; he held it carefully
like precious glass in his palm. This love was triumphantly
something more and thus it would not be, ever, less.

He felt quite certain he could fly.

"SAVE THE LETTERS," my mother had said to me. "Alice
might want them."

When we first moved to Chardin in 1973, and shortly
after Alice was born, Anton and my mother had a fight. She
left the house in a rage. We, her daughters, were in school. It
was a nasty fight as theirs always were—rooted in jealousy
and lack of trust. She stayed away all day, waiting for our
school to be over so that she could pick us up. She took us
first shopping for dresses and then for food and then to a
movie and only then did we go home. She did not tell us
about the fight. At home, Anton stood in the living room in
front of the fireplace, in front of a charred heap of slide
carousels and melted slides. A thick black path of burn

scarred the mantel and the stone above it, rising to the ceiling like a long black tongue lashing out. They had been fighting, as they often did, about whether she was still in love with our father. The slides contained pictures of their marriage and of our childhood—the only existing pictures of us as infants and toddlers with our parents. Anton stood in front of his mess, red-eyed, crying. For years my mother would try to scrub away the black tongue. That night she kneeled at the charred heap to see if there was anything she could salvage. A few days later, in a grand declaration of love, she took all the letters my father had written to her and tied them together with ribbons in a neat bundle, stuffing rocks in some of the envelopes. With Anton she drove to the Delaware River (five miles from Chardin) and as Anton watched she dropped them in. Even so, my sisters and I were still in his life. We would always be in his life. He could not get rid of us, permanent, perpetual (Jane and I even look like our father) reminders of our mother's past, haunting him as he walked through his own house, unable to take a different route.

As he lay dying, on my last visit to his bedside, just before leaving, I crawled into bed with him, put my back to his chest, wrapped his arm around my shoulders, and demanded that he love me.

CHAPTER TWENTY-TWO

The Beast in the Belly

AT THE END EVE WOULD tell her Cooper daughters a story. A rainy misty late November morning. All the leaves off all the trees. Mud in the fields from the fall rains. Anton's body lying in the bed. His hands at his side, his mouth open but not moist, waxy rather. His big blue eyes sinking into his big round head. She would clutch their arms, pulling them close as she told them of a trip to Italy the year before he got sick. The trip to Italy had its own photo album, leather bound, recording all the fun they had had. Down the driveway, the cold rain spit on their necks.

THEY ARE IN A SMALL TOWN south of Rome, staying in a *pensione*. The names are unimportant because they wouldn't have remembered them either. Neither one spoke Italian, but Eve tried. She was good with languages. Anton, with his Texas accent, referred to Italians as "Eyetalians."

Dinner in a little trattoria. Carpaccio and mozzarella di bufala and prosciutto di Parma and figs and vitello tonnato and everything fresh and seasonal. "I love the way you eat only what's in season," Eve says and Anton agrees.

They're in Italy visiting Kate, who is back in the country for divorce proceedings from her Italian husband. Kate, however, is not with them. She has suggested that they go off for a few days because she's in the midst of legal paperwork that is boring, and frankly her idea to have her mother and Anton there to help her out emotionally was a bad one. She's sent them off and now they're in the restaurant in the small town south of Rome. They share a bottle of wine with dinner and finish it before they finish dinner so Anton orders another. Eve doesn't want him to but says nothing because she understands happiness and understands what happens when he is denied something he wants. He orders the bottle and she smiles and inside she actually feels alive and grand. She loves it when he gets what he wants—an excited expression spreads over his face and it is as if he owns the world. A big smile on a big face and he inflates with a kinglike feeling. King of the universe. She loves that about him—his appreciation for satisfied desire. The restaurant is dark and there are a few other couples and only one waiter, zipping round. Little candles flicker on all the tables. Eve flirts with the waiter when he brings the dessert, tiramisù, which Kate has told her means "cheer me up." Kate has told Eve that she's been eating it ever since she and Gianni decided on the divorce. Eve tilts her head up to the waiter and though she's fifty-seven her hair is still blond and still curly and the gap between her teeth still alluring. Her green eyes sparkle as she tries out her Italian. As usual, the waiter falls in love with her and they talk about what the very special things to do are in this town.

When the waiter leaves, Anton tries to engage her in a conversation about his book. Anton toasts Eve and his book and talks about how in Italy the women seem more at ease with their sexuality. He speculates on virgin women, wondering if the first orgasm births self-consciousness. Eve pretends to listen. She says, Oh yes, and, How interesting, and, Wow. For years she has practiced the art of this. He talks on about banishing the irrational, the beast in the belly, the male ideologist's desire to divest himself of all contamination by this irrational urge for the other, the female. Of all illusions, the illusion of woman is supreme, Nagarjuna wrote.

Rather, she's thinking of Ian. A picnic in France when the kids were tiny. Just thirty years ago and one country to the west. A book he sent her years later for their wedding anniversary, long after they had divorced. It traced wine routes in France—the one they had taken, he had highlighted with an orange marker. She had had to look closely through the book to find it. But it was there like a treasure. Then she followed it over the pages and it was as if she were still in the blue Peugeot with him, with the rolling vineyards of Burgundy and the emerald hills, the fields of heather, the constant blue sky, the stone monasteries. The fresh smell of hay, of grapes, of lavender, of soil, of baking baguettes, of chocolate. He still loved her then, when he sent the book; she knew it and grew warm inside with a strange kind of hope—not a hope of reconciliation but of permanence. She had told Kate about the underlining in the book and Kate had suggested it first. "He still loves you, Mom," she had said. That was all Eve had ever wanted from him, to know that he still loved her. She wondered about his love now, in Italy in the restaurant— how it seeped out of him through the highlighter to the pages of the wine book, a trail of love nearly hidden there as a secret. She imagined him wanting to control it, but being unable to as the book, then the route in the book, and finally the pen had carried him back to that road in France. She remembered small roads everywhere, getting lost in the tangle of them, her bright smile, Ian's frustration with the roads dissipating with her enthusiasm for them. "You want a straight road," she laughed, and he laughed, too—at himself. She saw Ian at home with his practical wife who used powdered milk and clipped coupons to save dimes, the wife Eve could never have been. Of course, she knew there was much more between them. Ian had become a successful scientist with dozens of achievements to Anton's one failure. She wished deeply and somewhere she could have found a way to make Ian happy simply because she imagined it would have been less painful.

Anton's eyes are red and his mouth dry and he eats more tiramisù. "Agnes would have listened to me," he says. "With Agnes I could have talked about my book. You're not listening, babe." For half an instant she wishes he would die. Agnes, always Agnes. For twenty-five years she has not been Agnes. Then she pours herself a very full glass of wine. She has been doing this for years, drinking lots so as to keep him from drinking too much. She understands happiness, understands it perfectly, the need to compromise.

After dinner they stroll back along the tiny streets to their *pensione*. Full dark and late and overcast, not a star or the moon in the sky. Anton stumbles; he's drunk. His hand goes down the back of Eve's pants to her bottom and she smiles like a young flirtatious girl and sneaks away. "I love your bottom," he says. She thinks, Oh lord, he's going to want sex. She hates sex. She can say that quite honestly. I hate sex. I hate sex with this man. He sneaks up on her again and grabs her from behind and kisses her wet and sloppily on the neck and mentions his book and how women have all the control and power to refuse a man. "It's a gynocracy," he declares. "Men are rendered powerless, at the mercy of the female. Heartless Estella can't be bothered with remembering Pip in his youth, whereas she is his eternal queen. Over the centuries as in some kind of purdah, men have repressed the need so as not to desire. The beast in the belly." Eve hears this and imagines the devil alive in the gut of man.

The streets are impossibly narrow and the night moist, almost wet. Somewhere, on some other street, a car zooms by. Then silence again. Window boxes spill red geraniums and ivy and the smell of the flowers is a large one, though not sweet. You can hear their steps on the cobble streets. You can hear the echo ringing through the tiny town. Full dark and everyone else asleep. A fingernail moon appears through a thinning veil of clouds and the black sky. Anton wants to discover some dark alley and make love in the open air. "Come on, babe, be daring," he insists.

The first time they made love back in 1969 was in the woods behind the old shack where he practiced therapy, where he taught her how to trust—to fall backwards into the arms of strangers without hesitating or looking behind. He knew each fragment of her vulnerable mind; they had been working together for three months. It was dusk and he pulled her clothes off gently and she let them come off as easily as skin off fruit that wants to be peeled and it seemed there wasn't an inch of her that he had not kissed and she had never been so thoroughly kissed like that before, so absolutely, so positively kissed. Cars rushed by on the road, unaware. She was thrilling and warm, hot even, in the cold wet grass. And there was a tremendous silence and in that silence Agnes was obliterated. Their bodies collapsed against each other and they believed, both of them, that in each other they would find an answer. "A second marriage," he whispered quoting from Samuel Johnson, "is yet another instance of the triumph of hope over experience."

And here in Italy on the cobblestone street she does not want him to touch her. She is done pretending. She has known for years that he has had affairs. She stopped caring when she realized Agnes wasn't gone, that she lived on in his mind and guilt. His great love, his intellectual equal. Perhaps Agnes was the one person who could have helped him achieve the promise of his life's work. Eve had wanted him to be strong. He had promised to be strong. But she knows what happiness is and she knows she'll force herself to pretend. She sighs, resigned. And he reads it perfectly, that sigh. He rips his hand from her pants and his nail catches her skin, scratching it. He walks ahead. She, too, is drunk, and tired. She wishes she could disappear back to Rome and crawl in bed with Kate and fall asleep. She wishes that she and Ian were still lost on those windy wine route roads with Jane and Julia asleep in the back of the car. How definite it had all seemed.

Anton falls into silhouette. By the time we're in bed he'll have forgotten about this, she hopes. Infinite hope, the depths of hope, the triumph of hope.

In the small cozy room with a double bed and an armoire with a full-length mirror, windows looking out onto rooftops, he lights a joint. Looking into his face is a hard thing to do. His head, round like a globe, is suspended sloppily above his thick neck. His lips are thick and fat and wet. It disgusts her to think that he ever gave her pleasure. His eyes are slits and shot with very thin and delicate red threads. He looks at her and offers the joint—almost as a dare. "No thanks," she says and takes off her shirt. "I've had too much to drink."

"No thanks," he says, mocking her. "No thanks." She takes a deep breath and sits on the bed and unfastens her bra. "NO THANKS," he screams and approaches her with the

joint in his hand. She remembers a time in Mexico when he
almost hit Julia and Jane. She remembers a time in the
Waldorf-Astoria in New York when he almost hit Kate—the
back of his hand smashing against the wall. She remembers a
time out west when he successfully hit her, another time at
home. He approaches her on the bed and shoves the joint
into her mouth, holding her neck with one hand and pressing
the joint into her mouth with the other. She looks up into
him, her head cocked as it had been while she was flirting
with the waiter, yet her expression is mangled from the pressure of his hand. He makes her take a deep long drag, which
is hard since he's holding her neck. She coughs. Then he
makes her take off her bra. Her big breasts dangle there,
rolling into the rolls of flesh that are her stomach. She is like
a child with a woman's body crouched there on the bed, awkward. She understands happiness. Her head starts shaking, it
does that when she is overtired and anxious—slight, gentle,
steady shaking. Sometimes she holds it to make it stop. She
clutches her breasts and wishes him dead. Thank god Kate
had decided not to come. She catches her profile in the mirror—an old fat lady on a slumping bed. All the wrinkles on
her face like scars. Tears drip off her cheeks. She thinks of
falling in love once when she was nineteen with a friend of
Ian's. His name was Hari Kapoor and he had picked her up
from the train station in London and driven her to Cambridge to see Ian in the hospital. She had come from Paris
where she was spending her junior year. Hari was a light-
skinned Indian Brahman who had grown up during the end
of the Raj on a coffee plantation in southern India. He was
tall and elegant and young with slick black hair and a fine
Eton accent. Her skirt was pale blue and ankle length and she
had worn white bobby socks. She had been a virgin. His eyes

had held her, she had seen herself in her skirt and bobby socks shimmering in his eyes and it was as if a box of butterflies were set free in her chest.

She wants to cry to Anton, wants him to open up and embrace her and hold her and kiss her head and slightly graying hair and hold her and tell her he loves her and that everything will be all right, that she is a good and worthy woman—that he has loved her more than he ever loved Agnes. She wants him to rise into the big tall strong man she had thought he was when she'd made love with him in the onion grass, when it had seemed life was theirs for the making. Her will, his strength. Her kids, his kids. The beauty and hope of family. Say simply, What brought us here?

These damn breasts hanging like eggplants, dangling down her chest, hitting her stomach. She feels small and young and alone. Anton comes toward her, gently now. His chest is bare and she thinks of it slopping into her stomach as he thrusts against her. Her head is still shaking. The room smells of dope. Her face is stinging with the tears. She sees his back in the mirror. An apologetic please-forgive-me,-babe look lights his tender eye. But she has no generosity left. "Are you going to force me to have sex?" she asks, feeling for a moment strong. The words seem to echo. *Force me, force me, force me.* His body begins to swell as it has a thousand times before. She thinks of her littlest, Alice, his girl, too, and the reason she would never leave, saying, "Pop," as she tells a story of punching Anton in the mouth when he had tried to threaten her. "Pop. I popped him. No one, not even my father, will ever pop me."

Anton's swelling is different this time though. It is slower and more complete. It seems to begin at his feet, rising up his body until it possesses him entirely. She thinks about the beast. No longer contained by the belly? The light in the room is dull yellow, low voltage.

"Listen here, babe, I don't need you. I can find love a million other places. I don't need this." As he shouts the swelling increases. It seems this time he might burst. She tries to quiet him, but that makes him yell louder. He is transforming, becoming something other. Before long he is throwing things. He throws the porcelain water pitcher standing on the dresser. It shatters. He rips the sheets off the bed. "I can find love elsewhere," he repeats. He throws pillows, whacking them until the feathers are released and the bedroom is white with down. "You've never loved me, always wanted me to be something other, never cared about my work or dreams, never believed in them." He throws chairs and glasses and Eve's suitcase. Her clothes scatter on the floor. "If it weren't for Alice this would have ended long ago," Anton says. "Admit it. I want to hear you admit it. I want to hear you say you never loved me, that in fact you've hated me, that I wasn't Ian, that I wasn't good enough, that I wasn't a success like Ian, that I was a failure, a disappointment. I want to hear you admit that you were too afraid to leave so instead you punished me."

In minutes the room is destroyed. She begs him to stop, warns him that he'll wake people up. She is not afraid for herself. She is more concerned with the consequences, that they'll be deported, that Kate will find out and be humiliated in front of Gianni's family. "You just shut up," he says. His big hand pulls back for a smack. She notices tears in his bloodshot eyes. She notices his whole face is wet with them. His hand instead of hitting her, hits the armoire mirror and the glass rains onto the floor. Blood shoots from his hand. Feathers stick to it. Shards of glass stick to it. Still, he continues to destroy everything that can be destroyed. She sits on the floor and picks at the glass. The dull yellow light shatters, too. The room goes dark.

When Ian left, she went to see Anton Furey at the recommendation of a friend. He was a local therapist come to town from Dallas, Texas, with the idea of starting a commune. He had five children and a failing marriage. He was a philosopher, writing a treatise on love and sexual equality. He taught her how to trust and he taught her how to love and together they tried to create a commune of another sort. Now she picks up glass in the dark, piece by piece. Anton collapses on the bed, hiding not at all that he is weeping.

Walking down the driveway in the cold rain, Anton on his sea of white pillows, Eve telling this story to her daughters one by one, she would see that his life ended there in Italy. She needed to repeat the story to understand where she fit. Agnes and Ian gods of some juvenile dreams. Anton understanding for once and permanently the failure of his quest for a true and equal, ideological love. "Can't you say that I'm wrong?" he had asked her in the dark room, hoping. "Can't you say that you did love me, that you believed in my book, in me, that you weren't trying to punish me?" She continued to pick at the glass, dropping it into the wastebasket. The beast was captive no more. It had, in fact, devoured him quite completely.

The manager of the *pensione* opens the door without bothering to knock. Light from the hall fills the doorway. Eve grabs a blanket and covers herself. She's too humiliated to look at him. In Italian, he tells them to get out of his hotel. A few minutes later the police arrive and a few minutes after that Anton and Eve are presented with a bill for damages totaling one thousand dollars. A few minutes after that Eve is left alone with Anton in the night, no moon, no stars, in some little town in Italy with absolutely no place to go. Their luggage is heaped over the backseat. Eve thinks of that hotel room and the second bottle of wine at dinner and the feeling she had as she agreed to give him what he wanted. That feeling of utter happiness that had spread through her because he was happy, spread through her like an answer, as it had so many other times.

Back in Rome, Eve would tell Kate that they had had a fantastic time, that she loved Italy. Back in New Jersey she would have pictures of the trip developed and blown up and she would make an album for Anton for his birthday: ITALY 1993.

She knew happiness.

With the second daughter, as they walked down the driveway, she would bring a black umbrella to shield them from the biting rain, but otherwise the walks and the story would be exactly the same. An apology to the dead?

IN THE CAR on that Italian night, a little Fiat and everything damp and close inside, they drove around and around and around. They drove until dawn. Wheels on pavement, rain on glass, windshield wipers scraping and something horrid emerging from the depths of Eve's soul. Anton's bloody hand was bandaged with a sheet, glass still inside the wounds. Light cracked through the dark sky. At some point earlier, Anton had talked about Freud. Knowing the thoughts of great men on love and sex had been his life's work, of course. We are never so defenseless against suffering, Freud had written, as when we love, never so helplessly unhappy as when we have lost our love object. Eve had no idea what happiness was. And the man who taught her how to trust and the man who taught her how to fuck in the long wet onion grass, he was dead, and she had been killing him and for such a long time now.

CHAPTER TWENTY-THREE

Farther India

"IMAGINATION JERSEY CITY HALL," the grandmother would say, sitting in her chair in the living room at Chardin. "Imagination Jersey City Hall." It was perfect iambic pentameter and thus easy to remember, easy to roll off the tongue. Her white hair spun into a beehive, blue eyes piercing whoever passed by. She'd make a circling gesture with her hand, holding it near her ear. She'd screw up her face (crazy-like) and say, "Imagination Jersey City Hall." Nobody knew what it meant. The grandmother had been married at Jersey City Hall, quickly, after threatening her man (who had not yet proposed) with a vanishing act to Paris. He was a tall dark Bostonian. "Blue-blooded," she would say. "Eleven generations Lynn. A refined and elegant man." The ploy worked and he married her and soon thereafter came this inexplicable line, "Imagination Jersey City Hall." She would repeat it into old age. She would repeat it to anyone for the pure craziness of it. The whole family repeated it to indicate they were going a bit crazy themselves. As Anton died, the Cooper sisters would mimic the gesture with their hands and say it:

"Imagination Jersey City Hall." They used it as a way to give meaning to some situation that seemed beyond meaning. Death, for example, or say, shark cartilage hidden in fruit smoothies or Tibetan mushrooms Federal Expressed in from the Far East or cryosurgery in Russia or the Bahamas or macrobiotic spas in Massachusetts, bovine cartilage and pancreatic enzymes.

For Alice the meaning of the line was simple: It held everything her grandmother had hoped her marriage and life would be, would have been, as she stood on the steps of Jersey City Hall dressed in her finest silk, an ostrich feather in her hat from Bergdorf's, with the tall dark Bostonian at her side. As she moved forward the meaning of the line shifted. She looked back at her younger self, standing on those steps dreaming. Crazy foolishness filled her head along with a lifetime that spanned the twentieth century with all its wars and spaceships to the moon.

The grandmother had grown up in Montana, child of a woman who was an itinerant schoolteacher who traveled for months on end to the far corners of the state. She had affairs with congressmen and senators. She played the harp like an angel and knew most of Shakespeare by heart. She was a free soul who would not be burdened by her two daughters. She left them in Helena, Bozeman, Miles City, to fend for themselves. In Butte they swung high on swings to peek inside the windows of a brothel so that they could spy the little Irish whores who came to town on the five o'clock train, get a sense of what they were doing in there. They came to town all dressed alike in tidy but threadbare dark blue capes with hoods. The next dawn on the early train out they left.

The grandmother never went to high school. She was too busy seeing to it that her little sister, Anna Jane, had the opportunity. Instead the grandmother read the magazines and dreamed of tall dark blue-blooded Bostonians who would surprise her with extra extra river water diamonds from Tiffany's in New York. She read Edith Wharton and Henry James. She read and read and read. All of Shakespeare and all of Milton and all of anyone she could get her hands on. The East blossomed in her mind as a place where life happened, a place of sophistication and class and arrival. She wanted to arrive there. Imagination Jersey City Hall.

Her mother, as well, was a medicine woman of sorts. She knew the herbs that brought on the scarlet flow. She broke the crystal of her Elgin watch to scoop out the venom in her leg from snakebite. She knew how to make poultices and during the flu epidemic of 1918 she cared for the sick and dying. On the Lame Deer Indian Reservation she cured the children of lice. From this the grandmother learned. She had a will, the determination of ten thousand worlds. She rode wild through the plains of eastern Montana on horseback. When all the young men were off at war she learned to drive the horse-drawn plow and cut all that great Gallatin wheat. Wheat as far as she could see, but what she dreamed of was buildings and New York City, rising from the water like a song.

In 1922 when the grandmother was eighteen years old she asked her sister Anna Jane to take entrance exams for nursing school on her behalf. When Anna Jane did well, the grandmother changed her name to Anna and departed Montana for Brooklyn Hospital, to dreams of tall buildings and dashing young men—leaving behind Anna Jane (who was now just Jane), leaving her mother to her senators and her congressmen and her harp—going to a future all her own. Imagination Jersey City Hall.

Later, much later, she would tell her granddaughters that she had learned a thing or two. "If I don't like the way something unfolds, I reimagine it the way I'd rather have seen it happen. Memory doesn't dictate truth."

ALICE ON ROUTE 22 in Newark in the soft gray drizzle of the early morning. She walks to Newark Airport, cars splashing her with muck, walks through endless parking lots of endless superstores and all the blinking decorations of a far-off Christmas. It is not cold. She doesn't feel wet, though she is. She keeps walking, stepping lightly until she's in the airport. The magnificent emptiness of that hour. She can hear her own feet plodding over the floors. A plane lumbers into the sky, but even they are few. She watches more planes from the departures lounge, thinks seriously about getting on one. A mechanized voice over the loudspeakers instructs cars not to stand at the curb. Fly to London, London to Delhi or Bombay. She has a credit card and her father's alimony check. She even has her passport and a valid visa. A few weary travelers deplane. How long ago, it seemed, when she was on her way. Her family appeared coming together, pulling apart like Rodinia—mythic supercontinent. She was weary herself. She sat down heavily in a chair and closed her eyes. She imagined she was in India, India becoming her Jersey City Hall, India of foolish dreams, India—fairyland, the sunny country of common sense. She pictured it this way:

On a plane to India, in India, driven through the streets of Bombay by Luca, down away on the rocky roads of the subcontinent, dressed in a sari perhaps. A bindi on her brow, gold lamé sari beckoning. The soft comfort of the Ambassador, Luca steady and determined behind the wheel. Chardin back there, behind her. Same as it had always been. "The weeds," Eve saying to her daughters. "Help me with the weeds." Getting her daughters to weed, they'd been weeding for years. "If we could only conquer the weeds." Weeds between the bricks by the outdoor pool. "We could get the moss to grow and wouldn't that look nice." The sounds and smells of India coming through the windows of Luca's car. Cardamom and cinnamon and curries and the sizzle of fat and the heat and the humidity and the dust. And out there someone is dying and out there a pretty little woman is dancing a love dance in the midst of flames in the center of a lotus flower that drifts in a lotus pond. Ganesh has been spotted drinking milk in a miracle that has the temple mobbed and a pack of wild wolves eats small children in a small village and a movie star is kidnapped and another has become a politician though many believe him to be a god. And they drive past floating palaces and bird sanctuaries and ancient empires on the edge of an emerald river, past the burning *ghats*. ("The whole town smells like steak," a sister had said. "That's gross." "It's the most religious place I've ever been." "Well then you've never been to Pennsylvania or Kansas.") Into the desert, proud and arrogant spreading out around them. Luca steady behind that wheel. Alice slumped forward.

"Please, please Alice. Straighten up," Luca says, and she loves that he cares. "You could have good posture." Like a mother, a father. "You're an angel come from paradise to answer my prayers." All she has ever wanted to be for anyone is an angel come from paradise to answer prayers—that was her job, pencil-size, of course. She was that for her father, she knows. She laughs at herself, looking out the window at the vast expanse of nothing because she had always prided herself on needing no one—like the desert so proud and independent, almost arrogant, in its self-sufficiency and solitude, too spiteful to envy more fertile land.

Sanjay Deep becomes a chatterer carrying on about the

state of Indian cinema and his wife who will only act in Hollywood who says Indian films are all sexist. Alice likes this phantom woman and agrees with her and hopes she gets to meet her. "But there is no difference between your cinema and ours. It's all fantasy. You're just more literal," he says—lilting emphasis on *literal*.

"I love the way you move your head," she says suddenly and boldly. His head moves in rhythm with his words, a figure eight. When he smiles, he flashes a perfect set of white teeth and two dimples. "I don't blame your wife," Alice says. And then they're talking and he wants to know about her, wants to pry her open like an oyster. She's the traveler once again, outside of time. She has a way of deflecting that makes her mysterious, learned from all that poker playing, knows how to reveal nothing and attract curiosity. But now she talks. It spills out, all that she kept hidden for so long. She was always good at hiding things, even from herself. As a child she would even hide little treasures simply so that she could find them later. And though her brothers and sisters traded in each other's secrets like currency, she reveled in telling hers to no one, relished watching them as they tried to decipher her. But now everything she'd managed to hide comes forth: father mother sisters brothers Lily even and the Italian maid Finny the bastard and she the only one of both sides. Dad, she smiles and uses the present tense: A priest who becomes a Gestalt therapist, has dreams of writing a book on love and of founding a utopia, creates a family instead. Hit mother, mother needs stitches, doesn't ever finish his book, hurts sisters—God knows how, and don't want to know though on his deathbed he tries to will me to listen to his confession as if I were a priest with the power to save him from hell to which he was sure he was destined. Was what he did to the

Cooper girls something big or the simple fact that he did not love them because you do not really, deeply, truly love those that are not your own. She and Luca pass a field of flowering sunflowers, the moon sets and then rises again, and they are back in another desert filled with camels.

"The camel goes well with the desert, appropriate animal for the desert," she says to Luca. "It, too, has a sense of proud indifference, head held high, with only the dip in the neck to suggest weakness—with only a dip in the neck to give a sense of weight. Those long, awkward legs, weak knees, lips that foam, hoofless feet of solid soft pads—the only friendly thing about the camel."

"Don't find metaphors for yourself in the camel," Luca says. "You're softer than that."

"I didn't want him to confess to me. I don't want or need to know anything more about him than I already know," she said, crying.

They drive for days and for days she talks. Luca patient and steady. "Very colorful," he says about her family. The indoor pool and the architect who designed it and the rest of the house and the Omega Point and high dreams of paradise on earth and an orchard with succulent white peaches and a baby cherry tree with sweet baby cherries and berry fields and a berry farmer who betrays her father. And his book languishing on note cards like a girl in the thick of a hot summer day on a chaise by a pool, unable to get up.

"He believed in nothing at the end."

"Who would blame him? It's not nice to die. We always think it is the other who will die, not ourselves."

She presses her face into the window glass. It's night with a chill. They are above the Ganges—strong brown god—and thousands of kites cupping tiny glittering candles illuminate the world like stars. And she can see (sort of) both the exquisite beauty and the knowledge that who she is and who she would have become are in the stories she recites. She misses Chardin, sitting on the deck with a late summer breeze, overlooking the birds and the field and all of her father's romantic notions.

A Texan who swims in pools of beer and fights Indians and wins big pots of money in high-stakes poker and who has a head so big he can't find a hat to fit it until he visits a hat store in Ireland on a whim and finds a hat so big it is being thrown away since there is no head big enough to fit it in all of Ireland. A man who couldn't finish a book who developed a rage that ate him from the core, an anger she has in her own fists. Smash the brains out of something, a desire to kill. "I killed my father because I didn't want to know anything more because I wanted to save him (and myself) from the impostor," she said. "And I am an only child when a short time ago I was the center of nine and now there will be no family where a short time ago its primacy had been certain to me." She saw it like a precious plate, her family, tossed up into the air to shatter on the ground. Saw them fighting like beasts, tearing at the flesh of each other. A little boy saving toy soldiers for the daughter he will someday have. Who sends her a clown from the sky. "I had not understood that the integrity of the family had been certain only to me."

"Don't be sorry for yourself," Luca says, almost snaps. "All those sisters and brothers of yours certainly wouldn't be hanging around through his death if this family weren't certain for them."

"What do you mean," Alice says, a little annoyed at his insight.

"He had dreams," Luca adds.

"Yeah." Alice sighs ironically.

"Who doesn't?" he asks. And with that her father seems suddenly very ordinary. "Who is passionate and vital and dreamless?"

"Doesn't it mean more if you succeed at some of them?" She realizes that question is stupid as she asks it. If a thing is worth doing, she thinks. "You accomplished yours," Alice notes.

"How could you know?"

"All the movies."

"I've made dreams, but don't be certain cinema was my dream. Do you know where my wife is?" He pauses for a moment, sucks in the air. Blue sky all around them. He watches her, as she ponders this notion—what do we know about another person's desire—eyes off road as he drives and drives. "Why aren't Chardin and your family exactly where you left them?" he adds. He watches her watch her reflection in the window glass. She wipes away tears from her cheeks and pinches them. Her dreams of India and the promise of Indian movies float easily out a crack in the window and dissolve in the air.

"He's not gone," Luca says simply, and takes her back to Chardin.

ANTON GAVE ALICE a map once because she had decided to start a collection. She loved maps; they indicated both the way out and the desire to contain. Landowners love maps of their land. Emperors love maps of their empires. She had a map of Chardin, but mostly she had road maps of the United States. She had one map of the Isle of Man—a name she loved. She imagined it, as the name promised, as an island of men. She reasoned that of course then there existed an Isle of Woman. She imagined the two islands drifting together to make one—the way that land drifts, Rodinia pulling apart coming together again as Pangea; India crashing into Tibet; Madagascar to Africa; Scotland drifting from America. The map her father gave her was an antique from 1860—bought at a store that sold only rare maps—and depicted the lands of Hindoostan and Farther India, all the possibility that spread out beyond India. It was to be a place where the great civilizations of Asia, the Chinese and the Indian, merged and converged in perfect harmony. The Omega Point? Engraved and hand-colored by S. Augustus Mitchell of Philadelphia, the first great American cartographer. The perspective was godlike, the colors defining the countries pastel pinks and greens and blues against a creamy background. Etched in shades of gray, a panel of roses, lilies, and lotuses decorated the border. Even so, the lands of Farther India floated just above the surface of the paper, hovering over the Bay of Bengal and the Indian Ocean, the northeastern territory crashing into the delicate border of flowering vines. The land indeed was in motion, about to take flight—either because it would not be contained or because the vision of the empire would not be contained.

Later she would retrieve the map from the depths of storage boxes that held her childhood and she would frame it and hang it on the wall of the living room at Chardin. That would be much later, when Alice was an environmental lawyer (who wanted to be a famous movie star), working on a massive project to save open space in New Jersey from the grip of sprawl. She would choose a wooden frame painted with a silver distressed hue and a flowering vine design to echo the border. A frame that would contain the failure of an empire and all its dreams—how we run after them, all of us little emperors, like lepidopterists with their nets in those fields of rare butterflies, we run for the answer and the hope of beauty or at least of something more.

CHAPTER TWENTY-FOUR

The River

THEY SAY OUR EXTREMITIES die first—fingertips, fingers, wrists, toes, feet, ankles, shins, calves. Blood receding, death slowly creeping up your body, possessing you bit by bit, inch by inch, until it owns you finally and completely. Like an empire that dies from its outer territories first, slowly moving inward to the core. They say, as well (this magical universal *they*, this all-knowing, omniscient *they*), that our vitality is weakest in the night and that for this reason so many births and deaths occur in the early morning hours, those quiet lonely hours when it seems not only the whole world is asleep but the entire universe, when even the owls and the bats and the katydids and the moths are asleep, when even the stars seem to have vanished and the moon is gone.

Anton died at this hour. The same hour he was born, in fact, sixty-four years earlier in Corsicana, Texas—before the birds, before the light. He died in bed next to Eve. He sat up. The room was dark. He sat up quickly, with a strength and resolve he had not had in months. The gesture woke Eve. She tried to make him out but could see nothing. "I can't breathe, babe," she heard him say. "Help me, I can't breathe. Help.

Please, babe." Then he was choking. She searched for the light, afraid to find it. She wanted it to stay black forever. She did not want to see his face, those eyes. She heard his body move. It pulled the sheets, tightening them over her. He was writhing. Death was at his brain, his eyes, his neck, his throat. His mind was swimming, in a fog, swirling. No thoughts in it. No room for thoughts. Death was taking possession of his chest, his ribs, his lungs, his heart. *Where is the damn light?* He was wetting the bed, he was shitting—he hadn't been able to pee or shit easily in weeks. He was shitting easily now. She could smell it. The body does not die gracefully. They, our famous *they,* say the body voids completely when it dies. The muscles relax, releasing the bladder and the bowels. His voice planted itself firmly in her mind. Help me. Help me. Help me. It was the call of the peacocks. This was the way they sounded when they cried. HELP ME. Help me, babe, please. As if it were up to her, as if she could save him by finding the light. She knocked over bottles of pills and a glass of water searching for the light, afraid, but she knew he was already dead. His struggling stopped and quiet spread over the room. A tremendous stillness. Except for the smell she would have thought she had had a bad dream.

She was alone with Anton (save her ninety-year-old mother who was asleep at the other end of the house), as she always knew she would be. She had known that she would be alone with Anton when he died from the moment he was diagnosed. Even when the house was filled with all the kids. The kids, like the extremities that die first, receded from Chardin to their homes, their lives.

When she found the light she did not turn it on. She had imagined that she would be afraid next to his dead body, but she was not. It was just a body. Rather, she was relieved, a deep and guilty relief. Her hair was a mess. Her breath smelled. She wanted to brush her teeth, stand up, get dressed, go to work. *I've got to work,* she thought. *But what will I do with the body?*

She thought of her first three baby girls (the fourth was his, completely and absolutely) when they were still babies, their little pink bare bodies. She thought of them picking daffodils, she thought of them helping her dig up myrtle for the lawn all dressed alike in summer jumpers, near the old water tower deep in the woods behind their house, how the sun cut through those trees like a prism, dappled light. Then she wondered again how she would get rid of the body.

She lay back down for a minute to think, lay her head into the soft down pillows and beneath the covers she searched for Anton's hand. I'll just hold it for a while, she thought. When she found it, she lifted it to her chest and held it there. It was his left hand, swollen with a blood clot for a month. The first extremity to go. She pushed the hand into her chest. The hand was soft, but cold. She rubbed it with her hands, trying to warm it up. Then again she pressed it to her heart. She felt it, a weight there—her life pounding into the utter stillness of that hand. The weight of it sank into her heart, becoming heavier and heavier. "I'm sorry," she said. Her words hung in the air. Was his spirit in the air, in the wind? She had honestly believed that the cancer could have been reversed. By sheer will, they were going to escape this one. Residual omnipotence. As if in saving him, she would have been able to show and prove her love.

She lay there for a long time. The night turned pale and soupy with a thickly clouded dawn. A chorus of birds one by one began to sing. The thinnest film of light blessed the morning. She was tired. She kept her eyes shut, keeping out the light. He does not like to be alone, she thought. He was alone, watching television when she got home—just as if he were well, she'd thought. They'd watched *King Kong* on television. "All those actors are dead, too, babe," he had said in the middle of explaining that Alice had been there but had had to leave. She could see that Alice had been there; morphine patches covered his arms; in the hamper, morphine-stained pillowcases hid. Eve peeled off the patches and threw them away, worried for her daughter.

"Where is she now?" Eve wanted to hold Alice as if she were still a baby.

"I failed her in this," Anton said. A clarity Eve hadn't seen in a while and thus she should have known because our famous *they* speak of the lucidity that comes just before death. "Tell her she got rid of the impostor."

"The what?" Eve asked anxiously.

"Promise?"

"You'll tell her."

"It's not so bad as I thought, babe." He was thinking about his death, the most important experience of his life, an understanding that made it not so bad, that made it his entirely and exclusively. His little girl held his arm, whispered into his ear—gently he was leaving. It was gentle, a closing of the eyes that was all.

HE'S AFRAID TO be alone, Eve thought. The birds kept singing, a whole chorus, an entire orchestra—finches, of course, and robins and woodpeckers and indigo buntings. They reminded her of making love to Anton in the long onion grass, her clothes falling off, his kisses, how it had seemed she was reaching toward the universe to become part of it, part of some infinite and wonderful and exquisite new world. Pure sensation and every nerve awake, and though she thought she could hear the voices of her daughters, yelling for her, to show her something magnificent that they'd found—a fiddlehead fern, she imagined. *Did you know, Mommy, that ferns and asparagus are the oldest plants in the world? They were here before anything else. Matteuccia struthiopteris, you can eat them, a spring delicacy. Let's eat them, Mom.* She imagined her daughters finding her like this and though she was embarrassed to have the thought and though she felt it was wrong, possibly even criminal, it intensified her pleasure. She needed to cry out—she saw them standing above her, Jane's angry brown eyes on her—his lips sealed her mouth and she screamed into his mouth. The onion grass was cool and wet on her warm skin. And daffodils flowered everywhere—charity May, February Gold, Jonquilla hybrids, Peeping Toms. The little feet of her girls, those little feet thumping into the ground in search of treasures, geranium white with red cups in a treasure, little wonderful things, in their hands, a bouquet of fiddlehead ferns and daffodils for her, coming closer, closer. The dirt in her back with acorns. His lips in her ears, his lips on her neck. A radiant spring sun. She could no longer hear the girls. They vanished. This was too glorious, too impossibly sweet.

She called her daughters first, from the phone in the kitchen. "I'll be right there," Julia said. "I'll get Kate and be right there." All efficiency and business. "I love you, Mommy. I'll be right there." Next she called Jane. Dawn approached like a battalion of soldiers, creeping up from the vast fields as if the light were rising from the earth itself. The world was utterly still. She lit candles in the kitchen. She lit all the candles she could find until the kitchen and dining room flickered with candlelight. The birds sang wildly. She imagined they sang Beethoven, big and hard and full and romantic, for Anton.

"What do I do next, Jane?" Eve asked, crying into the phone. Jane was crying, too. Eve's face was creased and beaten; it seemed she'd been crying for fifty-eight years. She wanted her daughter to take her hand and lead the way. She was mad at Jane for not being here. The day promised rain, but even so as the sun lifted over the horizon a thin slip of clear sky bled orange, a nick of promise before it disappeared behind the thick clouds. "He doesn't like to be left alone," Eve said. "He's so scared to be alone, he doesn't want to die alone. I should stay with him—shouldn't I try to keep him warm?" The receiver was wet with tears and drool.

"Have you called Alice? She's staying with Caroline. Isn't she with Caroline?" Jane asked abruptly.

"I don't know."

"You need to be a mother now, Mom," Jane said.

"A mother and a father," Eve said with self-pity, hating herself for the desire.

"You need to think of Alice," Jane said, wishing she were holding the girl in her arms, protecting her from the final stab of this.

"I don't know where Alice is," Eve said. "She was here last night with Dad. She was supposed to be here." Eve wanted Jane to fix it all. She wanted Jane to find Alice and tell Alice and comfort Alice. She wanted to tell Jane about the morphine, get Jane to worry this out for her. "She tried to kill Pop," Eve said. "But don't tell the others," she added, knowing everyone would now soon know.

"She what?"

"Morphine, morphine everywhere. It didn't work, but she thinks it did."

"One of us should be with her...one of us should tell her. She'll need one of us with her," Jane said. Jane would find Alice, Eve knew that. "I'm afraid of what she'll do if she's alone. She might hurt herself."

"Don't alarm me, just today please." Eve sat in a child's chair by the phone, even though there was a big chair just next to her. But she wanted to become small, retreat, be six again. "You've gotten so big now I'll have to give you pills to keep you small," she had said to each one of her girls. How she'd hated it when they'd grown too big to pick up, how it felt like a robbery. No, no, not yet. She pressed the receiver into her cheek, looking out on bird feeders that Anton had erected so many years before. By the window he kept a guide to birds, always hoping to identify the rare species. Beyond the bird feeders was their night garden—they had planted it together. A garden that bloomed entirely at night—jasmine and brugmansia and moonflower, evening scented stock, magnolia, lavender. It had taken them years to make it perfect and they'd sit there late at night and watch the flowers open, breathing in all the fragrances. "Will you find her for me, Jane, please? Will you find Alice?" Then Jane wanted to know exactly when and how he had died. "Not now," Eve said simply. "Please just come. Please find Alice and come."

"Don't let them take the body away before we get there," Jane said. "I want to see him. Don't let it be taken away." She was crying, which made Eve cry more. Eve imagined Jane would want to be sure to see the body so that the picture of it could stay in her memory as a memento mori and also so that she could be sure that he was dead. The phone was wet and cold against her lips. "You're going to need to be strong for Alice, Mom. This can't be all about you." Sometimes it was as if her daughters forgot that she was real, capable of pain. She put down the receiver. She wanted to curl into bed and for just this once have Jane drift her fingers through her hair while she cried. She didn't have the will left to protect.

Slowly and meticulously Eve built a fire, crossing the kindling, stuffing it with paper, just the way Anton had shown the kids. "Let it breathe, babes, a fire's got to breathe." She wanted the house to look nice. She fluffed the pillows. She put the dog outside. She swept up the ash on the hearth. She straightened the photo albums and books on the coffee table. Then there was nothing left to fix.

She took a candle and walked to the back of the house, through Anton's library, to her mother's room. She would crawl into bed with her mother. She had never crawled into bed with her mother, not even when she was a child. The house was cold and quiet. It was her house now. The thought rang through her with more guilt. I'll make it just as you dreamed, she said to Anton. She had to call Laurence and tell him. Her daughters were always crawling into bed with her, curling up with her.

The blinds, thick raw blue silk, were closed. The room was dark and crowded with objects from the house her mother had once had. Last Morrow, it was called. A Victorian mansion in Maine. Bone china figurines of girls and boys frolicked on the shelves. Velvet pillows backed the velvet love seat. Gilt-framed mirrors hung on the walls. The grandmother had wanted to put as much as possible into the small room. "I can't be without my things," she had said when they were fixing it up. Eve watched her mother from the doorway. Her long white hair was out of its bun and net, hanging loosely, and thinly, at her chest. The sheets were pulled up to her neck. She breathed quietly. Her hands were clasped at her waist.

"Is that you, Eve?" she said after a while.

"It's me," Eve said. Her mother sat up with some difficulty. She stared at her daughter. Eve knew what her mother was thinking: how old her daughter looked, how weathered her once-gorgeous girl was. "It was that man's fault. He was a good for nothing. He worked you to the bone," she had so often said, calling him Ben for years and years when she knew perfectly well that was not his name. "You're not work-brittle, Ben," she used to say as he sat at the dining-room table drinking his coffee from his big mug, sitting there in his red robe, the paper spread before him. She didn't care to understand his pain, of course.

"He's dead?" her mother finally asked. Eve stood there like a little girl, arms hanging heavily at her side. Her mother patted a spot beside her on the bed and Eve sank into it and then against her mother. They didn't say anything for a while. Her mother simply held her, gently rubbing her back.

Eve remembered her mother at Father's funeral. She could still see them in the small church in Hasbrouck Heights. Her mother stared straight ahead with unwavering, unblinking, tearless eyes. Eve had been mad at her mother for not crying, as if it proved she had not cared. The church looked over the marshes to New York City and there was so much stained glass, made by Italians at the turn of the century. The Italians had been imported from Italy just to make the stained glass. Ian had told her that when they came to see the minister about the service. Ian had always known details like that. She hadn't paid attention at the time, but it was what she remembered most from those days surrounding her father's death. The Italians and her mother's tearless eyes.

The minister made them wait a long time before he would see them. "I don't see the point" is what he had said as they walked into his dark office. "Your father was not religious."

The minister was an austere man with a shock of white hair and small eyes set close together and deeply in a large face. "The close-set eyes of a liar," Ian had said afterward. Eve laughed, the first time since her father's death. Eve could see the two of them as if they were standing in front of her, a young couple struck by a first sadness—ordinary sadness, ordinary loss—trying to make something light of it. They would have been younger then than all three of her Cooper daughters were now, but older than Alice. At the time though, the sadness had not seemed ordinary; it had felt as if she, too, had died, as if a trench slowly, emphatically, opened in her heart and pulled everything that she had been and would be into it until there was nothing recognizable left of her. She had not wanted to get out of bed. She had not wanted to kiss the babies. She had not wanted to eat.

The minister wore black, of course, right up to his neck. It would seem those eyes of his could get lost in the flesh of his face. Ian tried to persuade him as Eve cried. This church didn't want her father. "Isn't it your job to welcome souls?" Ian had asked. The minister gave Ian a look with those eyes that said, "You know it's too late for his soul." In a few years Ian would be gone, off to Canada with Camille, setting Eve's life on an utterly different course. But this day, he held Eve so gently as he persuaded the minister. She had never felt that sort of warmth and tenderness from him. On the day of the funeral, his arms continued protecting her, allowed her to suffer, held her up in the pew, during the limousine ride. His hands warm in her curly hair. His lips quiet against hers. She had been young. She kept thinking of that, young then with her three little girls. He had seen to it that the girls were dressed as Eve liked, that there was someone to care for them so that Eve didn't have to worry and so that he could be entirely for her. He tried to make sure that she ate. He tried to make her laugh. "The close-set eyes of a liar," he'd repeat to hear her laugh again. It didn't seem so long ago when they were married. She remembered him holding her close, their sides pressed together, walking into the church, seated in the pew—he had held her so close it seemed he would never have wanted to let her go. She longed to be held by him today, to call him and tell him, to see him arrive for her, organize the wake, the funeral, the days for her.

"What do I do with his body, Mother?" Eve asked, sitting up. The candle she had brought to the room glowed on their faces and Eve's shone like a jewel, refracting the light.

"Eve," she said. "Eve, darling, you must call the hospice immediately and then the undertakers. Let the girls take care of the undertakers, but you must call the hospice. They'll clean him up before everyone gets here." Her mother had volunteered as a hospice nurse when she was in her early eighties in Maine. One by one her friends all began to die, so she decided to help them. She held Eve a little longer, warm and soft, their fleshy bodies meshed together, patting Eve, holding her tight against her chest. Her baby daughter, her little girl. Eve wished she were at home again, her childhood home on Larkin Lane, her father chasing her into the kitchen in a game of hide-and-seek. She wished for her father, the big leather chair he liked to sit in. How much of her life had changed since he died. "It's all right, darling, it's all right," her mother said. She ran her hands over Eve's. She examined Eve's hands, held them up to the candlelight. "Such perfect cuticles, beautiful half-moons beneath your nails. The perfect shade of pink, nice hard nails." Just love me, Eve wanted to say. But then understood that perhaps she was. Her mother took a file from her bedside table and began to file Eve's nails and she filed them until each one was rounded. Just the sound of the emery board on nails. Eve would have allowed her to do anything in order for her mother to love her. "He doesn't like to be alone, Mother. He made me promise I'd never leave him alone." Her mother filed and buffed and a long time passed, it seemed.

"Ian loved me," Eve said. "He loved me and I didn't know how to love him back. I just thought he'd always be there. We had those three babies." Eve felt like one of her own daughters, how they'd lie in bed with her and tell her all their secrets. She had never confessed a thing to her mother. She ached, she wanted to split in half. Her mother continued patting her. All those years. Twenty-five to be exact, somehow vanished—as if they had and had not existed, as if she were reading about them just now in a novel. No more real, and less permanent. What would her father think of her? She saw her three daughters waving good-bye to Ian's parents and her parents as she and Ian and the girls sailed off to Europe on the *Queen Elizabeth* because Ian was afraid to fly. They stood at the guardrail waving furiously, all dressed alike in outfits she had sewn herself. How proud she was of her sewing. "I loved Ian. I didn't love Anton. I didn't love Ian. I loved Anton. I don't know how to love. What's wrong with me, Mother? Help me, Mother." Help me, help me, help me. "You don't need to figure it out just now," her mother said. He had sat up and struggled for his last breath and couldn't find it and asked her to help him find it but she couldn't and thus he died and now he lay in bed alone and twenty-five years had passed and she had stopped loving him and now she loved him. "Stop," she screamed.

WHEN JULIA AND KATE arrived, Eve was curled up in bed with Anton, clinging to his arm. The grandmother was sitting in the rocker, watching over Eve. Nicholas and Caroline kneeled by Anton with Bible and rosary, saying a novena. Nicholas had set up his 16 mm on a tripod to film, though the camera was off for now. The hospice people had come and fixed Anton up, changed the sheets. One of them stood at the closet, boxing up Anton's oxygen. It was raining outside now and though the birds darted about, they were no longer singing. Anton's hands were neatly folded at his chest. The room was dark, lit only by the candles. The sliding door opened onto the deck and the sound of the rain.

"Some hot tea," the grandmother said to the girls. The girls ignored her. "Listen to me," she persisted, but soon gave up. "Be nice to your mother."

Julia and Kate kissed Eve and rubbed her back and then fell to their knees and kissed Anton. His cheeks were still warm, the blood draining slowly, his body becoming like lead. The room was still and thick. The candles hissed and flickered.

"Someone must call Lily," Eve said softly. "But I don't want her coming over." She felt cruel, felt her tongue hot and sharp. She thought, How healthy everyone looks—life flourishing on their faces.

"Has Alice been called?" Julia asked. Her face too puffed. All their faces puffed. "Jane is looking for her," Caroline said, without looking up. Finny and Timothy were on their way, but Sofia refused to come. Eve didn't welcome her there anymore. Ever since Sofia carted off the furniture in the U-Haul she was unwelcome. But since she refused to come to her father's funeral, which of course she would have been welcome to, it gave Eve more reason to spite her. Julia searched the Yellow Pages for undertakers and then called a few to negotiate a price. Mr. Moon and Jackson Jessie. "He'd like the names," she said with her smile.

"Don't bother," Nicholas said. "They're all franchised." He fiddled with his camera now to start shooting. No one seemed to notice or mind the camera by the bed, capturing the loss of Anton's face becoming like porcelain now, as delicate and breakable. Even so, later the images would shock. No one would remember that they had been taken—when why or how. Images that would bring back this day after Anton had come silently forward with them, slowly returning to his former self. "Death portraiture was common in the nineteenth century," Julia would explain later, in defense of Nicholas. "We just don't like death anymore—sweep it up out away."

"Can't we just bury him here?" Eve asked. "He'd want to be buried here." She looked at her children. They all considered the notion. He'd been dying for months, but no one had thought about what they'd do with his body once he actually died. Eve worried about how much burial costs would be and then felt guilty for worrying about that and noted all the healthy faces of the children again.

"Caroline," Eve said. "I tried, Caroline. I tried to save him. I thought that I could."

"It wasn't up to you, Eve," she said with a half smile and Anton's blue eyes. Eve couldn't look at Caroline's eyes. She wanted Caroline to love her. She wanted all of Anton's kids to love her. She wanted them to love her more than they loved their own mother. She wanted to be thought of as good; she wanted it to be acknowledged that she had tried.

"Someone has called Agnes?" Eve asked, feeling generous for thinking of Agnes.

The others arrived. Timothy, his wife, Finny, Jane along with her husband, James. Everyone adored her James, especially the grandmother. He busied himself making food for everyone, cleaning the dishes, seeing to it that everyone had what they needed. He swept the kitchen, took out the garbage, made sure the grandmother was comfortable, had hot tea whenever she asked for it. She'd always been in love with James, his English accent made him noble in her estimation—even if he was a painter. "I can tell by looking at you, son, that you'll make history." "Why, Grammy, I already have," he'd say, teasing her.

Jane hadn't found Alice. She wasted no time telling her sisters about the morphine. Then everyone knew about the morphine, a sizzle of drama at first, like water dancing in hot oil, until it became just one more detail in a long list of details. They waited for Alice to call while everyone hugged everyone, as if they could hug Anton back into them, hug up the moment. I love you I love you I love you, Kate repeated to Anton's lips. Her Jimmy, too, was there, sitting on the edge of the bed sifting through poems and reading them as they proved appropriate. Anton had come to love this short blond wiry man and, in turn, Jimmy had loved him back. "Such good men you girls have," Anton had said, and for them, when he praised them, it was always like they had won the prize.

Kate kissed Anton's lips. She dragged her fingers through his hair, along his scalp to comfort him. "He feels very here, very present," she said to no one. "He's still in the room." Julia wiped a cool cloth over his face. She straightened his collar, picked the dried catarrh from his lips and nose. She cut hairs that were too long. Eve watched her daughters, tending to him, loving him. You don't love him, she had often accused them—as if their ability to love him affected her own.

"He's building a Chardin in the sky for all of us," Julia said. "I can see him already finding the perfect cloud."

"So he made it to heaven after all?" Nicholas asked.

"Don't be sentimental, babe," Finny said.

"I need a pool, a small pool, big 'nough for twenty-five people or so and heated so I can hold therapy sessions there," Timothy said with a Texas accent. He wore a suit. On a private jet he'd flown in from Dallas where he lived now, running his mother's oil business. Rich, normal. He'd always wanted to be normal. As a ten-year-old he had taken himself out of free school and enrolled in a private school to which he had to wear a uniform, a tie, and polished shoes. His ambition became wealth so that he would grow up and have plenty for his father, so that his father could continue to live in the style he had become accustomed to and beyond, so that his father would not have to worry. Timothy told the other kids now that he earned so much money it wasn't worth his time to bend over and pick up a hundred-dollar bill. He had heard that about Bill Gates, that it wasn't worth his time to pick up a five-hundred-dollar bill.

"A cloud would be a more appropriate setting for the Omega Point."

"Who'll be next?" Nicholas asked.

"You," Kate said, staring at his skinny, bony body. Nicholas prided himself on being very thin.

"You can pick the hundred up for me," Caroline said to Timothy.

"I read that people with low body weight have a far better chance of living past one hundred," Nicholas said. Relief was palpable in the room, spreading through each one of them slowly and definitively as if they'd made it to the top of a mountain. The release of death being over, for now anyway, lifting like many beautiful bubbles in a champagne flute. They were giddy, all eager, all filled with the exuberance of life again.

"He outlived pancreatic cancer patients by a long shot," Julia said. "It's because he wanted to bring us back together before dying."

"We're together," someone said.

"Were we ever apart?" someone else asked. Sofia remained unmentioned although Eve thought about her. She can come if she wants, Eve thought. She looked around the room at all the children, wondering how long this family would last, glad for the breath of humor.

Anton's eyes sank and the skin became elastic and stiff, then waxy then blue. The hours passed and the air in the room thickened and the candles burned down and were replaced and the room smelled of them. No one left the room. Each minute a stolen minute. His dirty clothes still lay in a heap on the bathroom floor. His clean clothes still hung in the closet, so big, belonging to someone who had been gone for a while now. His ascots and his Irish cowboy hat. All the pills and experimental remedies, the oils for massage, the special straws, and all the Bibles and rosaries. The remnants of his book, the boxes of index cards with their scribblings. Gray, gray day. To each person entering the room Eve apologized for not being able to save Anton. She refused to leave the room. She held his hands. It rained a deluge. The grand-mother rocked in her chair.

YEARS FROM NOW, Anton neatly dead in his unmarked grave, Eve wandered Europe with a new lover. "If ever you think it's over when you're sixty," she'd say to a daughter, "you're wrong. It can just be beginning." Traveling Europe, lighting candles for her dead husband with her new lover at her side. For her dead husband's soul. Lighting candles in Chartres, the Duomo, St. Paul's. She was not religious, never had been— one more area where their minds had no chance of meeting.

She lit a hundred different candles, setting them next to other candles for other lost souls—feeling with it that she was at least trying. Making up for the unmarked grave? At night she would look at the universe and wonder, wish that Anton were up in the heavens fully entwined with Venus, making love to Venus, discussing his theories of sex and sexual equality and love with Venus. Perhaps even learning a thing or two.

In France, Italy, Spain, England, she lit her candles—with each one feeling just a bit more free.

ALICE DROVE UP the driveway in Anton's blue Toyota. Her face long, her eyes big and drooping, her lips a bluish gray, her clothes wet and rumpled. She said she had spent the night in Newark, wandering the highways—dramatic as she liked to be. She told them that she had known that Anton was dead and that she had wanted to be alone—mysterious as she liked to be. The secret of his murder, she believed, was firmly and deeply buried within her. The others did not let her know that they knew. She did not want to see her father's dead body. Eve tried to encourage her, tried to say that she would regret not seeing him later when it was gone. "It?" she said to her mother, and sat down on a stool just outside his bedroom door, close enough to be near, yet far enough so she could not see. Her sisters and brothers flocked to her, surrounding her with kisses and words of courage and the promise that this day, this moment, this pain, would pass.

And five, six, eight years from now they'd all be at Chardin for a party. Thick hot June day and the garden thick, too, with red poppies and gigantic purple iris—the kids fighting about the incompetence of the president, teasing each other about a mass baptism for all the kids. Eleven grandchildren, blooming youth, darting about on the lawn, owning the place—as if their existence had always been a certainty. Chardin so firmly theirs. A party to celebrate eleven-month-old India Furey—blue-eyed, black-haired daughter of Alice with a round face like a putto. "As if sculpted by Bernini," Julia declared. All the older grandchildren fawning over her. And Sofia there (after much fighting on Alice's part with Eve in Alice's attempt to unite her family again) with her three boys in their ironed sailor suits, dressed as Eve would like. An apology of sorts. Her three little boys swarming at her feet as they studied their mother's childhood home. "What a magnificent place for kids to grow up," one guest would say. And to Alice, Sofia would say, "I'm glad I had boys. Eve likes boys. She'll like my boys." The moment, the dread of Anton's death now an abscess surrounded by the tissue of time. "We'll get Father O'Brien to baptize them in the pond, full immersion." "That's hypocrisy—we're not religious." "We'll get him to baptize you, Alice." "I was already baptized, by Pop in the indoor swimming pool." Her pop firmly resurrected, filling her up inside. "It's as if Anton has been resurrected in her," the Cooper sisters would say to each other.

Alice would lie on his grave, imagining a mailbox there to mark it—ordinary silver-colored mailbox with its red flag erect. A mailbox in which anyone could write letters to him and read the letters sent to him. She would tell him of the new kitchen and the barnyard that Mom fixed up as he had dreamed. She would tell him that the new kitchen extended from the house like the prow of a ship and that half the house was shingled and that Laurence was there to make all the designs and that the Cooper girls still argued with Eve about practicality. "Fix the sewage system before these expensive renovations!!" "But they always succumb to the beauty of Mom's creations," Alice would tell her father. She would tell him that the barnyard was filled with sheep and ducks and goats and pigs and a cow for milking and steer for meat and chickens both for eggs and meat. "Mom's worried about mad cow, wants to grow everything she eats herself." And she'd tell him about mad cow and hoof-and-mouth and she'd tell him that the Indian government wanted to have all the cows of Europe shipped to India in order that they not be slaughtered. She knew he would appreciate the size of that dream. Moved forward in time, the great morass of days sailing into better days. She would tell him of India's eyes, the devouring intensity of them, how she'll eat you up with them, how they shimmer like star sapphires radiating wisdom. Her baby girl, her life, her love explaining to her her father's love. "Don't ever be sentimental, babe. You can be romantic but not sentimental," he had said to her. And she would laugh, hearing the words as if they were coming forth audibly from his grave. Lying on the soft grass above him, she would then imagine him with his head on the pillow that Caroline had brought to him in the funeral home. His favorite down pillow. His brain dust by now with all the time that had passed. But his bones still beautifully white and intact. The cancer never made it your bones, she'd think, lying there understanding finally the Promise of long ago. It's all right; it can't be anything else but all right.

BUT NOT TODAY. The undertakers had come in their dark undertakers' suits, Jackson Jessie and Mr. Moon. The kids kept repeating the names. The undertakers stood in the dining room waiting patiently, rubbing together their black-gloved hands. They had with them a stretcher and a bag. The grandmother sat in her chair near the fire. Julia discussed funeral fees and what they could afford. "Something simple," she said. "Discreet."

"We want a cheap job," Nicholas said with his blond smile. This even was not going to crack him. His father was dead. That's what happened. Nothing unique, bizarre, special. A dead father and he the oldest son. A cheap job. Very cheap.

"A pine casket," Jane said. For her the motivation was different. Her mother would be paying the funeral bills. Cocky perhaps, they both were, with the release.

"Some hot tea, please," the grandmother asked of Jane's James who brought it to her. "Piping hot, madam," he said, but inside he was waiting for this to be over so that he could take Jane back to their world. "Why have you all got the name James? I think that Julia and Kate were hoping to copy you," she said although she did not know Julia's Jim. He had not come because he was too new a boyfriend and it wasn't appropriate for him to be dragged through all this. He was at her home waiting for her to return, there to open up for her again the world beyond her family.

"Is that your grandmother?" one of the undertakers asked. He had a bright patch of white hair on the crown of his head, otherwise he was bald. His eyes were jolly and greedy.

"They've got their eyes on Grammy," Julia whispered to Kate.

"How many plots would you like?" the other asked, making a mental note of all the people gathered there. "All of you the kids?" He had a small notebook in which he jotted down notes. He was younger than the other, but still over fifty, and more somber. Liver spots flecked his pale face. "Lot a kids," he noted.

"We have to ask," the first one said. "Out of respect. The yard's filling up."

"The grim reapers," Kate whispered back.

"I think the rest of us will be cremated," Julia answered.

Just outside his bedroom door, Alice sat on her stool. It was her body that was there, that was all. Her mind was somewhere else entirely. She was impervious to the love of her sisters and brothers, who leaned over her and kissed her and asked after her night. She would not let them in, not yet. Just her body there—she was talking to Luca about dreams. The undertakers brushed past her with the bag and the stretcher. Eve held Alice's shoulders and begged them to wait. "My daughter needs to say good-bye. She hasn't said good-bye yet." They hovered at Alice's back, but she could not feel them.

"The body is ripening, Mrs. Furey." Just a job for them, of course.

"Alice," Eve said gently. Alice's arrival had turned Eve into a mother again, gave her a job, a purpose. Eve wrapped her arms around Alice as if she were still a small child. Alice was hers, what she would always have of Anton's, exclusively. "You got rid of him."

"What?" Alice asked, listening now.

"Dad told me to tell you. You got rid of the impostor."

THE FUNERAL WAS at St. Agnes's by the side of the road and yellow roses filled the altar, sent by Ian. A minivan of yellow roses. It all came together fast. The house was empty and then it, too, was filled with yellow roses—also sent by Ian. *I'm with you,* he wrote on the card. And that was something. Eve always counted the somethings. The girls wrote the obituary for the paper—some warm words about the passing of a poker-playing Gestalt Jesuit Texan. The house was empty and then it was filled and then they were driving in a caravan to St. Agnes's Church by the side of the road. Eve felt a bit like a queen. Anton wasn't there yet when she arrived. A bagpiper played in his kilt, the bleating of his pipes filled the parking lot. She looked for the hearse. She saw a sea of people and they came to greet her. It seemed all the merchants from town were there—the butcher, the pharmacist, the waitress from the coffee shop, the funny woman who sold ducks. For a moment Eve worried they'd ask her for money, then realized that today was the one day they would not. It felt like a wedding. She and Anton had married each other three times: twice in Haiti, the first on the balcony of the Oloffson by a priest named Rossignol; the second in the hills between Port-au-Prince and Jacmel. The third wedding was at Chardin only a few years before by a judge. She didn't remember marrying Ian. Her mother had organized it all. She remembered feeling that it was her mother's marriage and not hers and her mother hadn't even liked Ian. She loved him only after he left Eve. "You should hitch your wagon to a star, Eve," she had said when Eve first dated Ian, a high school girl in love with a college sophomore. Eve remembered the photographs of herself in the white veil and the silk gown with one hundred tiny silk buttons running down the back and the train that lifted into a bustle. Her mother had thought the gown too revealing at the chest and had sewn in a piece of lace to hide cleavage. Twenty-one, just graduated from college. All her friends married that year. They were each other's bridesmaids. She went to over a dozen weddings in 1957. Twelve years later she sank her diamond in a tall blue glass jar. Now she waited for Anton to arrive. It took a year to plan a wedding and only a few hours to plan a funeral.

Inside the church a soloist sang Ave Maria and the people congregated. Father O'Brien held Eve's hands. The family had

known him for years. A progressive Catholic priest who believed that women should become priests and who spoke of
God in the feminine. All the boys were dressed in black, ready
for their roles as pallbearers. The day was crisp and bright,
everything so exact, but cold—all the trees naked. Timothy
had flown in his wife's entire family. One of her sisters had a
black eye. She was there with her husband, a big man in a
shiny suit and cowboy boots and a cowboy hat, which he
removed upon entering the church. Eve wondered, Had
the husband given the girl a black eye? "Don't take it," she
wanted to warn the girl. Ave Maria. Julia held a Bible. The
other girls all held poetry. The bagpiper piped. So like a
wedding.

"I wonder if Dad will be on time today?" Nicholas asked.

"This is the one day of his life he'll be on time," Jane said.

The children were comfortable with each other. Somehow
this surprised Eve.

The hearse arrived, driven by the older undertaker. Caroline had taken a few things down to the funeral home for
Anton. His favorite Irish tweed suit to be dressed in, his favorite down pillow for his head to rest upon. "He always likes
pillows," she said. Shakespeare, Shakespeare, Shakespeare.
Some Beethoven and some Mozart. Pictures of the family.
Alice as a baby. They removed the casket from the back of the
hearse, those grim reapers with the black leather execution-
ers' gloves. They had managed to sell her a plot beside Anton.
Father O'Brien led Eve into the church, leading her toward
the black spider of widowhood, a different sort of marriage.
"Who are all these people?" she asked. People kept approaching her, holding her hands warmly. She saw the lady who had
sold them countless ducks. They'd bought ducks just a few
months before when Anton was sick, but well enough to go

for a drive. He had wanted to buy ducks. They'd bought a dozen ducks.

Father O'Brien's hand rested on her head, softly, with all the warmth of a kind heart. He patted her. Such a handsome man, she thought. Eve was sure that he was not celibate. She wished that she could ask him. He had a round soft face with big light brown eyes (that were not close together) and thick white hair—lots and lots of it, wild and crazy and daring. "It will be all right, Eve," he said softly to her, and handed her a handkerchief and only then did she realize that she was crying.

Father O'Brien sat her in the first pew. Now she felt like the mother of the bride at her daughters' weddings. One by one her daughters rose and read, rose and read. She could see them in her wedding gown—one hundred silk buttons racing down the back. Jane had been modest, leaving the lace at the chest. Kate had removed it. Julia had designed her own alteration for the neck. After each wedding it was vacuum-packed and put away in a box with a clear plastic window so that a sense of the dress could be admired without disturbing it. Both Julia and Kate, along with herself, had divorced. Bad luck dress. Who else would wear it? She had saved all their baby clothes, too, all those sweet dresses from Best's. And none of them had had children yet. Close to forty years, but the dresses had been so darling she hadn't been able to give them away. The children could have read all day. *I learn to go where I have to go.* Roethke, Thomas, Heaney, Shakespeare, Dickinson, Hopkins. Their voices seemed to say nothing though, just their pretty mouths opening and closing. Father O'Brien spoke about fear and asked everyone not to be afraid and he spoke about Anton in heaven with God teaching him a thing or two about sexuality, telling him that for the most part God had it right. Did he go to heaven? she wondered. She didn't believe in all that. Eve felt a hundred souls behind her, all weeping. Looking at Father O'Brien speak, Eve was certain he was not celibate. If he were, she decided, it would be a waste. Then singing, communion, prayers, singing again. The voices lifted off the roof of the church and the crisp blue sky sneaked off with the day.

THE LINE OF CARS with their headlights blazing spanned two towns. The graveyard was on a hilltop and Anton's grave looked out toward the Delaware. A soft yet chilling wind snaked through the white tent erected over the casket and the grave, carrying with it the song of the bagpiper. "Danny Boy" rose and fell on the back of the breeze, through the trees, in the grass up into the sky. Alice collapsed with a fist of dirt clutched tightly in her palm. The dirt was from the yard at Chardin, and she'd held it throughout the service. "He's in there and it's dark," she said to no one. She was a blur for Eve. Someone take care of the baby, Eve thought. They were all singing "Danny Boy," all their beautiful mouths filled with it. *All our wars are merry and all our songs are sad.* She saw Alice in the wedding gown. No no. Alice wouldn't wear the dress; it wouldn't make sense for her to wear it. Would she ever marry, have a child? She's such a baby. She'll never be anything but the baby. Alice cut in half, split open.... *When summer's in the meadow.* Eve heard her newborn wailing— someone take care of the baby. Overhead vultures circled, big and black and hungry, soaring on those same waves of air with the song. Ian kneeled beside Alice. He held her back as the casket lowered. Ian was tall enough to be her father, Eve noted. Why didn't he shave off that crazy beard? He does love Alice, Eve thought. His gesture like proof. The cold breeze sneaked up Eve's legs. Alice did not want to let go of the dirt. All the children surrounded the casket and then slowly it sank away. "It's dark in there, can't there be some light. It's so dark in there." "It's okay, Alice," Ian said. The wind blew and it seemed snow might come as the clear blue day grew pale. *And if you come, when all the flowers are dying.* And through the trees you could see the cold Delaware and the steeple of the Catholic church rising from the town. Alice leaned so deeply into the grave, grasping after the casket, as if she could grasp back more than the casket. Ian held back her hair. She was shaking. She let go the dirt, her father's work. Her daughter broke in half. Eve could see her splitting and there was nothing she could do to stop it, shattering down the middle a thousand fractured parts shining in that dying light. Eve wondered if the baby girl would make it. Push, Anton instructed her. Push hard, pretend you hate me, babe. Hate me, babe. She cracked with the pain and then she heard the wailing newborn catching her first drink of air. Anton held her first, all concern for the warmth of her, this magnificent life.

They would go home to a big party of the grand Anton kind—serape rolled back, a champagne fountain and a waltz or two. Kate would tell Eve later that a strange woman attended, a funeral crasher with a broken arm. She'd read his obituary in the paper and had come because, she said, "The life had sounded interesting." She sat on the edge of the sofa with a canapé in her fingers and a glass of champagne, feeling right at home and had Anton been there he would have greeted her with a smile, his gold tooth shining, and asked her all about herself and they would have smoked a joint and become fast friends and he would have learned that she did not have a broken bone but instead osteosarcoma and a pretty bad prognosis and that she had taken to crashing funerals in order that she could imagine her own. The life had sounded interesting—a poker-playing, Gestalt Jesuit Texan.

> And all my dreams will warm and sweeter be
> If you'll not fail to tell me that you love me
> I'll simply sleep in peace until you come to me.

IN HER BED ALONE, late at night—dreaming that Anton was still alive. Awaked by it, the image of him, of forcing him outside on a warm October day—less than a month before he died—because she believed if only he pushed himself a little harder, if only she pushed him a little harder. She had imagined all the love that would have been hers if she could have saved him, how that would make her feel finally worthy. I'm sorry, she said to the night. A strong wind made the bamboo scrape against her windows. All the kids gone again now. She alone. A widow now. Twenty-five years gone by. Somehow passed but not passed at all, as if they had not existed or had been lived by someone else and she had simply read about them. She sees the children crying at the edge of the grave. The bagpiper and the white tent flapping in the November breeze. The vultures spilling from the clouds. The Delaware River lying beneath the hill, cold and ominous, grown fat on smaller rivers creeks a mountain lake rain snow air, flowing to the sea as it had for centuries, millenniums, unaware of the lives passing here, the great dramas being played out on its shores as people stroll through the antique shops of time and their lives. Lives affecting effecting infecting other lives, the great morass folded into the fabric of all life, absorbed as plate tectonics kneads the earth into itself. Something old becomes something new leaving behind scars perhaps, remnants of what was—emphatically over—if that. The kids stood at the grave grieving the loss of a mighty person who had shaped them. He was gone, they'd be gone, their children would come and go, carried forth through stories and genetic memory and the transmigration of souls until they were all neatly kneaded away. For better for bad for worse for good a part of them had died. Weren't they grieving for their own lives, too?

Eve worries in her bed that Anton's children will drift away. By mutual agreement Sofia already had. Would she come back? Would Eve care? What had she and Anton worked for? She understands the laws of blood, but hadn't they somehow, perhaps with the sheer number of years, worked through that?

At the funeral party there had been champagne and toasts and Anton's hand had come down and his fingertips had gently pressed into the soft flesh of her shoulders. "This was beautiful, babe," she could hear him say. Alice with that clump of dirt, the vultures circling, the uncaring river that Eve wanted to will to care. "But the beauty's in its not caring, babe," she could hear him wisely explain. He was there with her late at night, a sliver of moon pasted to the starless sky. All the kids leaning into his grave, as if they wanted to fall in with Anton. Do you love him? she had asked her daughters repeatedly. Little girls piling into the back of a turquoise camper filled with the Furey children, headed for the promise of Alice.

They *had* accomplished that, Eve thought, and drank in a long sip of air like finding water in a desert. They will be back, all nine of them will keep coming back, sucked back, swallowed back, brought back on the waves of love and life—somewhere she was certain. She sank into the pillows and listened to the deep sounds of night, lit by the thin sliver

326 M A R T H A   M c P H E E

of moon refracting light like a spray of stars. The wind continued to scrape at the windows, tussling the bamboo like hair. Anton believed in the big empires of the future. So did she—yours if you could run fast enough. Flow on, she thought, thinking of the river and of all those other rivers, of all that she would do in the morning. Flow on. She was not afraid. Chardin was just the beginning of the dream.

"But what about my book, babe?" she could hear him ask, providing his lines now. How he loved the wind in the bamboo, how it made him feel he was somewhere distant and exotic. She imagined his book, saw his book everywhere—in the collages and index cards. His grand ambition rising from the depths of him to save the lovers of the world, remnants of some lost Atlantis. His book was every inch of him, his daughter even, his children, her children, his air. His book was all around her. His book was here. It was him, and she defied the wind to tell her that that wasn't something.

Martha McPhee first explored the fate
of the fictional Furey-Cooper family
in her acclaimed debut

Bright Angel Time

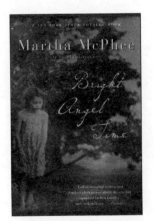

0-15-602934-0
$14.00

Set in the early 1970s, this magical first novel marked not only
the introduction of the Furey-
Cooper family that is revisited
in *Gorgeous Lies,* but also the
auspicious debut of Martha
McPhee's stunning literary talent. Eight-year-old Kate and her
sisters adopt a new life on the
road when their divorced mother
falls in love with someone new,
and a decade when values and
mores were turned upside down
is seen through the eyes of a very aware child.

"Blessed with a poet's ear for language and a reporter's eye
for detail, [Martha McPhee] proves with this volume that
she is also a gifted novelist, a writer with the ability to surprise and move us."
—Michiko Kakutani, *The New York Times*

"A gorgeous novel with subtle things to say about America
in the wake of the first divorce boom."—*Newsweek*

Harcourt | HARVEST BOOKS

www.HarcourtBooks.com